A FAMILY SCANDAL

You can never leave a bad man behind...

Mavis Pugh has had a hard life. Despised and abused throughout her teenage years, she turned to the first man who showed her kindness. But Alec quickly revealed himself to be a violent bully. When Mavis escapes from Alec, she thinks the worst is behind her. Moving to a large family house with her two children is more than she ever dreamed of, and when handsome signwriter Tommy takes an interest in her, she can't believe her luck. But unbeknown to Mavis, Alec is watching her and her family, just waiting for the right time to make his next – and final – move...

A FAMILY SCANDAL

A FAMILY SCANDAL

by

Kitty Neale

Magna Large Print Books
Long Preston, North Yorkshire,
BD23 4ND, England.

British Library Cataloguing in Publication Data.

A catalogue record of this book is
available from the British Library

ISBN   978-0-7505-4445-0

First published in Great Britain 2016 by Avon,
a division of HarperCollins*Publishers*

Copyright © Kitty Neale 2016

Cover illustration © Roux Hamilton/Arcangel by arrangement with
Arcangel Images

Kitty Neale asserts the moral right to be identified as the author of
this work

Published in Large Print 2017 by arrangement with
HarperCollins Publishers

Magna Large Print is an imprint of Library Magna Books Ltd.

Printed and bound in Great Britain by
T.J. (International) Ltd., Cornwall, PL28 8RW

I would like to dedicate this book to the memory of Hardip Bhamra, who sadly died in 2015.

He has been described by his colleagues, friends and family as a beautiful soul, a modest, gentle, kind and honest man; a devoted husband and father who is survived by his wife, Marianne, and daughter, Kristina.

Hardip Bhamra was also a talented artist who could create beauty with just a few strokes of a brush, and now, every time I see a wonderful sunrise or sunset, it reminds me of him and some of his wonderful paintings.

Chapter One

Peckham, Spring 1965

'Pete's done us proud, ain't he?' Lily Culling grinned at her daughter as she looked around her new kitchen with delight. 'Mavis, look at that, proper hot water and everything. And a new cooker too. It's the first time I ever had one of those. I'll be able to do some lovely sausage and mash on that, Pete, your favourite.'

Pete beamed at his wife but shook his head. 'It's only what you deserve. God knows we've waited long enough for it. I'm only sorry it took ages to get it all finished. I wanted it done while Bobby was still young enough to keep out of mischief but look at him, there's no stopping him now.'

Bobby paused when he heard his name, but then carried on chasing James and Grace around and into the patch of garden at the back of the house. He was two and a half and into everything. It didn't help that he was the youngest of the household too and spoilt rotten.

'It's lovely to see them playing together,' Mavis said. 'It's funny to think that Bobby is the youngest. He's their uncle, but I doubt he understands that.'

'Well, love, it is a bit complicated,' Lily replied. 'How do you explain to a two-year-old that you're my daughter from my first marriage, and that he's from my second? Same mother, but different fathers so you're his half-sister. Not only that, you already had James who is now eight and Grace who is six when I gave birth to him.'

'It's enough to confuse anyone.' Pete commented.

'I'll explain it, all to him when he's older,' Lily said as she once again looked around her new kitchen. 'Oh, I love this house, Pete. You've done a wonderful job of converting it into two generous-sized flats.'

'I love it too, Mum,' said Mavis. 'James and Grace will have their own bedrooms instead of sharing. It's not like when I was their age is it? I remember that damp, old kitchen in Battersea and you didn't have anything modern or new then.'

'Don't remind me.' Lily shuddered. 'Your dad off gambling all our money away, me never knowing where the next penny was coming from and if I'd be able to feed you or not.' She patted her hair, reluctant to remember those days of extreme poverty. She didn't intend to go back to that hand-to-mouth way of life. Even though she was well into her forties she still took care of her appearance, using the peroxide often enough to stop the roots showing through, determined nobody would notice if she was going grey or not. She prided herself on keeping her figure – not something many women who'd had a child at her age could boast of. 'Still, you didn't know no different when you were little. And half the stuff was still rationed. Those three out there don't know they're born. Nothing but good times ahead for us now, pet. You just see if I'm not right.'

Mavis smiled and crossed her fingers. 'Hope so. Now we're here it's a fresh start for all of us.'

'That's the spirit,' said Pete, proud of all he'd done to keep this family together. He was a bricklayer by trade and had worked his fingers to the bone until he'd had enough money to set up his own company. He had started off by doing small jobs but finally was in a position to go for the bigger projects, and that had all been down to his own hard graft. Now he'd found this big house and finally got it done up. Nobody else need know about the enormous loan that had made it possible. Good times were on their way for his business and nothing was going to spoil it. He'd done all this without a helping hand from anybody, and still had to pinch himself when he realised he really was married to Lily and he'd given her the life he'd always known she deserved. He certainly wasn't going to worry her by telling her about the loan. There were no flies on Lily, but he knew it was his job to be the provider for the family, and that was exactly what he intended to be.

'Best thing about this place is there's a decent pub just round the corner,' he said. 'I fancy a pint and reckon I deserve it after all that lifting. You coming to join me, Lily, just for a change? See if we can get to know any of the new faces?'

Lily turned to her daughter. 'I might go, just the once. It's something to celebrate, after all. I won't be long. You'll be all right, stopping here with the kids?'

Mavis nodded. 'You go and have a good time.

You worked hard for this and helped to pack a lot of my stuff too when I was busy sorting out James and Grace. Don't worry about me. Tommy will be over later to see how we got on.'

'You got a good man there.' Lily approved of Tommy. When he'd first come on the scene she hadn't been sure about him as he'd been a bit of a tearaway in his youth, but he'd turned into a real tower of strength for Mavis just when she needed one. 'Be giving him a tour of your new bedroom, will you?'

'Mum!' Mavis quickly checked that the children were all out of earshot. 'Don't go saying that. It's all very well for you, but I'm not rushing into anything. Tommy knows that. So don't you go putting ideas into his head.'

'You've been seeing him for ages, and if you ask me the man's a saint to wait for so long.'

'Mum!' Mavis warned again.

Lily grinned and then winked at her husband. 'Come on then, Pete. I might let you show me a good time, an' all.'

Pete caught her round the waist, grinning from ear to ear. He might not be much of a looker, with his boxer's face and skin still scarred from teenage acne, but he loved her mum, thought Mavis. He'd done them proud all right and she was grateful to him for that. 'You go on, I'll make sure Bobby goes to bed on time.'

'And we'll be back before it's James's bedtime so you won't have to worry about leaving any of them on their own in a different part of the house.' Lily grabbed her handbag. 'See you later. Don't do anything I wouldn't do.' She allowed

14

Pete to open the newly painted door for her and they were gone.

Well that didn't rule much out, Mavis thought ruefully. How different her mother was to her. Lily had begun her affair with Pete not long after Mavis's father had gone missing, which Mavis, a lonely teenager at the time, had found unbearably hard and impossible to accept. By the time her father finally reappeared, close to death after years of gambling and drinking had ruined him, Lily and Pete had been living together. They'd only married after Mavis's dad had died and when Lily was heavily pregnant with Bobby. It had scandalised the neighbours when they eventually found out, but then they had moved away to Peckham and a fresh start.

Mavis had to open a few cupboard doors to find the teapot. She remembered when she was a girl that her mother would use the same tea leaves several times as they couldn't afford fresh. Mavis grimaced, remembering how dreadfully clumsy she had been which had tried her mother's patience. She'd also been considered backward because she couldn't learn to read and write.

As she made the tea, Mavis found herself thinking about Rhona Foster and knew she would miss having her vivacious friend and neighbour popping in from next door now that they had moved away from Harmond Street. Rhona wouldn't have thought twice about showing Tommy her bedroom, Mavis thought. Though they had become friends, they were as different as chalk and cheese.

Everything had changed for Mavis when she'd married Alec, James and Grace's father. After leaving school with no qualifications she'd helped his snobbish mother run her house. It was Alec's mother who realised that her inability to read and clumsiness wasn't caused by lack of intelligence. It was due to word blindness, and though she had never learned to read, she had managed to overcome her clumsiness. No, she wasn't backward, Mavis thought ruefully, but she had been very naïve and what she hadn't realised was that she was being groomed by Alec's mother to be his perfect submissive wife. Because she'd been desperate to get away from Lily and Pete, she'd fallen for it – and ended up in a terrible abusive relationship.

When the domineering old woman had died, Mavis had found the courage to leave Alec. He'd sold the house that he'd inherited from his mother two years ago, hadn't given Mavis her share of the money, and moved out. He'd disappeared without a trace, but nobody was sorry to see the back of him. Except that, as she had no way of making contact with him, she couldn't get a divorce.

'I'm thirsty. Can I have a drink please, Mummy?'

'Of course you can,' Mavis said, smiling fondly at her son. 'Orange juice?'

James nodded and as she mixed the juice with water, Mavis's mind was still full of memories. Grace could hardly remember her real father and James's memories of him were fading day by day. That was a good thing as Alec had beaten James badly, although not as often as he'd beaten her. Mavis shuddered as she recalled the pain of the frequent bruises she'd had to keep hidden for so long.

'I want some juice too,' another voice demanded.

'Grace, you won't get anything unless you ask for it properly,' Mavis said sternly.

Grace looked sullen for a moment, but then said, '*Please* can I have some orange juice.'

'That's better,' Mavis said approvingly and when Bobby appeared she made him a drink too.

Once finished they all ran off again, while Mavis poured herself a cup of tea and then stood sipping it whilst watching the children through the kitchen window.

James was now running around without a care in the world. He was still a thoughtful little boy, often seeming older than his eight years, and he wasn't as withdrawn and fearful as he'd once been. As for Grace, even when a toddler she'd always said exactly what she thought – nobody had ever had to teach her how to put her foot down. She was more like her Granny Lily than anyone else and Lily was very fond of her granddaughter.

Mavis smiled ruefully again. As a girl she had found school hard, which had led to her being friendless and awkward. Grace on the other hand was fearless. She was a force to be reckoned with, and her teachers didn't know whether to praise her for her willingness to speak up in class or to punish her for never shutting up. Yet she was generous and kind-hearted – there she was now, making sure Bobby was all right after he'd taken a tumble. Mavis started, wondering if she should rush out, but Bobby didn't cry and she could see he'd only grazed his knee. He was made of tough stuff, the spitting image of Pete right down to the squashed nose. He'd known nothing but love all his short life and responded by loving everyone right back.

Mavis decided she'd finish her tea and then call them in as the light was fading and it would be getting cold, even if they were running about like champion athletes, exploring every nook and cranny of the new garden. She'd give them something to eat and a Corona fizzy drink for a treat to mark their first day in their new home. Then Tommy would be here.

Tommy. Her heart flipped over. Despite what Lily said, Mavis wouldn't be giving him a tour of her bedroom in the upstairs flat, no matter how much she might want to. It wasn't so much that Mavis craved respectability; she'd done that once and a fat lot of good it had done her. It was fear that held her back, along with the fact that she doubted she could ever completely trust a man again, even Tommy. He appeared perfect, kind, and caring, but Alec had seemed kind too. All that changed when she married him and she had been through too much to risk making the same mistake again.

'I'm not bloody having it!' Rhona Foster, screamed in frustration as they neared the end of their shift. 'How the hell do they expect us to do the same work but faster? Whose bright idea was that? They can stuff it, I'm not going to do it.'

'Yes you are and you know it.' Jean Barker, at twenty-six – seven years older than her hot-tempered colleague – had seen and heard it all before. Anyone could tell from a glance at her that she took no nonsense, from her sensible shoes to her tidy brown hair, now hidden under the regulation scarf they were all meant to wear on shift, though the younger ones often ignored the rule. 'It won't make any difference what we say. You've been at this factory for three years now, Rhona, and can you remember a time when the foreman ever listened to us? So we got to put up with it and get on with it. Unless you want to lose your job, which I can't see your mum being very happy about. I sure as hell don't want to lose mine.' She began to fold the cardboard boxes that had been stacked flat in the back room of the factory. 'Come on, let's make a start.'

'Rhona's right, they're picking on us,' moaned Penny, who at eighteen was the youngest of them, a year younger than Rhona and half a head shorter. She shook her mass of wavy blonde hair. 'It's not fair. I'll break me nails. I don't know why we have to lift those horrible filthy things anyway.'

'It might have something to do with someone round here chucking the foreman's nephew last week,' Jean said. 'I'm not casting aspersions, just saying. There he was, thinking it was love's young dream, and then he gets the old heave-ho before he even knows there's something wrong. Get bored, did you, Rhona?'

Rhona shut her eyes in exasperation. 'For God's sake. He was awful. Hands like a wandering octopus, and he kissed like a flabby sponge. Couldn't dance, couldn't get me backstage. What earthly use was he? I only went out with him 'cos he said he could get free tickets to the Talisman club and then it turned out we had to pay anyway. Good riddance to him. I'd rather stack boxes than get stuck with him for another evening, and that's saying something. Sorry, girls, that's the truth.'

'So my nails get ruined 'cos you chucked Andy Forsyth?' Penny glared at her friend.

'You don't seriously expect me to make up with him for that?' Rhona glared back. 'And put your scarf back over your hair or you'll get it full of dust and then you'll blame me for that as well.'

'I hate wearing it. It makes me look like me Auntie Rita and she's nearly fifty.' Penny made a face as if she couldn't imagine anything worse. But she did as she was told, because getting factory dust out of her curls took ages and she hoped to have better things to do with her time. She noted that Rhona still hadn't put her own scarf on.

'Well, you should be used to it,' said Jean without sympathy. 'Get on with it, Penny, or we'll be here until Saturday, and I'm sure you've got other ways to spend your weekend than finishing off this lot.'

'I know I have,' said Rhona and gave them a wink as the thought of what was in store brightened her mood. 'I've found myself another hot date. He's gorgeous, he plays the guitar and guess what he's got backstage passes to?'

Jean shook her head as she really didn't care, but Penny was beside herself with curiosity, her curls bobbing up and down. 'Where? Go on, don't be mean, what are you up to? Has he got a friend, can I come? Aren't you going to tell us?'

Rhona pretended to turn away but she couldn't resist her moment of triumph. 'I'm going all the way up to North London to see the Rolling

Stones. How about that?'

Jean shrugged, as she couldn't see what all the fuss was about. Penny screamed and quickly covered her mouth with her hands. Rhona glowed. 'Yep, he's called Kenneth and he knows everybody, I mean everybody, and he's going to introduce me to the band and everyone behind the scenes. So why do I care about this stupid factory?' She tossed her hair, which she tried to style like Brigitte Bardot's, though that wasn't easy working in such a place. She liked it when people said she looked like the film star though – and there was a reasonable resemblance, as Rhona's eyes were dark and wide, and her hair a similar blonde. 'You heard it here first, folks. He might be my ticket away from all of this.'

Chapter Two

Tommy Wilson checked the sign at the end of the street to make sure he'd come to the right place. It wasn't as if this was his first time in Peckham, but he wasn't as familiar with the area as he was with his old stamping ground, Battersea, or with where he lived now, over in Wandsworth. Still, he thought as he thrust his hands in his jacket pockets against the cold, with luck he'd be seeing a whole lot more of this road. If this was where Mavis lived then this was where he wanted to be.

He still counted himself lucky that she'd agreed to go out with him, even though they'd been dating for a year and a half. He knew Mavis was the one for him. But he'd treated her so badly when they were kids growing up on the same mean and dingy street that he wouldn't have blamed her if she'd said she wanted nothing to do with him.

When they'd met again as adults, it was soon clear the attraction ran deep on both sides. But the timing wasn't right. He had just got divorced from his wife, Belinda. He hadn't wanted to admit it but inside he'd been a mess. As for Mavis, she'd been married to that cold fish, Alec Pugh. What a useless excuse for a man he had been – or still was, wherever he was. A coward as well as a bully. Tommy clenched his fists at the memory. He couldn't abide men who abused their physical superiority and beat women and children. He seethed at the thought of anyone laying a hand on Mavis in anger.

He checked the numbers on the front of the houses. He was nearly there. The buildings were of three storeys, with tall windows, and it didn't look too bad a place at all. After Alec's disappearance, Mavis had rented a small house on Harwood Street for a couple of years, not too far from here, next to her mother and Pete. Although it was a step up from Battersea it had been too cramped for her and two growing children. But these places, even though they were still terraced, looked much bigger. Mavis had said the road had a dog-leg bend and they were in the corner of that. Here it was – just as she'd described it. The front of the house was, if anything, narrower than those around it but Mavis had said around the back, because of the bend, there was a bigger

22

garden than those of the neighbouring properties. So it would be ideal for the kids, and she and Lily would still have lots of space for a washing line and maybe even some vegetable beds.

Tommy smiled to himself. He couldn't quite see Lily getting her hands dirty planting up tomatoes.

For a moment he wondered what it would be like to work in the garden with Mavis. He'd build them a couple of raised beds, and he'd show James how to hammer them together at the corners, or maybe they could get a shed... He shook himself. First things first. He was always getting carried away with dreams of the future but before any of that could happen they had to sort out the present. He was sure Mavis felt the same way about him as he did about her, but he couldn't blame her for being cagey. She'd been badly hurt and he had to let time take its course and heal her deep wounds.

Again Tommy felt a surge of anger at Alec Pugh and his brutal behaviour. Calm down, he told himself. This is a day to celebrate. New house, new start. He fingered the little box he carried in his pocket and pictured Mavis's beautiful face when she saw it.

'Sure you don't want anything stronger, sweetheart?' asked Pete, picking up his empty pint glass and standing, stretching to ease his aching back. 'I'll have one more of these then we can get home. This isn't a bad local, is it?' He gazed around the lounge bar, all polished brass and dark wood. 'I passed it by loads of times when we were doing the house up but never came in. See what we were missing out on.'

'I'll stick to bitter lemon,' said Lily. She'd never been one for drinking – she'd had enough of that from her first husband who, if he wasn't gambling away their rent money, was blowing it down the pub. 'I like it in here. At least I'll know where to find you from now on.'

'I can't keep away from you for long, you know that.' Pete eyed his wife appreciatively. He was a lucky man and he knew it. He was under no illusions about his looks and yet he was married to a stunner. All those years of waiting had been worth it. He felt on top of the world. His own business, the most gorgeous woman in London and, just when he'd given up hope, a son of his very own who was the spitting image of him. A pity Bobby hadn't inherited his mother's head-turning looks in some ways; but Pete knew plenty of blokes who were far more handsome than him yet it hadn't brought them happiness.

No, when times were tough, Pete thought, it was all about character, that's what got you through. That's what had got him to where he was today. If anyone deserved a second pint it was him: he owned that whole house, and he'd fitted it out to keep his family safe. He pushed to the back of his mind the uncomfortable thought that it wasn't exactly bought and paid for. He'd be able to meet the mortgage without a problem just as soon as the big construction project was confirmed, and it was well-nigh one hundred per cent certain that it would be. He was proud that his company was the front runner for it – who'd have thought a bricklayer like him could end up doing so well? No need to worry, and certainly no need to share that bit of information with Lily.

Lily watched him, nursing her small glass in her hand. She didn't want to admit how tired she was. Everyone said moving house was one of the most stressful things you could do, and God knew she'd had to do it often enough. This was different though: no more renting, getting by in sub-standard places with dodgy landlords and dodgier agents. They now had their very own place – and with Mavis safe above them, she could keep an eye on her beloved grandchildren too. Guiltily, Lily recalled how she hadn't lavished love on Mavis when she'd been a child. She hadn't been able to understand why her daughter had been so difficult and awkward, but nobody had heard of word blindness then. Now Lily intended to make up for it by devoting herself to James and Grace, and ensuring Bobby wanted for nothing. Blimey, fancy being a mother at her age. No wonder she was tired. She just didn't have the energy to cope with a very active toddler and move house.

'Here you go, girl.' Pete put a glass of bitter lemon in front of her. The bright lights of the pub reflected in the cloudy liquid. 'We might want to take our time over this. I've been thinking about what you said earlier. Maybe Mavis will be giving Tommy a tour of her new bedroom.'

Lily eyed him above the rim of her raised glass. 'No, Pete. I don't think so.' She sighed. 'Mavis ain't like me, not in that respect. Once bitten twice shy, that's her problem, and as it was so hard fought, she doesn't want to give up her independence.'

'Yeah, I know, but Tommy won't wait forever.'

'Well nothing is going to happen at the moment, that's for sure. Mavis is looking after the kids. Bobby will have gone to bed by now but James won't and I bet Grace is playing up with her first night in her new room by herself.'

'Ah, well.' Pete settled on the red banquette beside her. He took a swig and got foam all over his top lip. 'We'll maybe make the most of our new privacy when we get home. I did those dividing walls extra careful. We won't have neighbours with a glass to the wall this time spying on us as we did in Battersea.' He raised his eyebrows hopefully.

'You devil, Pete Culling.' Lily felt a rosy glow spread through her. 'And at least we don't have to worry about making Bobby a new brother or sister. There's advantages to this getting old malarkey after all.'

'I don't want to go to bed!' Grace yelled, struggling as her mother tried to hug her. 'I hate my room! There's monsters behind that cupboard!'

'There, there.' Mavis knew the tantrum would subside if she gave it enough time. Typically Grace, who'd done nothing but complain about having to share a room with her brother, was now kicking up a storm faced with being left to sleep on her own. She'd get over it soon enough. She'd chosen the colours for the room herself – purple walls and pale green woodwork. It might not have been the choice of most other little girls but Mavis had to admit the colours went well together. Maybe her daughter had an eye for such things even at such a young age.

26

'Stay with me, Mummy.'

Grace gazed up and Mavis felt her heart constrict with love. Still, she knew she couldn't curl up beside the girl on the new bed with its smart white headboard, as James was still up, minding Bobby in his room below. Instead she drew out a battered teddy from behind the pillow. 'Look who has come all this way to stay with you. Recognise him?'

'It's Little Ted!' Grace exclaimed, and the tears stopped. She'd taken a fancy to the children's TV programme *Play School,* which she'd been able to watch when visiting their old neighbours, the Bonners, and Little Ted was her favourite toy on it. So she'd named her own teddy after him. Mavis was hoping to get a television for the flat but thought it best not to mention it until it happened, or Grace would be inconsolable.

The doorbell rang and Mavis had to take a moment to realise what the unfamiliar sound was. Back in Harwood Street everyone just banged on the door, but Pete had insisted they had a bell, so that Mavis would be able to hear it from the top floor. 'Right, time to say night-night. See if you can race Little Ted to be first asleep.' She kissed the top of her daughter's head as Grace snuggled down, pulling the new purple eiderdown up to her chin. 'Sleep tight.'

'Mmmmmm.' Grace was already seriously challenging Little Ted to the prize.

Mavis paused at the mirror in the hallway, checking her hair, even though she knew she'd hardly be expected to look glamorous after a day moving house. Her dark curls were flattened where they usually bounced attractively but her blue eyes had that sparkle which always appeared when she knew she'd soon see Tommy. Brushing the dust from her cardigan, which she'd thrown over her shift dress, she ran down the stairs. Although it had only been a couple of days she didn't want to be parted from Tommy for a minute longer.

She could see his silhouette through the glass panels in the upper part of the front door that both flats shared. He was tall, and also had dark curly hair, which he kept quite short or it would have got in the way. Tommy had trained as a signwriter, but now he managed his own firm and didn't do so much of the painting himself. He ran the business from a yard not far from where they'd grown up, much to the disgust of his meddlesome mother who couldn't get over the fact her son had gone through the disgrace of a divorce.

Tommy grinned broadly as she opened the door and immediately stepped in and took her in his arms. 'Hello, gorgeous.'

'Stop it, Tommy, the neighbours will see!' Mavis reached around him and pushed the door shut again.

'Thought you didn't care?'

'Not normally, no, but why give them something to gossip about if we don't have to.' Mavis led him into Lily and Pete's flat. 'Come and look around. James is through there, minding Bobby, so we'll leave that room till last. But here's the living room. Have a seat while I make you a cup of tea.'

Tommy looked around at the three-piece suite

clustered around the electric fire in the tiled grate. 'Very nice, but I'd rather be with you. Show me the kitchen.' He followed her through to the back of the house. 'How did the move go? Everything unpacked yet?'

'You must be joking.' She pointed at a pile of boxes, still bulging with their contents. 'We've only got as far as the essentials. I haven't even found my own teapot, I've just used Mum's.' She handed him a cup and reached for one herself. 'Haven't found a matching set yet, but I don't suppose you'll mind?'

'Hardly. I'd drink out of tin cans as long as it was with you.' He pulled her close again. 'I love to see you so happy. Give me a kiss, a, proper one.' He bent his face to hers. 'Listen, I've got something for you.' He reached into his jacket pocket.

Mavis rested her head against his shoulder. 'Silly, I don't need a present.'

'I know you don't but I wanted to mark the occasion.' He drew out the little box.

Mavis gasped. For a moment she hesitated and an uncertain look came into her eyes. 'What ... what's this, Tommy?'

'Go on, open it.'

With trembling fingers she took off the lid, to reveal a sparkling gold chain attached to a small locket. 'Oh, Tommy.'

'Do you like it?' He could hardly keep the eagerness from his voice. 'I know it's not your birthday until April but I saw it in a jeweller's window and I knew it would look just right on you. Do you want me to fasten it for you?'

'Please.' Mavis took a deep breath and tried to

calm down. For a second she'd been struck with fear and yet it was mixed with desperate hope. Now she felt stupid for having overreacted. It was a beautiful present, and from the name on the box it must have been expensive, but it was a necklace. 'There's a mirror over the fireplace so let's go back to the front room where I can see it. Thank you so much, Tommy, that's really thoughtful.'

She led him into the sitting room and switched on the table lamp in the corner near the mantelpiece. Now she could see how lovely the present was, and that it sat perfectly just above her collarbone. How well Tommy knew her. He stood just behind her and gazed at her reflection in the big mirror. He bent his head so he could whisper in her ear.

'You look gorgeous. Is it all right?' His eyes were bright with pleasure.

Mavis turned around so he could kiss her again. As he dropped his head and his lips met hers, she told herself not to be ridiculous, but couldn't help a shudder of relief tinged with disappointment. She'd thought just fleetingly that it was a ring in the little box and he was going to ask her to marry him. Mavis knew she couldn't say yes – she didn't know when she would be free. She was overwhelmed with a need to give herself to this man who loved her and understood her, who she believed would do anything for her. But after what she had been through with Alec, she couldn't.

Not yet. Maybe never. She just couldn't.

Chapter Three

'And then he left me there, stranded!' Rhona was outraged. 'Can you believe it?'

'I hope you told him where to get off,' said Penny loyally. 'I hope you rang him this morning and gave him a right earbashing. What a thing to do. Anything could have happened to you.'

'And I was freezing!' Rhona continued. 'I had my new miniskirt on and how was I to know we were going there on his motorbike? Then I had to get night buses home. All the way from bleeding Enfield. Can I have one of your fags?' She reached across the scratched wood coffee table to her friend's handbag. 'I left my last packet in his jacket and I've not had a change to buy any more. I made him give me it to wear once we got there, and now the bastard has got them, and I hope he bloody chokes.'

'Serve him right,' said Penny. She'd come round as soon as breakfast was finished to see how the night had gone and to share in the excitement, only to find her colleague furious and swearing vengeance. Kenneth had made good his promise to take Rhona to see the Rolling Stones and then to get her backstage after the concert. His claims to know the band's crew weren't idle boasts. The trouble was, he'd been asked along to the after-show party but it had been made clear extra friends weren't welcome, even those as young and glamorous as Rhona. It turned out the band had more than enough of those kinds of followers already. So Kenneth had dropped Rhona without a backward glance, leaving her to make her own way back to the other side of London late on a Friday night, without so much as a cigarette for comfort. Of course he hadn't answered his phone that morning. Someone in his shared digs had taken the call, not best pleased to have been woken before midday, but Kenneth was nowhere to be found. He'd be sleeping off his hangover somewhere safe from Rhona's rage.

'Was it worth it though?' Penny wondered. She pulled at her own miniskirt, which she'd got from the market. It looked all right but the material was cheap and scratchy, and too flimsy for the chilly spring weather. Still, she wouldn't give in and change it, as it was important to have the right look even round her friend's house on a Saturday morning. 'You did see the Stones, after all. I'd kill to see them.'

'Mmmmm.' Rhona prolonged the moment. It had been a fantastic gig, she had to admit. The energy of the band had been electric and she'd been totally mesmerised by Brian Jones. She definitely wouldn't have minded being at the party with him. Damn that Kenneth for denying her the chance. 'They did loads of their singles, like "Time is on My Side" and "Not Fade Away". I danced till my feet were sore. Everyone was singing along, you've never seen anything like it.'

'I love those ones.' Penny was wistful. If only she could get a date who'd take her to concerts like that. It would be worth the bad journey home to be able to say she'd seen the Stones. Everyone was talking about them and she was sure they'd be properly famous for ages. 'Give me those cigarettes, I'll have one meself.' She paused as Rhona's mother came into the room.

'Morning, Penny.' Marilyn Foster was a lively woman of nearly fifty, with an uncontrollable frizz of brown hair. 'Nice to see you. Have you had any breakfast? I was out cleaning earlier so I'm making some toast now, do you want any?'

'No thank you, Mrs Foster,' said Penny politely, pulling her skirt further down her thighs. She was a bit in awe of Rhona's straight-talking mother.

'Well, you're always welcome.' Marilyn made for the door again. 'Rhona's going to be lonely without Mavis nearby so you must feel free to drop in at any time.'

Rhona pulled a face as her mother went out. 'She thinks I'm still at school sometimes. I don't need to have her making my friends for me.'

'Course you don't,' said Penny, taking a deep drag. 'Ah, that's better. No, but you will miss her though, won't you? You and Mavis were really close.'

Rhona nodded. She was guiltily aware that she'd been the one person who wasn't delighted when the news came that Pete had finally bought the big house and the family would be moving from Harwood Street. Mavis had come round thrilled to bits and Rhona had had a hard job trying to appear enthusiastic. For some reason, though they were polar opposites in temperament, she and Mavis had got on like a house on fire. Maybe it was because they were so different. Rhona's wild years had started when she was sixteen, when she'd discovered the joys of dating all available gorgeous men, and she had even tried flirting with Tommy before the penny dropped that he was interested in only one woman.

Mavis hadn't judged her, unlike all the other women and even girls her own age who'd found out – and it wasn't as if Rhona made a secret of her enjoyment of sex. Mavis had been baffled, more than anything. Having had such a bad marriage, which she'd entered into when she was just sixteen herself, she couldn't understand why her friend bothered. Rhona had tried to explain the fascination: the thrill of the chase, the knowledge that your body drove men mad, and the fun that was to be had. But Mavis was unconvinced. Her priorities lay elsewhere, but she enjoyed hearing Rhona tell of her exploits, maybe because she herself wanted nothing more than to stay home to look after her beloved children. Rhona sighed. Even though Mavis hadn't moved far away, it wouldn't be the same in future.

'No point in sitting around moping,' she said now. 'Right, that's Kenneth done for. I wouldn't go out with him again if he came round here begging on his hands and knees. I'd shove him back out the door and sing him "It's All Over Now". What are you up to tonight, Penny?'

Penny shrugged. She didn't have a date and had no plans, much the same as every Saturday night, though she hated to admit it. 'Not sure. Why?'

'Let's cheer ourselves up and go down the Talisman club. We don't need no men to get us in, we've just got our wages so we can pay for ourselves. What do you reckon?'

Penny's eyes shone. 'I'd love to ... but me mum–'

'Don't worry about her. Say you're staying round here. Mum won't mind, she just said you're welcome any time. Then neither of us will be stuck trying to get home alone. I don't fancy that two nights in a row.'

'OK right, you're on.' Penny pulled a face. 'What'll I wear? I got this new skirt but nothing to go with it.'

'Let's go and sort that out right now.' Rhona got up and drew the old dressing gown she'd been wearing more tightly around her. 'I'll just go and get out of this then we can go down the market and see what they have to offer. Can't have you showing me up,' she said, though she wasn't averse to having a friend slightly less attractive than herself. Rhona had no doubts about why men made a beeline for her, but it often helped to have a willing accomplice who didn't threaten to steal the best-looking guy in the room. Penny fitted the bill perfectly: pretty but not stunning, friendly but not too confident, curvy but not drop-dead sexy. It wouldn't hurt to get her dressed up a bit.

'Lovely. I haven't been down there since I got this skirt.' Penny stood up. 'I might look for some new false eyelashes as well. Now that I've got the hang of them I feel naked going out without them.' She giggled. 'First time I tried them my mum screamed the house down – thought it was a big spider in the basin.'

'Can't say I blame her,' said Rhona, 'but it's a good idea. Might get some more meself.'

Mavis was already getting to know her new local market, armed with a list of items needed for the house. It was daft, she told herself as she recalled the familiar ache she always felt when she had said goodnight to Tommy. What she wouldn't have given to have him stay the night... Pull yourself together, she muttered. It's not as if he hasn't made it obvious he'd like to stay, but you don't let him and you know why perfectly well. So stop feeling sorry for yourself.

For some reason she'd never really explored this market, even though it was just round the corner from Peckham Rye station. She'd often come down Rye Lane to get to the big shops, and had window-shopped at Jones & Higgins, although she knew that such fine goods would never make their way into her cramped rented house. But now – why not? She might have to get most of her list from the market but perhaps she could treat herself to one or two things from the prestigious store where the more well-off members of the local population bought their homeware.

Meanwhile she had to buy a tea strainer. When she'd got round to unpacking her own crockery and kitchenware it was nowhere to be found, and she couldn't keep running downstairs to borrow Lily's. Grace wanted a new purple pencil case to match her room. She also wanted a purple dress and coat along with a matching scarf for Little Ted, but Mavis had pointed out that the pencil case would be the most useful and she couldn't have everything. The little girl had sulked for a minute over breakfast but soon cheered up when her mother had tuned the wireless to Radio Caroline. Grace was already a dab hand at singing along with the pop songs, effortlessly learning all the words.

Mavis stopped to check the price of some cleaning materials, which were bound to come in handy. 'Do you three for the price of two on those,' said the stallholder. 'Genuine Ajax, that is, none of your cheap imitations you'll get elsewhere. Got a lot of floors? This'll sort you out. My missus swears by it.'

Mavis nodded and agreed to take three, reckoning that if she didn't need them all then Lily surely would. 'And some dusters, while you're at it.'

'Throw them in for nothing,' offered the stallholder, picking up a small packet. 'Now how about some rubber gloves? Lovely soft hands, you got,' he added as he took her money and lingered for just a moment too long.

'Thanks,' said Mavis, moving hastily away. Rubber gloves could wait. She made a note to get any scouring powder elsewhere in future. She felt like running back to the house but told herself not to be silly. It was only a bit of harmless flattery, the bloke was just a bit on the creepy side. No doubt other women loved it and kept coming back for more. Anyway she'd have to get Grace something or there'd be tears and recriminations all weekend. Then if she got her daughter something it was only fair to find a little present for James too. He was so good, he hardly ever complained when Grace got more attention, so she had to try extra hard to make sure he didn't miss out.

All around her the crowds were growing, bargain-hunting women and men enjoying their morning off, young children being dragged along by their parents, one getting a clip around the ear for trying to take a piece of fruit off a stall. 'I was only lookin',' the boy wailed. Mavis couldn't blame him; the display was colourful and would have tempted anyone.

'You keep your thieving hands to yerself,' snapped his mother, smacking him again. 'You'll go without yer dinner if I catch you doing that again.'

Mavis looked away. After witnessing what Alec had done to James, she couldn't bear to see a child being hit, even if it wasn't anything more than a light tap. Lord knows she'd been on the receiving end of it herself, first from her mother, then from her husband, and she never wanted to be in that position again.

Noticing a stall selling toys and stationery, Mavis wandered over when she spotted a flash of purple. Exactly what Grace wanted – a plastic pencil case. She picked it up and added a set of coloured pencils for James. They'd come in handy for school even if he wasn't as keen on drawing as his sister. Thankfully the stallholder took her money without trying to get to know her. He was engaged in conversation with another customer, something about some old roads being knocked down to make room for new houses. The same thing was happening in many parts of London; houses being demolished to make way for towering blocks of flats.

Turning to walk away, Mavis thought she saw a familiar face, which stopped her in her tracks. An older woman slammed into her back. "'Ere, what do you think you're doing?' the old harridan roared. 'Almost made me drop my bags, you did. You wanna watch what you're about.'

'Sorry,' Mavis said, shaken and distracted. It couldn't have been who she thought it was. He didn't live round here – he'd left Battersea years ago and as far as she knew he had no reason to come back to any part of South London. Maybe it was a trick of the light – he'd have changed a lot since she last saw him. What would it have been since she'd last seen him? Ten years? She was jumpy after the creepy stallholder, that was all it was.

Clutching her shopping bag tightly, Mavis headed in the opposite direction, trying to enjoy the spectacle of the Saturday morning market in full swing. There were some teenage girls laughing at a clothes stall, holding up dresses in the latest styles, hurriedly copied from the West End shops and run up in cheaper fabrics. One of them waved around a miniskirt that was little more than a pelmet, giggling wildly. Another had a top in sharp geometric patterns that was an exact imitation of something Mavis had seen on *Top of the Pops* when she'd been round to her friend and former neighbour Jenny Bonner's. It made her think of Rhona and her outrageous outfits. She wondered how her young friend would get along now she'd moved away from Harwood Street. Don't be daft, she told herself. It was high time Rhona went out with girls of her own age, and she might even be relieved not to see so much of Mavis. Mavis had always felt herself to be very staid in comparison to her energetic young neighbour, but she knew she'd miss her. It wasn't just for the gossip and scandalous stories; underneath the good-time girl exterior, the young woman had a heart of gold. She just preferred to keep that a secret, in case some man decided he'd like to break it.

Feeling better, Mavis headed back towards the main road, Peckham Rye. There was still time to pay a visit to the high-end store of Jones & Higgins. But she'd gone off the idea. Maybe when she did go, she could drag Jenny along – her house had a few good-quality things in it and she'd know what a fair price was. The decision made, her mind turned back to that oddly familiar face in the crowd.

If her suspicions were right, Mavis knew she had every right to feel uneasy. What in heaven's name would have brought Larry Barnet to Peckham?

Chapter Four

Jenny Bonner stared at her husband. 'Do you really have to do this? What about me? What about Greg? He's only ten. It'll be a big change.'

Stan Bonner rubbed his head, pushing his hand across his receding hairline. He'd known this wasn't going to be an easy conversation. 'I realise that, love. It's not ideal. But if I want to get on in the firm there's no getting away from it. I've got to travel more, and as I said, it'll often mean staying away for several nights in a row.'

Jenny shook her head, worried and upset. For a moment she had the horrible thought that this was Stan's excuse to get away from her, that maybe there was another woman in his life. Then she came to her senses. Stan loved her and wasn't the type to stray. 'When does it start, Stan? Are you sure there's nobody else who'll do it?'

'That's not the point, love.' Stan tried not to show his impatience. He wasn't happy either but he knew what would happen if he didn't agree to do as his boss asked. 'Plenty of the others would do it. The thing is, they picked me out. That means they like me and I could be in for a promotion. That'd be good, wouldn't it? Get you more things, and for Greg too.'

Jenny could tell she was on a losing streak but tried again. 'What about Greg? He'll be doing his eleven-plus soon. He'll need you here to help him. I didn't stay on at school for long enough to be of much use. He'll get all those practice papers and then he'll fail because his mum wasn't clever enough to show him how to work them out.'

Stan came across the kitchen and put his arms round her. 'Don't say that, love. He's a bright boy, and he'll be fine. You're bright too and it wasn't your fault you didn't stay on at school. Your mum needed you to go out to work, to earn money to help her out.'

Jenny leaned against him and seemed to sag, the fight going out of her. 'I won't like it when you're away. I'll miss you.'

'I'll miss you too, but we want a good life for Greg, don't we? I'll be earning more money, and if I get promoted we'll be in clover.'

Jenny nodded, her head pressing against her husband's shoulder. She loved her house – it was big for three of them, and to begin with they'd hoped there would be more children, but none had come and now they were used to having lots of space. Greg had his own bedroom and there was a spare room. Stan was an insurance salesman and had a little space he called his office, though now that he was going to be away from home for long periods, it would hardly be used. 'I suppose if you get promoted, it'll be worth it.'

'That's the spirit.' Stan pulled back so he could look into his wife's hazel eyes. 'I'm doing it for you two. This chance has come just at the right time. Greg's old enough to understand, and he's not so little that you have to run round after him anymore.'

'I liked running round after him.' Jenny gave a sniff. He'd been an adorable little boy, and she never begrudged him a minute of her time. She didn't like to think of him growing up and getting independent. But Stan was right. That wouldn't be far away.

'I know you did. You were, you are, a wonderful mother. I'm proud of you.' Stan gave her a squeeze, thinking again how he'd miss her gorgeous curves while he was on the road. 'It'll break my heart spending nights away from the pair of you. You know that. But you'll be fine. You could ask Tommy over, if that would make it easier.'

Jenny hugged him back. 'I might. He must get lonely in that flat down in Wandsworth. He hasn't really got any mates there, and Mavis will be busy sorting out her new place. He might be glad of a few evenings round here.' Jenny had been close to her cousin Tommy when they were little and when his marriage had failed his mean mother had refused to take him in, even temporarily, so he had come to stay with them. That had been two years ago, but the cousins had stayed close, particularly when Tommy had started to date Mavis, Jenny's great friend and former next-door neighbour from when she'd been married to Alec. 'I'll ask him.'

'You do that. I'd feel better if I thought you weren't on your own every evening when I'm away.' Stan was relieved. It looked as if he'd be able to accept his boss's proposal with a clear conscience. 'I suppose there's still no sign of him staying over in Peckham?'

Jenny shook her head, pulling away from her husband. Her brown hair, which these days was cut in a neat bob, swung around her face. 'You know very well that Mavis won't do anything until the whole mess with that evil husband of hers is sorted out, and that might take years. It's a crying shame.'

Stan pulled out a chair at the kitchen table and sat down. He'd never had much to do with the Pughs when they'd lived next door and had found it hard to believe what had gone on only a few yards from their own happy home. 'Yeah, what a bastard, 'scuse my French. It'd be better off for everyone if he washed up dead somewhere, wouldn't it? That would solve everything.'

'I wouldn't wish that on anybody – but yes, you're right. After what he did to Mavis and James, it would be no more than he deserves.

43

Mavis has had to bring up their children without a penny of support from him, despite all that money Alec will have gained from selling the house.'

The sound of 'Please Don't Go' blasted out from the Talisman club as Rhona and Penny pushed their way through the entrance lobby. Penny had been worried that she wouldn't get in as she knew she looked younger than she actually was, but the doorman had taken one glance at her blonde hair and curvy figure and waved her straight through. She giggled nervously as she surveyed the crowd. Everyone seemed very sophisticated and confident. She straightened her shoulders. They were no better than her and she wouldn't stand in a corner waiting to be asked to join in.

'Shall we dance?' she shouted in Rhona's ear, struggling to make herself heard above the twanging guitar booming from the speakers.

'Let's get a drink first,' Rhona shouted back. She didn't want to seem too eager. That might put some men off and she wanted to have the chance to scout the place properly before deciding who was worth bothering with and who wasn't. 'If we wait until later the bar might be too busy. This way.' She led her friend around the tables crowded on the edge of the dance floor and across to the bar. The floor was already a little slippery from spilt drinks but she didn't care. 'Oh baby, please don't go…' she sang to the song under her breath, as she headed for a gap in the press of people attempting to catch the bar staff's eyes. She had a rule: to buy her own drink to begin with, and not to rush into accepting one from the first man who offered. She didn't want to risk getting stuck with a total moron for half the evening. She'd mentioned this technique to Penny on the way here on the bus. They'd sat at the back on the top deck, smoking and getting themselves in the mood for a proper night out. Penny had been slightly unsure of her new top but Rhona had assured her it was exactly right, and not too low-cut at all.

Penny had clearly forgotten the plan as when Rhona turned around to check what she wanted, her friend was already chatting to someone, their heads pressed close together. Rhona sighed in annoyance. This was no good. Their eyes hadn't had time to get accustomed to the dim lights of the bar, and the man could be anybody. She stared at Penny's bright blonde hair, willing her to look up, concentrating hard.

Something in her attitude must have got through because Penny glanced up and saw her, and then turned to the man in the shadows and pointed at Rhona. She moved away, giving him a little wave.

Good, thought Rhona. She didn't recognise the bloke but she didn't think much of his dress sense. He wasn't sharp enough to be a Mod, looked too conservative to be a rocker and he didn't have any of that cool air of the jazz fans. So he was ruled out on every count. 'What are you drinking?' she shouted at her friend when she was close enough to hear.

'What are you having?' Penny shouted back. She wasn't sure what to choose. She didn't want to look a fool by asking for the wrong thing.

'Babycham,' shouted Rhona. 'Have you ever had it? The bubbles go up your nose, you'd like it.'

There was a brief pause as one track came to an end before Wayne Fontana's 'Game of Love' began to play. Penny swayed around to it, teetering a little as her knee-high boots had higher heels than she was used to. 'Lovely. I'll try that.'

'You stay here, and remember what we agreed,' Rhona said, before turning and expertly wriggling her way to the bar. The vivid pattern of her mini-dress stood out against the dark jackets of the men – and Penny noted that it was mostly men doing the buying the drinks, with most of the women sipping from glasses. Some seemed to have halves of beer, which Penny didn't fancy. Too bitter for her. She didn't mind shandy but thought it would be much more sophisticated to have Babycham like her friend – if Rhona was having it, it must be all right. She tapped her foot to the rhythm of the music and, bearing in mind their agreement on the bus, tried not to catch the eye of any of the men. The man who'd first approached her had been OK but she was sure she could do better.

The song was over by the time Rhona re-appeared with two glasses of the sparkling drink. 'Here you go. A filthy sod at the bar tried to pinch my bum. I told him what he could do.' Rhona knocked back a gulp. 'Right, let's find a good spot and check out who's here. This way.'

Penny once again allowed herself to be led through the crowd, smiling at the people whose gaze she met but not stopping, taking her cue from her more experienced friend. Finally Rhona found somewhere acceptable. They stood with their backs to one of the walls, a little behind a row of tables, and from there they could see all of the dance floor and most of the people sitting around it.

Something by the Kinks came on. Rhona nodded in approval. She didn't like clubs where they played anything as long as it was in the charts – she preferred music that sounded new, as if it had been written for her generation. She found herself singing along again, lost in the sounds, but then reminded herself to concentrate. She was here for a purpose, and if she didn't watch out Penny would wander off and get picked up by any old idiot. It was fine to appear to be lost in the music – some men liked that – but you had to be fully alert behind the mask.

'What about them?' Penny nodded to a table where two young men were sitting, both in sharp suits, deep in conversation.

'Hmm, let's wait. No, they're no good.' Rhona pointed to two young women weaving their way to the same table, both in tiny miniskirts. 'They've just got back from the cloakroom over there. Nothing doing for us in that direction.'

Penny scanned the dance floor. 'Him? I like the way he dances ... oh no, maybe not. Look, he thinks he's on the telly, look at him go.' The two girls stared at the strange dance and then burst into laughter. The man carried on oblivious, clearly convinced he was God's gift to women everywhere.

The song ended and another one started up, with some dancers returning to their seats and other people taking their places. The floor grew more crowded and the spotlights moved around, illuminating geometric patterns on the dresses and shirts, light catching the more bouffant hairdos, or picking out the glossiness of the hair gel favoured by some of the men. Penny finished her drink and clutched the empty glass.

'Fancy another?' A slim-hipped young man approached them, smiling broadly.

Rhona met his gaze and cocked her head. 'You asking her, me, or both of us?'

The man's grin grew even wider. 'Oh, both of you. Definitely both. How could I choose between you two lovely ladies?'

Rhona assessed him even as she continued flirting. 'That's cheesy, that is. You got to do better than that.'

'I'm wounded,' said the man. 'I meant every word from the bottom of my heart. What'll it be?'

Penny giggled but said nothing, waiting to see if Rhona would allow him to buy them their next drinks.

Rhona made her decision. The shirt was good, the trousers were the right shape and hugged his body quite promisingly, and the hair was almost but not quite like Brian Jones's. He'd do. 'Seeing as you're so sincere, we'd like Babycham,' she said, giving him her best upwards glance. Then she looked away, as if suddenly shy.

'Coming right up.' He took their empty glasses and as he did so, his fingers brushed Rhona's. 'Pleased to meet you. I'm Gary.'

Jean clocked on at the factory on Monday morning and looked around for her team. She was early and so didn't really expect to see everyone there but it was a shock all the same to find she was the

48

only one in, with ten minutes to go until the shift was due to start. She tucked her straight brown hair back under her scarf, buttoned her overalls and pitched up her sleeves. After Rhona's outburst at the end of last week, and the way Penny clearly looked up to her and followed her every move, Jean was concerned that the two young women wouldn't make it in.

As if he'd been listening to her thoughts, Mr Forsyth, the foreman, came whistling through the door to the factory floor. His round red face shone in the few beams of sunshine that penetrated the dusty windows.

Jean groaned inwardly. As if Mondays weren't bad enough, she now had to deal with the boss in chirpy mood, who was definitely a morning person, which she wasn't. 'Hello, Mr Forsyth. Did you have a good weekend?' She reached in her pocket for her headscarf and shook it out.

'I did indeed, Miss Barker, I did indeed.' He rubbed his hands as if he couldn't wait to start work. 'We saw my brother and his family. I think you know my nephew Andy?'

With a sinking feeling Jean wished she'd never asked what she'd thought was a harmless question. 'Not well, no,' she said, 'but I've heard of him.'

'And would that have been from your young colleague Miss Foster?' The foreman didn't wait for an answer.

Jean nodded and made a noncommittal noise. From what she knew of him, Rhona was better off without Andy Forsyth. He was good-looking, as all her boyfriends seemed to be, but he had a vindictive streak and could be thoroughly unpleasant when crossed.

'And where is Miss Foster this morning?' Forsyth went on. 'Here come our two most reliable ladies, but I don't see Miss Foster anywhere.' His eyes narrowed. The good mood hadn't lasted long.

'Oh, she'll be here, don't you worry,' said Jean, crossing her fingers and hoping she was right. 'Morning, Margot, morning, Alma.' The two older women nodded and moved away to hang up their coats. It was still chilly and spring seemed to have forgotten it was due to arrive.

'Well, she'd better be,' said Forsyth. 'I'm keeping my eye on that young woman. But I'm needed for an important meeting with the manager, so I shall leave you to it for now.' He bustled off, all importance and swagger.

Important meeting with the manager my arse, thought Jean. With the biscuit barrel more like. Still, Penny and Rhona were cutting it fine.

They burst through the outer door together with a minute to go. Rhona looked as if she hadn't had time to brush her hair, her coat was done up the wrong way and she was breathing heavily as if she'd been running.

'Blimey, you're taking a chance getting here with only a minute to spare,' said Jean. 'You do realise Forsyth has got it in for you after you dumped Andy? He's been down here checking. You'd better watch your step or you'll be out on your ear.'

'Oh, I'm not worried about him,' gasped Rhona. 'I just overslept a bit, that's all. We're here now. Go on, Jean, pass me my overall and I'll be ready in a tick.'

'Good weekend, was it?' Jean did as she was

asked, arching an eyebrow. She could make a fair guess at why the girl was in such a state.

'The best,' grinned Rhona. 'Thanks, you're a star. Right, I'm ready to go.'

Jean wondered if her colleague would be safe to work near machinery but decided it wasn't her problem. 'OK, let's make a start. You and Penny get down to the packing end of the production line.'

Rhona and Penny set off to their appointed places, Rhona leaning heavily on her friend.

'You could have landed me in it,' hissed Penny. 'I'm all right to work even if you aren't. I never should have waited for you on the corner.'

'But you wanted to hear what happened yesterday, didn't you?' Rhona laughed. 'Just as well 'cos I never would have told this lot the details.' She grinned. 'It was worth it, even if I can hardly stand up today.'

'Rhona! That's disgusting.'

'I only meant with tiredness. Seriously, we didn't go all the way. Not on our first real date, and that in the afternoon.' Rhona smiled dreamily at the memory. 'I didn't mean to stay up half the night with Gary, and we were only talking. Well, and having a drink or several.'

'You better suck on some more mints before Forsyth comes by,' Penny advised her. 'I can still smell it on your breath. He'll notice it at once and you don't want to be giving him any excuse to fire you. Turning up half drunk when you're operating machinery is asking for trouble.' She pulled out a stool and sat down at the conveyor belt.

Rhona collapsed on to the stool next to her.

'Sorry. But you did enjoy the other night, didn't you?'

'Yeah,' Penny admitted. 'It was great. Shall we go again or will you just want to be with Gary?'

Rhona jumped to catch a tin that almost made it past her. Damn, she thought, she really was going at half speed today. She'd better sort herself out or it wouldn't just be her who was in trouble; it would mess up the whole shift. She liked her co-workers and didn't want to get them in hot water if she could help it – but she wouldn't be giving up her nights out for anybody.

'No reason why you can't come along when I next go out with Gary,' she said kindly. 'He might have other friends for you to meet. He's bound to have, he knows lots of people. We've definitely got to go back to the Talisman. They play all the best music. How about next weekend?'

'You sure I won't be a gooseberry?' Penny wasn't completely convinced. 'I don't want to cramp your style or anything.'

'Not much chance of that,' said Rhona, tossing her head.

Chapter Five

'Next time your van breaks down on a Friday for God's sake don't wait until Monday to tell me,' groaned Tommy. It was all very well handing over the day-to-day work of signwriting to his team but that relied on them having some common sense.

Now it looked as if Jerry had none. The big man stood by the stationary van, looking helpless.

'Didn't want to bother you,' he muttered.

'Well, you were going to have to bother me at some time and if you'd done it on Friday we could have fixed it over the weekend and had it up and running this morning,' Tommy told him, wondering if the message was getting through. 'Now we've got a client who's going to think we're unreliable. That's the last thing we want.'

Jerry shrugged. Clients weren't his problem.

Tommy thought fast. 'Right, you'd better have my van. Come back to the yard with me, and bring your stuff.'

'What, do you mean I have to carry it all?' asked Jerry, frowning. 'It's heavy.'

Tommy gave him a straight look. 'It's not far. Good job you only live a couple of streets away. The exercise will do you good.'

He set off without looking back to check that Jerry was following him. He certainly wasn't going to offer to help carry anything after all the trouble the big man had caused.

Turning into his yard, Tommy ran into the office which stood at the back of the premises and came out with a set of keys to the van parked beside the main gate. He opened the back doors and took out some boxes. They contained his own materials, which he still sometimes painted with, but he didn't want Jerry to use them. The man was a good signwriter when it came down to it, which was why he'd taken him on in the first place, but he was always losing things and was completely disorganised.

Jerry came puffing along the pavement and nearly collapsed as he staggered into the yard. 'That's all I'm taking. I couldn't manage it all. Shall I sling it in there?' He nodded to the open van doors.

'Yeah, better put your foot down.' Tommy watched as his employee threw his gear into the vehicle, his thinning strands of sandy hair plastered to his head with sweat despite the chilliness of the day.

'I'll be off, then.'

Tommy nodded, watching as Jerry backed the van up to the office and turned it before leaving the yard. He realised he'd better ring the mechanic straight away or else he might not get the broken van ready for tomorrow, and they had a lot on.

Before he could go into the office to use the telephone, a voice called out to him.

'If it isn't Tommy Wilson. It is you, Tommy, isn't it?'

Tommy turned around and looked at the figure, whose face was indistinct because the late morning sun was behind him. The voice was sort of familiar but he couldn't place it. He shielded his eyes and could see it was a man, almost as tall as him and heavily built. There was no point in denying who he was as there was a big sign over the gate saying 'Thomas Wilson and Company, Signwriters', so he went towards the stranger and said, 'Yeah, that's me. Who wants to know?'

The man stepped forward. 'Don't you recognise me, mate?'

Tommy squinted and moved so that the shadow of the overhead sign fell across the man and suddenly he could make out the features on his face. He was definitely familiar but he just couldn't place him. 'Yes, of course, it's...' He ransacked his memory but nothing came.

The man laughed. 'It's me, Larry. Larry Barnet.'

The penny dropped. Tommy gasped in surprise. He hadn't seen Larry since they were about fifteen. He thought about telling his former friend that he hadn't changed a bit but that would be an out and out lie. The man had filled out, of course he had, but he was carrying a lot of weight around his middle and his hair now formed a widow's peak. His nose was a bit red, the sign of a heavy drinker most likely. But his clothes were tidy and he wore a tie, which looked new.

'Larry. What brings you back here? I thought you'd gone for good.'

Larry shook his head. 'Long story, mate. You got a minute? This is your place, isn't it? You done well for yourself.'

'Yeah, well, not bad,' said Tommy, unsure if he wanted the man on his premises or not. The two of them had hung around together when they were schoolboys but it was a time he'd have preferred to forget. They had terrorised some of the local girls and he was now deeply ashamed of what he'd done. Now he was older he could see that it had been cruel and the thought of anyone doing something similar to Grace made him very angry. But maybe Larry had changed, as he himself had.

'Come on in to the office if you like,' he said. What harm could a quick cuppa do, he thought. 'It's just across there.' He led the way through the yard, with Larry right behind.

'Nice place you got here,' he said admiringly. 'Good location. Bet it brings in a fair amount of business.'

'We do OK.' Tommy switched on the kettle as his old friend sat down on a swivel chair. 'Milk, sugar? Yes, we've been here for a couple of years or so. I was a one-man band for a while, but it's better with a team. I don't have to work seven days a week anymore for a start. How about you?'

Larry shook his head and laughed. 'Bit of this, bit of that. You know. Import, export.'

Tommy leaned back against a filing cabinet and raised his eyebrows. In some circles that could mean anything from selling a few black market cigarettes on a stall to major smuggling and tax evasion. He'd no reason to think Larry was involved in anything criminal and yet the man's father had been sacked for stealing from his place of work, which was why the family had disappeared from the Battersea area to start with. Larry had always been a chip off the old block and close to his dad. Well, it was none of his business. He didn't intend to get sucked in to Larry's schemes and once they'd had their tea he'd wave him goodbye and that would be that.

'Ever think about the old days, Tommy?' asked Larry, stretching out his legs and putting his arms behind his head, making himself at home. 'I missed the old place something rotten for ages when we moved. It's good to have an excuse to come back. Not that I'll be back here to live, we're out in Kent now. Me mum – remember her? – she won't ever want to breathe in this smoggy air again, she loves it out there. But you can't live on fresh air so I'm doing a bit of business round here for the time being. We should get together one evening for old times' sake.'

Tommy smiled noncommittally. 'Maybe.'

Larry cocked his head. 'We had some good times back then. Used to enjoy ourselves, didn't we? Chasing all those girls? Remember flashing them in the park and hearing them scream?'

Tommy looked uncomfortable. He didn't want to be reminded of what he'd done.

'I think now we should have gone further, you know,' said Larry lazily. 'Half of them were too scared to know what we were doing, and most would never have told their mums once we'd threatened them properly. We missed a chance if you ask me.'

'I'm glad we didn't,' said Tommy shortly. 'We were stupid back then, didn't realise what could have happened.'

'Exactly my point.' Larry laughed wolfishly. 'All those schoolgirls and that big park ... what a wasted opportunity. Still, there were two that told on us, weren't there? Two that got us into trouble. That snooty grammar-school kid, what's her name ... Sandra. That was it. Always thought she was too good for us. Should have taught her a proper lesson while we had the chance. And her friend...'

Tommy had a sinking feeling that he knew what was coming next.

'...the stupid one. Dumbo, we used to call her. Her mum was friends with ours, weren't she? Good-looking kid but thick as two short planks. I wonder what happened to her.'

57

Tommy said nothing.

Larry looked at him. 'Don't suppose you know?'

Tommy still said nothing.

'Ah, that's it.' Larry smiled, a calculating expression on his face. 'You do know. Still round here, is she? Is she still a looker? Filled out, has she? By the looks of you, you know the answer to that one. Is she still stupid?'

Tommy reached across and took his guest's empty cup. He set it carefully back down on the countertop beside the kettle and old jam jar that held the sugar. Then he walked to the door and opened it.

'Tommy, Tommy,' said Larry, swivelling round on the chair. 'I only just finished me tea. Don't tell me you want me to go already?'

'Best you do,' said Tommy, his voice strained.

'And why's that, Tommy?' teased Larry. 'Don't like thinking what I might do to Dumbo if I came across her? It'd be no more than she deserves. And you don't need to answer my questions. I already know where she is. Peckham, ain't it.'

Without thinking Tommy reached across and grabbed the man's shirt front and held him so that the shiny new tie was tight across his throat. Larry struggled, taken by surprise. He was the bigger man but Tommy was lean and strong, and fitter from years of hoisting heavy signs around. He stared at Larry, eyeball to eyeball.

'You try anything and you'll be sorry,' he said with an icily. 'You lay one hand on Mavis and you'll wish you hadn't been born. You get me? You understand? Don't just splutter, give me a proper answer or you'll live to regret it.' He kept on staring into the man's face.

Larry tried to break free but the tie was too tight and choked him every time he began to turn away. He was sweating and his red nose shone. Tommy noted in disgust that he had greasy pores when you looked up close. So Larry cared about his clothes but not enough to look after himself properly. All style, no substance. That shouldn't have come as a surprise to him. Well, if he was all surface bluster he'd be easy to intimidate. He loosened his hold a little.

'You understand me?' Tommy repeated, without dropping his gaze.

Larry gasped noisily for air. 'Yes, I get you. For God's sake, Tommy, it were only a bit of banter. It's not as if I care what Dumbo's up to or who she's up to come to that.'

Tommy let go of the man and thrust him away. 'Don't calling her Dumbo. Her name is Mavis!'

Larry gained his footing and, as though to regain some dignity, he straightened his tie as he said, 'Yeah, well, you're welcome to her.'

'Door's that way.' Tommy didn't move, but followed the man with his eyes as he attempted to stroll nonchalantly across the yard and out of the gate. When Larry reached the pavement he turned and gave a half-wave. Then he disappeared behind the tall surrounding wall.

Tommy slumped into his desk chair and put his head in his hands. What had come over him? He hadn't done anything like that for years, not since he was in his teens at least. Part of him was glad he still had the strength to command such a situation – he'd have looked pretty ridiculous if Larry had been able to get away and then had clocked him one. But in another way he was horrified that he'd reacted so immediately and could have lost control at any moment. Was that the sort of man he wanted to be? It usually took a lot to rouse his temper, and he had thought he'd mastered it, but when it came to Mavis it was a different matter. He'd seen red and would have gone to any lengths to defend her.

Still, he guessed that in one way it had worked – Larry would be unlikely to try anything with Mavis now. It was then that Tommy remembered the broken-down van and his intention of ringing the mechanic as soon as he got back to the office. Damn it, Larry's visit hadn't only made him lose his temper, he'd wasted all that time and now he might lose a day's work if it couldn't be repaired. Forcing himself to breathe more slowly, Tommy reached for the phone.

Chapter Six

Rhona hadn't told Penny about her next date with Gary because she didn't want to make her friend jealous – or not more than she was already. When they'd agreed to go to the Talisman at the weekend Rhona had already known that she'd be seeing Gary in the middle of the week, but she didn't want company this time. Tonight was just for the pair of them.

Normally Rhona wouldn't worry too much about a date. She liked to get ready and dress up but knew she was attractive and didn't waste time wondering if she looked good enough. She knew she did. She was well aware that the men she dated went out with her based solely on her appearance and played the same game. First and foremost they had to look good, and she liked it if they could take her to the sort of places she loved best – clubs or pop concerts. She liked her boyfriends to be fun. She was after a good time and assumed that's what they were after too. Serious questions like personality and reliability didn't come into it. But with Gary, she found herself wondering. Something about him made her take more notice of what he said than she usually would, and he intrigued her.

Rhona put on her false eyelashes and plucked her eyebrows with extra care that evening, spending ages in front of the mirror checking they were even and dark enough without being too heavy. She wished the lighting in her bedroom was better, but there was only the dull light bulb inside the battered shade that had been there for as long as she could remember. Just before leaving she checked her diary, ticked the date and reached into her bedside cabinet. This was where she kept her precious stash of the Pill. She was meticulous about taking it, even though she knew of plenty of girls who only did so when they remembered. Rhona had no intention of leaving such things to chance. She knew what everyone thought of her – that she was irresponsible, to put it kindly – but she backed up her love of a good time with stringent precautions. She wasn't going to get pregnant.

She couldn't repress a little shiver of anticipation at the thought of Gary waiting for her at Oxford Circus tube. They'd be in the heart of the action and they'd draw everyone's attention, she just knew it. She wondered what he'd be wearing. She pulled on her highest patent boots and zipped them up, careful not to snag her nylons. Her mother always went on about how hard they'd been to come by during the war, but as Rhona had never had any trouble getting any she didn't understand what all the fuss was about.

Tying the belt on her new mac tightly at her waist, she grabbed, her bag and ran downstairs.

'What time are you gonna be back?' called her mother from the kitchen.

'Not sure. Don't wait up,' Rhona shouted as she ran out of the front door.

Nearly an hour later, Rhona was getting cold as she stood at the exit to the tube. She knew there were lots of ways out of this particular station but she thought they'd been clear when they'd made their arrangement: the exit closest to Liberty's. Rhona had never been into the grand old shop but she knew where it was and liked to gaze into its windows – not that she'd have been seen dead in any of the fabrics they displayed. 'Maybe when I'm thirty,' she muttered. Where was Gary? Surely he hadn't stood her up? He'd seemed so keen on Sunday. After Kenneth's poor performance nearly a week ago, she was beginning to wonder if her luck had turned and she'd lost her touch.

'Hiya, beautiful.' There was a tap on her shoulder and she turned around and there he was.

'Gary!' She hoped she didn't sound too eager. Men didn't like girls who were desperate. She grinned and made her voice casual. 'Thought you might've had second thoughts.'

He pulled back and made a face. 'With you waiting for me? Never. No, I admit I did set off a bit late 'cos I'd had to go round to my old mate Jeff's place, but then there was some problem on the Camden Road and all the traffic was backed up. I got the bus, I'll know better next time. Jeff's a great bloke but not worth me missing a date with you.'

He put his arm around her shoulders and pulled her close to him. Rhona could smell his aftershave, warm and spicy, and the smell of his body mixed with it – he must have hurried to get here, knowing he was running late. Good, he was still keen.

'Fancy a drink somewhere?' he asked. 'I know a quiet pub round here then we can go on and catch some music in that basement bar I told you about.'

'Sounds fab,' said Rhona, wanting to undo the top button of her mac as it looked better in a deep V shape but she was too cold. 'I could do with something warm.' She giggled.

Gary steered her down the side of Liberty's and into a back street, where in the orange glow of a streetlight she could see a pub sign swinging in the chilly wind. It was an old-fashioned place with leaded windows and deep green paintwork outside. As he held the door open there was a low buzz of conversation from the small crowd inside. Even though it was a weekday evening the place was far from empty. Gary elbowed his way through to a vacant table and they sat on raised stools.

'Here, I'll just take my jacket off and then go to the bar. Babycham again?' he guessed.

'I'll have a rum and blackcurrant,' Rhona said. 'That's what the Beatles like, I heard it on the radio.'

'Wow, OK,' Gary whistled. 'I'll stick to the bitter if it's all the same with you. Back in a mo.'

Rhona leaned back cautiously and lit a cigarette, wondering if she would actually like the new drink. She'd have to pretend she did whatever happened. If the Beatles had it then she'd do her best to enjoy it, as it would mark her out as somebody in the know. She wondered what the Stones drank. Kenneth could have told her, but she wasn't talking to him.

Gary came back bearing his pint and a small glass for her and she thought again how like Brian Jones he looked. She smiled involuntarily. 'Cheers,' she said, raising the glass and sipping. That wasn't too bad. Oh, no. Wait a minute. It had an aftertaste she wasn't at all keen on. She managed not to pull a face and resolved to get used to it. She couldn't go round having Babycham all the time, everyone drank that.

'So shall I put something on the jukebox?' Gary suggested. They could hear it playing above the murmur of conversations around them. 'How about something by the Beatles if you've started ordering their favourite tipple?'

Rhona laughed. 'It doesn't mean that I like

their music the best. I don't mind it but there's other stuff I prefer. Like the Stones. They're ... I don't know, wilder.'

'Oh, you like wild things?' Gary gave her a sideways look. 'I might have known it. I could have predicted that from the first moment I saw you.'

'Cheeky.'

'True, though.' He tapped his beer glass against hers. 'To wild times.'

She tossed her hair, now it was free of the coat collar. She'd put on new earrings and they swung around her neck. 'Wild times,' she echoed.

Gary took a gulp and sighed. 'That's better. Sorry to keep you waiting like that, I really mean it. I kept thinking you wouldn't be there. I wouldn't have blamed you, a cold night like this, being stuck there on your own, and you hardly know me.'

'Got to know you quite well on Sunday though, didn't I?' Rhona said, with a little smile at the memory. If she had her way that would be just the start. She'd been very restrained, not jumping into bed with him at his first suggestion. Didn't hurt to make them wait a little bit, but it had taken all her willpower to say no.

'You did,' he breathed, waving away the smoke from her cigarette that was drifting between them. 'We could do that again. How about coming back to my place after the bar? We can be as wild as you like.'

Rhona sighed wistfully. 'I'd love to, Gary, I really would. But I've got work tomorrow morning and my boss has got it in for me at the moment – don't know why, he's a mean old sod. I can't get away with being one minute late. So I'll need to get back to Peckham.' She paused. 'And as I live with Mum and Dad I don't think I can sneak you in. That wouldn't be right.'

'Pity.' Gary took another gulp of beer. 'I don't want to get you in trouble…'

'No, I can do that well enough on my own,' Rhona assured him.

'I bet you can.'

'So not tonight.' She gazed at him and her eyes sparkled. 'Maybe another time.'

'Soon?'

'I'd like that,' she said, looking down in an attempt at modesty.

'I know what I'll put on,' Gary said suddenly. 'Marianne Faithfull. I bet you like her. And it's because it's just come to me who you look like. You're a dead ringer for Marianne Faithfull.'

'Me?' Rhona hadn't heard that one before, but she could hardly object. The sexy, sultry young singer was high in the charts and was drop-dead gorgeous. For a moment she suspected Gary was spinning her a line but then she told herself to relax. She'd just been given a huge compliment by a very attractive man. She gripped the table top. 'Yes, go on, see if they've got her new single.' She watched him as he sauntered across the floor towards the jukebox, and a thrill went through her. He was special. She'd never met anyone quite like him, and she was a bit scared, knowing that no man had ever affected her in exactly this way before. 'To wild times,' she said quietly to herself.

Mavis proudly put away the last of the crockery

from the evening meal in her kitchen, pleased with the way she'd organised everything now it was all unpacked. The smart cupboard doors were a pale green, which she'd picked out when Pete gave her the choice. She thought it would remind her of parks and gardens. Now she could look into their own garden from her kitchen window on the first floor and imagine how it would be in summer, with tubs of flowers and vegetables. She sighed contentedly.

'So you're settled in?' asked Tommy, who was sitting at the kitchen table, his elbows on the grass-green Formica surface. 'It feels like home now?'

'It does. The children love it, and Grace has stopped worrying about monsters,' Mavis said with a note of relief. Of course she should have expected that Grace, having complained solidly about sharing with her brother for two years, would then kick up a fuss when she finally had a room of her own. But it had only lasted a couple of nights.

'It's a big improvement on Harwood Street, or Wandsworth for that matter,' said Tommy. 'You'll never want to come over to my flat again.'

Mavis laughed. 'Don't be silly. We won't see less of each other now I'm in here, will we? It's no further away from your place than the old house.'

'No, only teasing. Anyway, now that the baby-sitters are right downstairs, if anything, this set-up means we can see more of each other. Or I bet you could get Rhona over. Grace would love that, she can play with those false eyelashes.'

'Of course,' said Mavis, but her mind was wandering to what had happened at the weekend.

'You'll never guess what,' she began. 'The other day, Saturday it must have been, I was down Choumert Street market and I thought I saw a face from the past.' She grimaced. 'Larry Barnet, but surely it, couldn't have been him?'

'Larry?' Tommy kept his face expressionless. He didn't want to give anything away about the incident in his office. Had Larry seen her too? Had he sought him out deliberately to wind him up, rather than just walking past the yard and recognising him? 'You sure?'

'Well, not totally, but it did look like him, though he had less hair and was bigger than I remember,' Mavis said nervously. 'I really hope he hasn't moved to this area. You know he made my life a total misery for a while and I know you were part of it, but he was the ringleader.'

Tommy rubbed his chin and looked away from her. It sounded like Larry all right. Should he tell her what had happened? No, she'd be more worried than ever and he could tell she was getting herself all worked up. That wasn't fair, not when she'd been so happy earlier in the evening.

'Forget about it,' he advised her. 'Larry Barnet's been gone from South London for years and good riddance to him and his family, bunch of criminals that they are. You don't want to be thinking about him. He's in the past, love. Why would he show himself round here? He never had anything to do with Peckham. It must have been someone else. Like you said, you could have made a mistake. People change a lot in, what is it? Ten or twelve years?'

'Yes, I know.' Mavis bit her lip.

'Come here,' Tommy said, opening his arms to her. She went across to him and sat on his lap, resting her head against his. 'Forget about it,' said Tommy, stroking her back. 'You've got nothing to worry about on that score. I love you and won't let anything happen to you.' His face set in determination. 'I will never, ever let anyone hurt you ever again. Trust me. Nobody is ever going to harm you. I'll see to that.'

Chapter Seven

'You sure you don't mind me tagging along?' asked Penny, battling along the street against the driving wind that Saturday evening. 'Oh, this is ruining my hair. I don't know why I bothered. You got any hairspray on you?'

'No.' Rhona wasn't managing much better. 'Let's go to the ladies as soon as we get inside and we can fix ourselves up all over again. I can't have Gary seeing me like this.'

She gave a sigh of relief as they finally approached the door of the Talisman club. This time it was easier to make out the layout in the dim lighting and they both pushed their way across to the ladies, only to find that everyone else had had the same idea. The small room was full of young women bemoaning the state of their appearance and jostling for a view in the steamed-up mirror. Rhona and Penny ended up doing each other's make-up and hair in a corner, but eventually they were satisfied that the damage had been repaired and that they were ready to do battle on the dance floor.

Gary was waiting by the bar and Penny nudged Rhona. 'There he is. Oh, I like his shirt.'

Rhona nodded in agreement. Gary's dress sense was one of the things that had made him so attractive in the first place. He'd pulled out all the stops tonight, looking better than ever. She eyed him hungrily.

'Hello, beautiful.' He smiled when he saw her and pulled her close to him. 'Hi, Penny. What can I get you both?'

'Babycham please,' said Penny.

'I'll have rum and blackcurrant,' said Rhona, giving him a conspiratorial glance.

Penny looked at her with suspicion. 'What's this? Rum? You don't usually drink rum.'

'It's my new thing,' Rhona told her, as Gary nodded in acknowledgement and turned to buy them what they wanted. 'The Beatles love it. I'll let you have a sip if you like.'

'Yeah, I'll give it a try,' said Penny dubiously.

Gary returned with their drinks and Rhona offered her a sip of the new favourite. Penny tried it. It was disgusting, thick, sweet, and far too strong. 'Nah, you can keep it,' she said, grimacing. 'I don't care who likes it, I'm not having that again. Give me Babycham any time. Thanks, Gary.' She raised her glass to him.

'My pleasure, doll.' Gary grinned broadly, knowing he was getting some envious looks for having a blonde on either side. He edged them away from the crowded bar to a vacant table. Sandie Shaw blasted through the speakers and Rhona hummed along.

'I really like her,' she said as they took their seats. 'I wonder if she writes her own songs?'

Gary stared at her for a moment and then laughed. 'I shouldn't think so,' he said. 'Not big hits like she's had. You need a man to write music like that. Women aren't much use at the serious stuff.'

'Why not?' Rhona asked. She hadn't thought she'd said anything out of the ordinary and wondered if Gary was winding her up. 'I mean, it's not that hard, is it? You just need to be good at music.'

'It takes more than that,' Gary said with an edge to his voice. 'I've been playing the guitar since I was seven, and you've got to be really good to get noticed by the right people to get anywhere. You need talent and luck. Girls are all right to sing the songs and look good at the front of the band, you get the right sort of attention that way, but you don't want them behind the scenes. They don't take it seriously. Take it from me.'

Rhona didn't know what to say to that. She'd obviously touched a nerve. What was so strange about a girl wanting to write music or play the guitar?

'Are you a musician, then, Gary?' Penny breathed, stepping into the gap. 'I hadn't realised.'

'Yeah, I've played with several bands but I don't have a regular one at the moment,' he said, relaxing again. 'There are a couple who want me to play with them but I'll have to see. They got to be doing music that I'm into. I don't want to play any old thing just to be popular. I need to be

71

doing interesting stuff, new stuff.'

'That sounds exciting,' said Rhona, moving her chair closer to his. 'I bet anyone can play the boring old songs. It takes something special to play the sort that nobody's done before.'

'Exactly,' said Gary, lifting his beer. 'You got to be one step ahead all the time if you really want to make it. It ain't easy at all, let me tell you.'

Rhona's eyes shone with expectation. 'Would you teach me to play, Gary? I'd love to have a go. I've never had the chance before.' Suddenly she was seized with the desire to try it out for herself. What harm could it do to see if she was any good?

Gary laughed and patted her knee. 'Sure, why not. You can have a go when you come to my place. Just don't go getting your hopes up 'cos it takes a long time to learn how to play the guitar really well. But you can have a bit of a play around.' He raised his eyebrows suggestively.

'You're on,' said Rhona eagerly. Gary just got better and better. A gorgeous man who'd teach her the guitar – things didn't come more perfect than that. 'I can't wait.'

Jenny had just checked that ten-year-old Greg had put his light out. He was staying up later and later and if she didn't put her foot down he'd be reading comics all night. She suspected he had smuggled a torch into his room so he could read under the bedclothes, but short of bursting in on him every now and again she couldn't very well stop him, and besides it wasn't a school day tomorrow.

She came back down to the living room and collapsed on to the sofa beside Stan with a big sigh.

'That boy of ours is changing by the minute. I bet he's not gone to sleep and was just pretending a moment ago. He'll ruin his eyesight if he keeps on reading under the blankets like that.'

Stan put down the letter he'd been holding. 'He'll be all right, stop worrying. He's getting older, it's only natural his interests are changing. You can't wrap him in cotton wool.'

'I know.' She glanced at the piece of paper he'd set aside. 'What's that?'

'Ah,' Stan paused. 'I was going to talk to you about it.'

'What?' Jenny's eyes widened in alarm. 'What do you mean?'

'It's all right, no need to panic.' Stan took a deep breath. 'The boss called me in yesterday to talk about my new territory. This is just a letter confirming the changes. I'll still be covering parts of London, but also the southwest.'

'Do you mean southwest England?' Jenny gasped. 'They don't expect you to go down as far as Land's End, do they?'

Stan laughed, 'No, love, that's Cornwall, but it'll include Dorset, Somerset and maybe parts of Devon.'

'Devon, but that's still miles away. You'll be gone for ages if you have to drive that far.' She folded her arms. 'Oh, Stan, I know you've got to do it, but honestly, it's not what I want. I hate the thought of you going away. I really hate it.'

Stan put his arm around her. 'It won't be so bad,' he said reassuringly. 'It could be much worse. What if I had to go to Scotland?'

She turned and stared at him.

'No, no, I won't have to do that,' Stan said hastily. 'There's a whole different team covering the north of England and Scotland. And it won't take me too long, I'll go down the A303 and be there in next to no time. It's meant to be beautiful.'

Jenny shrugged. 'I wouldn't know. I've never been.' Stan waved the letter. 'Well, here's the thing. Would you like to?'

'What, go to work with you?' Jenny asked, shaking her head. 'I don't think so, Stan.'

Stan shut his eyes briefly, wondering if she'd deliberately got the wrong end of the stick. He was trying to see this as a positive change and knew his life would be easier if he could talk Jenny round. He hoped what he had to say next would do it. 'Not to work, no. But obviously if I have to stay over for a few nights then I'll put up in a hotel or somewhere that does bed and breakfast. There may be occasions when you could come too and we can turn it into a nice weekend away. How do you fancy that?'

'What about Greg?' Jenny asked at once. 'We can't leave him on his own.'

Stan sighed. 'Nobody said anything about leaving him on his own. He could stay with Mavis, couldn't he? Or Tommy. Or my mum would have him.'

Jenny thought for a moment. 'He'd rather stay with Mavis. Not being funny or anything but your mum will make him go to bed at seven o'clock and won't let him watch telly. And now that James has got his own room, Mavis could have him easily...'

Stan brightened up. This was going better. 'He'd really enjoy that, wouldn't he? I know he still misses having James next door.'

Jenny nodded. 'He does. And Mavis wouldn't mind.'

'We'll do that, then, as soon as we can. When the weather gets a bit warmer.' Stan gave her a smile. 'I'll have to do a few trips first and then I'll get to know where the best places are. We haven't been away just the two of us since our honeymoon, have we?'

Jenny giggled. 'How could we? First we had no money then along came Greg and our lives were never the same after that.' She looked up at him. 'Maybe this new job won't be so bad after all, Stan Bonner. We could have a second honeymoon.'

He gave her a look. 'We could. We could have a whole series of them. Fancy a bit of practice, Mrs Bonner?' He stroked her face and noticed how her eyes lit up.

She slapped his thigh. 'Nice try, Stan, but you'll have to wait. Like I said, I reckon Greg's still awake. And I know he's growing up fast but there are some things he shouldn't know about just yet.' She didn't trust the sound-proofing in this house, solid though the walls were. 'Shall we see what's on the telly?'

'Suppose so,' said Stan, releasing her. He stretched out. He could wait if he had to – he knew Jenny was as keen as he was. 'Is *Dixon of Dock Green* on?'

'That'll have finished.' Jenny waited for the set to warm up. 'Or we could just listen to some music. Pass me the *Radio Times*.'

Stan got up and put his arms around her, nuzzling her neck. 'I don't care. I'm only waiting

75

till I can get you upstairs.'

'Shhh, what if Greg hears you saying that?' But Jenny knew he wouldn't. She hugged her husband. A second honeymoon in Devon – wait till she told Mavis.

Chapter Eight

Rhona turned on to her side and watched the patterns change on the unfamiliar curtains as the orange streetlights threw shadows from the tree branches outside the window. The light slowly changed to the dull grey of dawn. She raised her arms over her head and stretched luxuriously, savouring the memories of the night before. Gary had been everything she'd hoped for, passionate and considerate and the most exciting man she'd ever been with. They'd spent all Sunday afternoon in bed, then managed to go to a fish and chip shop round the corner for a quick bite to eat, before falling back into bed again and staying up half the night. She'd only had a few hours' sleep but she felt wonderful. Idly she tried to work out just how long she'd, slept ... oh no.

It must be Monday morning. Slowly the, cogs turned in her brain and she realised she was meant to be at the factory in Peckham in half an hour and she was still in Gary's bed, in his flat near Finsbury Park, the other side of the city. She was going to be in deep trouble. Penny might cover for her for a short while but she wouldn't be able to do so for long. Jean would notice at once, and the loathsome foreman Mr Forsyth had been making a point of turning up at the start of their shift and making sarky comments. She still hadn't been forgiven for dumping creepy Andy.

Rhona swore under her breath and heaved herself out of bed. The bedroom was cold. There was a one-bar electric fire in the corner but she didn't have time to switch it on. Blindly she groped around for her clothes and struggled into them. They'd raise a few eyebrows at the factory but there was no way she could waste more time by going home to change first. She'd just have to hope she could get her overall on before everyone noticed her low-cut top.

Gary stirred. 'Morning, doll. Make us a cup of tea, will yer?'

Rhona groaned. What a romantic way to start the day. 'I can't,' she hissed. 'I'm late for work, I've got to run.'

'Nah, babe, come back to bed and I'll make you forget all that,' said Gary, and she could just about make out in the gloom that he was opening his arms to her. It was very tempting. But she thought of her mother's face if she got the sack and forced herself to zip up her boots.

'Got to go.' She kissed the top of his head. 'Thanks for a fab weekend. See you Wednesday.'

Gary half-sat up and kissed her back. 'Wednesday it is, babe. See you then.'

As she opened the bedroom door a shaft of light from the landing showed her that he'd already curled up to go back to sleep. She wished she could stay with him, spend the day with him, messing around in bed, playing his guitar and making the world go away. Reality was waiting for her in the shape of a freezing cold morning and crowded buses all along the Seven Sisters Road. Grimly she reached for her purse and forced herself to walk as far as the bus stop, where she shivered in her thin mac, designed for looking good, not keeping warm.

Finally she managed to get on a bus and wedge herself into a seat, next to a middle-aged man in a suit who looked at her with barely veiled contempt. She could feel the disapproval rising off him. Miserable old git, she thought. Then she smiled to herself. Bet I've had more fun this weekend than you've had in your entire life. Bet I've done things you didn't even know were possible. She couldn't help giggling and quickly smothered it, pretending to cough. The man edged away from her, an even more disdainful expression on his thin face. Rhona didn't care. It gave her more room. Her thoughts drifted back to the night before and she sat daydreaming happily as the windows fogged up and the overcrowded bus made its slow way down the busy road.

'What time do you call this?' Jean hissed as, over an hour later, Rhona eventually made it to her shift. The only good thing was she'd got to her locker and into her overall before anyone could spot what she had on underneath – or, more like, what she didn't have on.

'I was delayed,' said Rhona, trying to keep a straight face.

Jean stared at her. 'Come on, you can do better

than that.'

'Well, it's true, I was,' said Rhona, unable to stop herself from smiling. 'Oh, all right, I had further to come this morning and got the timing all wrong. I got here as fast as I could. Don't take on.'

'It's not me you've got to worry about,' said Jean, retying her scarf tightly. 'And you smell of drink again. For God's sake go to the ladies and tidy yourself up. A few more minutes won't make any difference now, the damage has been done. Your absence has been noted. You'll be on a warning, and it'll be worse if Forsyth sees you in a mess like that.'

'OK, thanks.' Rhona dashed for the door to the ladies.

Sure enough Mr Forsyth strode over to her as the bell rang for the mid-morning tea break.

'Miss Foster. My office, now, if you please.' He strutted off, full of his own importance, which left Rhona little choice but to follow him. She pulled a face and smoothed down her overall.

'Wish me luck,' she said to Penny. Jean heard her.

'He won't sack you now, surely, not in the middle of a shift. I don't know how we'll get everything finished if we're a person short.'

'We'll soon find out, won't we,' said Rhona nonchalantly and strode off after the foreman, a little unsteadily in her high-heeled boots.

Lily groaned as she dropped the heavy laundry basket on to the paving slabs. What with all the upheaval of moving she hadn't managed to do the washing for ages and now she was paying the price. Her arms ached with the weight of it but at least she finally had a decent length of line on which to hang it all. Pete had put that up as a priority. It had been threatening to rain first thing this morning but now it was brightening up and there was a good breeze, even though it was cold. Still, it was too good an opportunity to miss and now she'd got it all done and had run it through the wringer, there was a decent chance it would get dry enough to iron later. She reached for her peg bag and noticed that her new neighbour was doing the same thing next door.

Lily had seen people going in and out of the houses around her but hadn't had time to meet any of them. She'd had her ups and downs with neighbours over the years and wasn't in a hurry to get to know the new ones. Back when Mavis was young she'd thought her next door neighbour was a good friend but she'd turned out to be a judgemental gossip who'd spread rumours about her relationship with Pete. So even though they were a legitimately married couple now, she was still wary of rushing into anything. On the other hand, here was a chance to make an acquaintance.

'Morning,' she said brightly, going over to the fence that divided the two back gardens. 'Good day for it, isn't it?'

'Might be if it doesn't come on to rain again,' said the woman on the other side, her expression sour. 'I don't trust it to keep dry.'

'Lily Culling.' Lily introduced herself, wondering if the woman was always this miserable.

'Muriel Burns.' The woman nodded – they

couldn't exactly shake hands as the fence was in the way. 'You just moved in, then?'

'Yeah, that's right,' said Lily. 'Got here Friday before last. Takes a while to get it all sorted out, doesn't it?'

'I wouldn't know,' said Muriel. 'I was born in this house and never lived anywhere else. When I got married to my Reggie, he moved in with me and Mum and Dad. Now they're dead and buried it's just us.'

'It's a big place for just two of you,' Lily said. 'We done this place up into a couple of flats.'

'I know,' said Muriel. 'I heard. I couldn't hardly have missed it.' She gave Lily a hostile glare.

Lily ignored it. 'Me and Pete got the lower flat, with our little boy Bobby, and my grown-up daughter, Mavis, has the upper one with her two kids. They're old enough for school now.'

Muriel looked interested for the first time. 'Oh, is that little boy yours? I've seen him out here playing, from the kitchen window. I just assumed he was the little brother of the other two.' She peered at Lily more closely. 'Surprise, was he?'

Lily bristled. 'He was someone we waited a long time for,' she replied, although the truth was nobody had been more surprised than her to find she was pregnant again in her mid-forties. 'He's our little angel.' She shot a direct look at her neighbour.

'I'm sure he is.' Muriel didn't seem convinced. 'Come far, have yer? Where was you before?'

'Oh not far. Just a bit north of here, still in Peckham, but once we were blessed with Bobby the place was too small. Then Mavis needed a larger place too what with her kids getting bigger, so it made sense for us all to come in together and yet have our own space. It was the ideal solution,' preened Lily, sure that Muriel couldn't possibly find fault with it.

She had a good try, though. 'Bit odd your daughter having kids older than your son, isn't it?' she asked. 'Don't they find it funny? I bet they get teased for it at school.'

'Not at all.' Lily shook her head. 'Mavis's two love Bobby, and help to look after him. He looks up to them and plays with them. It's good for him to have older kids around him, it makes him more grown-up for his age.'

'Hasn't Mavis got a husband, then?' asked Muriel.

Blimey, thought Lily, the blasted woman had been paying close attention. She'd probably been taking notes. 'No, Alec isn't with us anymore,' she said, injecting a note of sadness into her voice and daring the woman to question exactly what that meant. 'Still, they've got Pete and they love him, so they won't miss out.'

'Very fortunate, I'm sure,' said Muriel. 'Well I can't say I'm sorry that your building work is finished. It drove me round the bend, all the banging and drilling. There should be a law against it.'

'All finished now,' said Lily brightly, thinking that she'd have to start hammering in nails for pictures to annoy the woman in payment for her unkind comments.

'Glad to hear it,' said Muriel. 'Right, I'm done here. I'm gonna get back indoors. Pleased to meet you I'm sure.'

She turned and hurried back through her kitchen door before Lily could say anything else. The grumpy woman looked anything but pleased.

Chapter Nine

'Oh, it's nice here.' Rhona looked around Mavis's living room with approval. 'You've got it looking lovely already. It's nice to see the picture you sketched of James and Grace on display.'

Mavis glanced at the little sketch which Tommy had insisted she framed. She'd done it quickly, she remembered, but there was something about it that captured the characters of the children and she was quietly proud of it.

'Now that you've got all this space, it must be easier for you to work from home. Are you still getting plenty of orders?'

'Yes, quite a few, and though I've insisted that I pay rent for this flat, Mum and Pete won't take much, just a couple of pounds,' Mavis said, finding that she had a little more money to spare nowadays. She earned money by doing sketches of children, and had started with just those at Grace's playschool. Then, thanks to word of mouth and a bit of local advertising, the orders grew. She now offered a framing service too, which gave her a decent profit, and though it didn't happen very often, she occasionally got a commission to do an adult portrait which paid well.

'You could do a sketch of me. I've got someone

who might like to have it.' Rhona grinned, throwing herself down on her friend's new sofa and resting her head on one of the crocheted cushions that had been a moving-in present from Jenny Bonner.

Mavis sat down beside her. 'Is that the young man you were talking about before we left? Andy, wasn't it?'

'God, no. He's off the scene.' Rhona pulled a face. 'He was a waste of time.'

'Wasn't he your boss's son or something?' asked Mavis, concerned.

'His nephew. I should have known they'd be alike once I got to know him. Old Forsyth has put me on a final warning, just because I've been late a few times. His nephew was useless and had wandering hands, and not in a good way so I gave him the push.'

'Won't that cause trouble at work?'

'No more than I'm in already. Anyway that seems like ages ago and I've met a real dreamboat now.' Rhona's expression changed. 'He's not like all the others, Mavis. You'd like him. It's why I haven't been round before, 'cos I see him most of the weekends and in the week if we can manage it, only he lives up in North London so it's not so easy. But he's gorgeous, I mean, just like Brian Jones, and he wears dead trendy clothes, and he's teaching me the guitar. All right, a chord or two anyway. He's a musician, well, he has to work in an office at the moment, but that's only till he gets his big break. That's bound to be soon, he's so talented. He's really special.' Her eyes shone.

'He must be,' said Mavis, impressed. 'You don't

usually talk about your boyfriends like that. Don't tell me you've actually fallen for this one?'

'He's different to the others, he really is. I haven't felt like this before. He makes me tingle all over. He treats me like a princess, he's a real gent.' Rhona sighed with pleasure. 'You'll have to meet him, you'll get on. I just know you will.'

'Maybe.' Mavis thought she might not have much to say to an up-and-coming musician but if he made Rhona happy then that could only be a good thing. 'I hope you're being careful?'

Rhona gave her a direct look. 'Now you sound like my mum, but I ain't stupid. If you can't be good, be careful, that's what I always say.'

'And how long have you known him?'

'Almost two weeks. Two wonderful, perfect weeks.'

'Almost an old married couple, then.'

'You're laughing at me and I know I probably deserve it but you wait and see. Gary's different,' Rhona insisted. 'Talking of dishy men, how's Tommy? Now you're in this huge flat are you going to let him move in?'

Mavis's face clouded over. 'It's not that simple, and you know it.'

'It's about time you gave in and had a bit of fun.'

'We do have fun.'

'Not the sort of fun I'm talking about. You still don't go to bed with him, do you? Is it the worry about getting pregnant?' Rhona asked. 'You needn't, you know. You wouldn't even have to tell the odd little lie like I have to. You can go and get the Pill all legit, since in theory you're still a married woman. You wouldn't have to say that the man you're planning to sleep with isn't your husband.'

'Rhona, it sounds terrible when you put it like that,' Mavis protested.

'It isn't terrible at all,' Rhona replied. 'It makes sense. You love Tommy, he loves you. I hate to see you missing out when you could be having such a good time, that's all. Believe me, it's really different when you're with a man you love. I know that now. You're missing out, Mavis, you really are.'

'It's not that simple,' said Mavis, shaking her head. She had been bossed around all her life, manipulated and beaten, so was it any wonder that the fear of losing her hard-fought independence held her back.

Pete pushed open the door to the public bar and breathed a sigh of relief. He'd come back to his old local in Battersea and was pretty sure that nobody he knew from those days would be in here at this hour of the day. He didn't particularly want to talk to anyone, just to have a few moments on his own to think over what he'd just been told.

The place was nearly deserted and weak sunshine came in through the grimy windows, falling on the scarred wooden stools that ranged along the length of the bar. The barmaid, not the one he'd known all those years ago, was wiping glasses with a bored look on her face. She took her time finishing her job and coming over to him but he didn't mind. For once there was no hurry. He watched motes of dust dancing in the narrow sunbeams and vaguely noticed that the whole place could do with a clean, but it didn't worry him. There were worse things in life than a slightly dirty pub.

'What can I get you, love?'

Pete paused. He wasn't much of a drinker compared to some, and certainly not in the middle of the day, but he hated ordering halves and didn't have to rush back anywhere. 'Pint, please.' He nodded to the beer he fancied.

She barely glanced at him as she reached for a glass from the shelf behind her, and ambled to the pump. Slowly she filled the glass and finally wandered back to him. She took his money and gave him his change then turned her back, obviously not wanting to make conversation. Pete was relieved. He took a seat at the end of the bar furthest away from her and went over his meeting earlier that day.

It had begun well enough. He'd come to it expecting to be given a start date for the big new project, in which many of the substandard old terraced houses in Peckham were to be pulled down and replaced with modern ones. His company was perfectly placed to build them and over the past few months he'd been given to understand there were no real competitors for the contract; it was just a case of when it would happen.

On the surface nothing had changed. He'd been welcomed, everyone was all smiles and slapping each other on the back. Yet when he asked direct questions, such as when the all-important start date would be, there'd been a lot of beating about the bush and fudging. He just couldn't make any headway. It didn't make sense, and finally he'd said so.

He'd been assured that there was nothing to worry about, it was just a question of the right person at the council signing it all off, no problems at all. Pete wondered if that was all there was to it and wanted to ask if somebody else was being lined up behind the scenes but they'd explicitly told him that no other company was in the running for the job. It was just a question of waiting for the final thumbs up.

So Pete had come to the quiet pub to think things through. He never used to be much of a worrier; he did his work and did it well, took the money and came home to Lily. Now he could feel all that might be changing. He had Bobby to consider; he couldn't just up and leave for greener fields elsewhere if things went wrong. It wouldn't be fair on Lily and of course there was Mavis with her two kids too. They all depended on him and more so than ever now they had the big house.

Well, they were safe as long as that contract got signed soon. He sighed. He hated relying on other people. Council politics, politics of any kind, had never been his thing. He couldn't be doing with all the bureaucracy, the waiting around, the feeling that you had to say the right thing at the right time to the right person. It was all very frustrating, but he'd have to grin and bear it. When it went ahead, the project would bring in the best money he'd ever had.

An internal door from behind the bar opened and he could hear voices.

'...better if you can start in ten days' time then,'

a man was saying. Then the speaker came through the door. Pete recognised him as the landlord, who now looked balder and more careworn than the last time he'd seen him, a few years ago. 'Here, Patty, get this gentleman a drink. You'll be seeing a lot more of him as he's going to do the signs when we get this place done up.'

The barmaid nodded in a bored way and reached for another pint glass. 'This one all right for you, love?' she asked without any interest in the answer.

'Thanks,' said a familiar voice, and Tommy came through the bar door. Pete groaned to himself. Of all the pubs ... but it made sense. Tommy's yard wasn't far away and the place definitely could do with smartening up. Of course they'd ask the local sign writer. It was just his luck that he'd come in today at exactly the same time.

Tommy caught sight of Pete and did a double take. He made his way over. 'Didn't expect to see you in here,' he said. 'Not your usual stamping ground, is it? You drowning your sorrows or celebrating?' He said it as a joke but Pete had to remind himself to smile, as he wasn't honestly sure which of the two he ought to be doing.

'Passing the time, more like,' he said. 'Cheers, Tommy. No, I had a meeting not too far away so I thought I'd have a look in for old times' sake. How about you?'

'Well as you can see, this place isn't in good nick,' said Tommy, drawing up a stool to sit beside him. 'They're gonna do it up and they need a new sign and lettering for outside as the old paintwork is peeling off and you can hardly read it anymore.'

'Not changing the name of it, are they?' asked Pete, keen to get the subject away from why he was in there. 'I hate it when they do that. I always think it's bad luck.'

'No, it's staying the same,' said Tommy. 'I know what you mean. But they'd have said or I'd have to come up with a new design. No, I just have to do a better version of the old one.'

'So you coming over to ours later? Mavis didn't say.'

'No.' Tommy shook his head. 'Not tonight. I'm going to see Jenny and Stan. Something about changes to Stan's job. I bet they ask me to babysit or something.'

Pete raised his eyebrows. Babysitting was a woman's job as far as he was concerned, though he never minded looking after the three kids at home. 'Young Greg's a good boy,' he observed. 'He can always come round to ours and Mavis will see to him. James would love that.'

'He would. I'll tell them,' said Tommy. He drained his glass. 'Right, best be off.' He looked at Pete and caught something of his mood. 'You sure everything's OK?'

'Never better,' said Pete as cheerfully as he could.

'You seem a bit quiet tonight, babe,' Gary said to Rhona as she slumped against the wall, apparently glad of something to lean on in the crowded basement. They were waiting for the band to come on, and the place was hot and stuffy. 'It's not like you. I've known you, what...' he paused to think 'about six weeks now, and I've never seen you at a loss for words. Don't tell me you're not looking forward to the music. It'll be right up your street.'

Rhona smiled wanly. 'Of course I'm looking forward to it. I've been looking forward to this lot for ages. I've just got a bit of a sore throat, that's all.'

'Comes from singing along to The Who so loudly,' joked Gary.

'That was days ago. It can't be that. I don't know, I'm just a bit run-down,' said Rhona, tucking her blonde hair behind her ear. She felt terrible but wasn't going to tell Gary that. She'd wanted to come to this basement bar in Soho ever since she got wind of it opening and already it was absolutely the place to be seen in. She would die rather than admit how bad she felt. Perhaps she had been overdoing it – staying out late with Gary and yet still managing to get to her morning shift on time, or almost, but Penny was getting better at covering for her. It meant she didn't have to go home early, even if she felt like death warmed up.

'Get you some of that blackcurrant drink you like, shall I?' Gary offered. 'Blackcurrant's good for colds, it's got vitamin C in it, everyone knows that. So it'll be like medicine.'

'Thanks.' Rhona summoned up the energy to flash him a smile. He was so kind to her, she mustn't let him down. Maybe he was right and the drink would help. She had to snap out of it or he'd get bored and she couldn't bear that. She forced herself to stand up straight and look around at the crowd. Everyone was sharply dressed, and nearly everyone was young and good-looking. They had a strict door policy about who could get in, you had to fit, be the right sort and Rhona felt a burst of pride that she was part of this scene, the hippest crowd in the whole city. She'd made it. She had a gorgeous, generous musician boyfriend to get into places like this on his arm, and she knew the sort of envious glances they got as a couple. So why was she feeling so down?

A young man made his way over towards her. He wasn't very striking-looking – if you were feeling mean you'd call him plain, thought Rhona, wondering why he was heading for her. She hadn't shown him any interest, and she looked away from him now, while keeping a check on his progress from the corner of her eye. His clothes weren't trendy, his hair could do with proper styling and his eyes had none of the audacious promise Gary's had had from the word go. He must be aiming towards some friends near her. All the same he got closer and closer and then he was standing beside her. She didn't react.

'Hi. I'm Jeff,' he said. She pretended she hadn't heard.

He looked at her and smiled, she noticed while not revealing that she'd seen him. You'd think he'd get the hint, Rhona thought in annoyance. She wanted to save every ounce of her quickly fading energy for Gary, not waste it on some hopeless case.

Gary came back with the drinks. 'Here you are, doll. Get that down yer, it'll sort you out,' he said. 'This is my friend Jeff. We go back a long way. We were at school together.'

So that was why the man was here. She pretended she hadn't realised he was standing next to her and turned round. 'Pleased to meet you,' she said, her voice a croak.

'Gary's mentioned you. You live up in North London too, don't you?'

Jeff made as if to answer but Gary got in first.

'You're getting one of those husky voices,' he grinned. 'You'll be more like Marianne Faithfull than ever. Jeff, you should hear her go on, she thinks girls should write their own songs, don't you, Rhona?'

Rhona groaned inwardly. She was in no mood to argue that point again and was too tired to make a joke of it. 'Well I don't see why not,' she croaked, smiling brightly as she didn't want to provoke a row, though she hadn't changed her mind. 'If they can sing them, then why not write them as well? I'd be no good though.' She shrugged apologetically at Jeff. 'I can only play a few chords and as you can hear I can hardly talk let alone sing.'

Jeff smiled back. 'I thought you always sounded like that. Nothing wrong with a husky voice...'

'You'd look the part on stage all right,' Gary told her. 'They'd all pay good money to look at you. Lucky I don't have to.' He gave her a squeeze. 'Leave the writing to me and Jeff.'

'Oh, are you a musician too?' asked Rhona, more out of politeness than anything. But before Jeff could answer the lights went down and a cheer went up as the band walked out on the small stage. Rhona leant her weight against Gary, glad of his strong arm around her. He shouldn't tease her like that, but he was only having a bit of fun. She sipped her drink, which she'd almost come to like. She felt worse than ever.

Chapter Ten

Next morning Rhona could hardly get out of bed – her own bed, not Gary's, even though he'd asked her to come home with him. If she'd been feeling better she would have really enjoyed the evening before as the music had been fabulous. But if she was honest with herself she'd rather have spent the evening in bed. She couldn't admit that to anyone. Or maybe she could have said it to Mavis, but Mavis was no longer two shakes away. She'd tell her when she got better, and they could have a good laugh about it.

Meanwhile she somehow had to get herself ready for work, as she wasn't going to give Forsyth the satisfaction of sacking her. She wanted one day to have the pleasure of telling him where he could stick his job. Her fantasy was that if she hung around the music scene enough she'd be noticed and asked to be a backing singer, or dancer. While she didn't have a definite plan in mind, Rhona had a growing conviction that she could do something more than hang around looking good. Who knew where being in the right place at the right time might lead? Maybe it could be her ticket out of the factory. Something had to be. She'd die of boredom if she was stuck there for ever.

This morning Marilyn Foster took one look at her daughter as she came downstairs and shook her head. 'My God, Rhona, what you been up to now?' She poured her some tea. 'You better have this and see if it helps. Blimey, what you been doing? Smoking too much and wrecking your voice? Hanging round till all hours in those smoky clubs again? You have, I can smell it on your hair. How are you going to work like that?'

Rhona shrugged and slurped her tea, desperate for the hot liquid to numb her agonising throat. 'It's not that,' she whispered. 'I don't feel well. I lost my voice last night and it wasn't the staying out that caused it.'

'In that case I think you should go back to bed.'

'No, I'll be all right,' Rhona croaked but unable to eat any breakfast, she made do with another cup of tea. It eased her throat just a little and then, despite her mother nagging, she left for work.

She slowly dragged herself along the familiar route, pulling her scarf tight, but it didn't help. She felt chilled, even though the days were getting warmer and it would soon be Easter. Glancing at her watch as she approached the factory door Rhona saw that by a miracle she was on time. Even better, the first person she saw when she went inside was Jean, putting on her overall.

'Blimey, you look terrible,' said Jean. 'What on earth were you doing yesterday? I've seen you looking rough but this takes the biscuit.'

'I'm not well, it's not anything to do with yesterday,' Rhona protested, only it came out all wrong. 'It's my voice. It'll be all right soon, I just need to take it a bit easy today. Can I do that?'

'You better stay out of Forsyth's way or he'll find a way of making it worse for you,' Jean predicted. 'As it happens someone's got to go round to the store room to sort out anything that's nearly out of date. It won't be heavy lifting and you won't have to speak.'

'Yes please,' said Rhona.

By the time the tea break came round Rhona was exhausted. She'd tried to make sense of the vast array of boxes in the store room, but she'd come down with a headache so bad that she couldn't read the labels properly. The room was quiet and warmer than the factory floor and before long she'd been unable to resist the urge to sit down on one of the dusty chairs, just for a minute. She propped her arms on one of the grimy shelves and rested her head on them. Ten minutes later, as Penny came through the door unannounced, that's how she found her friend: fast asleep and snoring gently.

But she hadn't come there alone. Mr Forsyth stood just behind her and looked over her shoulder. Penny did her best to shield his view, but he could see over her head. He allowed himself a quick, sharp intake of breath before bellowing at the top of his voice, 'What's the meaning of this? What do you think you're doing?'

'Wha...' Rhona slowly raised her head, totally confused.

Penny backed away, not wanting to be part of this.

'You've abused my trust once too often.' Forsyth was going red in the face, getting worked up and vengeful. 'I've given you chance after chance even though your timekeeping has been appalling, and you ignore it. You've already had your final warning. This time, Miss Foster, you are sacked.'

Stan pulled into the car park in Honiton so that he could eat his sandwiches before the long drive home. His landlady had kindly made them for him, even though he'd offered to go out and get some, or buy bread and cheese to make his own. She wouldn't hear of it, and had fussed over him, insisting men shouldn't have to make their own lunch. Stan had smiled to himself, wondering what Jenny would have said about that. He was grateful, though, because the landlady had made him a pair of doorstoppers stuffed with cheese, ham and lots of pickle, just how he liked them.

This was his second trip to Devon and he was getting to know his way around a little. For his first trip he'd only gone as far as Exeter, which had plenty of potential customers who had taken up all his time. On this occasion he'd gone further afield, heading for Newton Abbot and Torquay. He was growing to like the scenery, the green hills and the sweep of the bays. There were plenty of hotels too, which made him remember his promise to Jenny that they spend a long week-end in the county. Visitors were plentiful in this run-up to Easter, and with the schools on holiday Greg could come too. There were children everywhere he looked, enjoying themselves, just as Greg would do if he came with them. He'd love the beaches, Stan was sure, even though they'd never taken him to one. He realised his son had never seen the sea, and this had brought him up short. What sort of father was he, not taking the boy to the seaside?

He was glad he'd been recommended the bed

and breakfast as when he'd arrived the landlady, Mrs Hawkins, had assured him lots of places were full at this time of year. 'And they put up their prices for Easter,' she'd said, 'not that I blame them, but you've got to be careful.' He began to plan ahead. If he came down and worked the Thursday and Friday, then Jenny and Greg could get the train after school on the Friday evening and he could collect them from the station at Newton Abbot. The landlady had shown him a small single room that would be just right for Greg, and she'd seemed very keen to meet the boy. 'My grandchildren are around the same age,' she'd said. 'I can tell you all the things they like to do. He'll have the time of his life.'

Stan took a big bite of his sandwich, which was as delicious as it had looked. He'd fallen on his feet with the kind landlady. She'd told him of a friendly pub where he could have a decent pint after a long day calling on customers, and provided slap-up full English breakfasts. She'd been in the area ever since getting married to a Torquay man and knew everyone. She regaled him with tales as he ate his fried egg and excellent sausages, of town scandals and local eccentrics. 'We get all sorts down here,' she'd remarked. 'Some come to retire, others because they've been on holiday in the summer and think it's like that all year round. They don't last long, not when they see the rain we get in winter. Then there's those who love the walking, or sailing. Then others I don't understand at all. There's one bloke, been here a couple of years, who runs a shop and won't let women in! Can you imagine? How he's going to keep a business afloat with that sort of attitude I wouldn't like to say. When you deal with the public you've got to take the rough with the smooth, and I should know, present company excepted of course.'

Stan smiled to himself now, as he finished the last crust and scrunched up the paper bag. He checked his map. Yes, nice and easy, up the A30 then the A303, all the way to London and home in time for the Easter long weekend with Greg and Jenny. His smile broadened as he thought of how Jenny would react to the ridiculous idea of not being allowed into a shop.

Tommy pushed away his account books with a sigh of satisfaction. He was relieved to have finished them all in one session and that meant he could spend some of Easter with Mavis and some with his cousin Jenny with a clear conscience. He'd just been paid for the job at the pub, and he considered it well worth the money as the place looked a whole lot smarter now. The landlord had given the bar a lick of paint inside as well, along with buying new tables and chairs. He'd also sacked the surly barmaid and got in new staff. Tommy had ended up getting to know them quite well after working there on the signs for a number of days; he had decided to do it himself rather than ask Jerry or one of the others, as he needed to keep his hand in.

One of the reasons the barmaid was sacked, apart from being completely uninterested in most of the customers, was that she'd been caught taking from the till. Tommy had overheard it all, hidden as he was behind the scenes, preparing the new wooden sign to be hung. The barmaid had protested she hadn't meant to and the money wasn't even for her but for her new boyfriend, who was going to beat her if she didn't do what he said.

Tommy knew this was true. He'd been packing away his equipment one day and had paused for a breather in the little hall behind the bar where he'd been told to keep his bags. The barmaid, Patty, must have assumed she was the only person on the premises, as he could hear her singing to herself, unusually cheerful. Next thing a man's voice could be heard, shouting as he came in from the street. Having heard it himself recently, Tommy recognised who it was at once. Larry Barnet. He decided to stay put and keep quiet.

Larry immediately started having a go at Patty, asking her when he was going to get the cash, demanding she hurry up about it or he'd give her another taste of the back of his hand. Patty's cheerfulness vanished and she'd sounded frightened. Larry threatened her some more, warning her not to think he wouldn't hurt her. He then began to reel off names of places he'd robbed, men he'd done the jobs with, and who for, adding that they couldn't fence the stuff yet until a local policeman that he named had been bribed to look the other way. In the meantime he needed money from Patty to live off.

Tommy had stood stock still during all of this, listening hard. He didn't like hearing a woman being treated in this way, even though she had barely bothered to acknowledge him all the days he'd been there. If things got physical he decided he'd come out and defend her, knowing what a

100

coward Larry really was, like all bullies. But as long as things didn't go that far, he'd stay hidden.

Now he drew towards him another piece of paper he'd tucked into the account book to keep it safe. He'd written down the names of the locations Larry had mentioned and the policeman's name: Sergeant Fenton. He hadn't done anything with the information, not yet anyway. He intended to hang on to it for insurance. He didn't know why he felt it would be useful, but something told him to bide his time. This piece of paper could be dynamite.

Chapter Eleven

Lily had just rounded the dog-leg bend in the street when she saw her neighbour Muriel heading towards her. Lily was feeling relaxed after a lovely family Easter, during which she'd fed the children too many chocolate eggs and indulged them far too much, but what were holidays for if not to spoil your nearest and dearest? Besides she'd got the eggs at a last-minute bargain price from Woolworths and it had been worth it to see the kids' faces. Mavis had painted them Easter cards and they'd had an egg hunt in the garden, which hadn't been very difficult as James found everything almost at once, but it had been fun to plan. The kids had insisted they do the same next year so it had been a big success all round.

Now she decided she'd speak nicely to her

miserable neighbour and not pretend to be too busy, which is what she'd found herself doing after their first conversation in the garden. Muriel's coat was flapping open to reveal a faded cotton printed apron beneath, a look which Lily thought made her seem years older than she was. She herself wouldn't be seen dead going out like that. She patted her hair, which she'd carefully sprayed into place before leaving the house earlier that morning. 'Had a good Easter, did you?' she began cheerfully.

'Not particularly,' said Muriel. 'I heard your lot out in the garden, running wild. I take it you don't take send them to church on Easter Sunday then.'

'It was better to let them work off their energy outdoors, seeing as the weather was right for it,' said Lily, refusing to be riled. 'Which church do you go to? I wondered whether to start Bobby at Sunday school when he's a bit older, be good for him to make friends his own age.'

'Oh, I don't hold with any of it,' Muriel snorted. 'Organ fund this, roof repair that. If they're so high and mighty they can put their money where their mouth is. They ain't having any of mine.'

Lily thought the woman contrary. If she didn't go to church, why had she brought up the subject? 'I'll think about Sunday school when Bobby's more the right age,' she said. 'He ain't three yet.'

'I take it your daughter doesn't attend either, then,' sneered Muriel, her eyes narrowing.

Blimey, thought Lily, what's that about? Had Mavis done something to add to the neighbour's sourness? It didn't seem likely. 'No, not really,' she said neutrally.

'Thought as much,' said Muriel. 'Not what with her having that young man round all the time.'

So that was it. Lily drew herself up to her full height, hefted her shopping basket on her elbow and looked her neighbour direct in the eye. 'There's nothing wrong with my daughter seeing a young man and he only visits, he doesn't stay overnight.'

'I'm glad to hear it,' snapped Muriel. ''Cos if I had a house full of children I wouldn't allow no hanky-panky going on in front of them and that's a fact.'

Lily reckoned a bit of hanky-panky would have done Muriel the power of good, but she doubted if the older woman had ever gone in for that sort of thing even in her youth. Some people just didn't have it in them to enjoy themselves.

'Tommy has been a tower of strength to all of us in what has been a very difficult time,' she replied, choosing her words carefully. 'He's a pillar of the community, owns his own business, doing very well too. So I won't have him badmouthed in my own street. As long as we're clear about that.' She fixed her gaze on Muriel's mean face.

'Ain't she lucky to have found such a paragon of virtue,' Muriel snorted. 'Well I can't stand around here gossiping all day. I've work to do.' She turned and sped down the road, nose in the air.

For the thousandth time Lily cursed Alec for leaving Mavis in such an impossible situation. If Mavis could get a divorce, then she'd be free to marry Tommy, but instead he'd just upped and disappeared. It was the cruellest thing he could have done, which was no doubt the reason for his actions. Lily cursed under her breath. If she were ever to catch sight of him again, she'd tear him limb from limb.

Mavis knew she was running late as she hurried back from Peckham Rye and its shops. Tommy was coming round for a meal and she'd run out of milk of all things, and then she'd decided while she was out she'd get some nice vegetables to go with the pork chops. She'd also seen some lovely cooking apples, going cheap because it was the end of the day, and she could almost taste the delicious sauce she could make with them. So she had a full shopping bag as she made her way home, hoping that Tommy hadn't already arrived. Though she was still a little unfamiliar with the area she'd noticed people coming in and out of a side alley and reckoned it could be a useful shortcut. It would save her a few minutes. She'd told Lily she'd be back at half past and it was already twenty-five to.

The clouds had been threatening all afternoon to land some late April showers and now they obscured the sun as she turned into the alley. Mavis almost stumbled as the ground quickly became uneven. The walls were high on either side and there wasn't much light. She hurried on, banging one elbow against a jutting-out piece of stone as the passage narrowed. She hastily checked her sleeve as even in the gloom she could make out that the stone was slimy. Better not to think about what that might have been caused by.

There was a sudden rustling behind her and Mavis jumped involuntarily, turning round to look just as a long, narrow tail disappeared under some abandoned newspapers. A rat. Where there was one there would be more she remembered someone telling her, and she glanced around nervously. She knew they would be unlikely to hurt her and would be trying to get away but that didn't mean she had to like them.

Ever since having James and Grace she had done her best not to show any fear when confronted with insects or animals, in case she made them frightened as well. It wasn't always easy and it didn't always work; Grace was petrified of daddylonglegs, even though nobody else in the family was bothered by them. Mavis had no idea where that had come from, certainly not from her, but as long as everyone was careful to shut the windows before it was dusk and remembered to check the bathroom before Grace went in, there was usually no problem.

Mavis smiled now as she remembered Tommy carrying one out in an empty tin so that Grace wouldn't see. It was about the only thing that did scare the girl, though. Once, when Rhona had been babysitting, a big spider had run along the edge of the carpet and Grace had thought nothing of catching it in a hanky and asking Rhona to open the window so she could put it outside. Rhona had told Mavis she'd been the one shaking in a corner. Now Mavis turned once more and began to walk along the narrow alley, treading carefully, making sure not to bang her bag against the walls, which would bruise the lovely apples. She reminded herself that the rats would be far more wary of her than she ought to be of them.

Maybe this wasn't such a shortcut, she thought, as the winding path seemed to be taking much longer than she'd thought it would. Then again that was probably because it was unfamiliar. The first time you went anywhere it always seemed to take longer. She glanced at her watch. It had only been five minutes, though it felt like far more. She rounded a corner and could see that the walls opened out on to a bright street at the end. Not far now.

There was more noise behind her but she didn't turn round, not wanting to see more rats or whatever scavenging creature it was. She forced herself to ignore it, to concentrate on getting to the end of the alley which was so close now. Then she felt something on her shoulder. She screamed.

'You always was a squealer.'

Terrified, she spun round and came face to face with the person she'd seen in the market weeks ago, the person from her past, the last person she ever wanted ever to see again: Larry Barnet.

'What ... what...' She couldn't get the words out.

'Lost your voice?' he taunted. 'Didn't do that all those years ago, did you, telling on me and Tommy to our mums.' He grabbed her hair as she tried to flinch away.

Mavis tried to answer back but couldn't. Her protests froze in her throat. She twisted, attempting to break free.

'Trying to get away? I don't think so.' Larry's breath was hot on her face and she could smell drink on it, beer mixed with something stronger, whisky maybe. It was foul and sour. 'We've got unfinished business, Dumbo. Bet you still can't read, can you?' He held on to her hair with one hand and blocked her way with his other arm, pressing it across her shoulder and into the wall behind. She was backed up against the brickwork, the sharp corners jabbing into her as she tried to wriggle out of his grasp.

'I'm gonna show you what you missed out on all those years ago,' he said, leaning in closer. 'Now it's your lucky day 'cos you're about to find out.' He released her hair and moved his hand down towards his flies.

Mavis acted without thinking, throwing her bag to one side, unbalancing him, then slamming her knee up and into his groin. Before he could grab her, she was off, down towards the end of the alley. The clouds parted again and a beam of light fell on the dark pathway, and as she dared to look back over her shoulder she could see Larry curled on the ground, gasping in pain.

'You bitch!' he managed to get out. 'You're gonna pay for that. I'll get you, you've got it coming to you big time.'

Mavis came to an abrupt halt as a silhouette appeared at the end of the alley.

'Mavis! Are you all right? What's happened?'

'Tommy!' She fell into his arms. 'I ... I...'

Tommy took in the scene in the alley, the man on the ground, the shopping bag spilling its contents, Mavis shaking and now sobbing into his shoulder. It didn't take a genius to work out what had gone on.

'Shush, you're safe.' He held her tightly for a moment, catching his own breath. He'd been rushing along the street, thinking he was late and she'd have had the meal ready and waiting. Then he'd heard the sound of someone running down the alley and seen who it was. The horror of what might have happened flashed before his eyes.

'You're OK now, it'll be all right,' he soothed her, stroking her hair. 'I'll make sure of it. Come on, let me pass. This has gone far enough,' he muttered, running down the slimy path towards the curled-up figure. He bent and clutched Larry's collar, dragging him upright even as the man moaned and protested.

The material of the flashy shirt ripped under Larry's weight but Tommy just gripped him by the throat and forced him back against the mouldy wall. Larry groaned and tried to fight back but Mavis had totally winded him and he didn't have the strength to stand, let alone land a punch on his old school friend. 'Lemme go,' he rasped. 'That bitch kneed me.'

'Shut up,' Tommy snarled. 'You deserved it.'

'I didn't mean nothing by it. I was only going to teach her a lesson.'

'I know what you were going to do. It's bloody obvious. You've got your flies undone. Old habits die hard,' Tommy snarled, his face contorted with disgust.

'You was no angel yourself so don't you come all high and mighty with me.' Larry was getting his energy back and sounded hard done by.

'Yeah, well, I grew up. And now I'm going to teach *you* a lesson.'

'Are you? I'd like to see you try to–' Larry didn't finish as Tommy's fist connected with his ballooning gut. He bent over in agony, retching. The smell of sour beer filled the confines of the alley.

Tommy stood back, waiting for him to finish, watching as the man collapsed into the pool of his own vomit. 'I warned you, Larry, but you didn't listen. Did you have a few drinks and it made you feel brave so you decided to have another go at Mavis? Brave man, Larry, very brave. But this stops here, so listen, and listen well. You stay away from Mavis or your friends might find out about your big mouth.'

Larry turned his smeared face up to meet Tommy's gaze. 'You don't know my friends. They aren't the same as back in the old days. You leave them out of it.'

'Trouble is, I do know who your friends are, Larry. I've been doing my homework. I don't know if you're in any state to remember, but you've been boasting about some jobs you've been doing. Who you were with, who for, and where the stolen goods are. You've even been stupid enough to boast about the bent copper who's taking back-handers.'

'I don't know what you mean.' Larry tried to sound convincing but it was more of a reflex response. His expression began to change as the penny dropped that he was in very serious trouble.

'Yes you do, Larry, and when your friends are nicked, they'll want to know who grassed them up.'

'You wouldn't.' Larry's mouth began to tremble. Even after an afternoon's drinking he recognised a serious threat when he heard one. 'Come on, we're old friends. You wouldn't want a woman to come between us. Specially not Dumbo...'

Tommy made to hit him again but stopped himself. He forced his hand back into his pocket, almost shaking with the effort. The information he had on Larry was a far bigger weapon, gratifying though it would have been to smash his ugly face to ribbons.

'I reckon you've got about twenty minutes to clean yourself up and get on the next train out of here,' said Tommy as steadily as he could. 'I'm making an anonymous phone call, and then there won't be anywhere in South London where you'll be safe. All your friends, all those valuables you've got hidden away, your bent copper, they'll all be uncovered, and I'll put it about that it was you and your big mouth that got them nicked.'

Larry gulped and tears of weakness trickled down his filthy cheeks. 'No, come on, for old times' sake...'

'I'm done here,' said Tommy with finality. 'I've got better things to do than stand in stinking alleyways with fat blokes covered in their own sick. You should have listened to me, Larry. You made the mistake of not taking me seriously, but now you know better. If you're not gone in the next few, minutes you're dead meat.'

With that Tommy turned and walked back towards the opening into the street.

'Was that all true?' It had taken Mavis a while to recover, but now that she was home in her own kitchen, she'd begun to think through what she'd overheard.

Lily, was fussing around, taking over the cooking as Mavis was too shaky. The apples had been lost along with the milk and vegetables, but Lily had carried up some potatoes and carrots from her own kitchen as well as a jar of apple sauce. It might not be what Mavis had planned but it was better than nothing.

'Afraid so,' said Tommy. 'I knew he was back and thought I'd done enough to warn him off, but obviously not.'

Mavis shuddered. 'I dread to think what he'd have done if you hadn't turned up when you did, Tommy.'

'I don't know about that. It looked as if you'd landed a good blow yourself. He was writhing around on the ground in agony.' Tommy gazed at her with admiration.

'Good,' said Lily, flipping over one of the chops. 'I didn't know you had it in you, pet. You look as if you wouldn't hurt a fly, then you go and knee that bastard in the balls. I'm proud of you.'

'I didn't think, I just reacted,' said Mavis, scarcely believing it herself. She'd always been so timid before. 'I just did it. I didn't know he'd fall like that. I just ran.'

Lily turned down the heat under the pot of potatoes which was threatening to boil over. 'And are you really going to ring the police, Tommy?'

Tommy shrugged. 'There's not much point in saying you're going to do something like that and then not following through, though it goes against the grain.'

Lily moved to the sink to drain the carrots. She put them on plates, added the potatoes and finally the chops. 'Right, here you are. I'll get the kids in from the garden and your two can eat with us, Mavis.'

'Thanks, Mum.'

There was a moment of silence after she had gone, but then Mavis sighed and shook her head. 'I don't know what to say, Tommy.' She reached across the table for his hand. 'It's really only sinking in now. And you had all that information up your sleeve, just in case he came after me? I can't believe it. You won't be in any trouble from those people, will you?'

'No,' said Tommy, hoping it was true. He'd be very careful when he made his phone call. 'All I'll do is point the police in the right direction, and I'll make sure my name is kept out of it. If I don't carry out my threat, Larry might find out and I won't have that bastard hanging round tormenting you. I should have stood up to him years ago, but better late than never.' He stroked her hand. 'I'd do anything to keep you safe, Mavis. I won't let anyone hurt a hair on your head. You are the most precious person in the world and I'm here to protect you.'

Mavis gasped and tears ran down her cheeks once more as the reality of it hit home. She knew with her head and her heart that he meant it. 'I'm ... I'm sorry,' she blurted. 'I should be happy, not crying. I'm just so ... it's all too much.'

'Mavis,' Tommy said, 'you can cry all you like, you've had a horrible fright, but it's not going to happen again. I love you and I'll protect you. Nothing will change that.'

'I love you too, Tommy,' she said, 'and I'll never forget what you did for me.' She smiled through her tears as he pushed his chair back and came around the table to hold her tightly. She had thought that she could stand on her own two feet now that she was independent, but as Mavis rested her head against his warm body she relished how safe she felt in Tommy's arms.

Slowly the thought came into her head that here was a man she could absolutely trust with everything – even with her life – and at last the wall of ice, the fear and defensiveness she had built around herself after Alec's years of mistreatment, started to melt.

Chapter Twelve

Rhona sat propped up in bed, gazing blankly at her bedroom window. She'd been ill for four weeks. To begin with she'd been so sick she hadn't registered what was going on, although everyone around her seemed to be very worried. Then the doctor had pronounced it was a bad case of glandular fever. She'd barely left the confines of her room and hadn't even cared. Now, as the blossoms on the few small trees outside proclaimed it was May, she was beginning to show signs of recovery. The rash, sore throat and fever had receded and although she was still unbelievably tired she could at least bear to sit up against the pillows for a few hours before going back to sleep again. She wasn't well enough to be bored yet, so wasn't worried that she didn't know what the future would bring.

Her mother was fighting the battle on her behalf to get her job reinstated, but Rhona decided not to think about it. She wouldn't be going near any production lines in her current state.

For the first time since she'd fallen sick she was glad to hear the knock at the door, followed by Penny's voice in the hallway. Moments later her friend poked her head around the bedroom door.

'Blimey! This is a surprise! You're sitting up.' Penny grinned as she put down her shiny patent handbag, which looked new, and tucked her mass of curls behind her ears. 'You feeling better, then?'

'A bit,' admitted Rhona. 'I still feel like death warmed up but that's an improvement. Well, anything would be, to be honest. You wouldn't believe what the last few weeks have been like.'

'You've really been in the wars. I'm glad you're on the mend. You'll be back on the dance floor in no time now.'

'Maybe, but I can't imagine it. I've sort of lost interest in everything. I haven't even been listening to the radio. Mum has the Light Programme on and that's about it.'

'You're kidding!' Penny couldn't hide her astonishment. 'You won't have heard any gossip then and there's been a few police raids round here. And you love music, the charts and going out to the nightclubs. I'd have thought you'd be climbing the walls to get out of here by now.'

'I've been too tired to care,' Rhona couldn't seem to make her friend understand, 'and I couldn't dance if you paid me. It's good that you've been going out without me though, I wouldn't want to think I've ruined your social life.'

114

'I'm glad you said that. I wondered if you thought I was mean, having fun while you were stuck in here,' said Penny, a guilty expression flitting across her face. 'But everyone's been so nice, I haven't felt lonely.'

'That's good then,' said Rhona. 'I meant to ask, how's Gary? He's been really quiet. I thought he might have got in touch.'

'Oh yeah, he said get well soon,' Penny replied. 'He definitely asked me to tell you that.'

'That's nice of him. It was just that I thought he'd do more,' said Rhona. 'Maybe he's one of those blokes who gets embarrassed if someone's ill, you know, they don't know what to say in case it's the wrong thing and so they do nothing. I just didn't think he was like that. Oh well.'

Penny shifted in her seat. 'Shall I say something to him if I see him?'

Rhona shrugged again. 'No, don't bother. He probably thinks I'm infectious or something and hasn't got in touch in case I ask him round. I don't want him to think I'm all clingy or anything.' She forced a broad smile. 'Anyway, what do I care? He's a free agent.'

'Exactly,' said Penny. 'We're not tied down, are we? Young, free and single, that's us.'

'Yeah.' Rhona sighed. 'Except this last month I've felt like a pensioner. Never mind, it'll be over soon and then world, watch out.' She slumped back, exhausted by the effort of talking.

Penny watched her anxiously. 'You all right? Are you feeling bad again?'

'Nah, just tired. Tell me what you've been up to.'

Penny gazed at the floor as if trying to work up the nerve to say something. Then she glanced up again. 'I've ... I've met someone.' She blushed.

'Wow. Good for you. Is it serious?' Rhona was impressed; she'd only been out of circulation for a matter of weeks and Penny had been hanging on to her coat tails up till then; now the girl was out there making a life of her own. 'Was it at a club, or a concert, or pub, or what? Not at the factory, was it?'

Penny snorted. 'Don't be daft. You know what a bunch of weirdos the blokes are at work. No, I met him at the Talisman club.'

Rhona nodded. That made sense. Lots of the men there had been giving Penny the eye, and once Rhona herself was off the scene she'd have got a lot more attention. 'Is he good-looking then? Bet he's a fab dancer.'

'Yeah, he really is. He's a dream boat.' Penny didn't elaborate.

Rhona wasn't sure why her friend wasn't saying more but if Penny wanted to be coy about it, then that was her business. Rhona didn't have her usual energy to fire questions until she got to the heart of the matter.

'The thing is ... the thing is...' Penny was nervous now. 'Oh, I don't like to ask.'

'Come on, this is me you're talking to.' Rhona tried not to be annoyed. How scary could she be, in her condition?

'OK, well, the thing is ... he's asked me to go all the way with him.'

'They all do that.'

'I know. But this time ... this time, I want to.'

'All right, as long as you're sure,' Rhona said. 'You don't want some sweet talker to persuade you into going to bed with him then you wishing you hadn't done it.'

'Yeah, I know.' Penny wrung her hands. 'He's not putting any pressure on me, he just said it was up to me to decide. But I need your advice. About ... you know.'

'About sex, you mean?' Rhona asked.

Penny nodded.

'I've told you what happens.'

'I know.' Penny nodded. 'You've told me far more than Mum ever did, but ... but I'm nervous. I've heard that it ... it will hurt. Is that true?'

Rhona could feel the exhaustion creeping up on her again but she made an effort to hide it. 'It'll be your first time, so it might, but not much. Just don't let him rush you. Make him wait until you're ready and then you'll be fine.'

Penny leant forward impulsively and hugged her friend. 'You're a brick, you are, Rhona. You're kinder than what I deserve.' She picked up her patent handbag. 'That's a weight off my mind, that is. Mind you, I'll have to make sure my mum doesn't find out. She'd go mad.'

Rhona didn't doubt that. She remembered the almighty row that had broken out when her own mother had found out what she'd been up to. 'Let me know how you get on. I want all the details.' She grinned at her friend.

'Oh I will,' said Penny, hugging the bag to her chest.

'Do you really think it will be all right?' Jenny was

117

trying not to get too excited. 'Your landlady won't mind? And Mavis is OK to take Greg?'

'How many times have I told you?' Stan was part exasperated by his wife's worries and part happy to see her so pleased. 'Mrs Hawkins can't wait to meet you, and Greg too when he's finished for the school holidays. Meanwhile it makes more sense for him to stay with Mavis and then you can ride down in the car with me. We can have a proper long weekend, and he won't miss school.'

'I can't wait,' Jenny exclaimed, her eyes shining.

Stan beamed, proud of what he'd achieved. He'd asked his boss if he had any objections to him taking Jenny with him for a weekend, pleased when there were none. In fact his boss was so delighted with the results of his first few trips to Devon that he had said the firm would foot the bill for a double room.

'Do I need to buy anything special?' Jenny went on. 'It's warmer down there, isn't it? Maybe a sunhat?'

'Oh that's it, any excuse to go shopping.' Stan pretended to be annoyed. 'They do have shops down there, you know, and while I'm off visiting my clients you could have a look round and see if there's something you fancied. You could get one of those sexy sundresses, show off your figure. You might get a tan.' He raised his eyebrows. 'Then I'd have to check just where it ended, wouldn't I...'

'Shush, Greg will hear.' Jenny pushed her husband's hands away, but she didn't mean it. She could just see it now: sunshine, the sand, maybe they'd take a blanket down to the edge of the sea, and she could get one of those halter necks... She gave herself a shake. They wouldn't be going for a couple of weeks yet, but she couldn't wait.

The painted sign above the door of the narrow-fronted shop read 'Collier's Collectibles'. Stencilled on the glass of the door in fine gold lettering were the words 'Rare Stamps'.

From his position behind the counter the owner of the shop smiled. He didn't have to add 'No Women' to the shopfront. Any ladies who tried to come in soon thought the better of it, as it was immediately evident that they were unwelcome. That was exactly how he wanted it. It was his all-male kingdom, uncontaminated by the female form in any shape except for the occasional figure or head on one of the many stamps he was so proud of. Fortunately for business, most serious collectors were men. He ran his hand along the beaten brass strip that edged the counter, pleased to see there was no dust on his fingertips. He did make one exception to his all-male rule, as his cleaner was an old woman who lived nearby, but she had to come and go when he wasn't on the premises. He couldn't have borne to see her touching his property.

To all appearances, the proprietor was a mild-mannered man in his early thirties, with mousy brown hair which had started to thin increasingly rapidly of late, and a tidily trimmed moustache. His clothes were neat and nondescript, his Crimplene trousers keeping their shape no matter how much lifting of heavy catalogues he did during the day. He brushed them now out of habit, but there were no longer any dog hairs clinging to the fabric. His beloved Labrador, who he'd named Hunter, had died three months ago. He still missed him and was often surprised at just how big a gap the dog's death had left in his life. After what he'd gone through, he had thought he would never be able to feel affection for any living thing ever again, but the dog's unswerving devotion had broken down his defences. Still, he reminded himself, it was understandable. The dog had been male. Females, even dogs, were not to be trusted and could not be loved.

He had not always been like this. Until she had died, he had adored and worshipped his mother, even though he knew she was prone to be controlling. But she had been ill for many years and he'd made allowances, always believing that she had raised him as well as possible after having to cope with being widowed so early in her marriage. That was before he had found out everything he had held as true, was in fact a tissue of lies. His mother had made up the entire story of her past – there had been no husband, and he himself was actually a bastard, which meant that his whole life as Alec Pugh was based on thin air.

He didn't even know his real name, something he'd discovered only after his mother had died, and so he was never going to find it out now. In an act of rebellion, he had chosen the name Charles Collier, and moved to an area of the country where nobody knew him. He was safe to reinvent himself here, far away from everyone who would have mocked him if they had found out, laughing at his superior ways and manners that had all been founded on lies.

He had no regrets about severing all contact with his wife and small children. They deserved to suffer. Mavis had taken them when she'd walked out on him, all because he gave them all the discipline they so badly needed. Mavis had ultimately refused to respect his position as head of the house and he certainly didn't owe her any of the profits from selling the family home. He hoped she'd gone back to the poverty he had misguidedly rescued her from when he'd agreed to his mother's idea that he should marry her. Walking away from his former life and leaving her in limbo was the best thing he'd ever done.

As far as he was concerned, Alec Pugh no longer existed. The man he had once been had suffered betrayal beyond imagining, and it made him shudder even now to recall the details of his mother's web of falsehood. She had built him up to be something he wasn't, filling his head with false notions and tying him to her with a bond of unbreakable guilt, which had been shattered only by her death.

During his first weeks and months in this new location, he had endured some very dark times, when his mind had clouded over and he had thought he would be unable to bear the weight of it all. But now he had settled and Charles Collier was doing increasingly well. Now he watched the crowds walking along outside his window, most of them ignoring the small shop. He didn't mind in the slightest; he was interested only in similar-minded men who shared his obsession with rare stamps. The common hordes were of no import-ance to him as they wandered by, licking their ice creams and swinging their brightly coloured buckets and spades. Some were eating chips with their fingers from greasy newspaper as they passed, in a show of unforgivably bad manners. His mother would never have approved... Angrily he brought himself up short. No matter how hard he tried, the bloody woman was still festering in his mind, still infecting his thought processes. In frustration he thumped the countertop and turned away, just as a shortish woman with bobbed brown hair caught the corner of his eye.

It wasn't that her hair was striking, but she wore a dress that stood out from the rest of the holiday makers as it was in bold geometric patterns. She had paused to reach into her handbag and he looked at her more closely. She was facing away from him but he could see that it had a nipped-in waist and almost obscenely thin shoulder straps. He hoped she got sunburnt; she was asking for it in a skimpy top like that. It shouldn't be allowed. He would never have permitted his wife to go out in public so brazenly, flaunting her flesh for all and sundry to see. It wasn't decent.

He shook his head. He hated the very idea of Mavis, the cold, scheming bitch. At first she'd seemed so malleable and innocent that he'd believed his mother when she'd strongly hinted the young girl was attracted to him. His mother had been adamant that he should make his move and win the girl, despite his nervous misgivings. Of course he'd been set up, he saw that clearly now. His wife had never loved him, but had just used him to get a house that was far more comfortable than the hovel of a place she'd been brought up in, in a more respectable area, and then she'd gone and spawned two little copies of herself. He'd insisted, quite reasonably, that the children must be seen and not heard around the house as he didn't want them to disrupt his habits, but they had refused to obey. The little girl in particular had taken to answering back almost from the day she'd started to talk. She had deliberately ignored his rules, which he'd only made so that she would learn her place in society. Nobody liked an uppity girl, and he hadn't wanted that for his daughter. As for his son, his lack of politeness had been a big disappointment too. He'd had to beat the child to get him to understand what acceptable behaviour was. He hadn't done it for pleasure, but for the boy's own good.

Then, after all the effort he'd made, the things he'd done for them, his wife had still left him and taken the children. How that hurt him even now. Not because he'd loved them but for the social blow it had dealt him. His standing in the community was in smithereens. He should have shown her who was boss much more forcefully. He had exercised his God-given right to punish her severely when she had displeased him but it hadn't been enough. She'd somehow retained enough independence of spirit to walk out on him. Maybe her appalling mother had had something to do with it – she was common as muck and if he had had his way there would have been no communication between them. In that way too he had been disobeyed.

The woman in the bright print sundress turned a little and he caught the profile of her face. No.

It couldn't be. He must be imagining it because he'd been thinking of the past, of his family. There must be thousands of young women of similar appearance and it was a trick of the light, or he needed glasses. It couldn't be who he thought it was.

The woman turned so that she was almost facing the shop as she drew out what looked like postcards from the bag. There was a post-box a couple of shops along and Alec realised that she was going to head towards it to send her cards. Was one of them to his wife? This woman was almost definitely who he thought she was. She was their former next-door neighbour. She and her husband and horrible, noisy little boy had moved in while his mother was still alive. She had been friends with his wife, had probably encouraged her treachery. She wore her hair differently now but it was definitely her, with that irritatingly cheerful expression and big mouth. Many a time he'd thought he'd like to wipe the smile from her face.

He stood back a little in case she noticed him, although he knew it was unlikely at this time of day – the sun would be reflecting off the panes of glass at the front and he'd be all but invisible. Still, he drew to one side, keen to avoid her gaze. The last thing he wanted was for her to recognise him and go home tittle-tattling to his wife.

He hoped she'd post her cards and go, but she glanced at her watch and stood as though waiting for somebody. Of all the meeting places she could have chosen, she'd picked the pavement right between him and the sea. Other tourists wandered past, but he could see she was still there – her dress stood out in its gaudy pattern.

Then another familiar figure swept into view, catching her from behind and twirling her round. It was her husband, the one who used to make such a clatter when he mowed their lawn and left it untidy at the edges. There he was now, in what seemed like smart trousers but with his shirt-sleeves rolled up and his tie half undone. Unlike his wife he wasn't dressed like a typical holiday maker and Alex feared the man now worked in the area.

He shuddered even more as the couple hugged and then kissed, brazenly, right in front of his window. He was worried that sudden movement might attract their attention or he'd have dashed into the back room pretty sharpish, and then froze as the two of them broke away from their energetic kissing and the man pointed at the sign above his shop. Alec couldn't quite lip-read what he was saying to the woman, but he was turning to her and nudging her and then they both fell about laughing. The woman pointed as well and shook her head, wagging her finger at him as if pretending to tell him off. The man said something to her and she looked up at him, then he kissed her again with enthusiasm.

Alec felt weak with anger. How dare they mock his shop? What was so funny about it? His was a respectable business and they had no right to stand outside it behaving so repulsively and obscenely and then insulting his property like that. With a repressed howl of rage he hit the counter-top again and then with great restraint slowly made his way into the back room, all the while seething inside. He must not let it disturb his peace of mind. He must not let the dark days return.

Pete stood at the kitchen sink, rubbing his chin with anxiety. Things weren't quite going to plan. They'd moved into the new house at the beginning of March and it was now June, and yet the big contract still hadn't been confirmed. He'd had further meetings and written more letters, but had come no closer to a start date as the mysterious person in charge at the council seemed to be away a lot. Pete knew he was being fobbed off with excuses but didn't know why. What made it worse was that he couldn't share it with anybody. Lily would do her nut if she found out the house was mortgaged to the hilt, but he had no intention of telling her. Mavis had no experience of this sort of thing and anyway it was his job to protect both her and Lily, not to burden them with his difficulties. If Tommy had been family maybe he could have sought his advice but the way things stood it was anybody's guess when, or even if, he would ever get together with Mavis.

Pete knew Lily would be back any minute. She'd only popped to the shops to get some last-minute items for Mavis, who was cooking a big meal upstairs. Jenny and Stan had just got back from their holiday and were coming round to tell them all their news and to collect Greg, who'd been sharing James's room while they were away. He and James were out the back now, playing football, while Grace and Bobby were upstairs with Mavis, probably getting under her feet while

126

pretending to help. Pete realised he had to put a brave face on it and snap out of his bad mood; there was nothing to be done but wait it out. He had to believe that the project would still come off, and when it did his money worries would be over. If it didn't he couldn't quite bring himself to think of the consequences. It would spell disaster for all of them.

'Thanks, Mavis, that was a lovely meal,' said Stan, finally pushing his plate away.

'That pie was a good as your mother's,' Pete said.

'Yes, it was love,' Lily agreed.

Mavis smiled happily. Dinner had been a success; everyone's plates were clean and there wasn't as much as a single pea left.

'You'd love the coast in Devon, Mavis,' said Jenny, her eyes shining at the memory. 'All that fresh air and the sea breeze. It makes you come alive. I felt ten years younger, I really did.'

'You certainly did,' said Stan suggestively, nudging his wife.

Mavis gave a little frown. She could tell what they'd been up to for most of their long weekend but didn't want James asking questions – he was far too quick on the uptake.

'You'll love it too, Greg,' Jenny said enthusiastically. 'We'll take you with us next time you break up from school.'

Tommy, who'd been asked round as well, grinned and turned to his young cousin. 'So did you miss your mum and dad, Greg?'

Greg shrugged. He knew he was meant to say

yes but he hadn't really. 'Sort of,' he said, 'but I like it round here with James 'cos we can play football out in the back garden, and Aunty Mavis lets me have cake every day. If we're going to the seaside, Mum, why can't James come with us? Why don't we all go?'

'Funny you should say that, Greg,' said Stan. 'Your mother and I had the same idea. I always stay at the same Bed and Breakfast place when I'm down there and I get on with the landlady, Mrs Hawkins, like a house of fire. We actually thought it would be lovely for us all to have a holiday together, so I had a word with Mrs Hawkins...'

'Hang on a minute,' Mavis said, her voice was edged with worry. 'I'm not sure I can manage–'

'It won't cost the earth,' Stan butted in. 'Mrs Hawkins can do us a special rate for a large booking, especially if you and Lily come too, Pete. She can hold us a week in August, but only if we confirm it pretty quickly.'

'Really?' Pete perked up. If Lily had something like this to look forward to she wouldn't notice that he was worried, and though he had to watch their dwindling cash flow, it didn't sound like it would cost them much.

'Can we?' James was almost jumping out of his seat.

Grace squealed excitedly, 'My friend at school goes to the seaside every year and I want to go too.'

'You should go Mavis,' said Tommy seriously.

Stan turned on his dining chair. 'Tommy – you're included too of course,' he said.

Tommy turned to look at her, a question in his eyes, but Mavis lowered her gaze. It would be nice if he came too, but they would have to book separate rooms. She had the children to think about, but she didn't want to talk about sleeping arrangements while they were all gathered around the table.

Thankfully, her mother, as though sensing her dilemma came to her rescue as she said, 'It sounds like a lovely idea, but Pete will need to check his work schedule to see if he can take a week off in August. Ain't that right Pete?'

'Err, yes, but I...'

'Right then, Stan,' Lily interrupted. 'Can we get back to you tomorrow?'

'Yes, that's fine,' Stan agreed.

Mavis was hardly listening. Yes, she and Tommy would have to have separate rooms, but a part of her was wishing it could be otherwise.

Chapter Thirteen

'Rhona, you should have said something!' Mavis looked at her friend and thought how much she'd changed – she'd lost weight, her skin was pale and her hair had lost its bounce. 'I didn't even know you were ill until my mum bumped into yours in Woolworths, or I'd have come round before. Let alone that you had glandular fever. You poor thing, you've been laid up for weeks.'

'I didn't want to bother you,' said Rhona, shifting in her chair. She'd finally managed to get downstairs and was now able to sit in one of the old armchairs for half the day before going back to bed again. 'Anyway I wasn't up to seeing people for ages. I can't tell you how tired this has made me feel, so I wasn't really keen to have visitors.'

'Am I tiring you now?' Mavis asked anxiously.

'No, no, I'm on the mend. About bloody time too.' Rhona shook her head. 'I wasn't even bored before, I was so wiped out, but now I don't know what to do with myself. I'm really fed up with being at home.'

'I love being in the new flat and wouldn't swap it for the world but now and again I like to get out, see people, even if it's only down the market for half an hour. You need a change of scenery. How do you feel about going for a walk?'

Rhona looked dubious. 'I haven't left the house since Easter and I'm still weak. I don't think I'm up to it.'

'We could get a bus and that would give you a change of scenery. We could get off at the common. There'll be lots of people out, you'll enjoy it.'

Rhona cast her eyes down. It sounded so tempting. She could imagine what it would be like on the common, wandering along the paths that criss-crossed the open ground or sitting under the shade of a large tree. But it was no good. She tried to smile. 'Look, I'm sorry, but I don't think I'm strong enough yet. Another time, maybe.'

'How about that small park then? It's only a couple of streets away,' Mavis persisted. 'The fresh air would do you good, but if you feel a bit wobbly we can turn around and come back. You won't know unless you give it a go.'

Rhona thought for a moment. 'OK. Why not.

I'll lean on you and you can carry me back if you have to.' She flashed a smile. 'Just joking, Mave, it won't come to that.'

'I would if you needed me to. I've carried James often enough, and even Greg until pretty recently. I'm stronger than I look.'

Rhona gingerly stood up and tested her weak leg muscles. 'Give me your arm,' she said. 'We'll have a wander and see how we go.'

They set off, Rhona moving like someone four times her age, but she didn't give up and realised she was enjoying herself as they slowly made their way to the little park, where she collapsed on a bench. It wasn't a trip out on a bus, but that could wait. For now she could sit back and let the sunshine fall on her face. It was such a pleasure not to be inside the four walls of her small house. She sighed with relief. 'Thanks, Mavis. I wouldn't have made the effort without you urging me to give it a go.'

'I used to come here when Grace was really little. She liked chasing the pigeons.' Mavis smiled ruefully. 'When she goes back to school in September, she'll have a new teacher, one I've heard is quite strict, but that'll be good for her. Grace loves school, which is more than I ever did.'

'She hasn't got word blindness like you, then?'

'No, neither of them has. I don't know if it's passed on in families but I'm very glad they're both all right. It made my life a misery all the way through school.'

'Yeah, you said. Didn't Tommy tease you?'

'He did more than tease me, he was horrible back then. But he was egged on by his friend

Larry. He was the worst, but he's not around to bother me now.' Mavis thought back to the news of the raids the police had carried out after Tommy had given them his information. There was no way Larry Barnet would dare come back to South London again. She wondered whether to tell Rhona about the attack, and that now and again she still felt nervous, but decided the younger woman had quite enough on her plate at the moment. She'd tell her once her friend was stronger.

'And how's Tommy these days?'

Mavis smiled. 'Same as ever.'

'Still waiting for you to give in?'

'You've got a one-track mind, Rhona, but yes.'

'The man's a saint,' said Rhona, 'and anyone can see that he loves you to bits.'

Mavis watched a blackbird hopping along, looking for worms. She sat back against the bench. 'I've got some news. You'll never guess. We're all going on holiday in August – Jenny, Stan and Greg, Mum, Pete and Bobby, me and the kids and Tommy. We're going to Torquay, to a Bed and Breakfast that Stan knows. I've never had a proper holiday before and I can't wait.' She grinned broadly at the thought of it.

'Wow, that sounds fab,' breathed Rhona. 'I've never been to the seaside. You'd better send me a card.'

'The thing is,' said Mavis, 'I've found myself starting to wish that Tommy and I could share the same room.'

'What!' Rhona nearly fell off the bench. 'That's a turn-up for the books! You've always said you wouldn't. What's changed your mind?'

Mavis turned to face her. 'I've finally realised I can trust Tommy. I mean, it wasn't him, it was me who had the problem. After Alec I didn't want anything to do with that side of things ever again. What you said helped – made me think not every man was like Alec. And now I know Tommy cares for me, really cares for me, I think I want to be with him, you know, all the way. I don't want to spend the entire holiday thinking how gorgeous and loving he is and not be able to do anything about it. Does that sound bad?'

'No, it sounds good,' said Rhona at once, sounding more enthusiastic than she had done since falling ill. 'About time too, I'd say.'

'My family won't mind, they all think he's great.' She paused. 'There is one thing…'

Blimey, thought Rhona. She wondered what was coming next and if she was becoming the agony aunt of Peckham. She waited for Mavis to get up the courage to say what she wanted.

'I can't risk having a baby,' Mavis said in a rush, 'not until I'm married to Tommy. You take the pill. Could I get hold of it?'

'Of course. You go to the doctor – if you don't want to go to your usual one then try a different one, but like we said before, in theory you're still a married woman. It's not like you're single and trying to get hold of it like I was. Get yourself down there today so you're all ready when the time comes.'

'All right, I will. Now that's enough about me. What about this new man you were telling me about before you became ill?'

Rhona's expression grew confused. 'Gary? You know what, Mavis, I'm not sure what to think. I thought he was really keen on me, like I was on him. I even wondered if he might be the one, you know? He was so different to all the other men, and I reckon I let myself fall for him.' She stopped for a moment. Now she was feeling better, the sense of disappointment in him was even stronger. 'But I haven't heard a peep from him, well, other than my mate Penny passing on a message from him to tell me to get well soon. But otherwise not a dicky bird from Gary, no card, no flowers, nothing. It's like everything we did together never happened, and I don't just mean the sex. We used to talk about lots of stuff, like music. He taught me a bit of guitar. I thought that made us special, that we had a real connection.' She clenched her hands in her lap. 'Now it's sweet FA, and I don't know what to do about it.'

Mavis sat up in surprise. Rhona had never been uncertain about a man before, so this was a first. Her heart went out to her friend. 'Maybe he's waiting for you to get better,' she offered. 'Perhaps he thinks he'll be in the way.'

'Yeah, maybe.' Rhona blinked once or twice, willing herself not to cry. She never cried over men, that was her golden rule. It must be because she was still weak and tired. 'Men aren't good with things like sickness, are they? He's probably scared he'll catch it.'

Mavis privately thought that if Gary only cared about himself then Rhona was better off without him, but that wasn't what her friend wanted to hear. 'If he's on the telephone, now that you're feeling better you could ring him.'

'There's one in the hallway of his digs.' Rhona swallowed hard and pulled herself together. 'That's a good idea, Mave, I'll just give him a casual call and ask him if he fancies going out somewhere when I'm feeling up to it. He won't mind. I've never been one to let the man do all the asking anyway.' She gave a small grin. 'Or I might surprise him, wait until there's a concert on I know he'll be at and then just turn up, out of the blue.'

'Do you really think that's a good idea?' asked Mavis, unsure. She could well imagine what a man like Gary might be getting up to while his girlfriend was sick.

'Oh yes.' Rhona's eyes shone now with anticipation. 'The more I think about it, the more I reckon that's what I'll do. It'd give him a lovely surprise.'

Mavis walked back from the doctor's surgery towards her house, trembling with excitement. She'd plucked up the courage and got what she wanted, even though she'd had to tell a white lie. She was changing doctors, she'd said, because they had moved house and although they'd only gone from one side of Peckham to the other, she thought it would be too far to remain with her present doctor if one of the children became ill. She didn't want any more children at the moment because Grace had only recently started full-time school. No, her husband didn't have any objections. Mavis herself was certain it was the best thing for all the family.

The doctor had nodded; checked her blood

pressure and agreed to prescribe the Pill. She only had to come back for repeat prescriptions and regular check-ups to ensure it wasn't affecting her blood pressure. Otherwise she was free to go. Mavis wondered whether to tell Tommy but decided she'd try taking it for a while first, just in case she experienced any side effects. She wanted to be absolutely sure it would work before she broke the news to him. She wouldn't have long to wait, though, and everything would be ready for the August holiday.

Mavis closed her eyes for a moment, smiling as she imagined the look on Tommy's face when she told him.

Chapter Fourteen

'Mr Tambourine Man' was playing at full volume as Gary made his way back from the bar. 'Here you are, babe,' he said, holding out a glass.

'Thanks.' Penny smiled up at him, her eyes alight. 'Cheers.'

Gary raised his pint of beer and chinked it against her Babycham. 'Cheers.'

'To us,' said Penny, gazing adoringly at him. Gary smiled but didn't say anything. Instead he nodded his head to the beat.

'Fancy a dance?' Penny turned towards the dance floor, which was filling up with people swaying to the jangling guitars of the song. 'I like this one.'

'Know what you mean, doll, but I'll finish my drink first,' Gary said, putting his arm around her waist. 'It's thirsty work, taking a beautiful girl like you out.'

'Gary, you don't half say daft things,' Penny giggled, but she was flattered. He was the best-looking bloke in the whole club and she could see some of the other girls giving her envious glances, though she pretended not to notice. She didn't want to seem smug, but she definitely felt pleased with herself. She knew she wasn't as beautiful as some of them but it didn't matter, because Gary had chosen her. He had even given up on Rhona getting better to ask her out. Sometimes Penny felt a little guilty and a small internal voice would say that he'd been a bit impatient, but she was too thrilled to pay it much attention. After all, she reasoned, Rhona herself had said he was a free agent. She sucked in her stomach and pouted, trying to look like the women she'd seen in magazines. Sometimes she had to pinch herself at the thought that she'd come here for the first time only in March, and now, just four months later, she was with the sexiest man in the place. She'd really dressed up this evening, in new shoes that pinched her toes and extra-long false eyelashes that had taken ages to get right, but you couldn't go out looking any old how when you were meeting Gary.

The music changed to 'The Price of Love' but the dance floor stayed crowded. She moved in time to the beat, leaning against Gary. She felt him move his arm. 'Sorry...' she began, turning towards him to apologise, thinking he hadn't liked it. Then she saw why he'd dropped his arm.

Rhona was standing in front of them.

Penny's jaw dropped. Hastily she looked up at Gary. He was smiling as if he hadn't got a care in the world.

'Look who it is!' he said. 'Didn't realise you were better. Welcome back.'

Rhona just looked at him, raising an eyebrow. 'Hi, Gary,' she said eventually. 'I see you've moved on.'

'Well, you didn't expect me to stay at home just because you was sick, did you?' he said in surprise. 'I knew you wouldn't mind. We had fun but that was all it was, you know that. It's not as if we made any promises or anything.'

Rhona kept her cool. 'Of course not, Gary. No commitments either way. That's how we wanted it.' She directed her gaze at Penny, who couldn't meet her eyes but stared towards the floor, at her new high-heeled shoes. 'Well, I won't disturb you two love birds. See ya.'

'OK. See ya,' said Gary, an expression of relief on his face.

The chorus came on and the Everly Brothers sang in harmony, 'The price of love, the price of love...'

Penny didn't look up as Rhona swept across the dance floor to the other side of the crowded club. For a moment she hesitated. Then she slammed down her drink and went after her friend, leaving Gary bemused with his pint.

Rhona pushed her way into the ladies, which seemed to be empty. Then she looked in the

138

mirror and saw the door was opening again, and Penny appeared. She spun round.

'You've got a nerve coming in here,' she spat, any attempts at staying cool gone. 'What the hell do you think you're playing at? Getting off with my boyfriend as soon as my back's turned?'

'No, Rhona, don't be like that.' Penny tried to placate her. 'It wasn't like that, honest. We couldn't help ourselves...'

'Couldn't help yourselves, my Aunt Fanny.' Rhona threw up her hands in disbelief. 'Don't give me that, Penny. I get bloody glandular fever and you step over me to nab my boyfriend. Fine friend you are. And then you come round to my house and tell me you met someone! It was him all along, wasn't it? You had the nerve to sit in my own bedroom asking advice about if you should sleep with my boyfriend. Well you can sling your hook. You pathetic excuse for a friend. You wouldn't even have met him if it wasn't for me and first chance you get you go and cop off with him behind my back. Get out!' She pointed to the door. 'Get out of my sight!'

'Please, Rhona, listen, I didn't do it to hurt you.' Penny was gabbling now, tears beginning to fall from her eyes, magnified by the heavy make-up and enormous lashes. 'Really, we were just swept away. I came here one night and there he was–'

'I don't want to know,' snarled Rhona. 'You can dress it up any way you like, but you've done the dirty on a friend and there's no way back from that one. I don't care about your excuses, you can even believe them if you like, but I trusted you and you took advantage when I was down. You disgust me, just get out.'

'But I love him,' cried Penny, wiping her nose on her sleeve. 'You don't understand–'

'No, Penny, it's you who doesn't understand.' Rhona spoke very steadily now. 'Get this into your head. You've betrayed your best friend. Love's got nothing to do with it. Don't come crying to me when it all goes wrong, which it will, 'cos now I know Gary's a two-timing bastard who'll do anything as long as he can get his leg over. If you're happy with that, fine. And by the way you better get yourself another job 'cos Forsyth has given in after my mum wrote to the manager saying I was ill and I'm going back to the factory. If you're still there when I go back I'll make your life a misery and tell everyone what you've done.'

'You wouldn't.' Penny gasped in horror at the thought of having to tell her mother why she couldn't go back to work.

'You know I would and Jean will have your guts for garters for a start. So you better look elsewhere, you sneaky bitch. I never want to see your lying little face again.' Rhona pointed at the door once more. 'Now get out.'

Crying unstoppably now, Penny gave way to the force of her friend's anger and beat a retreat, pausing only to take a handful of toilet roll to wipe her ruined eyes.

Rhona waited for a moment after the door had slammed behind her old friend, leaning against the cool tiles on the wall. Her head was spinning. She'd come here thinking that she'd fall into Gary's arms and he'd kiss her in happiness at being reunited. Then they'd share a few drinks and maybe go back to his place, and all the magic of when they'd first met would reignite. How wrong she had been.

Slowly Rhona pushed herself upright and made her way to one of the toilet stalls. She locked herself in, pulled down the lid and cautiously sat on it, relieved it wasn't broken like some of them were. Only then did she allow the tears that had been threatening since she'd seen the couple to fall, and she sobbed into her balled-up cardigan, covering it in mascara. Despite all her experience of men she'd allowed Gary to get through her defences and now all her dreams were in tatters.

Rhona told herself off for being stupid enough to dream them in the first place, but it didn't help as for the first time in her life she felt her heart break. Gary had turned out to be a lowlife cheating scumbag and yet she couldn't stop herself from crying, for everything she'd wanted him to be but he wasn't. She cried and cried, for his betrayal and treachery – but also for the utter betrayal by a young woman she'd thought of as a trusted friend.

Chapter Fifteen

'Welcome back,' said Jean, as Rhona walked through the factory door for the first time since Easter. 'Didn't think we'd see you round here again.'

'I just couldn't keep away,' grinned Rhona. 'Mum kicked up such a stink when they tried to sack me when I was ill that the manager gave in. Thanks for the card. It was nice to know you hadn't all forgotten me.'

'Not much chance of that,' said Jean briskly. 'Here, better get your overall on. Blimey, it's too big for you now, isn't it? You've lost heaps of weight.'

'I know.' Rhona looked at the hated garment, which now hung loosely on her. 'I needed to come back to earn some money to buy new clothes. All my stuff just drops off me now.'

'You could pass for Jean Shrimpton,' said Jean, thinking that her young colleague was now far too thin. 'Well, I must say I'm glad to see you back. You know Penny's left, don't you? Handed in her notice in a hurry and was off and away, no real goodbyes or nothing.'

'Yeah, I heard.' Rhona made herself busy with her locker.

Jean watched her critically. 'You two had a falling-out? You was thick as thieves before.'

'Nah, not really.' Rhona wouldn't look at the older woman. 'I think she's got some new friends.'

'Maybe it's just as well, she was getting un-reliable,' said Jean. 'OK, Forsyth will probably be down in a minute but let's get you started on something.'

'Oh God, I could do without seeing him,' sighed Rhona. 'I bet he's still got it in for me.'

'He can't afford to have, what with Penny leaving so suddenly and no replacement yet,' Jean pointed out. 'Besides, I think he's forgotten all that stuff about you and Andy. He keeps going on about how Andy's turned over a new leaf, is bringing in proper money now, so they're all relieved. Perhaps he's settled down and grown up a bit.' She bit her lip – from the little she knew it didn't seem likely; Forsyth's nephew wasn't her cup of tea at all, but she wasn't going to ask awkward questions. If it got the foreman off their backs then she wasn't going to complain.

Rhona was surprised to find she didn't mind being back at the factory. She enjoyed Jean's company, not quite in the same way that she enjoyed Mavis's, but it was good to be with someone just a few years older than herself and not one of her mother's generation who didn't understand what was going on these days. Compared to working alongside Penny it was almost restful. It was also a bit of a novelty to be at work this early and without a hangover. Somehow things that had seemed so difficult earlier in the year, like keeping up with the production line when the conveyor belt was at full speed, suddenly weren't as hard. Maybe there was something to be said for staying in every evening and going to bed on time after all.

'Sorry I couldn't come round yesterday,' said Tommy, as he and Mavis strolled around Peckham Rye Common, enjoying the last of the day's heat and making the most of the light evening. 'Jenny asked me to go to her place. I think she gets lonely when Stan's not there, though she doesn't like to say so.'

Mavis tipped back her head to gaze at the sky, as the sunset was tingeing the clouds with pink and lilac. 'Can't say I blame her, it's a big house to be alone in, except for Greg.'

'He was in his room for most of the evening anyway. We're too boring for him,' Tommy grinned. 'Anyway, it'll be Stan's last trip before we all go away.'

'Not long now.' Mavis's eyes shone. 'I can't wait. I'm going to get myself a swimming costume.'

'Can't wait to see you in that,' Tommy said, drawing her to him. 'You'll have all eyes on the beach on you. But I want you all to myself. Talk about Jenny alone in a big house for some evenings – you have to take pity on me, rattling around that huge flat in Wandsworth.'

'Oh, I do.' Mavis knew his flat was bigger than many terraced houses, and one person alone in it could easily rattle around. She hugged him, as tightly as she could while out in public. This part of the common was very open and she didn't want to draw attention to them. Then again, they weren't the only couple out taking advantage of the gorgeous weather. 'So Stan will be sorting out arrangements while he's down there, I suppose.'

'That's the idea.' Tommy nuzzled her neck and then her face. 'We don't have to worry about any of that, do we? He's looking after it all.'

'I know.' She gazed up at him. 'But do we know how many rooms the place has got? I don't think he actually said.'

Tommy stopped and looked at her directly. 'Are you worried about something? Is it the kids? They'll love it, you know they will.'

'No, it's not that. Well, Grace will probably make a fuss about being in a strange bed but it'll last a few minutes then she'll be too excited to bother about it for long,' Mavis replied, making a

144

quick mental note to pack Little Ted. 'It was more ... it was more ... about where I would sleep. About where you would sleep.'

Tommy's expression grew puzzled. 'I assumed you'd share with Grace, and James would go in with Greg, and I'd take one of the single rooms. I hadn't thought that much about it to be honest. Trust you to start worrying about a thing like that. Relax. Grace will be fine.'

Mavis almost gave up, realising that Tommy had no idea what she was talking about. She'd held back for so long that he hadn't picked up on her hints at all. Now she turned to walk, slipping her arm around his waist as he draped his around her shoulder. 'She will, of course she will. I was just wondering ... well, you know ... whether we might...' Her nerve failed her. She couldn't just come straight out and say it. It sounded too cold and calculating, setting a date when they could finally be together, and she wanted it to be romantic, not scheduled in like an appointment at the dentist. She stroked his back, willing him to understand what she meant without her having to spell it out.

Suddenly Tommy came to a complete standstill. He turned to her once more and gazed into her eyes. 'Are you saying what I think you're saying?'

She gave a small nod, and he bent to kiss her, hard and passionately. She responded, arching up to him, holding him as tightly as she could, and to hell with whoever might be watching. 'Yes,' she managed to say after they finally stopped, breathless. 'Oh Tommy. I want you so much, you know I do. I just thought with Alec and everything ...

but now it seems silly. I love you, I want to be with you.'

'And I love you, Mavis, and I won't do anything you don't want me to.' He was serious now. 'I respect you too much for that. If you want to go on waiting until the future is clearer for us then that's fine but if not ... oh my God.' He shook his head. 'Let's go back to my flat now...'

'Tommy, we can't, not tonight.' Mavis smiled up at him, relieved that they were in agreement and he hadn't been shocked at her suggestion. 'Mum will be waiting for me to check on James.' She paused. 'But actually ... well ... maybe we could...' Suddenly it seemed silly to wait for the holiday. She was ready, she didn't want to put him off for any longer than she had to. 'Tommy, shall I come to your flat tomorrow?'

'Would you like to?' He could hardly believe what he was hearing. 'We could go to that little restaurant a couple of streets away, we could pretend we're on a first date or something like that.'

'First date? Now that is a shocking idea.' Her eyes danced. 'But I'm taking pity on you rattling round that flat, you see. I hate to think of you there, all lonely.'

'So you're doing me a good turn. Then it would be rude of me to refuse.' He kissed her forehead and hugged her again. 'I can't wait. I've waited so long for you, Mavis, even one more night seems like too much. But I will wait. My God, you are the most beautiful woman in the world and I'm going to make you happier than you've ever been in your life.'

146

Pete stepped away from the outer door to the bank, pausing to rub his handkerchief over his forehead. He was sweating with anxiety. He glanced around, making sure there was nobody on the busy street who might recognise him. He didn't want anyone to know he was in any kind of trouble as that would make his situation even worse than it already was. There was no getting away from it, he was now up to his neck in it.

The bank manager had been blunt. The mortgage loan repayments weren't being made. Pete would have to pay extra to keep it going or risk losing the house. Pete had blustered, assuring the manager that the big contract would be signed any day now, but he himself no longer believed it. He'd heard nothing for weeks. He had tried telling himself for so long that it would come right, but now it was all threatening to come crashing down and he'd lose everything he held so dear. And that included the faith that his family had placed in him.

Now Pete gazed along the street, wondering where it had all gone wrong. The project had seemed ideal. Peckham needed modernising – lots of the old housing stock was in a terrible condition, the officials were saying, and Pete reckoned he should know because he'd lived in some of it. Also, there had been bomb damage here, just as in much of the city. The whole area was crying out for new developments and he had been proud to think he was going to make a difference to his beloved South London.

He always cautioned others not to put all their eggs in one basket, yet he had gone against his own advice and risked more than he would usually have done. Pete shuddered. They'd all been so happy, moving into the new place, Mavis able to feel safe for the first time in years, the kids overjoyed to all be together, even Lily calming down a bit. He couldn't even begin to imagine what they'd do if he had to tell them they couldn't stay in the house.

The good thing was that Lily had been so caught up in planning for the holiday that she hadn't picked up on his mood. He'd expected her to turn on him over the past few weeks, demanding to know why he was so preoccupied, telling him to cheer up and not to be such a misery guts with a long face. Instead she'd been making lists with Mavis, checking with Jenny to decide who would bring what, and filling the kids' heads with all sorts of expectations. Bobby had just gone three and was old enough to join in with some of it, asking for a bucket and spade and announcing that he was going to sail on a boat. Pete realised he was too young to know what that really meant but he'd been delighted that his son was coming out with long sentences and excited at trying something new. He was such a happy little boy, grown-up for his years thanks to mixing with Mavis's children, and Pete's heart nearly missed a beat at the idea of letting him down.

So he had better make sure that he didn't.

'Come in, come in.' Mavis welcomed Rhona, who'd dropped by after her late shift had finished. 'I haven't seen you for ages. You look miles better.' She led the way into the kitchen, where Rhona pulled out a chair and slumped down at the table.

'Thanks. Not sure I feel it at the moment.' Then she pulled a face. 'No, that's not true, 'cos I was still in a bit of a state when I saw you last. I'm back at work now and while I'm there I can't think about anything other than keeping up. Then when I leave it hits me.'

Mavis was sympathetic as she turned on the kettle. 'Have you eaten? I've got some stew left over from our tea if you like.'

Rhona was about to say no then realised she was hungry. 'Do you know what, I'd love some. At least my appetite is back to normal now.' She grinned. 'As long as I'm not depriving you or anything.'

'If I hadn't wanted you to have it, I wouldn't have offered,' said Mavis, pleased to be able to do something for her friend. 'It won't take long to heat up. So how have you been?'

Rhona rested her hands on the tabletop and twisted them together. 'Oh ... you know. All right. Not so bad, could be worse.' She paused. 'You know when we went to the park and I said I'd give Gary a lovely surprise by turning up one evening? Well, I did it, but it was me who got the surprise and it wasn't very lovely.'

'How do you mean?' asked Mavis, making tea for both of them. 'Here, take the sugar, you need the energy.'

Rhona smiled wanly. 'Yeah, you're probably right. It all went wrong from the moment I got there.' She began to describe the disastrous evening at the Talisman, stopping every now and again as the emotions hit her all over again. 'I just didn't see that one coming, not in a month of Sundays. I can't believe he'd do that, or that Penny would either, and I can't believe I'm still letting it get to me.' She gave a quick sniff. 'Stupid, isn't it? He's obviously an idiot and I'm better off without him, but still...'

'He'd have to be a real fool, preferring her over you,' said Mavis loyally, resisting the urge to say she'd wondered about him at the time. 'Look, have some of this, it'll make you feel better.' She ladled the stew into a bowl, and cut a big slice of bread to go with it.

'Smells lovely.' Rhona wiped her eyes. 'I can't believe I was so stupid, dreaming of me being with him for ages, turning into Darby and Joan.' She sighed. 'It wasn't only that, though, I really, really did like him a lot.'

'I know, I could tell,' said Mavis. 'It's not fair, Rhona. You deserve better.'

'Do I, though?' Rhona took a mouthful of the stew and shut her eyes. 'That's lovely, Mave, you're such a good cook. But all of this has got me thinking.'

'Oh?' Mavis took a sip of her tea. Rhona seemed to have changed. She was quieter, more reflective, and seemed less desperate to have fun all the time. 'Thinking about what?'

Rhona scraped the last of the stew from the bowl and then wiped it with the rest of the bread, making sure she got every drop. 'Well, you know. What I was like before.'

Mavis cocked her head. 'How do you mean?'

'When I was dating blokes, I didn't even begin to think of how they felt. I just wanted to have fun and assumed that's all they wanted too. Most of them did, I'm pretty sure. But now and again one of them would get upset, or try to talk me out of finishing with them, or say that they wanted something more, and I just didn't get it. I thought it was daft and I didn't want to be tied down.' She looked at the empty bowl for a moment, and then back up again. 'So it serves me right, doesn't it? I wanted fun, I had fun. Then I meet someone who also wanted fun and I go and expect more. I should have known better. Gary never said it would be anything else so why should I be surprised? Yet you could have knocked me over with feather when I saw him in that club with Penny of all people.'

'Some friend she turned out to be,' said Mavis. 'You expected better from both of them so no wonder this has knocked you for six, and if Gary can't see what he's missing then more fool him.'

'You're too nice, Mavis,' Rhona replied, smiling through a fresh burst of tears. 'You don't go round treating people badly like I did, and in a way this is just punishment.'

'You're being too hard on yourself,' Mavis reassured her.

'No, I'm seeing myself from the outside for the first time. The way I behaved wasn't right, and I let work mates down too – not the bosses, I don't care a fig about them, but the likes of Jean. She had to work extra hard to cover for me when I went in still half asleep and hungover. That wasn't fair on her, she didn't deserve that, but she never let me down, unlike Penny.' Rhona paused, to take a gulp of tea. 'Then there's you. Thanks for listening, Mavis. You're a real friend all right. I can tell you anything and you never blame me.'

'It's what friends are for,' said Mavis seriously.

151

'Who knows, one day Penny might see what she's done and come begging for forgiveness. She's younger than you, isn't she? Maybe she just needs to grow up.'

'Maybe.' Rhona sat up straighter. 'Right, that's enough about me. What about you? How did it go down the doctor's? Are you ready for you know what?'

Mavis suddenly blushed and couldn't stop a huge smile creeping across her face. 'I'm more than ready. It all went fine and ... and ... we've done it already.'

'No!' Rhona squealed in surprise and delight. 'You never did! You sly thing. How did it go – no, I don't even have to ask, I can see it on your face. It was good, wasn't it. He's made you happy. Look at you, I can't believe I didn't see it straight away. Come on, Mavis, spill the beans. I want to know everything.'

Mavis gave her head a little shake. She wasn't prepared to divulge the full details of that very special evening, even to Rhona. She'd never experienced anything like it. Tommy had taken her to the little Italian restaurant near his flat, where the owner had treated them to extra drinks and desserts as he knew Tommy well. She'd been too nervous to make the most of it, even when her glass had been topped up. She could tell he was on edge too, yet eager to get her back to the flat. In the end they had almost run there, like a pair of teenagers. Once inside he had taken her in his arms and kissed her as she'd never been kissed before, and she had responded in a way she hadn't dreamed possible. They hadn't even got as far as the bedroom but had fallen upon each other on the big couch, where she'd clutched at the cushions and moaned as Tommy showed her exactly what she'd been missing. All the nightmare encounters with Alec were banished from her mind as Tommy explored every inch of her with infinite care, love and mounting passion. To her amazement she'd done the same to him, with no thought of embarrassment. It had all felt completely natural and right. When eventually they finished she'd lain in his arms and purred with pleasure. They had snuggled up, both satiated, but then Tommy had begun to laugh.

'What?' she'd asked.

'Nothing.'

'No, what? You can't get away with saying "nothing". What is it?'

Tommy had stroked her back and neck and then her face. 'I was just thinking, it's just as well we didn't wait for Torquay. I don't know what the B and B is like but I bet its soundproofing wouldn't have been enough to stop half the place hearing all that.'

'Tommy!'

'It's true. We'd have woken the kids, no doubt about it. Still, at least now we know. Next time we'll have to practise being very, very quiet.'

'Who says there's going to be a next time?' she'd giggled.

'I do,' he'd breathed. 'And so do you, if I'm not much mistaken. Because I love you very, very much and I'm not afraid to show you.'

Mavis had no intention of repeating any of this to Rhona. It was all too new and felt deliciously private. But she had to give her friend some credit. 'I'll tell you one thing,' she said now, leaning back in the kitchen chair. 'I didn't believe you when you told me how wonderful it can be, but now I know you're right.'

'I'm dead chuffed for you,' Rhona said, smiling.

Mavis felt that her friend's smile failed to hide her sadness and with a deep sigh she said, 'I hope you find someone to truly love you, Rhona, I really do.'

'I wouldn't hold your breath,' Rhona replied.

Mavis felt deeply for her friend. She wanted her to be happy, as happy as she was. She was already longing to see Tommy again.

Chapter Sixteen

Every so often Tommy forced himself to go back to his old childhood home to visit his mother. It should have been easy; it wasn't far from the sign-writing yard or Jenny and Stan's house. If things had been different he could have popped round after work, or when there was a quiet moment during the day, or on his way to see his cousin. However, Olive Wilson wasn't the sort of woman to welcome a son who'd been through a divorce, no matter how close he might be geographically. Tommy went to see her purely out of duty, not out of affection, because it was years since she had shown him any, and he kept his visits to a minimum, just to reassure himself that she was in reasonable health and wanted for nothing. That was about as much as he could bring himself to do.

Knowing it would be just like her to have an emergency when he was away, he dragged himself down his old street before the trip to Torquay. He'd have to tell her about it, though he didn't want to, but it would be worse if she found out from Jenny's side of the family. So he put a brave face on it and approached his old house. The paint on the door was peeling, just as he always remembered it. He'd lost count of the number of times he'd offered to help do it up but his mother always refused point blank. When I want your help I'll ask for it, she would always snap.

It was a warm evening again, hot even for August, and Tommy was looking forward to the sea breezes of Devon, but when his mother opened the door she was wrapped in a thick woollen cardigan full of moth holes.

'Oh, it's you.'

'Hello, Mum. I said I'd call round today.'

Olive looked at her only son with thinly disguised contempt. 'Well don't stand there cluttering up the doorstep. I suppose you'd better come in.'

She turned and went back into the dark hall without waiting for him. Tommy followed, trying not to get depressed at the sight of the dark brown walls, the exact colour they'd been while he was growing up here. To this day he couldn't stand that shade of brown.

'How have you been, Mum?' he asked as he went into the kitchen. This hadn't been painted for years either, and now that his mother was on

155

her own she didn't bother cleaning it very often. Many years ago Tommy recalled she had been house-proud but now there was no reason for her to be as he was about the only person who came to see her – she had driven everyone else away, one by one, by being mean, miserable or both.

'What's it to you?' she countered at once. 'If you cared for me at all you wouldn't have brought shame upon the family by getting divorced. You know full well I've never got over that and I never will. Don't think you can come round here and butter me up.'

Tommy shook his head. It was always the same. 'Change the record, why don't you,' he muttered beneath his breath but she was on to him like a shot.

'What's that?' she demanded.

'Nothing. Just wondered if you aren't too hot in that cardie.'

'What, so I can't wear what I want in my own home now?'

'No, I was only worried that you'd be too hot.'

'Hot? In this? Can't you see all the holes that are in it? I'm hardly likely to be too hot in that, am I? Now if you'd stayed with that Belinda, she could have got me some new ones and I wouldn't be forced to be seen out in this old rag.'

Tommy reminded himself to count to ten and not let her get under his skin. He had offered her money time and time again, only to have it refused. He also knew full well that his ex-wife would sooner have died than set foot in this place, let alone help his mother to choose new cardigans. The idea would have been laughable if he hadn't been face to face with this angry, bitter woman.

'Suppose you want a cuppa, do you?'

Tommy shook his head. He had no wish to put his mouth anywhere near one of the greasy-looking cups he could see draining by the sink. 'I wouldn't want to put you to any trouble,' he said instead. 'Anyway it's hot out, I'm roasting. That office gets like a furnace.'

'I would have thought you'd have got yourself another one, a fancier place by now if you're doing as well as you say you are. Further away from Battersea,' she said pointedly.

'I like it well enough where I am. Anyway it's useful for seeing Jenny and Stan.'

'Oh yes, I hear that you've plenty of time to go round there to see them. Suppose they're more interesting than your poor old mother.'

Tommy stopped himself from saying yes. He took a deep breath. 'You know Stan's travelling a lot now, going down to Devon.'

'Is he, now?' Olive's eyes were beady in the dull light from the grimy kitchen window. 'Nice work for them as can get it.'

'In fact he's found a good B and B and they're taking Greg on holiday there, to Torquay.'

'They spoil that child,' she snorted. 'It's not as if he's old enough to appreciate such things.'

'Mum, he's ten.'

'It's a wonder you aren't trailing along with them, seeing as you think so much of them. More than of your own mother.'

Tommy looked her in the eye. This was the moment to get it all out in the open. 'As a matter of fact, they've asked me to join them and I've said yes. I've never been, and everyone says it's beautiful.'

'Beautiful!' she cried in derision. 'What use is that when it comes to putting money in the bank?'

Tommy knew he had to continue and then brave the storm that would inevitably follow. 'They've also asked their old neighbour Mavis, her two kids, and her mum and family.'

'What!' Olive's head went back and she stared at her son as if he was mad. 'You're going away with that lot? That tart Lily Jackson, who's no better than she should be? And her daughter, Dumbo?'

'It's Lily Culling now,' Tommy pointed out, keeping his voice level with some difficulty. 'You know I told you ages ago she married Pete and they've got a little boy...'

'At her age! It's a marvel she hasn't dried up. Bet it's all gone south now.' Olive's expression grew even more malicious. 'As for that daughter of hers, Dumbo, she's as thick as two short planks. What you want to go away with that lot for?'

Tommy had managed to avoid mentioning Mavis to his mother in the time they had been dating, even though he had assumed word would have reached her somehow on the gossip grapevine. Maybe it hadn't. She knew he'd been keen on her ages ago but not how far things had gone since then. 'Mavis and Jenny are good friends, they have been for years. You know that. Besides, Mavis isn't thick. She's got a medical condition that stops her being able to read properly. She's got as much sense as anyone else and she's brilliant at art...' Tommy stopped before he said any more, but the change on his mother's face

158

showed that she'd put two and two together.

'Medical condition my foot. She's as daft as they come, Tommy, and so are you if you're mixed up with the likes of her. How you can do that after being married to a woman like Belinda...'

'Let's leave Belinda out of it,' growled Tommy, feeling his face grow hotter still with the effort of keeping his temper.

'How you all travelling down there, then?' Olive wanted to know.

'We're taking two cars. Stan's got his big estate from his firm and can take Greg and Jenny, as well as Lily and Pete. Then I've got a new car that's big enough for me, Mavis and her kids, and Lily's little Bobby.'

'So you've got yourself a new car to ferry that lot around? You must have it bad,' his mother said, her expression one of disgust. 'You're driving that thicko and her two brats plus that scrubber Lily Jackson's last-minute sprog down to Devon? Now I've heard it all.' She sank on to a spindly chair, seeming exhausted by all the revelations. 'Well, good luck to yer. You're gonna need it. You wouldn't catch me cooped up in a car with three little kids puking their way all the long journey down there. I'd sooner roast in hell.' She looked up at him. 'Hope you've got a strong stomach.'

Tommy had had enough. 'I'll be fine, don't worry about me.'

Olive barked out another mirthless laugh. 'Worry about you? That'll be the day. You don't know what worry is. When I think of what you've put me through, getting that divorce, and now you're taking on another man's litter...'

'Must be off,' said Tommy, before she could say anymore. 'I'll let you know when I'm back. Look after yourself.'

'Ha! Who else is going to do that, I'd like to know? Especially as my only son is now too busy with someone else's brats...'

Tommy could hear her voice echoing down the dark, mean little hall as he headed for the front door and let himself out. Once back on the street he drew in a deep breath. The air tasted much fresher than when he'd arrived, but that was because it had been so close inside the old house; his mother didn't believe in opening the windows, just in case germs got in.

Well, that was that over with for a while. Maybe he'd send her a postcard, Tommy thought. It might cheer her up. Then he shook his head. Who was he kidding? She'd probably rip it into tiny pieces. He sighed, aware that she was a sad woman facing old age on her own – and yet she wasn't that much older than Lily. If his mother was determined to be miserable then there wasn't much he could do about it, other than make sure she didn't actually harm herself.

Tommy turned back towards the yard, where he'd left the new car. Not long now before the holiday, and he'd have all those nights with Mavis in his arms. At once, his mood lifted.

'Are we nearly there yet?' Grace asked, bouncing up and down with excitement. She'd been asking the same question ever since they'd got on to the A303.

Bobby caught her mood and began clapping his

160

hands. 'Want to be there, want to be there,' he chanted.

'We are, or very nearly,' said Mavis with as much certainty as she could manage. Really she hadn't a clue as she hadn't been to Devon before, but they'd passed a sign for Newton Abbot so she knew from the large map spread on her lap that they must be close. She picked up the handwritten instructions Stan had given her for the final leg of the journey in case they got split up. She was glad, as they'd lost sight of the other car somewhere close to Exeter when Stan had overtaken a tractor while Tommy had got stuck behind it. James had been worried, but Tommy had laughed and said that's what they had to expect if they came visiting farming country.

'Here we are. Next junction,' said Mavis with relief. She'd enjoyed the drive, or most of it, and they'd broken the journey halfway and eaten their sandwiches, but she'd be glad to get to the guesthouse now. Her calves were aching, as she'd had to put one of their bags under her feet because the boot was full, and she could tell the kids needed to be let out again to stretch their legs.

Carefully she read out the list Stan had made, getting the children to watch out for landmarks as they gradually approached the seaside resort. James pointed at the palm trees. Bobby and Grace stared at them, unsure what they were. Tommy was probably just glad they were distracted, as she could tell he'd been a bit worried they would get lost. But now here they, were, in the street just as Stan had described it, and there was his car parked at the end.

Pete was standing by it, waving, as Tommy pulled up alongside. Mavis wound down her window.

'There's a parking space over there,' Pete grinned. 'Can you smell the sea air? Ain't it great? I tell you, I feel better already.'

Tommy pulled into the space, reflecting that Pete did look happier than he'd seen him in weeks – months, come to think of it. He wondered again what that was about, but decided it was up to Pete to tell him if he wanted to. He wasn't going to cloud their holiday by raising the subject.

Mavis held her nerve as they went into the B and B, keeping her fingers crossed that the landlady wouldn't ask if she and Tommy were married. She needn't have worried. Mrs Hawkins had clearly decided they were all to be on first-name terms, as that's how she addressed Stan and Jenny. Mavis had also wondered how her children would react when they saw the sleeping arrangements but all James cared about was that he was sharing with Greg.

Mrs Hawkins had found a put-you-up to place in one of the single rooms as an extra bed and the boys were fascinated by its mechanism, so the adults left them to it, with plenty of warnings not to stick their fingers in the hinges. Grace was to share with Bobby, in a little room connected to one the main double bedrooms. 'It must have been a dressing room once,' said Mrs Hawkins. 'I don't like to let it on its own but it's fine when there are families.'

'You don't mind being next to Granny's room, do you?' Mavis asked as her mother demonstrated how the dressing room door led in to their room.

'No, and I can look after Bobby,' Grace said, seemingly delighted to be in charge of him, whilst Mavis quietly slipped Little Ted under her daughter's pillow, just in case there were bedtime tantrums. A bathroom separated Lily and Pete's bedroom from the large one allocated to Mavis and Tommy.

Later, Tommy smiled broadly as he shut the door behind them and flopped with exhaustion on the big double bed. 'Did you see that? No danger of any sound getting through the walls? He patted the candlewick bedspread. 'Come and join me.'

Mavis giggled and lay down beside him, propping herself up on one elbow. 'Look at that view. I can't believe we're actually here.'

'I can't believe I'm actually here with you,' he said, his big green eyes suddenly serious. He traced the line of her cheek, her jaw, and then kissed her long and hard. 'That's better. I've been waiting to do that all day, you've no idea. You are a temptress, Mavis.'

'We've got all this time together,' Mavis breathed, lying down properly, raising her arms above her head and stretching luxuriantly. 'This room is lovely. Look at that high ceiling. I'm glad I don't have to dust the corners.'

Tommy snorted. 'Stop thinking about housework. You don't have to do any all holiday. Your only job is to enjoy yourself.' He bent over her and brought his face close to hers. 'Think you can manage that?'

She gazed up into his eyes and smiled. 'Oh I think so,' she said, as she reached to pull him closer still. 'But why don't you show me how, just to be sure.'

Alec Pugh stood at the window of his stamp shop later that day, thankful to see the last of a difficult customer. He knew the man was a serious collector and therefore good for business but he couldn't bear him. He was big and bluff, wore a loud tweed jacket and spent most of his time commenting on the women who passed by.

'Look at her,' he'd roar, rubbing his hands. 'She'd be a handful, wouldn't she? I'd like to see what she's made of underneath.'

Alec had forced himself not to react as he really wanted to, unable to bring himself to join in with light banter. He saw nothing remotely attractive in the curvy figures his customer seemed to prefer, and the very idea of seeing what any of them were like underneath their skimpy sundresses made his stomach turn over. Now he breathed a sigh of relief as the big man disappeared around the corner, having at least bought a selection of very rare stamps. Alec knew he should record the purchases in his ledger in his meticulously neat handwriting, but he allowed himself a minute to take in the view. When he raised his sights above the crowd he could see the big sky and the distant horizon, all a beautiful blue today. He sighed. Despite having to deal with obnoxious creatures like that customer, he'd made the right decision coming here. Battersea seemed a world away.

His attention was caught by the sight of someone he'd seen only a couple of months ago. He'd tried to obliterate the memory but now it came flooding back, the insult of the man with the pretty woman laughing at his sign. His old neighbour from Battersea days: Stan Bonner and that meddling slut, Jenny. And there she was as well, damn them straight to hell.

Before he could turn away in deep annoyance, it got worse. There was their horrible little boy, a bit taller now, but still full of irrepressible energy, most likely still making far too much noise. He was carrying a football, which was just typical. He'd be one of those ghastly children who played games on the beach, kicking sand into respectable people's faces, shrieking as he did so. He'd have expected no better from those parents.

Then his heart skipped a beat. The boy turned and it looked as if he was shouting to someone. Another boy came into view, younger, hair flapping, shirt untucked, and socks falling down around his ankles. But it wasn't the untidy clothes that bothered Alec. He stared at the second boy's face. It couldn't be. He'd changed, lost his baby roundness, but there was no doubt who it was. There, running along the pavement in Torquay, miles from where he should have been, was his very own son. James.

Following not far behind came a woman in very tight clothes with bright blonde hair that couldn't be, and never had been, natural. Alec felt the breath catch in his throat. It was his detested mother-in-law, the scrubber, Lily, and sure enough there was that child she'd had so disgracefully late in life, now running around, holding his little arms up to the man just out of his view, who most probably was the poor fellow who'd been sucked into marriage with the scheming bitch. Alec almost felt sorry for him, but then, it had been the man's decision to shackle himself to such a vile woman. He shuddered.

Finally in the small group came a couple, swinging a child of about six between them. For a moment he couldn't tell if it was a boy or girl as the little figure wore bright green shorts and a matching sunhat. Then he caught sight of her profile. Of course. Again a bit older, but there was no doubt that he was looking at his very own daughter, that uncontrollably rude little girl, Grace. Closest to him, holding her hand, was a tall man with very dark hair, good-looking, well set, casually dressed. He was partially obscuring the figure on the far side of the group, but then Grace pulled her forward.

Alec felt a loud hiss escape his lips and he staggered a little. There was a tightness in his chest as he fixed his gaze on the creature he had come to loathe most in the entire world.

There, strolling along without a care in the world, a happy smile on her upturned face, the breeze blowing through her dark, wavy hair, was his wife, Mavis.

Chapter Seventeen

Rhona slumped in the lumpy old armchair beside the empty fireplace in the little living room, wishing she had something to do. She was bored. Now that she wasn't friends with Penny anymore, she didn't have anyone to go out with, or anyone to visit. Mavis was away with all the family.

Jean had asked her if she wanted to come over after work and they could maybe go to the cinema but Rhona had sensed her colleague was just being kind. She knew Jean would be seeing her boyfriend. Rhona had met him a few times as he would come to the factory now and again to see Jean after one of their late shifts. He was nice enough, and Jean was obviously very happy with him, but Rhona couldn't see him being a bundle of laughs somehow. He was older for a start, in his early thirties, with a steady job and the odds were that he'd soon ask Jean to marry him and then they'd settle down and that would be that. Rhona wondered if she could persuade Jean to come out on her own, maybe to a bar in town, but it didn't seem very likely she'd accept. It wasn't her sort of thing.

Sighing, she flicked through the local paper, but none of the articles grabbed her attention. There was something about a corrupt police officer, a Sergeant Fenton, which vaguely rang a bell – perhaps something to do with a story about some raids Penny had mentioned back when they were still talking to each other. Rhona couldn't be bothered to read it. A summer sale at Jones & Higgins – big deal, she still wouldn't be able to afford anything. A market trader cautioned for counterfeit goods – Rhona glanced at his picture and recognised him as the one who always held your hand too long when giving you your change. Good, serve the dirty bastard right.

She came to the 'what's on' section, and sighed even more deeply. Usually these would be the first pages she'd turn to, eager to see what entertainment was on offer. Now she couldn't see the point. There wasn't much listed anyway; it was always quieter in August.

Then her eye was caught by a small advertisement for a bar she knew that wasn't much further away than the factory. They were having an open mic evening, so anyone who fancied trying out a few numbers could come along. Normally she would have turned up her nose at such things; she only wanted to see the cutting-edge, sharpest bands, not any old Tom, Dick or Harry who fancied they could have a go. But if she went along she'd be bound to see someone she knew. It was on Sunday, so it wouldn't go on till late, and she wouldn't have to work out how to get home; she could walk it.

Before falling ill she'd barely spent any time considering such things but somehow now she was more cautious. She'd felt she was invincible, no matter what hour she'd had to make her way across the vast spread of the capital; now though Rhona felt she wasn't. Still, she couldn't sit round here moping all the time. It was time to get back in the saddle – or at least back on the music scene.

'Sunday night,' she said to herself. After all, how hard could it be? She might even enjoy it. She'd missed her guitar lessons and now she had more energy she was pleased at the thought of getting back to what she used to love so much, music. Maybe she wasn't ready to break away from the factory into the big time but there was nothing wrong with seeing what was going on just up the road.

'Over here! Pass it over here!' James yelled, belting along the sand as fast as he could go.

'Goal!' shouted Tommy, shooting the ball past the pile of jumpers.

'No, it should be on the other side!' protested Greg, who'd failed to make contact with the ball as it shot past him.

'Nonsense! That was a goal, fair and square,' said Tommy, puffing a bit. The boys had kept him running around since shortly after breakfast. As he'd been up half the night making the most of his precious time with Mavis, he could have done with a rest this morning, but the boys weren't having any of it.

'Where's the ball gone?' asked James, spinning round. Then he saw that it had rolled off towards a pair of middle-aged holiday-makers who were reading the newspapers, sitting in striped deck-chairs. He trotted over, putting on his politest face.

'Please may we have our ball back?' he asked, remembering how his teacher had taught him to speak in school.

The man in the deckchair beamed. 'Of course. Help yourself. Aren't you lucky your daddy plays football so well? I bet he's shown you how to kick for goal.'

'He's not my daddy,' said James without thinking. Then he caught the expression on the woman's face and hastily added, 'He's my Uncle Tommy.'

'Well then, you're very lucky to have an uncle who's so good at football. Enjoy your holiday,' said the man, and went back to his newspaper.

James picked up the ball and strolled back to the others. He didn't want to think of his daddy, whom he'd grown to fear. He didn't particularly want another one. He much preferred Tommy, who didn't mind getting covered in sand, was not bad at football and never, ever hit him.

He glanced across to where his mother was sitting on a picnic blanket, chatting to Greg's mum. They had on sunglasses and straw sunhats with big brims, and were drinking tea from a flask. The landlady had packed them all a picnic hamper this morning and had been careful to ask the children what they wanted in their sandwiches.

'No cucumber!' Grace had shouted. 'I hate cucumber!'

James had groaned inwardly as he'd heard the same complaint all summer, and it was a pity as Granny Lily had managed to grow lots of cucumbers in their new back garden. He suspected if she hadn't then Grace would have demanded cucumber for breakfast, dinner and tea, because last year she'd loved it. He wondered if Granny would tell her off, but Mrs Hawkins had simply said, 'Well, I shan't put any in, then,' and made no fuss at all.

'Look at them, they love it here.' Mavis sat back, leaning on her elbows, peering at the boys over the top of her new sunglasses. She felt quite self-conscious wearing them but Jenny had told her to stop worrying and that she looked like Jackie Kennedy. Mavis was sure Jackie Kennedy never got sand in her sandwiches but on a beautiful day like this she wasn't going to protest. She was just relieved that it was all going so well.

'Yeah, I knew they would,' said Jenny, reaching into the hamper for a banana. 'I don't know about you but this sea air makes me famished. I must have put on a stone.'

Mavis shook her head, laughing. Her friend was slimmer than ever, and getting the beginnings of a tan.

'I didn't know how the children would react, seeing me with Tommy all day every day, but they don't seem to mind. It's all gone smoothly, or so far. Touch wood.' She tapped her hand on the little toggle holding down the hamper lid.

'Well, why wouldn't it?' Jenny pushed back her sunhat. 'They've known him for ages, and let's face it, he treats them better than their own father ever did. Look at him there, having a kick about, like a big kid himself. They love him because they know they're safe with him and they just relax.'

Mavis let out a sigh. 'I'm so relieved. You know, I kind of looked on this break as a bit of a practice run – for what it might be like if we ever get together for good. God only knows when that will be. I keep hoping for news of Alec so that I can at least file for divorce.'

'Before the seven years since Alec's disappearance and you can have him declared dead, you mean?' asked Jenny. 'That's a long time to wait. Still five years to go, aren't there?'

'Afraid so.' Mavis's face fell. 'It seems ages when you put it like that. But who knows, something might happen before the time's up. We could hear something definite, either way. That would help. Anything's better than not knowing.'

'You should get some legal advice, but in the meantime you're both happy. Any fool can see that you're made for each other, it's obvious,' Jenny said as she put the banana peel in a paper bag and shoved it back inside the hamper. 'What's Grace up to?'

'She's down there at the shoreline, with Lily and Bobby. They're having a paddle. She can't get enough of the sea now she's got used to how cold it is.' Mavis laughed. 'I reckon she thought it was going to be like a bath. She got the shock of her life when she first stuck her toe in. That, and the way the tide brings the waves back and forth, but now she loves it, and keeps bringing back shells. I don't know where she thinks they're all going to go when it's time to go home.'

'Don't even talk about it,' said Jenny, rolling on to her front. 'I could stay here for ever. No smelly tube trains, no South Circular. Imagine, just fresh air and blue skies.'

'You'd be bored, you know you would,' smiled Mavis. 'I'm sure it isn't sunny all the time either. I know what you mean, though. I bet loads of people settle down here when they've had enough of London.'

'Hmmmm.' Jenny knew the idea of staying was pie in the sky but it didn't hurt to dream. 'You know what, after that banana I could do with an ice cream. What do you say?'

'A ninety-nine?'

'Definitely.'

The two young women stood up, brushed the sand from their frocks and wandered back along to the shops above the beach, to the distant shrieks of the boys trying to save goals as Tommy kicked the football. Gradually the voices were drowned out by the racket of seagulls wheeling above. Jenny tucked her arm through Mavis's and they sauntered in the sunshine, enjoying the heat and the relaxed air of everyone around them. They had no idea that someone was watching their every movement.

On Sunday evening, Rhona forced herself to get ready. There was none of the excitement she used to feel when she knew she'd be meeting Gary, or before that when she'd prepared with military precision in case she got lucky with a new man. She almost gave up and went back down to sit with her parents to listen to the wireless, but Sunday evening programmes drove her mad. She could hear something that sounded like the strings of Mantovani wafting up the stairs now and that decided her. She couldn't put up with that sort of noise for a minute longer. She had to get out, mix with people of her own age group who liked the same sort of music – or at least, the nearest

Peckham could offer in that direction.

She hastily applied her mascara and didn't bother with false eyelashes. What was the point – she wasn't going to Soho now. She debated whether to change into a miniskirt but decided against it, choosing to stay in her dogtooth-check trousers instead. She wasn't likely to meet anyone who'd appreciate her legs in such a venue. And, she reminded herself, she wasn't as curvy as she had been. She'd have to get used to the idea of not attracting so much attention. In a way she was glad; she didn't particularly want to fend off men's idiotic comments this evening. She was going for the music, and that was all.

'You off, love?' Marilyn asked.

'You could always stay in with us and listen to a bit of the Light Programme,' Ian Foster suggested.

'Nah, I'm going to try the open mic night,' said Rhona hurriedly, picking up her old jacket with the frayed cuffs. 'It won't go on too late but don't wait up. I'll be fine.' With that she left them to it, desperate to get away from the cascading strings and syrupy tunes.

The air outside was hot as she made her way along the roads. She slowed down once she'd left Harwood Street behind, figuring there was no point in arriving red-faced and perspiring. She wondered if she might bump into a familiar face but everyone must be inside or else in their back yards. Houses had their windows open to let in any shred of a cooling breeze but nobody was about. Every now and again she caught the sounds of radios playing, some with the same unbearable programme her parents had been enjoying. Other

174

lucky households had a television set. She wondered if they would ever have one. Mavis was going to get one when she got back from holiday and Jean had said she was saving up for one to give her mum as a surprise. Rhona thought she would soon feel left out without one. Besides, if they did get one she would be able to watch *Top of the Pops.*

As she approached the bar she could hear the sound of a guitar being tuned over an amplifier, floating out through the open front door. People stood around the wooden tables outside, drinking beer or, from what she could see of most of the women, soft drinks. As she got closer she recognised a few of them from her days at school, and there were even a few who'd occasionally turned up on the music scene. She breathed out in relief. Maybe this wouldn't be so bad.

One of the girls drinking lemonade waved to her. 'Hi Rhona.'

Rhona smiled and went to join the group. She noticed that they weren't dressed in the height of fashion, but then berated herself for caring. It wasn't as if she had bothered to put on her glad rags. 'Thought I'd try this place for a change. What's it like? Have you been before?'

The girls fell over themselves to tell her about previous evenings, trying to outdo one another in their knack for spotting the best singer, who was bound to make it as a future star, and who'd managed to get a date with any of the performers.

Rhona smiled and nodded and forced herself to come across as interested, though she quickly guessed that there were no superstars-in-waiting likely to appear, and that the girls seemed desperate to date anyone who could pick up a guitar. She excused herself, saying that she wanted to get a drink, and ducked through the front door into the shady bar. Light was just about managing to filter in through the grimy windows but at least it was cooler in here. Edging round the customers standing and talking she didn't notice a tall figure making a beeline for her.

'Rhonda! Fancy seeing you here.'

Rhona squinted up at him, her eyes adjusting to the dimmer light. 'Hello, Kenneth,' she said reluctantly. She hadn't seen him since he'd abandoned her at the Rolling Stones concert months ago. 'It's Rhona.'

'Good to see you, Rhonda,' Kenneth went on, either unable to hear above the background noise or just oblivious to what she'd said. 'I always remember a gorgeous face. It's like you were named after that Beach Boys song, how did it go, "Help me, Rhonda, help me, Rhonda..."'

'Yeah, I was born a bit earlier than that, and it would have made you a child snatcher,' Rhona said, flashing him a smile. No point in picking an argument.

'Well maybe it's not *you* helping me, but I can help you,' he said cheesily. 'What will you have to drink?'

Rhona shook her head, finding it hard to recall why she'd ever found this fool attractive. 'Babycham, please,' she said. At least she could return to her favourite tipple now that she wasn't pretending to like rum and black.

She waited for him to get back from the bar, where a bored-looking young man in a disgusting

176

nylon shirt was serving the few punters who'd had enough of the sunshine outside. Ken got himself a pint at the same time and strutted back to her, as if he was doing her a favour. He reeked of aftershave.

Rhona accepted the glass and thanked him, knowing that a few months ago she'd have chucked the drink in his face for dumping her like that. Now she figured she might as well get him to pay if he was daft enough. Or perhaps it was his way of saying sorry.

'So what have you been up to?' he asked. 'Been to any good gigs lately?'

'Nah, not really,' said Rhona. 'What about you?'

'I've been taking a break from the big venues,' Kenneth said grandly. 'I reckon it's so much more authentic to see bands at small places like this. That way you really get to feel the music, you know?'

'Depends,' said Rhona noncommittally. 'I quite like the big stages, I like a big show. It's nice to see something local though, but to be honest I've no idea what this is going to be like.' She swirled her Babycham around. Somehow it tasted sweeter than she remembered it. It had been a long time since she'd had any.

'That's the whole reason to come along, isn't it,' said Kenneth, nodding vigorously. 'You might see the next Van Morrison or Ray Davies, on your own front doorstep.'

'Well that'd be nice,' Rhona acknowledged, 'but don't get my hopes up. Anyway you must go to lots of different venues, you've got your bike after all.'

Kenneth's expression changed. 'Ah, that's off the road at the moment. Just temporarily.'

Rhona raised her eyebrows. She knew it had been his pride and joy and one of the reasons she'd felt so cheated at being left to make her own way home that time. 'Really. What happened? You had a crash or something?'

Kenneth stared into his pint. 'Not exactly. No, it wasn't like that. Actually if you must know I got pulled over for dangerous driving and they found out I've never taken my test. So I'm banned until pass it, though I'm a good rider so that shouldn't take too long.' He shifted uncomfortably. 'You didn't feel unsafe on my bike, did you?'

'I didn't really spend long enough on it to find out.' Rhona eyed him balefully. 'I reckon you owe me big time for that.'

'Oh come on, I got you into the Stones concert.'

'Yeah, then you left me when you had the chance to go off and meet them. Had to make my own way home, I did. Anything could have happened.'

'And did it?'

'Of course not. I know how to take care of myself.' Rhona shook back her hair. 'That's not the point. You just took off.'

'You'd have done the same if you got the chance to go to the after-gig party with them,' he protested. 'It's not something you turn down.'

'Wouldn't have mattered, would it, 'cos you could still have got home on your bike. I had to take night buses and you know what they're like.' She pulled a face.

'OK, OK, I owe you. What do you want?'

Rhona thought for a moment. She wasn't sure

she'd be up for a party with the Stones these days, even if that was ever to come her way again. It seemed like part of another life. Then she remembered the one thing she'd really missed since splitting up with Gary. In fact, if she was honest, she'd missed this more than the man himself. It had taken the bout of glandular fever to realise the truth of it. This might be a golden opportunity and what did she have to lose? 'Back in the spring I started learning the guitar,' she said, her eyes lighting up. 'I didn't get very far but I really liked it. I'd love to have my own guitar then I could get a book and teach myself. Do you know anyone who might have one?'

'What sort?' asked Kenneth.

'I don't know. A normal one.'

'What, electric? A bass? Come on, there are different kinds.'

'No, a wooden one.' Trust Kenneth to start showing off and putting her down. She wondered what she'd ever seen in him, other than a way into concerts and to meet pop stars.

'An acoustic, you mean.' Kenneth nodded, as if to say it was too much for her to understand. 'Like Bob Dylan plays.'

'Yes, an acoustic.' Rhona wasn't going to be put off. 'Can you help? Don't worry if you can't, I'll find a way to get one.'

Ken seemed offended at having his expertise doubted. 'Of course I can help you, Rhonda.' He smiled as if he'd made a joke. 'In fact, you're in luck. I know a couple of the musicians who are on tonight and I think one of them is trying to sell one of his old guitars. He's doing well enough to get some better models.' Ken puffed out his chest as if his friend's success was something to do with him. 'Shall I introduce you after the evening's over?'

Rhona beamed. Maybe tonight wouldn't be a complete waste of time. 'Yes please,' she said.

Chapter Eighteen

Stan wandered along the seafront in the evening, savouring having fifteen minutes alone. He loved having his family down here but now and again it was a relief to get a break from them. Greg was overexcited all day every day now he had James with him, and the two of them were up with the lark demanding to be taken to the beach and then reluctant to go to bed. Jenny was having such a good time with Mavis that she let him get on with it. Stan had to admit his wife and her friend both looked stunning with tans and he felt himself lucky to be on holiday with two such gorgeous women, but the fact that Mavis had Grace with her added to his urge to get away for a short while. He was very fond of the child, and knew only too well what her first years had been like, but she never stopped asking questions. Pete and Lily were a help but Bobby was getting even livelier and often took all of Lily's energy, and when Stan came to think about it, Pete seemed to be lost in his own world for much of the time.

So Stan was in no hurry as he sauntered along, watching the sunset. Red sky at night yet again – it would be a good day tomorrow, Monday. Plenty of people would be returning to work but he had another couple of days to go. He'd timed it all on the advice of Mrs Hawkins, who had warned him that Fridays and weekends would be the worst on which to travel. 'Everyone goes then,' she'd said when they were arranging the booking. 'You want to avoid it if you can. If you've got the choice of travelling mid-week, you might as well take it.'

Stan had thought this very sensible and as both Pete and Tommy worked for themselves, it was no problem for them to arrange mid-week dates. He grinned, pleased with himself. This whole holiday was thanks to him, and he'd had the good fortune to meet Mrs Hawkins. She'd done them proud and was already suggesting that they come again next year. She'd taken to Greg and was spoiling him – spoiling all of them when it came to it. Well, he wasn't going to say no. They deserved a bit of pampering.

Looking up he realised he was on the stretch of road where he'd walked with Jenny that first time he'd brought her down here. His heart swelled at the memory. What a good time they'd had. It had reinvigorated their love life, no doubt about it, and unless he was much mistaken Torquay was working the same magic for Tommy and Mavis. Good for them, taking their chance of a bit of pleasure.

There was that strange shop that he and Jenny had found so funny, with its fussy sign. He'd found out afterwards that this was the very place Mrs Hawkins had spoken about on his first trip, where women weren't welcome. Good job they hadn't tried to go in – then again, Jenny was quite capable of taking on anyone who tried to tell her what to do.

He could see a figure moving behind the glass, though the card in the window said 'Closed' and something about him – it must be a him after all they'd heard – made Stan pause. He couldn't see very clearly, as the man was half-turning away, so the view was only of a partial profile, and the lettering on the window obscured much of the room inside. Yet Stan came to a standstill. Some instinct told him not to stare, so he pretended to be winding his watch and checking it, while out of the corner of his eye he observed the man in the shop.

The height was the same, the build was the same, and from what he could tell the hair was the same, though it was hard to decide the exact colour from where he stood. The man was a dead ringer for Stan's old neighbour, and Mavis's husband, Alec Pugh. Stan wondered if he should barge in to confront the man, but what if he was here on holiday too and disappeared again. Or what if it wasn't him after all? Stan wasn't usually a man to put off until tomorrow something he could do today, but he imagined what Jenny would say if she found out he'd messed this up.

The shop next door was a tobacconist and was still open. Stan had an idea, and before he could decide against it he went in, the door ringing a bell as he did so. A short, middle-aged man looked up from behind the counter.

'Can I help you?'

Stan would normally have asked for what he wanted and been on his way again without any attempt at conversation, but now he drew upon all his experience as an insurance salesman and set out to charm the fellow. 'Lovely evening,' he began. 'Should be good tomorrow, shouldn't it?'

It worked, and the shopkeeper was soon regaling him with all his tips for how to forecast the weather and what to do when the wind blew from offshore or onshore. Stan nodded, not having a clue what all this meant, but bided his time before bringing up the subject he wanted to raise. 'That place next door,' he said. 'It's not something you expect to see in a resort like this, is it?'

'Torquay prides itself on catering to all tastes,' the shopkeeper informed him. 'We have connoisseurs from all over the world beating a path to our door, you know. It's not all sun and sea. Mr Collier has been very successful, he tells me.'

'Oh, do you know him?' Stan asked innocently. 'Has he been here long?'

'No, no. He only came down here about two years ago. I understand he was in a totally different line of work up in London. That's what makes it even more remarkable that he's done so well.'

'I'm from London,' Stan said. 'Wouldn't it be a coincidence if we came from the same area?'

The fellow seemed to like the idea. 'I've been to London a few times, huge place, but let me see, what did he say ... he doesn't talk about it much, he puts all his energy into what he's doing now, he's very hard-working. Well, you can do that when you're a youngster, he's only about thirty. It was somewhere with a park ... Belsize Park? No, near the river ... Battersea. I believe it was Battersea.'

'Now isn't that funny,' said Stan. 'That's where

183

I come from too. But I don't know any Colliers.'

'He was a bit distant, reticent, when he first moved here, but nowadays we've become quite friendly and he did say that he didn't have any family,' said the old man. 'He once mentioned his mother dying shortly before he moved and, reading between the lines, I think that's why he left. He probably wanted to make a complete break after looking after his poor, sick mother.'

Blimey, thought Stan, they are chatty down here. He almost felt sad for deceiving the man and as another customer walked in he said, 'Don't let me keep you. I'll have a packet of Embassy please and then be off.'

He paid up and left, pondering what best to do. The man looked like Alec, was about the right age, had left London at the right time, even came from Battersea and had lost his mother fairly recently. But he called himself Charles Collier so surely it could all be just a big coincidence. What should he do? Mavis was desperate to track down her husband in order to get a divorce. He knew just how much it would mean to her. But should he raise her hopes?

Rhona's expectations had been pretty low, so she was surprised to find there were some good acts on that night. There had been a group of four lads who might still have been at school but they knew how to sing and did some decent cover versions of the latest chart hits. There was an older man who could really play the guitar, singing folk songs. Once she would have thought that boring, but now she could appreciate his skill, even if the lyrics

184

weren't to her taste. There was a duo in which the man played and the woman sang; she thought Gary would have approved of that. Then there were others who had friends in the crowd, including the people Kenneth knew. Privately Rhona thought they weren't as good as the schoolboys or the folk singer but she didn't say so. Kenneth had edged closer to her and even tried to put his arm around her at one point but she'd stepped away.

He hadn't seemed offended, and now that everyone was packing up he leant down to make good on his promise. 'There's a corridor round the back where they keep their equipment,' he said. 'The man you want to see is my friend, Mike, in the green shirt if you remember him? He knows you're interested in the guitar. I'd introduce you properly but I gotta go. Early start tomorrow.'

'That's OK,' said Rhona. 'I'm sure I can handle it myself. I can walk home from here anyway.'

'I didn't mean...' Kenneth was embarrassed.

'Joke, Kenneth.' Rhona sighed. 'I didn't seriously expect you to see me home, bike or no bike. Thanks for telling Mike about me. I'll see you around.'

He pecked her quickly on the cheek and went off in a hurry. Rhona smiled to herself. He probably had to catch a bus now, and they stopped running early on Sundays. He might have missed it already. Serve him right.

The crowd had thinned out while they had been talking and now there was hardly anyone left apart from the bored man at the bar, who had his back turned to her. She had never been backstage here before and wondered which door it was, as there were several. She wandered over to the nearest and went through. The corridor behind was dingy and dusty, which wasn't promising. There was one low-watt light bulb dangling from a frayed flex and as the corridor turned a corner it barely threw any light as she made her way along. It led to a stairway downwards, and Rhona hesitated. Ken hadn't said anything about that. Then again she'd got this far, and presumably as the place wasn't that big, all the rooms connected to each other at the back.

There was hardly any light now as she slowly went down the stairs, feeling her way along the wall, cringing when her fingers made contact with dust, slime and God knows what. She was glad she hadn't worn her trendiest clothes or they'd have got filthy. Then she found herself in what must be a cellar. She could make out the shapes of boxes and barrels. That made sense. So maybe they used one of the other cellars for the musicians' equipment. She edged along and after passing the barrels could see what must be a doorway. Now she got closer, Rhona could hear dim voices coming from behind it. She found the door handle and tried it. It was stiff – evidently this wasn't the right way in, but she turned it sharply, pushed, and the door suddenly opened.

She blinked at the bright light, unable to see at first. Then she took in what she'd burst in upon. This wasn't the room where the musical instruments were left. It was an office, with filing cabinets, a desk and what looked like a safe, the door of which was hanging open. She gasped. There were bundles of banknotes inside, some of which were neatly stacked but others lay in a heap. That could mean only one thing. She'd walked in halfway through a robbery.

Then she screamed as an arm grabbed her around the neck from behind and she felt something heavy make contact with her head. Everything went dark.

'Let's leave the girls to it,' Stan suggested to Tommy later that evening, as they all made their way back towards the B and B, having been out to stroll along by the harbour. 'What do you say to a quick pint?'

Pete overheard him. 'You can count me out, lads. I'm totally bushed.'

'Righto,' said Stan, thankful as he hadn't meant to ask Pete anyway. It wasn't an invitation to a boys' night out – he wanted to have a private conversation with Tommy and he knew that would be impossible at the guesthouse.

'Yeah, you go on,' said Lily, coming up behind them with Bobby in his pushchair. He was too big for it really but they'd brought it along for moments like these, and now she was grateful they'd thought of it as he was getting to be quite a weight to carry around. 'Let your hair down, it won't be long before we're back in the Big Smoke.'

Tommy gave Mavis a hug. 'You don't mind, do you? We won't be long.'

Mavis smiled at him. 'No of course I don't.'

Tommy nodded, relieved that Mavis rarely made a fuss. His ex-wife Belinda would have complained bitterly, not because she wanted his company all the time but because she hated the idea of him enjoying himself when she wasn't. He had a feeling that Stan had something on his mind and wondered what it was as they left the group at the B and B to continue to the nearest pub.

It was quiet inside and as Tommy went to the bar to order two pints, Stan headed for an unobtrusive table in the corner. Tommy carefully carried their drinks back to the highly polished table, finding that the seats were comfortable and well padded, unlike some of the pubs they sometimes met in at home. 'OK, Stan, what's up?'

Stan looked surprised. 'What makes you think that something's up? Why wouldn't I just fancy a pint?'

Tommy looked him directly in the eye. 'Come off it, Stan. This is me you're talking to. I know you, remember?'

Stan shrugged and then gave in. 'Yeah, well, it might be nothing. I didn't want to say anything in front of the rest of them as I might have got it all wrong, but I saw something earlier this evening and wanted to talk to you about it.'

Tommy was intrigued now. He took a sip of his beer, covering his upper lip with froth. 'Go on, then. Spit it out.'

'You'll never guess who I think I saw,' Stan said, then taking a gulp of his drink he poured out his story, relieved to have got it off his chest. He hadn't been able to enjoy the walk earlier, nor the fish and chips they'd had as they went along, as the strange scene in the shop had kept replaying over and over in his mind.

When he finally finished, Tommy stared at him. 'Are you having me on, Stan? Right here, along the seafront? That bastard Alec Pugh?'

'Straight up,' said Stan. 'I wouldn't joke about such a thing. Why would I? I think Mavis is a great girl, you know that, and she and Jenny are like sisters. I only want the best for her.' He grew embarrassed. He hated talking about his feelings. 'I know what she's been through, so when I saw that slimy git through the window I didn't know what to do. If it is Alec Pugh, I didn't want him to see me or he might do a runner again. How do you think we should handle this, Tommy?'

Tommy took a swig of beer while his mind turned, then he carefully put the glass down in the centre of his beer mat. 'OK, firstly, we have to find out for sure that we've got the right man. Until then, we say nothing to any of the others. We'll go there and watch him. He has to come out of that place at some time during the day, doesn't he? I'll think of something to give us an excuse to hang around there tomorrow. If it's not him, then there's no harm done. If it is...' He took another drink and realised all the beer was gone.

'Fancy another?' Stan was on his feet.

'Yeah, why not.' Tommy accepted gratefully, wanting a few minutes alone to work this through While Stan queued at the bar behind a party of tourists who had come in and sounded as if they'd just arrived in town, his thoughts whirred.

Assuming this Collier bloke was really Alec Pugh, what would he say to him? Tommy's instinct was to go in all guns blazing and have it out with him. He'd all but destroyed Mavis while she'd been married to him and was now ruining her chance of future happiness, not to mention the physical and emotional damage he'd done to his own children. Yet what good would that do? Tommy knew he had to go against his natural gut reaction to wreak revenge and concentrate on what would be best for all their futures. That meant getting the man to agree to give Mavis a divorce. That was the bottom line. Until she had that, none of them could move on.

Tommy knew he would have to approach the man rationally, and discuss it calmly. Losing his temper would achieve nothing. Alec was a coward, taking out his anger on those physically weaker than himself, but he was also manipulative. He wasn't Larry Barnet, to be outwitted easily with threats backed up with a show of brute force, but there was still the risk that when confronted, Alec Pugh would disappear again.

Stan was finally getting served, but it looked like he'd been drawn into conversation with the new arrivals, while Tommy quickly totted up how much he could offer Alec Pugh as a bribe. He knew the man wasn't hard up; that he had sold a house and left with the proceeds, but he must have spent a fair whack of that money to buy his business. Money talked, Tommy knew that, and surely he could raise enough to get Alec out of their lives once and for all. His bank account wasn't exactly large but since working on that pub refurbishment, word had got around and he had had plenty of expressions of interest recently. If even half of them turned into definite jobs then he would be able to put up a decent sum. If he could do it in two halves ... one upfront to show willing and a second payment when a solicitor confirmed the divorce proceedings were underway...

'Penny for them,' said Stan, setting down the beers. 'Blimey, that was harder work than I thought. Those people wanted tips for where to go when it rained, where to get the best ice creams, it was like I was the town tourist board or something. They wouldn't take no for an answer.' He paused, and took a gulp. 'How are you getting on?'

Tommy looked up at him. 'I think I've got it,' he said.

Chapter Nineteen

There were lights dancing around her head, something was digging into her side, and her mouth tasted funny. Rhona was slowly coming round but couldn't work out where she was. She could smell dust and mould and something else – acrid and unpleasant, like sweat. Her head hurt and she shut her eyes to keep away the lights but even so her vision swam in circles behind her eyelids. She wanted to groan but couldn't.

As Rhona's thoughts cleared it all began to come back to her. She must be on the floor of the cellar office in the pub, and she'd been gagged. There were footsteps near her face.

'She ain't coming round is she?'

Rhona thought the voice was familiar but she was too uncomfortable to place it immediately.

'Nah, she's still out cold,' said another voice. 'Anyone would be after what you did to her head.

She ain't waking up any time soon.'

'Good. Make sure she stays that way.'

'Yeah, we can't have anyone getting in our way, but what was she doing down here? I thought you said the place would be empty by now.'

'It should have been,' replied the first voice. 'It always has been before when I've checked it out. Sunday night it empties out at ten thirty; they lock up, and all the takings for the whole weekend get bunged in the safe. They don't open on Monday, so with any luck it'll be Tuesday morning before they find anything's wrong. I hadn't reckoned on everyone hanging around, nor that any of the punters knew about this office in the cellar, so how the hell did she find her way down here?'

'Could she have got a tip-off?'

'Who from? The only one to know apart from us was the guy behind the bar, and he wasn't going to say anything, or they'd know it was partly an inside job. He hates his boss, he wouldn't bother to help him in any way. No, I reckon this one likes to find and make trouble.' The feet came closer to her face.

'What do you mean? Do you know her or something?'

There was a pause. 'Yeah,' said the first voice heavily. 'I know her all right so it's just as well she didn't get a look at me before I knocked her out.'

Rhona forced herself not to moan, even though the gag was holding her mouth tight. Cautiously she opened her eyes a fraction. She could just about see through her lashes and make out the two figures. Now she knew why the voice had sounded familiar. One of the men was Andy

192

Forsyth. She hadn't seen him since she'd ditched him months ago.

He was moving around again now, putting bundles of what she thought must be the banknotes into a bag.

'What are we going to do with her?' the other man demanded. 'She's not a friend of yours, is she?'

'You got to be joking.' Andy zipped up the bag. 'I wouldn't call her a friend if you paid me a million. Seriously, she's trouble, but as long as she doesn't get a look at me, we can just leave her here.'

The other man turned and came back to where she was lying on her side. He bent down as if to touch her. 'Why don't we have some fun with her while she's out cold? You can go first seeing as you know her. She can't put up a fight now, can she?'

Rhona trembled at the threat and the lewdness in his voice. She was totally defenceless, her hands bound behind her. She prayed that he wouldn't come any closer. She couldn't stand it, being raped in this stinking cellar, and there was nobody to hear her even if she did manage to cry out for help. The man bent down and she felt his hand on her breast. Somehow she managed not to make a noise or react in any way.

'See? She can't do nothing. Do you want to have a go? She's a bit thin and there ain't much of a handful, but who cares?'

Rhona flinched as he moved his hand, dreading what was going to happen next. Was he going to touch her again? She tried desperately not to shake with fear. Now she couldn't see where he was unless she fully opened her eyes. She didn't know what would be worse – should she show them she was awake? Would that put them off or invite them to treat her even more cruelly? Would they take pleasure in hurting her? Or if she kept on pretending to be knocked out would it be worse, would they do whatever they wanted assuming that she'd know nothing about it? She didn't want to begin to imagine what that could be like.

'Leave her.' Andy spoke again.

'What? Are you kidding? A real live woman, not a bad looker, just lying here and nobody to stop us? Don't you want to fuck her? I will if you don't.'

'I said leave her.' Andy's voice had a harsh edge to it. 'I don't want her coming round, and anyway you don't want to go near that. She's been with half of South London. She's scum, she ain't worth it. God knows what you'd catch if you fucked her. I came close, but thank my lucky stars I saw sense and found out in time.'

'Nah, come on, she can't be that bad and I'm in the mood. We've got the money so let's celebrate and we can start with her.'

'Will you listen to me, for Christ's sake?' Andy snarled. 'She's worse than a dog. It ain't worth the risk. You'll be paying for it with a dose of the clap and that's if you're lucky. With this money we can go and buy ourselves any whores we like, and they'll be a darn sight cleaner than that bitch.'

'You're just saying that 'cos you don't want me to have her,' the other man said aggressively.

'For fuck's sake. Fine, be my guest, but if she starts to come round you'll have to knock her out again and quick. Just don't come running to me when you get scabs all over your dick. You'll be crying to your mother, you'll be in such a state.' Andy couldn't contain his impatience. 'Don't say I didn't warn you.'

'All right, all right.' The other man gave in. 'Let's go and give some of those women up in Southwark a seeing to. I know one I've wanted to try for ages and you wouldn't believe what I've heard she can do with her tongue.'

Andy picked up the bag. 'Turn out the light and let's go. Just check her ties and then we can be off. It's a relief she hasn't woken up or we'd be stuck with getting rid of her permanently and that's a complication I can do without.'

'We! It'd be you who'd have to put her lights out. She doesn't know me so I ain't got nothing to worry about,' the other man said as he tugged at the ties that bound her wrists. 'She's still out cold, but I'll make sure she stays that way.'

It was the last thing Rhona heard as a boot smashed onto her skull.

Rhona finally regained consciousness. She opened her eyes but that didn't do much good. It was completely dark, black, and she couldn't even see a glimmer of light. She groaned into the gag, finding it difficult to breathe and fighting panic. Her head was ringing with the pain and she couldn't think clearly. She attempted to bring some life back into her arms but they were bound so tightly behind her that all she could do was wriggle her fingers. Exhausted with fear, she felt like giving up. Her head was pounding and maybe if she just lay there she would lose consciousness again, and then she wouldn't have to think about anything.

Then her survival instinct kicked in and she gave herself a mental shake. Her thoughts began to clear. So, she couldn't move her arms, and her mouth was gagged, but she could breathe through her nose, which was good. What about her legs? She moved them, relieved to find that they hadn't been tied together or to anything else. She rolled over and managed to sit up, dizzy for a moment before she began to orientate herself. Where had she come in? She wasn't sure, but felt that the door was probably behind her and surely there'd be a light switch beside it.

Rhona tightened her lips in determination. Agonisingly she got to her feet, nearly falling without being able to use her hands and arms to balance. She stepped forward and if she hadn't had the gag between her teeth she would have screamed as a sharp corner dug into her thigh. It felt like a corner of something, maybe a table or desk. She couldn't remember the layout of the furniture as she'd only had a moment to take it in before she had been grabbed from behind. Now she kept the edge of whatever it was to one side and used it to direct herself forward, inch by inch. She was shaking with the effort, not to fall, not to panic. She came to the end of what maybe was the desk top and cautiously moved on, waiting to hit the next obstacle. There was nothing. She went on. Still nothing. Another couple of shuffling steps and her toes met something solid. She kicked it, and it made a dull thud, which she thought might be wood. She kicked to one side of it, and that made a rattle. It had to be the door,

Rhona thought, as she turned her back to it and moved her bound hands over as much of the surface as she could. She touched a panel, and then what felt like a frame.

Rhona tried to lift her arms higher behind her but they wouldn't move far so she turned again to face what she was sure, now, was a door. She brought her face closer, using her nose to search for the frame, and then moved to one side of it until she felt that she was touching the wall. Slowly, edging upwards, she moved her nose back and forth slightly from side to side until she felt the slight protrusion of a light switch. Rhona knew this was probably going to hurt so braced herself, and with nothing else to use other than her nose, she put her weight behind it, groaning and hoping that she hadn't torn her nostril as she managed to push the small toggle down. It worked. The light came on.

Rhona turned again, dazzled, as she took in the untidy office, the open safe – now empty – the overturned chair, the cabinets with their drawers agape. All she wanted was to get out of there, but to do that she had to get her hands free. She walked back to the desk, saw a telephone, but then her heart sank when she saw that the wire had been cut. Her eyes scanned the top of the desk, looking for something sharp amongst the various scattered articles; pens, a ruler, a stapler, but then her eyes lit up when she saw a paper knife. It took her a while to work out how to get it where she needed it, but finally she approached it backwards and wedged it into a corner of the desk drawer, making it fast by pushing the desk chair against it. Now, as long as she was careful not to dislodge it, she could move the knot against it. Gradually she cut through the material and, after what felt like hours, her hands were free.

The muscles in Rhona's arms protested against being forced into an unnatural position for so long and she moaned in pain as she rubbed some life back into them. She then set about loosening the knot to untie the gag which, when removed, turned out to be a disgusting piece of unrecognisable material. She threw it to one side in and looked around the office again, desperate for something to drink and to get out of the dank cellar. Her watch told her it was three in the early hours of the morning and all she'd had before the pub closed were a few glasses of Babycham. She went to the door again, turned the knob, only to find that it was locked. Desperately she scanned the room again and saw another door, which thankfully opened onto a small hall. But the door at the end of it was locked too. Rhona kicked it in frustration before her lips set in determination again and she hurried back to the office to grab the paper knife. She tried to use it like a key, but it was too thick to fit into the lock, so she wedged it into the frame and tried to lever the door open. Again and again she tried, but then the knife snapped and she fell back, exhausted.

There were no windows; there was no way out. She had heard the men say that the bar wouldn't be open again until Tuesday, yet surely the owner would turn up before then to bank the takings that had been put in the safe. It was her only hope, but until then she was trapped. Her parents wouldn't know she wasn't back; she'd told them not to wait up. Nobody would miss her for ages.

Thirst raged, and desperately Rhona looked around again, tried the desk drawers and at last, under some papers, she found a half-drunk bottle of lemonade. She brought it to her lips, but realising that she could be trapped in the cellar for a long time, she somehow managed to refrain from drinking all of it in one go.

Rhona held back a sob as she flopped onto the office chair, exhausted with terror and misery and only then did she think back to what the men had said. She didn't know what to feel. She'd been deeply afraid Andy's friend was all set to rape her, but then Andy had said those awful things about her. She was relieved and disgusted all at the same time. How dare he say that? What right did he have? But the other side of her could have cried at the shame, knowing this was how she was talked about. It didn't matter that they were two scumbag criminals; this was her reputation. Tears fell down her cheeks as she prepared to face a night in the stinking cellar.

'I've done it, Uncle Tommy!' Grace was shouting, jumping up and down and waving a big piece of paper. 'Come and see.'

Tommy laughed and went to do as he was ordered. He'd found the perfect cover for hanging around the seafront not too far from the stamp shop. For several days now they'd noticed an artist by the harbour, setting up his easel and selling charcoal portraits of visitors, which he'd sketch right in front of their eyes. Over the weekend he'd been very busy, but probably expecting trade to be quieter on Monday, he'd put up a sign offering a one-hour drawing lesson that was to start at eight thirty in the morning. The sign also said where he'd be setting up and Tommy was delighted to see that it would be just down the road from the shop. It was ideal. Grace had been desperate to have a go and Tommy had agreed at once, even though Lily had said it was a waste of money with the little girl being too young to know what she was doing.

Tommy knew he was probably making a rod for his own back in agreeing to her demands so readily, but he couldn't have come up with a better idea if he'd tried. So he'd volunteered to sit on a nearby low wall while Grace solemnly picked up her charcoal and got covered in it in moments. She didn't fuss, though, and had taken the whole thing very seriously, and while she was engrossed, Tommy had been watching the shop.

Nothing had happened for the first fifteen minutes. A couple of dog walkers went past, and a postman. Further away a few people were beginning to set up for another sunny day on the beach. Tommy had promised Grace that as this was their last day in Torquay, they would go down there later for a final paddle.

A few customers came and went to the tobacconist's next door, emerging with newspapers or packets of cigarettes which they shoved into their pockets. Gulls wheeled overhead, calling out to one another, sometimes swooping down to see if any food was on offer, then taking off again in search of richer pickings. The sun grew warmer and Tommy put on his sunglasses.

Finally, nearly half an hour after he'd taken up his position, a figure approached the stamp shop. Tommy drew in his breath sharply. He reminded himself to keep calm and take careful note of what he saw; he couldn't get this wrong. But there was little doubt in his mind that this was indeed Alec Pugh.

He'd never been introduced to the man but he'd seen him around when he'd visited Stan and Jenny's house, back before he realised it was Mavis living next door. There was no mistaking him. His hair was thinner, he was a little more stooped, as if working behind a counter had affected his posture, but it was Alec all right. Tommy exhaled heavily; he hadn't realised he'd been holding his breath. Now he had to keep his cool and get Grace back to the others before he could talk to the man.

'Do you like it?' she demanded, showing him what she'd done. 'Guess who it is.'

The artist beamed at him. 'She's very good. I wouldn't have believed how young she is if I'd only seen her picture.'

Grace nodded, as if this was only to be expected. 'Guess, Uncle Tommy.'

Tommy looked at the picture and was amazed. It was recognisably a head and shoulders portrait, just like the artist produced for the tourists. There was a mop of curly dark hair on top and the face had a big smile. 'Give in,' he said, to prolong the game.

'Silly!' Grace exclaimed. 'It's you! That's your hair.'

Tommy ran his hand through his wavy hair, so dark it was almost black. 'So it is,' he said. 'That's very clever. Shall we go and show Mummy and the others?'

'She should go to art classes,' the artist said as Grace took hold of Tommy's hand. 'Can't start them too young. Does the talent run in the family?'

'Yes,' said Tommy shortly. He didn't want to think about what he'd done as a teenager, destroying Mavis's own painting of her grandmother, out of sheer stupidity, he realised now. 'Her mother's very good,' he told the man.

Walking along with the little girl, he vowed he would make it up to Mavis by sorting out Alec Pugh. Maybe he could manage it so that she would never know. Somehow he was going to resolve this desperate situation and persuade the odious Alec to grant his wife the divorce she so desperately wanted. Then, and only then, would Mavis finally be free.

Alec Pugh gazed in fury at the two figures walking along the seafront. For days he had been watching the group of holiday-makers: his former neighbours, his detested tart of a mother-in-law, her thuggish husband, and worse, his wife and children, who seemed very cosy with this tall man. It had come to Alec that it was Jenny's cousin, who sometimes had taken up a parking space in their old road with his brash white van. What he was doing with them he hadn't been able to imagine, but after a few days it had become obvious. He and Mavis couldn't keep their hands off one another. They canoodled on the beach, they linked arms as they walked along, they held hands, and all of this in front of the children – *his* children. Now the man had the nerve to stride down the pavement holding hands with his daughter. *His* daughter.

Alec had absolutely no desire to have his wife back, much less his children, but he didn't see why another man should have them. That was too much to bear. His pride would not stand it. He felt less of a man as he stared at the receding man and little girl, who was skipping along. How dare they be so happy and carefree, when it was he who had brought that child into being? What right did that stranger have to hold her hand? He was most likely spoiling her, letting her run riot all over the place. Like all females, Grace needed discipline and that had been obvious from the very start.

Alec could feel something slipping in his mind, the old anger and the black pit of betrayal that had haunted him when he discovered first his mother's lifetime of lies and then that his wife had upped and left him. The world seemed to slip into a different kind of focus. He turned the sign on the door to 'closed', picked up his jacket and, at a safe distance, began to edge his way along the seafront, keeping the tall man with dark hair and little girl always within his sight.

Alec hated the way they were so at ease with each other, as if they were entitled to be happy. His daughter had never been like that with him. As soon as she had learned to speak she had answered him back, never obeying him without a fuss, her contrary nature calling out for correction and punishment. Alec ducked behind a tall van as the man glanced round, wondering if he'd been seen, but the little girl pointed and laughed, and he realised they'd been looking at a particularly daring seagull. The bird was rummaging in a litter bin, pulling out paper wrappings from fish and chips, and his daughter found that amusing, rather than the disgrace it really was.

Finally they wandered off and Alec moved surreptitiously behind them. His thoughts were whirring. Nothing seemed straightforward anymore. He'd once known exactly what was right and what was wrong but now the boundaries were shifting. He didn't want to think like this. He relied on certainty and yet here were people who deserved nothing but pain walking around flaunting their joy at being alive. It was all wrong. He had to fight it, had to get back to the world where things were clear in black and white.

He lost track of time as he tracked the man and girl along the bright streets, away from the main parade of shops, down some residential roads, past rows of guest houses. Finally they paused and turned, heading down a short garden path to a welcoming front porch. Alec peered from a safe distance, his heart hammering unsteadily in his chest, his anger rising once more. So this was where they were staying. A respectable establishment, by the looks of it – but the people staying there were anything but that. How he longed to punish all of them.

Chapter Twenty

Rhona stretched uncomfortably. She checked her watch; nine o'clock. She was amazed that she'd managed to sleep for that long in the office chair. Her limbs were stiff, and her back ached, but that was nothing compared to the pain in her head. She gingerly touched the spot where she'd been hit and winced, wondering if she was concussed.

Her stomach rumbled and she groaned. There was only the last of the lemonade, and if nobody came to bank the takings, it would somehow have to last her until the bar opened on Tuesday. Perhaps somebody would miss her and send out a search party. Her parents knew where she was going last night. Then Rhona thought about all the times she'd stayed out all night after going to a club, without warning her mum or dad. They'd begun by being furious, anxious, trying to ban her from leaving the house but she'd defied them until they gave up. At the time she had thought it was clever, that she was daring and a free spirit who couldn't be tied down. Now she saw that it had been stupid. They'd been concerned for her safety and she'd laughed at them. Now she was trapped and they'd be going about their morning business, thinking she was back to her old tricks again and that she'd show up that evening after work.

Nobody would be worried about her when she didn't turn up for work either. They'd just assume she'd reverted back to her old ways; that she'd been painting the town red all weekend and was now sleeping off the after-effects. Rhona clung to the brief hope that Jean would suspect something was wrong, but it didn't last more than a few moments. She'd let down Jean most of all over the months and years, and yet the woman had always spoken up for her to the management, even if she'd been sharp with her in private. Jean would be disappointed in her, but not surprised.

That meant she was stuck here and for a moment she almost cried in frustration, but then once again Rhona stiffened with resolve. She'd tried to force the door, but she'd been in so much pain and distress that she hadn't thought about the obvious. Andy and the man with him must have taken the keys to lock the door when they left, but maybe there were duplicates in case the originals were lost.

After half an hour of careful searching, first through the desk drawers, then the filing cabinets and finally under every surface in case they'd been hidden for safety, Rhona came up with nothing, except a small packet of shortbread biscuits and a bag of crisps in one of the cabinet drawers. Rhona was about to rip them both open when she stopped herself. If nobody came that morning, or she couldn't find a way out, the meagre amount of food would have to last her for twenty-four hours. She would have to ration them. Gritting her teeth, she carefully took out just two biscuits and put the rest of the packet on a high shelf so that she wouldn't be tempted to eat them. She then found a jam jar that had been used to keep elastic bands in, and poured a tiny amount of lemonade into it, while trying not to think of her mother's steaming porridge or eggs on toast, washed down with a cup of hot, sweet, tea.

Rhona slowly nibbled at the stale biscuits and sipped the flat lemonade. She vowed never to turn down her mother's cooking ever again. When she got out of here she was going to be grateful for everything her mother did for her, instead of complaining she fussed too much. She felt bitterly ashamed of the way she'd treated her parents, only now beginning to appreciate what they'd been through.

Tommy stood at the threshold of the shop, his nerve almost failing him when he thought of how much depended on the next few minutes. Then he told himself to get on with it. Standing there doing nothing wouldn't get them anywhere.

He pushed open the door and came face to face with the man who had abused and terrorised Mavis for so long. It was almost unbelievable. The man's skin was pale, his hair mousy and thin, his moustache neatly trimmed. Everything about him indicated he was weak. Tommy felt a surge of confidence, knowing he could easily beat him in a fight if it came to it, but hastily reminded himself that this would be the worst possible outcome. He had to stay in control, whatever happened.

'Hello,' he said 'Are you Charles Collier? I'd like a word with you.'

The man's eyes narrowed. 'Would you indeed? And what makes you think I'd want to talk to you?' He paused and his voice grew lower. 'I know who you are. I've been watching you and I even know where you're staying.'

Tommy nodded, trying not to be thrown off course by that unpleasant revelation. He should have seen that coming. If he'd been able to observe Alec, then logically Alec would have been able to see him too – and he would have had all week to do it. 'I think you'll want to hear what I have to say,' he began.

'I doubt it very much,' said Alec, brushing the long sleeves of his shirt as if they'd become dusty.

'I won't beat about the bush,' said Tommy, deciding to cut to the chase. 'It looks as if you've made a life for yourself down here and from what I gather it's been quite successful.'

Alec hissed at that, seemingly disturbed by the idea that someone had been talking about him. 'That's as maybe. It has nothing to do with you.'

'But it does,' said Tommy. 'I think you know why. You're still married to Mavis. She wants a divorce.'

Alec shut his eyes and his mouth turned down at the corners. 'I'll thank you not to mention that woman's name in here. She is nothing to do with me. She is a slut and a disgrace. I've seen how she acts when given the opportunity, her hands all over you and wearing those tight dresses, nothing but thin little straps holding them up, it's an affront to decency. Eating chips in public like a common whore. I washed my hands of her long ago.'

'Not legally, you didn't,' Tommy persisted, trying not to become incensed at the completely unfounded slur on Mavis's reputation. 'If you hate her so much why don't you divorce her and have done with it? Then you could … you could find yourself a different woman.'

That was the wrong thing to have said, Tommy realised, as the man's eyes grew bright with fury.

'How dare you even suggest such a thing!' Alec seemed to be having trouble breathing. 'All women are unreliable and untrustworthy. Don't come into my shop and speak such filth. Get out. I don't want you in my sight a moment longer.'

Tommy didn't move. 'If you think like that then divorce Mavis. Or let her divorce you.'

'Never!' spat Alec. 'It's a disgraceful suggestion. What if it were to become known that I had gone through such a shameful process? My reputation and business would be ruined. Now get out, I shan't ask you again.'

'You're here in Devon, using a different name, so I don't see how anyone would find out,' Tommy pointed out. 'Not only that, if you agree to a divorce, I'll make it worth your while.'

'What? You're trying to bribe me? How dare you. Get out, leave my premises and don't come back.'

'Bribe you? No. Look upon it as a bonus, something to expand your business.' Tommy gave the man a moment to take in what he was saying. 'Think about it. Don't turn it down out of hand. I'm sure you'd like to get in rarer stamp samples, appeal to the real specialists, but that costs money.'

Bingo. Tommy saw that this idea had hit home. Alec clearly craved to be known as a cut above the average stamp dealer. At last he had his bargaining tool. 'Think what you might make of this business if you had the reputation of offering only the finest, the hard-to-locate exhibits. You'd be the first person all the genuine collectors would call. Imagine it. Your standing in the local business community would rise.' He paused. 'I bet they're a bit of a closed circle, aren't they? Not used to welcoming outsiders? Just imagine if you could make a big donation to the Rotary Club or the Chamber of Commerce. They'd open their arms to you then.'

Alec shook his head but he was tempted. It had been more of a struggle than he wanted to admit, getting any local business contacts. His immediate neighbours barely counted. They weren't of the class he wanted to mix with. He fought with his instinct to get this obnoxious man out of his shop as soon as possible. 'I'll think about it,' he finally said, pursing his lips in reluctance. 'I won't promise anything. I can't just shut up shop you know, so you'll have to meet me after work, and make sure you come alone.'

'Fine. Name your place and time.'

'Six o'clock,' Alec said. 'In the car park at Marine Head.'

Tommy wasn't sure where it was but told himself he had plenty of time to find out. He turned for the door. 'Right, see you there,' he said.

'I don't understand, Tommy,' protested Lily later that day. 'You never said anything about this job before. What's so urgent that you got to think about work while you're on your holiday? Let 'em wait. Mrs Hawkins is cooking something special a little earlier than usual, and she's also offered to babysit so that we can all go out on our last night.'

'When a chance of work comes up, you have to

take it,' Tommy said, trying to keep his expression relaxed. 'That's right, isn't it, Pete?'

'What? Oh, yeah, absolutely.' Pete sounded vague and was clearly thinking about something else, as he had been for most of the last week.

'I'll have a quick bite with you, pop out to see these clients and then be back with you before you know it,' he promised.

'Well you make sure you are,' said Lily. 'I know what you men are like when you start talking business.'

'I'll be back before you know it. I just don't want to lose what might be a lucrative contract,' Tommy said, hating that he had to lie.

'Then you'd best go to meet them then,' Mavis said affably. 'If it drags on a bit longer than you're expecting, you can meet us in the pub.'

Tommy smiled, glad that unlike her mother, Mavis wasn't making a fuss. He then asked Mrs Hawkins if she would mind if he used the telephone to order a taxi.

When the meal was ready at five o'clock, Tommy managed to eat his in double-quick time and then apologised to Mrs Hawkins before bending down to give Mavis a quick kiss on the cheek. 'I'll see you soon.'

Tommy hoped that was true, though he had no idea how long it would take to get to Alec Pugh's chosen meeting spot, nor how long it would take to persuade the man. Still, he now had a clear idea of how far he could afford to go when he bargained with him. Whatever he ended up offering, it would be worth it. He'd already arranged for a taxi to pick him up and as he got into it, Tommy felt no regret that he hadn't told Stan what he was doing. He'd thought it through and decided against it as he didn't want to involve his friend more than he had to.

'Marine Head, mate,' he said. 'Can we get there before six?'

The driver shrugged. 'Depends on the traffic. Some days it's better than others. People are still coming home from work. What's the rush?'

Tommy tapped his foot up and down with impatience. That was the trouble down here – nobody seemed to be in a hurry. 'I've got someone waiting, that's all,' he said, striving to keep the strain from his voice. 'I'll need you to wait for me when we get there.'

The driver met his eye in the rear-view mirror. 'I don't know about that.'

'I'll make it worth your while,' said Tommy, his tension growing.

'In that case, fine, I'll wait.'

Tommy sat back. Most people had their price. It was just a question of knowing when to mention it. No doubt Alec would be the same.

The driver pulled into the car park, which was emptying rapidly as all the tourists made their way home after an afternoon of beaching or walking. There were hardly any vehicles left once he'd finished parking. Tommy looked around and at first couldn't see anybody. Then he spotted a lone figure on the far side of the area.

'Right, I'll be back with you as soon as I can,' he said, handing over the first part of the fare to the driver, who didn't seem to be very interested. He was already reaching for his newspaper and barely looked up.

Tommy strode towards Alec, who hadn't waited for him but had already set off along the cliff path. He struggled to reach him – the man was fitter than he'd thought, or perhaps he was just used to these narrow, uneven paths. Tommy cast a glance down to the rocks below. He wouldn't want to lose his footing here. Perhaps he should have worn something with a better grip than the new sandals he'd picked up from a shop on the seafront a couple of days ago.

Finally Alec slowed as he turned a bend in the path, the area now a little wider. 'I think this is far enough,' he said as he turned to face him.

'It's a strange place to meet.'

'I didn't want to be seen talking to the likes of you,' Alec said, his expression supercilious. 'There are no witnesses to our meeting here.'

Tommy's blood began to pound in his ears. 'You're no better than me. I'm a businessman too.'

'Is that so? All right then, let's talk business, or should I say, let's talk about my wife.'

When he thought of that smug face next to Mavis's, those pale hands touching her, hitting her, Tommy's head swam and it was all he could do not to reach out and grab the man around his neck. Somehow he managed to contain his temper and took a deep breath before saying, 'I said I had an offer to make you. Well, here it is.' Tommy named a sum that was actually half what he could run to but there was no sense in laying all his cards on the table if they were here to bargain.

Alec grunted. 'I have spent the afternoon contemplating what would happen if I agree to your proposal. My children would be in the care of a slut, and a man who is prepared to bribe me for her freedom. I have watched you with my wife, seen your disgraceful and lecherous behaviour in front of my children, and I don't want them tainted by such low morals. I've therefore already decided that I won't be taking your bribe money.' He turned to gaze out towards the horizon, as if Tommy was no longer worthy of his attention. 'Now listen to me. If you do not persuade Mavis to give me full custody of my children I will expose her for the adulterous slut that she is. I will prove that she is an unfit mother and she will never see the children again.' He gave a small, calculating smile. 'Also, the scandal when I name you is sure to adversely affect your business and you won't want that, will you? Two can play at this game. I've been checking up on you this afternoon while you've had your disgusting fun on the beach. You and my wife are adults and I can't stop you, but I will not have my children's minds infected with your degenerate natures. They require discipline and I now understand it is my business to see to that.'

Tommy lost control of his temper, pushed beyond the limit by these ridiculous slanders, but fuelled by the thought that the authorities might believe them. 'You don't give a shit about those kids,' he shouted. 'You beat them just like you beat Mavis and then you buggered off, without so much as leaving them two pennies to rub together. You haven't bothered to contact them since so why would you care now?'

'Because I have seen the error of my ways. It was remiss of me to abandon them to your lax care, but I can remedy that. It's up to you. Either you persuade Mavis to give me custody, or I take steps to leave my wife's reputation in the gutter where it belongs, and take you down with it. You have the choice. It's more than you deserve, but I am a fair and reasonable man.'

Tommy couldn't believe his ears. 'You piece of shit! You fucking bastard! You wouldn't dare!'

'I think you'll find I would,' said Alec. 'However, I appreciate that this has come as a shock to you. You thought you were coming here to buy me off, but that isn't going to happen so I'll give you until morning to think about it. You know where to find me! With that he turned and began to stride along the cliff path that soared above the now-deserted beach and rocks.

For a minute or two Tommy watched him go, not quite able to take in that the tables had been turned so completely. Then he gave himself a shake. He wasn't going to let this man ruin Mavis's life – he'd done enough to wreck it already. As the gulls circled above his head, he came to a decision. Gathering his resolution, he ran after the stooping figure along the precipitous cliff path. As he rounded a corner the sun glinted off a windscreen back in the car park but he was too angry to notice.

Meanwhile, the taxi driver, bored with his newspaper, had decided to get out of the driver's seat and stretch his legs. He began to wander towards the start of the cliff path. The air was still and the noise of the gulls carried from the faraway seafront.

Tommy broke into a sweat as he hurried after Alec Pugh, scarcely registering the jolt in his ankle as he narrowly missed slipping on an uneven stone. All that mattered was catching up with the bastard who thought he could ruin all their lives. Tommy couldn't allow him to do that. Too much was at stake. Mavis had been through enough. So had the children – and so had he.

Finally Tommy caught up with the man, and shouted, 'Wait! We need to talk.'

Alec swung around and nearly knocked him off balance with his outstretched arm, his eyes shining with a horrible intensity as he spat, 'There is nothing more to say. You won't change my mind. You are beneath contempt and I'll never agree to anything you suggest.'

Tommy caught hold of the man's arm and drew himself up to his full height, towering over him. 'It's no use you trying to twist away. We wouldn't want any accidents, would we? Your days of messing up Mavis's life are well and truly over.'

Stan tutted to himself as he stood at the bar. This was their last night out in Devon and Tommy hadn't turned up before they left the house. He thought it an odd time to have a meeting about a new contract, but who was he to doubt what his friend told him? All the same, it was a pity, as for once they were all out together without the children.

'And a bitter lemon as well,' he said to the barman, who turned to the shelf of soft drinks. Stan

216

lined up the pints for himself and Pete and the halves of cider for Jenny and Mavis. They'd joked that as they were in the West Country the least they could do was try the local brew.

Then he sensed someone close behind him. 'Get us one of the usual,' breathed Tommy, bending over to lean on the bar. 'I'm parched.'

Stan swivelled round to look at him. 'Blimey, what you been doing? I was going to say, make yourself useful and take these over to the girls, but by the state of you, you'll drop them. I'll get a tray. Seriously, mate, are you all right?'

Tommy screwed up his face for a moment then gave what looked like a forced smile. 'Never better. Just in need of a good pint.' He drank greedily from the glass the barman set in front of him. 'There was a fair bit of traffic out there, maybe there's been an accident or something, and not wanting to leave you all waiting I ditched the taxi and ran back, that's all. Must be more unfit than I thought.'

'Oh, right,' said Stan, thinking that Tommy had just spent a week running around the beach playing football with James and Greg, not to mention the exercise with Mavis after hours, and hadn't shown any sign of suffering before. 'Better get you in training once we're back home,' he added weakly.

Tommy appeared not to be listening, staring at his pint, but then he put his shoulders back and gave the forced grin again as he swept a hand through his messy hair. 'I suppose we should get these drinks over to the girls.'

'Yes,' Stan said as she looked directly at his

friend, 'but are you sure you're all right? You'd tell me if there was anything wrong, wouldn't you?'

'Course I would,' smiled Tommy. But the smile didn't reach his eyes.

Chapter Twenty-One

By Tuesday morning Rhona was desperate. She'd finished her meagre supply of food and the last dribble of lemonade the night before, so thirst and hunger raged. She was racked with non-stop stomach cramps too and with no other choice, her toilet had to be a rusty waste paper bin. She'd managed to sleep a little in the uncomfortable chair but was haunted by dreams in which everyone she knew kept turning their backs to her. When she woke up she felt even more stricken with shame, yet terrified that nobody would come to find her.

She had shouted and banged on the door that morning until her voice was hoarse and now all she could manage was a croak. Her watch told her it was ten o'clock. Why had no one opened up upstairs? Wouldn't somebody arrive to clean the place after the mess everyone had made on Sunday night? She strained her ears to try to catch any sounds from above, maybe footsteps or the hum of a vacuum cleaner, but there was nothing. Her nerves were becoming more and more frayed. She couldn't take much more of this and paced back and forth in the small room.

She jumped, thinking she'd heard something, but her hope died as she realised it was only her frayed jacket hem catching a pencil on the edge of the desk and knocking it over. Angrily she balled her fist and hit the desk. It hurt, but then so did her head. A sob caught in her throat but she forced it down. She would not cry. She wouldn't give Andy Forsyth the satisfaction.

Ten thirty came and then eleven o'clock. Rhona's pacing got faster and she dug her nails into the palms of her hands so hard they began to bleed, but it somehow helped with the hunger pains. She tried to remember all the words to every song by the Rolling Stones. She told herself that if she could do that, then she hadn't gone mad. She worked her way through all the hits of the previous year and the singles that she loved from the spring. It was only when she got stuck on 'The Last Time' that she thought she heard a noise. She froze. There is was again, a sort of dull thud.

Her heart started to race. Then she ran to the connecting door and banged on it with her fists. 'Help!' but her voice was only a croak. 'Help ... oh please...'

For one agonising moment Rhona thought whoever it was hadn't heard her. Then came the best sound in the world, as a key rattled in the lock and the door handle squeaked as it turned.

Slowly the door opened. A middle-aged woman in an overall and headscarf stood there, her jaw dropping open. For a second she couldn't say anything, then she gasped in shock. 'Oh my good God.' She stared at Rhona. 'What happened to you? Oh my God. What are you doing in there? What happened to your head? Who are you?'

Rhona couldn't answer as finally she gave way to her tears, and she sobbed in relief at the sight of her startled rescuer, whom she'd feared would never come.

'Of course we were worried sick,' said Marilyn Foster as she hugged her daughter. 'Trouble is, it's not the first time you've disappeared with no warning, so we made ourselves just get on with everything as usual and wait for you to come home. I'm so sorry, love, if we'd known we'd have been up to that pub like a shot.'

'No, it's me that's sorry,' said Rhona sadly. 'I never realised how worried I'd made you. I know now.' She hugged her mother back and then collapsed on to their old sofa. 'At least the police believed me when I told them I had nothing to do with the robbery. To begin with I reckon one of them thought I'd been part of the gang.'

'I should hope so too!' Marilyn exclaimed. 'I'd have given them what for if they'd tried to take you in. There are some right funny ones working in that station. Look at the state of you, any fool should have seen that you couldn't have done that to yourself. You sit still and take it easy, and the doctor will be here soon.'

Rhona snuggled against the cushion balanced on the armrest and yawned. 'I could sleep for a week. I had nightmares down in that bloody cellar.'

'Shall I make you something to eat?' asked Marilyn. 'I know they gave you a sandwich in the pub but that's not enough to fill you up.'

Rhona smiled, or as much of a smile as she could manage now that the bruising was coming out on her face where it had been shoved against the stinking cellar floor. 'Yes please. I'll stay awake for that.'

'I've got some pie left from last night. How about that?'

Rhona sighed with pleasure. 'I kept thinking about your cooking all the time I was down there. Some pie, and lots of bread and butter with it, and a big mug of tea. And have you got any tins of rice pudding?'

'Of course I have. You know I always keep some in as it's your dad's favourite. Would you like a dollop of strawberry jam in it?'

Rhona nodded. She didn't care if she never had Babycham again as long as her mum still gave her homemade stew and rice pudding with extra jam. She was out of that vile prison of a cellar, she was home, and nobody was going to hurt her anymore. Even if her head hurt, she was safe at last.

Tommy sat at his desk and groaned at the pile of unopened post that would have to be seen to before he did anything else. His legs were still stiff from the long ride back in the car on Tuesday, but he told himself to ignore them and get on with all the work that had accumulated in the last week. The holiday was over and he had bills to pay.

The phone rang and he was tempted to ignore it but knew he shouldn't.

'Tommy, is that you?'

'Stan, long time, no hear,' said Tommy. 'You putting off starting work as well? Not much fun being back at the coal face, is it?'

'No,' said Stan's voice, sounding tense. 'Have you seen the papers yet?'

'Are you joking? I've got a mountain of paperwork to get through. I can't be sitting around reading the papers.'

'Well, you might want to take a look,' said Stan hurriedly. 'Make it fast. You have to read the *Mail* before Mavis sees it. She'll be in a right state.'

'What are you talking about?' Tommy felt himself growing anxious in reaction to his friend's tone.

'There's a story in there about a body being found at the foot of a cliff near Torquay. They say it's a local man called Charles Collier and they've put in a photo of him. As soon as Mavis sees it she'll know it's Alec Pugh.'

'What? What did you just say?'

'Alec's dead, Tommy. He's fallen off a cliff on to the rocks and died. They don't mention his real name, but they say he ran a stamp shop so there's no doubt about it. You'll have to tell her.'

Tommy stood up and realised he was shaking.

'You still there, Tommy?'

'Yeah, mate.' He paused, running a hand across his face. 'Just a bit shocked, that's all. The *Mail*, you said? Not just whatever the local paper is down there?'

'Yes, it's all there in black and white, page five of the *Mail*, with a picture of that slimy bastard, which means everyone will recognise him. How about that for a coincidence? He goes missing for ages, then no sooner do we find him than he winds up dead. When I think about what he did to Mavis and the kids, I can't say I'm sorry. He made their lives a living hell.'

'He did that all right,' said Tommy.

'Look, I've got to go, I've got loads to catch up on as well, but I thought you should know as soon as possible.'

'Thanks, and I'll go over to see Mavis right away,' Tommy said and after saying goodbye he replaced the receiver.

Grabbing his jacket he left the office and ran to the corner shop, where he picked up a copy of the *Daily Mail,* and then the *Express* and *Mirror* as well. The woman behind the counter was keen to make conversation but for once he ignored her, running out again and getting into his van. He took a moment to catch his breath and then turned to page five of the *Mail.*

TORQUAY BUSINESSMAN FOUND DEAD AT TOP BEAUTY SPOT

Tommy pulled a face and thought how Alec Pugh would have loved his description, rather than plain old shopkeeper. The man's face smiled out, posed in front of his premises, with the 'Collectibles' sign in the background. There was no mistaking him. Everyone who'd known him in Battersea would recognise him at once, even though he'd aged a little. Tommy skimmed the story but there was not much to tell. The body of Charles Collier had been discovered by some early rising beachcombers on Tuesday morning at the foot of the local cliffs, but the paper didn't give the exact whereabouts. Nobody appeared to have seen the man fall and police were appealing for any witnesses to come forward. The reporter had managed to find someone to say a few good things about the deceased: how well-mannered he was, how the local community respected him. Tommy snorted. They couldn't have known him very well, then.

He picked up the other two papers. They had both run the story but in less detail, and the story wasn't sensational enough to make the headlines in any of the papers. Now though Mavis had to be told, and they would have to think about what to tell the children. Tommy turned the key in the ignition and set off for Peckham. He drove faster than normal, inwardly praying he wouldn't get pulled for speeding, but at last reached Peckham and found a place to park near the dog-leg bend of her road. He hurried towards her front door, just as her miserable neighbour was coming out.

'You're in a hurry this morning,' she commented sourly. 'Where's the fire?'

Tommy gave her a brief nod and after knocking on the door, Lily answered almost at once. Bobby was just behind her, looking as if he was about to be taken to nursery as he was dragging a colourful canvas bag along the floor behind him. 'Where's Mavis?' Tommy gasped. 'Has she seen the newspapers?'

'Not that I know of. Why, what's the matter?' Lily asked worriedly.

'There's something she needs to see.'

They turned as they heard footsteps coming down the stairs. 'Tommy! This is a surprise!' Mavis's face broke into a delighted smile. 'I wasn't expecting to see you until tonight. What brings you here so early?'

Tommy's mind went blank. He didn't know how to begin. 'I've got something to show you ... tell you,' he blurted out.

'Come upstairs then,' Mavis invited.

'I've got to take Bobby to his playgroup, but it's just around the corner so I won't be long,' Lily said, leaving with obvious reluctance.

Tommy followed Mavis upstairs, and after holding her in his arms for a moment she lifted her face for a kiss, then saying, 'What is it that you want to show me.'

Tommy bit on his lower lip and frowned. 'Mavis, you'd better sit down.'

Her smile faltered. 'There's something wrong, isn't there? What is it, Tommy?'

Tommy gently pushed her onto a chair at the table, and then sat down next to her. He pulled out the newspaper, turned it to the relevant page and placed it between them. 'There's no easy way to say this, love. Alec is dead.'

Mavis's face didn't alter. It was too much to take in. 'What did you just say?'

'Alec is dead. Look, here it is in black and white.'

Slowly Mavis pulled the newspaper towards her. She looked at the page, looked away then looked back again. Her hand went to her mouth as she saw the picture and as she still struggled with her letters, Tommy read it to her.

'Oh God, what a terrible thing to happen.' She shivered, but then began to babble, 'Torquay, that was just down the road from where we were

225

staying last week. We could have bumped into him. Thank God we didn't and that the children didn't see him. It doesn't bear thinking about...' She glanced up, saw Tommy's expression and her eyes narrowed. 'Tommy, you knew. You saw him, didn't you?'

Tommy couldn't deny it. She knew him too well. 'Yes, it's true. I did see him and so did Stan. It was only towards the end of our holiday. We didn't say anything because we knew it would upset you.' He watched her carefully, waiting to see what her reaction was.

Mavis was in shock, not knowing what to think. On the one hand she suddenly felt desperately sorry for Alec. He'd been a vindictive cruel husband and father but nobody deserved to die like that. He must have lain there for hours in the darkness, his body mangled on the rocks. She'd seen those cliffs, and could imagine only too clearly what the scene must have looked like. She half-closed her eyes to block out the picture in her mind. Yet on the other hand ... this was the day she'd been waiting for, for two long years. It was the end of her time in limbo. She had wanted a divorce, but not to find out that Alec was dead, yet dreadful as it was, she was finally free. It was all too much. Before she could stop herself a sob broke from her throat and in the next moment she was in Tommy's arms, crying unstoppably. The tears ran down her cheeks and soaked his shirt.

'There, there, you don't have to cry.' Tommy stroked her back and held her as she wept. 'He can't hurt you ever again. He can't touch the children, none of you have to live in fear of him anymore.' He rested his face on the top of her head. 'You're all right now. I know it's a bad way to die but you don't have to be afraid from this day onwards. Don't be sad for him, he didn't deserve it.'

Mavis gave a gulp and the tears slowly stopped. 'It's not that, Tommy. It's the shock, I suppose. Relief as well, mixed with guilt that I feel relieved. Not knowing where he was all this time preyed on my mind. I kept expecting him to turn up one day, to threaten me, or to try to take James and Grace away.'

'Well you won't have to worry about that anymore,' murmured Tommy, shutting his eyes in thankfulness that she would never know how close to the truth that last fear came. 'He's gone, Mavis, gone for good. You're too kind-hearted, he doesn't deserve your tears.'

She shook her head and looked up at him, her eyes still glistening. 'I'm not crying for him, really I'm not. It's sad though, because he was the father of my children and now he'll never know how they grow up.'

'His choice,' said Tommy abruptly. 'He disappeared, so that was his loss, and now he's lost his life.'

'I know, but I wouldn't have my two wonderful children if it wasn't for him. You're right, I do see that, it was his decision not to have anything to do with them. I can tell them the truth; that he's dead, and then they won't be thinking about him turning up again either. I don't really think it ever entered Grace's head, but I could see how James flinched when anyone ever mentioned his father.'

She paused and gave a big sigh, tipping back her head. 'No, the more it sinks in, and though it sounds awful, the better I feel.'

'Good,' said Tommy.

'And now, at last, I'm no longer a married woman,' Mavis said. 'It's really true. I don't have to lie, or keep quiet and let people make assumptions. I'm a widow, I'm free. Tommy, I'm free.'

'You are.' Tommy brought his mouth close to hers and kissed her very softly. 'You are absolutely and totally free to do what you like. How does that feel?'

'In light of Alec's death, it still feels wrong to say it, but I feel bloody marvellous.'

'Mavis! You never swear!'

'Maybe now I'm a widow I do.' She smiled up at him. 'I can do what I like without fearing in the back of my mind that he'll come back to make my life a misery again. And you don't have to worry about going on holiday with a married woman.'

'I liked it,' said Tommy with a wicked look on his face. 'With one particular married woman anyway.' Suddenly he knew this was the moment. He'd always thought it would be a perfectly planned occasion, yet here was the chance he needed. He paused and grew serious. 'In fact I liked it so much I want to do it again.'

Mavis shot him a look, puzzled.

Tommy smiled gently and kissed her again. 'Sorry, I'm talking in riddles. I've waited so long to say this that it's coming out all wrong.' He took a deep breath. 'Now you're free ... what I wanted to ask you was ... oh Mavis, you know how I feel about you. Will you marry me?'

For a moment there was silence. Mavis gave a little gasp, and then she beamed at him, happiness radiating from her. 'Oh, Tommy,' she breathed. 'Of course I will. I'm the luckiest woman alive to have you. Let's do it as soon as we can.'

Tommy swept her off her feet and danced with her, twirling her around the kitchen. 'For richer, for poorer,' he chuckled. 'Then you won't have to have his name anymore either. You can be Mavis Wilson.'

'Mavis Wilson. Yes. That sounds much better. I never did like the name Pugh.' She hugged him tightly around his neck. 'Rich, poor, none of that matters as long as we're together.'

Tommy set her down and held her close. 'That's exactly howl feel too. I'll never hurt you, Mavis. I'll do everything in my power to keep you safe. I'll never let the bad times come for you again,' Tommy said firmly, meaning every word.

Chapter Twenty-Two

Rhona had wondered what sort of reception she would get when she went back to work, thinking perhaps everyone would assume she'd been skiving. So she returned to the factory before her head wound had properly healed and still bearing signs of the bruising, wanting to get back into a normal routine as soon as possible and to forestall any trouble. Her worries were unfounded. When she got there, everyone greeted her like a hero.

'You've done me a favour,' beamed Jean. 'Getting that slimy Andy Forsyth arrested was the best thing you could have done.'

'No! I didn't give them his name!' Rhona cried, horrified. She'd been careful to say that before she had seen her attackers, she'd been hit on the head from behind and hadn't mentioned anything about coming to before they'd left. She knew only too well what happened to snitches and she didn't fancy the repercussions. Being beaten up once was bad enough.

'Sorry, that came out wrong,' said Jean, still grinning like the cat who got the cream. 'That barman cracked under police questioning and confessed everything. My fiancé heard all about it. The police raided Andy Forsyth's place and as the daft sod hadn't had the sense to hide the money, he didn't stand a chance.'

'I hope they put him away for a long stretch. Prison's too good for the likes of him,' Rhona said as she rubbed her head where it still hurt.

'But that's not the best bit,' Jean went on. 'It was all too much for our foreman. He'd boasted about Andy getting on in the world and looked down his nose at us, so when he heard what had happened to you he went crazy. He barged into the manager's office and started shouting, accusing you of putting Andy up to it and demanding your dismissal. The manager was none too happy and sacked him on the spot.'

'What? You're kidding.' Rhona couldn't imagine the pompous foreman losing his temper like that. He'd been deliberately mean to her, but had never shown any signs of doing anything to jeopardise his own job. 'I can't believe it. He was always such an arse-licker around the boss. Has he really been sacked?'

'Yes he has. He had to empty his locker and go.' Jean held out her arms. 'And guess who the new foreman is now?'

Rhona shrugged. She had no idea who the boss had chosen for promotion. It would be one of the men from the other shifts. She looked across to Alma, who had been standing watching them, a smile on her face. Rhona frowned. What was she missing here? 'I haven't got a clue.'

'It's me!' Jean exclaimed. 'They've put me in charge! What do you think of that?'

Rhona gaped. 'But you're a woman!'

Jean snorted. 'Well, I know that. So what? Just because they haven't had a woman foreman before, doesn't mean they can't change. Aren't you pleased for me?'

Rhona nodded hastily. 'Of course. It's fab. You were more or less in charge anyway. Old Forsyth was in the canteen more than he was with us, except when he wanted to pick on me.'

'It's been winding me up for ages,' Jean said, 'seeing that old fool lording it over us and not having the faintest idea what was going on half the time. I knew I could do his job better than him. The money will be better too so I can get married a bit earlier. I'm over the moon.'

'Congratulations,' said Rhona, and meant it. Jean would make a great boss – she was fair, she was straightforward, didn't take any nonsense and knew exactly how everything worked around the factory. 'It's a real turn-up for the books and the best news I've had for ages.'

Jean smiled. 'Thanks. So now, as your new boss, I suppose I should ask if you're really well enough to start work this morning.'

'You bet I am,' said Rhona. 'I've been stuck at home for long enough.'

'In which case, get your skates on.'

Alma stepped forward. 'Jean, aren't you forgetting something?' she asked. 'That other thing that happened.'

'Oh yes.' Jean spun around. 'Sorry, in all the drama of Forsyth getting the push and me getting promoted it slipped my mind. Penny was here.'

Rhona stopped in her tracks. 'Penny? What did she want? I hope you told her to sling her hook.'

'Not exactly,' said Jean. 'She wanted to see you, actually.'

Rhona raised her eyes heavenwards. 'Did she indeed? Well she can go on wanting. I don't want to see her, that's for sure.'

'We didn't think she looked very well, did we?' Alma said, turning to Jean. 'She was always such a lively young girl when she worked here, but now she looks sort of washed out.'

Rhona pulled on her overall and said dismissively, 'I'm not interested in what she looks like.'

Alma made as if to say something more, then seemed to think the better of it.

'Right,' said Jean. 'Now you've caught up with everything that's been going on, we'd better make a start. I'm telling you as your boss to get cracking.'

On Sunday afternoon Tommy gritted his teeth

232

and forced himself to walk along the familiar pavement to his mother's door. He knew he had to get this matter over with. She would be furious if she wasn't one of the first to know about him and Mavis.

His mother opened the door with her usual lack of affection. 'Oh, it's you again.'

Tommy nodded. 'Can I come in?'

'I suppose so.' She led the way down the dark hallway to the kitchen where the remains of her lunch sat congealing on the draining board: a fatty piece of a pork chop surrounded by a greasy gravy. Tommy looked away.

'I can guess why you're here,' she scowled.

Tommy took out a small box wrapped in a brown paper bag which he'd been carrying in his pocket. 'I brought you something.'

Olive looked at it scornfully. 'What's that? Something from Torquay?'

'Yes, I thought you might like it.' He held it out to her.

She took it and opened the paper bag, which she then carefully folded and tucked in between two jars on the dresser before looking properly at the present. 'A souvenir from Devon,' she read. 'What is it?'

'It's fudge, Mum. You like fudge. You get a lot of it down there.'

'That was before I got me false teeth. It sticks to them something awful.' Olive pulled a face as she plonked it on the table. 'Can't touch it now. I hear there's lots of things happening in Torquay by the sounds of it.'

'Yes, there was lots going on. We went to the

233

beach and visited–'

'That's not what I meant,' Olive interrupted. 'You must have seen this piece of news.' She picked up a copy of the *News of the World*. 'Here. Have a read.' She leant back and folded her arms, pitching up the sleeves of the old cardigan full of holes.

Tommy took it and realised it had been folded so that one article was uppermost.

DEAD BUSINESSMAN
USED FALSE NAME

He read on. It had emerged that the body found at the foot of the cliffs was not that of Charles Collier. It had been an assumed name and the man's real name had been Alec Pugh. The same photo smiled out at him. Tommy shook his head. Well, anyone from Battersea who'd seen the Wednesday papers would have known anyway. He noted that this headline was much bigger than the earlier ones, probably because despite the event being several days old, it added a whole new layer of mystery to the story.

'Well?' Olive fixed him with her beady eyes.

'Well what?'

'That man was married to Dumbo Jackson, wasn't he?'

'Her name's Mavis, and like I said before, she's not dumb. She just has word blindness.'

'So you keep saying. So now the brats have lost their dad. How very convenient.'

'What do you mean by that?' Tommy tried to breathe steadily, reminding himself as he did on every visit that his mother was a lonely, malicious woman who had nobody else to take out her bad temper on. Still, he could feel his heart begin to pound.

'I mean, you lot go on holiday to Torquay and he winds up dead. Bit of a coincidence, isn't it?'

Tommy shook his head. Trust his mother to try to make something out of nothing, to create suspicion. He reminded himself that she hadn't been there, she couldn't have known anything beyond what was in the papers. 'I didn't know he was there. Mavis didn't know either until she saw the papers in the week.'

'You expect me to believe that?' Olive asked indignantly. 'You suddenly announce you're off to Torquay, then while you're there the husband of the floozy you've taken up with falls off a cliff and dies. It don't take a genius to work out what went on. You better be careful. I won't be the only one thinking what a stroke of luck it was for you.'

'Are you saying it wasn't an accident?' Tommy could feel his temper rising despite all his good intentions and fought to stay calm. There was no point in saying something rash now, it could land him in really hot water.

'I'm saying it's all a bit fishy.'

'Come off it, Mum. You know me. I'm not going to go round pushing people off cliffs just because I don't like them.'

'So you didn't like him, then?'

'I didn't say that! Stop looking for the worst possible explanation. Alec Pugh was walking along a narrow cliff path and fell off the edge. It's sad, but there's no more to it than that.'

'It's going to take more than a bloody box of fudge to convince me of that,' snapped Olive.

Tommy could have slammed his fist on the kitchen table in frustration. He'd wanted to share his news about his engagement, even knowing that his mother wouldn't be happy, but he hadn't expected her to all but accuse him of causing Alec's death. 'Mum, it was an accident. The papers don't say it was anything other than that and at least it means Mavis and the children can get on with their lives. He made them a misery, you know.'

'Yeah, well, I can't say that surprises me. His mother was a stuck-up old bag,' Olive mused. 'Like mother like son no doubt.'

'Yes, and after what she went through, Mavis deserves something better,' said Tommy, steering the conversation back in the direction he wanted it to go in. 'Mum, I came here to tell you the news. I asked Mavis to marry me and she said yes.'

For a moment Olive was lost for words. Her hands went to her throat and her eyes widened. Then she found her voice again. '*Marry* her?' she shrieked. 'Have you lost your bleeding mind? Dumbo Jackson? Her with those two little brats, and you tell me this just after they find her husband's body? Have you gone stark staring mad?'

'No, Mum, I've never been more serious in my life,' Tommy said, keeping his voice level. 'I love Mavis and she loves me. I'm sorry it took such a sad event to make it possible but I've wanted to ask her for ages. Can't you make an effort to welcome her and the children into the family? After all, she's going to be your daughter-in-law.'

'God in heaven, in case you've forgotten, I've already had one,' spat Olive, going red in the face as she ranted on. 'You were just like this the last time, love this, and love that. Fat lot of good that did. Two shakes of a lamb's tail and you're splitting up with Belinda, bringing the disgrace of a divorce on the family. Now you want to marry that idiot whose mother is a right tart and take on her brats, while their own father isn't even cold in his grave. That's if there was anything left to bury after they scraped him off the rocks.'

'Mum!'

'Don't you "Mum" me. Take a good look at yourself, Thomas Wilson, and ask yourself what people are going to be saying about you. Her husband dead, Dumbo marries again just after – what does it look like?'

'It's not like that,' protested Tommy, but it was like banging his head against a brick wall. Once his mother had an idea in her head there was no shifting it – it didn't matter if he was her son or not.

'My God, you're dafter than I'd imagined,' breathed Olive. 'Here, take your blasted fudge and get out before everyone knows you're here. All you do is bring trouble to my door. There's going to be one hell of a palaver about this, just you wait and see, but go ahead, marry that fool of a woman. Just don't come crying to me when it all goes wrong. You make your bed, you can lie on it. Now get out.'

Chapter Twenty-Three

Rhona was leaving the factory gates after her shift on Monday, her mind on the story she'd seen in the paper yesterday and what it meant for Mavis. She'd rushed over to check that she knew and if she was all right, but Mavis had been fine, more than fine in fact. She'd had a few extra days to adjust to the news, and the wonderful thing was she was now formally engaged to Tommy. Rhona couldn't bring herself to feel sorry for Alec, and was delighted that Mavis was at last out of limbo. Even James and Grace didn't seem too bothered; Grace had had a hard time understanding what someone being dead meant, but neither was sad at the idea of never seeing Alec again.

So Rhona was miles away when she caught sight of a figure leaning against the wall on the opposite side of the road. She groaned to herself. This was the last person she wanted to see, but there was no way of avoiding her, short of turning round and going back inside the gates, which would be stupid. Sighing, she decided to find out what the girl wanted.

Penny made her way across the road, huddled into a light coat, her expression miserable. Her hair was flat and looked like it hadn't been washed in a while. Rhona thought that if she hadn't known better, this didn't look like someone who could steal their best friend's boyfriend.

'Hello, Penny.'

Penny looked up in what might have been relief at not being ignored. 'Rhona. I came to see you. Actually I came last...'

'Yeah, I heard.' Rhona stood still and folded her arms. 'What is it that you want exactly?'

Penny shuffled her feet and looked uneasy. 'It's a bit ... well, I can't quite...'

'Spit it out.' Rhona wasn't in the mood to make things easy for the young woman who'd betrayed her so badly when she'd been in no state to do anything about it.

Penny glanced around, checking to see if anyone was close enough to overhear. Then she plucked up her courage and came out with it. 'Rhona, I need your help.'

Rhona raised her eyebrows. 'Blimey. You got a nerve. Why would I help you, when you went off with Gary?'

'Please, Rhona. I haven't got anyone else I can turn to.' Penny gazed at her imploringly. 'I can't talk to Mum, and everyone at my new job down the fruit and veg warehouse is miles older so they wouldn't understand. You're the only person who would know what to do.'

Rhona thought this sounded like trouble, but in spite of herself she was interested. She should send Penny away with a flea in her ear, but instead said brusquely, 'You've got the time it takes me to walk home.'

'All right,' Penny said, but struggled to keep up. 'Please, Rhona, slow down. Sorry, I'm just a bit tired.'

Rhona slowed her pace, noting that though

Penny had always been fair-skinned, she now looked an unhealthy shade of white. She was also breathing heavily and a bit of Rhona's hardness to-wards her softened. 'You obviously can't talk and walk, so when we get to my place you'd better come in.'

'Oh, thanks, Rhona.'

When they arrived at the house, Rhona shoved open the door and headed for the kitchen where her mother looked up in surprise when she saw their visitor. 'Penny, I didn't expect to see you here.'

'Hello,' Penny said weakly.

Marilyn looked at her daughter, but Rhona just shrugged. Sighing, she said, 'Cup of tea?'

'Yes please, Mum, I'm parched,' said Rhona at once.

'No thanks,' said Penny. 'Could I have a glass of water?'

'Yes, and I'll make the tea,' Rhona said, staring meaningfully at her mother, willing her to leave them alone.

Marilyn got the message. 'Now you're back I'll just pop out to see if they've got anything at the bakery going cheap at the end of the day. You never know.' She picked up her bag and went out of the back door.

Rhona handed Penny her glass of water and indicated the kitchen chair. 'So, what's up?'

Penny sat at the kitchen table and put her head in her hands. 'I don't know how to begin.'

Rhona made herself a cup of tea and sighed impatiently. She already had her suspicions, but said, 'I can't help you if I don't know what the problem is.'

Penny raised her head and wiped away a tear that was trickling down her face. 'Do you remember when I asked your advice about ... about...?'

'Sex!' Rhona snapped.

Penny lowered her head, nodded and stammered, 'I ... nearly did what you advised, but ... well...'

Rhona took a sip of her tea to compose herself then put her cup down. She suspected that this was the problem during their walk from the factory. 'So you're telling me you're pregnant.'

Miserably Penny nodded. 'I think so. I hoped it was just that I'm a bit run down or something, but I've missed two of my monthlies now. Oh, what am I gonna do?'

Rhona bit down the answer that came to her lips. She just didn't have the heart to berate someone who was clearly in desperate straits. 'So you didn't take precautions then.'

Penny began to cry properly. 'I did try. But sometimes I just forgot. You know, when you get carried away...'

'So you just trusted to luck,' Rhona said sharply. 'That was a silly thing to do.'

'I know that now...' Penny sobbed as she wiped her face with a grubby hanky.

'What do you expect from me?' Rhona asked.

'I don't really know. I just needed to tell somebody, and everyone else would have said it's my fault for going all the way before marriage. I knew you wouldn't judge me like that.'

Rhona sat down opposite her former friend. 'Have you told Gary?'

Penny shook her head. 'I don't know what he'll say. He's so busy at the moment. He's trying out all these different bands to play with so I don't want to worry him.'

'He's going to have to know some time,' Rhona pointed out. 'After all, when your belly swells he's going to notice.'

'I'm scared of how he'll react, and I know that he'll never agree to marry me,' Penny started crying again. 'And I can't tell my mum. She's never met Gary, but she doesn't like me going out with him, and when she finds out I'm pregnant she'll go crazy.'

Rhona didn't want to admit it, but she felt she wasn't exactly blame-free. She'd encouraged her friend to go ahead and enjoy herself, even telling her how to protect herself against pregnancy. All right, Penny had been lax, but it could so easily have been her in the same position. She also knew that Gary would never agree to marriage. He liked a good time too much to get tied down and he'd deny that he was the father. 'Look, this has come as a bit of a surprise, and I need time to think about what you can do. Leave it with me, but don't go home with a face like that or your mum will know something is up. Come over to the sink and give it a wash.'

She stood to one side as Penny did as she suggested, and handed her a towel. 'That's an improvement already. Go home, have a bath, do your hair and don't give up just yet. We'll come up with something.'

'You're too good to me,' sniffed Penny. 'I don't deserve it.'

Rhona thought about the night in the cellar and what the two men had said. She knew she couldn't blame Penny; just like she had been, her former friend was only out to have a bit of fun. The difference was, she'd got caught out, whereas thankfully, Rhona had never found herself pregnant.

'I'd better go before your mum gets back.' Penny hung the towel on its hook again.

'Yeah, that might be best.' Rhona led the way through to the front door. 'Come on, chin up.'

'Thanks, Rhona.' Penny leant forward on the doorstep and gave Rhona a hug, before turning and hurrying down the street.

Blimey, thought Rhona. If anyone had asked her before, she would have said she never wanted to see Penny again, and that if she got herself in trouble then that was her look-out. But when it came to it, Rhona couldn't abandon her old friend.

Chapter Twenty-Four

Mavis sat at her mother's kitchen table, writing a list of what she'd have to do to plan a wedding. She knew the whole thing would take a while, as there would be so many legal matters to sort out, but she refused to let them weigh her down. Her first marriage had been rushed, she'd been so desperate to get away from Lily and Pete at the time, and Alec's mother had sorted out all the arrangements. Now she could have it all exactly how she wanted it. Maybe they should have an engagement party? Or would that be seen as disrespectful, after Alec's dreadful accident? She'd ask Tommy later.

Lily came in from the garden with a handful of late tomatoes. 'Look at these, pet. Fancy some of these in a cheese sandwich? I could eat them straight off the plant, they're that sweet.'

Mavis looked up and raised her eyebrows. 'Don't say that in front of the children. It's taken all summer to get them to understand they should bring things in and wash them, not just stuff them in their mouths.'

'Ain't no one here to see now though, is there?' said Lily. 'Here, go on.' She offered one to Mavis, who bit into it.

'That's lovely. I'm so glad we planted them. It's good for the kids to have fresh fruit and veg.'

'Not like when you were a nipper, eh?' said Lily wistfully. 'We only had what was left at the end of the day from the market and a lot of that was rotten.' She looked at her daughter, sad for a moment. 'I wish things had been better back then, that I had behaved differently, but still, I suppose it's no use crying over spilt milk. We do all right now, don't we?'

Mavis nodded. 'Yes, Mum, and as you say, there isn't much we can do about the past, except perhaps learn from it.' She briefly shut her eyes, determined not to let all the misery of her childhood flood back to spoil her happiness now. 'I've nothing to complain about. We've got our new home, the kids love it, we're all healthy and, best of all, Tommy and I can now plan our future. I was

244

just wondering about that in fact. Should we have an engagement party?'

Lily set down the rest of the tomatoes and beamed. 'Damn right you should. Never pass up the chance of a party.'

The hall door opened and Pete came in, struggling out of his jacket. 'Blimey, it's still warm out there. What's all this about a party?' He tugged his arm out of the sleeve and an envelope fell from his pocket and skittered across the floor.

Mavis bent over to pick it up. 'Look, you dropped this.' She peered at the print on it but as usual the shapes of the letters swam about and made no sense. She concentrated on the image in the corner. Pictures she understood; it was words that confounded her. 'Isn't that the symbol for the bank?'

Pete hurriedly threw his jacket on the back of a chair, reached over and snatched it from her hand. 'Oh, that,' he said with forced cheerfulness. 'That arrived while we were away. I must have stuffed it in my pocket and forgotten about it. They're just offering me a higher interest savings account. Tell you what, I could do with a cuppa but first I'll hang this jacket up.' He quickly made for his bedroom and headed to the big old wardrobe which stood solidly in the far corner.

Wiping his brow he leant against the wooden frame. That had been a close one. He should have left the letter from the bank at the office along with all the others. This one was even more urgent, piling on the pressure for him to increase the loan payments. He was one step away from a final notice and yet he was no closer to a solution.

What if it had been Lily who'd picked it up? She wouldn't have handed it back so readily and then his terrible secret would be out and they'd know about the threat hanging over them. How could he bring himself to give them the news? He couldn't bear to ruin their happiness. The safety and security of his family meant everything – but what if it all came tumbling down around them?

On Friday Rhona found herself working late, helping Jean out again. She found she didn't mind. In the old days she'd have had a date or concert to go to and would have complained bitterly, but she had no plans for the evening, which would be the same as any other night now. She'd go home, her mother would have dinner ready and then she and her parents would sit around listening to the radio. She might read a magazine but somehow fashion didn't seem as important as it once had. The pages would be full of what coats and footwear were the right style for autumn, which was just around the corner, but she couldn't bring herself to care anymore. What did it matter if boots were meant to be knee-high or not? Even though all the trendy boutiques were only a bus ride away, and Swinging London was the talk of the world, she could not bring herself to be interested.

'Doing anything this weekend?' she asked Jean.

'We might go and see *The Sound of Music*,' Jean said, checking off something on her clipboard. 'I've seen it already, but as my mum hasn't I said I'd take her.'

'That's nice of you,' said Rhona, who hadn't

seen it and didn't intend to either. 'Bet she's pleased about your promotion.'

Jean laughed. 'She is, but my dad doesn't know what to think. He likes the fact that I'm going to be taking home more money and is glad for me that it means I can bring the date of my wedding forward, but he doesn't believe women should be in charge of anything. He says I'm too irresponsible and that I'll lose my head in a crisis.'

'You!' Rhona exclaimed. 'You're the least likely person I know to do that.'

'He thinks that applies to all women,' said Jean. 'Doesn't matter if they're like you and me or someone famous, he still thinks they shouldn't be boss and should know their place. I tell him he's old-fashioned but he won't change his mind.'

'But he still likes you bringing home your wages,' Rhona commented.

'Yeah, he doesn't see the problem with that,' Jean said. 'Anyway he'll go down the pub for a pint with his mates so me and Mum can enjoy ourselves. Might get some fish and chips to round off the evening.'

'Now you're talking,' said Rhona. She glanced across the room to where a door had flown open. One of the young boys who worked on the late shift was standing there.

'I've got a message for you,' he called. 'You're Rhona, aren't you? There's someone waiting outside for you and he says he can't stay long.'

'Ooh, you kept that quiet.' Jean raised her eyebrows. 'Who's this, then?'

'I don't know,' said Rhona, puzzled. She hoped it wasn't Kenneth, thinking he could have a second shot after that Sunday evening. He may not have heard what happened after he left, so she couldn't blame him, but she didn't particularly want to see him, much less go on another date with him. 'Did he leave his name?'

'No,' said the boy, staring at his feet, looking embarrassed.

'What did he look like?' Rhona asked.

'Oh, you know – normal. Brown hair,' said the boy hopelessly.

Jean shook her head. 'Well, that's a fat lot of use. You'd better find out who the mystery admirer is, Rhona. We're almost done here and I can finish up on my own.'

'You sure?'

'Yeah, go on. I'll see you on Monday.'

'OK, thanks. See ya.' Rhona grabbed her bag and light jacket and made her way to the main exit, wondering who it could be.

When she saw the man she still didn't know who he was. She searched her memory, trying to place him. She knew she'd seen him somewhere but not exactly where, or when. His face was pleasant enough but there was nothing about it to make him stand out. His clothes weren't bad, but they were nothing special and she could see now why the boy hadn't been able to describe him very well. He was just, well, ordinary. She approached him hesitantly.

'Rhona?' he asked.

'That's me,' she said. 'I'm sorry, I...'

'Don't worry, I'm sure you don't remember me,' he said. 'I met you in a bar in Soho earlier this year.'

He had a nice smile and Rhona smiled back but she was none the wiser. She'd met a lot of men in Soho bars in the early part of the year so this didn't really narrow it down.

'The basement bar near Soho Square, it was,' the man went on, as if he could tell she still didn't have a clue. 'You were with Gary, and you were losing your voice.'

'Oh, yes,' Rhona remembered that Gary had teased her in front of a friend, and they'd talked for a few minutes before the band came on, but that had to have been the only time she'd seen this man, 'I know what night you mean, but I still don't think...'

'I'm Jeff,' the man reminded her.

That was it. She nodded. 'Hi, Jeff. Why do you want to see me? In fact, how did you know I work here?'

A look of concern appeared on his face. 'Well, that's the thing,' he began and now he sounded awkward. 'Penny mentioned it.'

'Penny? You know Penny?'

'A bit. I met her through Gary. She said she used to work here and that you still do, and as I don't know where she lives, I thought you might be able to tell me.'

Rhona wondered how well Jeff knew Penny, and whether it was well enough to know that she was pregnant. She had been racking her brains for a way to help her, but hadn't come up with anything that didn't involve a back-street abortionist, something she would never suggest. 'That depends. Why do you want to see her?'

'I've got some news to pass on to her, something she'd want to know, and this was the only way I could think of to find her.'

Rhona looked at him more carefully and had a sense of foreboding that this wasn't going to be good. 'I see,' she said slowly. 'Well, you'd better tell me what this news is.'

Jeff met her eyes and nodded. 'Right. Well, the thing is,' his voice sounded heavy with apology, 'what it is ... Gary's done a runner.'

Rhona sat in the lounge bar of the pub a few roads away from her house, trying not to notice how sticky the floor was. Jeff had suggested going to the bar closest to the factory but Rhona had said no to that idea very firmly, without explaining why. She barely knew the man and didn't want to go into the whole story of being attacked and left in the cellar. Still, she'd agreed to have a drink with him while he told her what he knew of Gary's disappearance.

He sat opposite her, slowly drinking a pint of bitter while she sipped at her orange juice. Her head still hurt now and then and she didn't want to have anything stronger in case it made it worse.

'OK, tell me again. I can't quite make sense of it,' she said. It wasn't that she particularly cared what Gary was doing with himself these days but she knew, even if Jeff didn't, how important this might be for Penny.

Jeff shifted uneasily in his seat. It was as if he didn't want to be disloyal to his friend, yet knew Gary's girlfriend wasn't going to find out the truth any other way unless he told her. 'You know he was trying to get in to several bands,' he began.

'Yes. Or, well, no. He said it was the other way round; that they all wanted him and he was trying to decide between them.'

Jeff raised his eyebrows. 'Maybe he thought that if he could get you to believe that he'd start to believe it himself. No, he'd always manage to talk himself into having an audition, but when they heard him play, they'd turn him down.'

'Oh.' Rhona was surprised. 'But I thought he was good, and he taught me some guitar too.'

'Did he?' Jeff asked. 'How many chords did you learn?'

'Three or four.' Rhona tried to remember.

'And then did he tell you that you'd better stop before learning anymore, and to just practise those to begin with?'

Rhona stared at him. 'Yeah, that's just what happened. How did you know that?'

Jeff took a swig of his pint. ''Cos he doesn't know many more chords himself. I'm not saying he isn't musical, but he hates practising. He could be miles better if he put the work in, but he never does.'

'So what's he doing now then?'

'He finally got asked to join a group and he jumped at the chance. They don't care that he doesn't play well. They like how he looks.'

Rhona snorted, remembering how Gary always maintained that women were in bands to look good while men did all the actual work of playing and writing songs. 'And he's up and left, just like that?'

'Yeah, he said they didn't want to wait around, they're off on tour,' Jeff explained. 'He didn't

251

even give in his notice at work. He got the offer in the afternoon and was gone by the evening. If this all works out then there's a chance that they'll be asked to tour with Herman's Hermits.'

'But Gary hates Herman's Hermits!' Rhona exclaimed, almost knocking over her drink. 'He says they're for bored housewives and have no soul.'

Jeff spread his hands. 'What can I say? It's his one shot at the big time. He's been given a chance and he's grabbed it with both hands.'

'Without telling Penny.' Rhona sighed heavily and thanked her lucky stars that she was no longer involved with Gary. He'd only cared about himself, she saw that now. She'd been a piece of arm candy he was happy to be seen with, but no more than that. He'd have done the same to her, abandoning her without a second thought.

'Yeah, without telling Penny,' Jeff echoed. 'So I thought somebody had better tell her, or she'll turn up at the Talisman and wonder where he is. I didn't like to think of her standing around, not knowing what was going on. I'm sorry to be the bringer of bad news. Gary's impulsive like that, always has been, even when we were kids together at school. It's just how he is.'

Rhona slumped in her seat. Jeff was being very sweet about this, and clearly was trying to be loyal to Gary while disagreeing with what he'd done, but he had no idea how much depended on this conversation. Penny was pregnant and had now been left high and dry. Even if Gary hadn't known about it, he was still meant to be her boyfriend and they'd been together all summer. She looked up at Jeff. 'What a bastard.'

252

Jeff shrugged. 'Well, he's waited a long time for this. In some ways I can't blame him.'

'I can,' said Rhona decisively. 'He's dumped her without a backward glance. Bet he's hoping to pull loads of girls on tour – they'll be all over him like a rash once they see him on stage. He'll be doing very nicely thank you and she'll be breaking her heart over him.'

Jeff nodded. 'Yeah, it's tough on her, I do realise that. That's why I came here. So are you going to give me her address so that I can break the news to her? The sooner she hears the sooner she can get over him.'

Rhona shut her eyes briefly. If only it were that simple. Jeff had only seen Penny in the Talisman when she was dressed up to the nines. If he saw her now, looking washed out and wan, he might guess and she didn't think Penny would want anyone to know that she was pregnant, especially now that Gary had deserted her. There was only one thing for it. 'I'll tell her,' she said. 'It will be better coming from me.'

'But won't that be hard on you?' asked Jeff. 'I mean, I know you and Gary were an item for a while and I'm not daft. When you weren't on the scene for a while, he soon gravitated to Penny and that must have hurt. Will you be OK?'

Rhona stared at him in amazement. She wasn't used to such sensitivity from men and it temporarily disarmed her. She blushed. 'Don't worry about me. She did me a favour really, showing me what Gary was like underneath all the trendy clothes and big talk. Anyway, I've made up with her, so I'll be fine. It's her I'm worried about. The

253

only thing I really miss about Gary is the guitar lessons.'

Jeff laughed. 'And they wouldn't have lasted long anyway. Are you serious about learning? Properly, I mean, not just strumming along to whatever's in the top ten? If so, I could teach you?'

Rhona's eyes brightened. 'Top ten? No thanks. You'll be asking me if I like Herman's Hermits next.' She paused and shuddered, remembering what trouble she'd got into just trying to track down a guitar to buy. She was ready to give up the idea after that – the attack, on top of the glandular fever, seemed to be fate's way of telling her girls weren't meant to play music after all. However, something shifted and her instincts told her there was nothing dodgy about Jeff. She could trust him, she was sure, and he didn't seem about to make a pass at her or offer her lessons if she'd sleep with him first... He cared about Penny, even if she was only his friend's girlfriend, so he must be decent and she came to a decision. 'If you mean it, yeah, I'm interested. When do we start?'

Chapter Twenty-Five

On Saturday morning Mavis was cleaning the kitchen, getting the chores out of the way before taking the children for a picnic. The sun was shining and it made her hope for a real Indian summer. Now they were closer to Peckham Rye Common and the park beyond they could easily carry their hamper over to the big stretch of grass, and the boys could take a football. Jenny was bringing Greg over to join them, and as Lily wanted to go to the hairdresser's to get her roots done, she was only too glad to let Bobby come along too.

The doorbell went and Mavis assumed it would be Jenny. Humming to herself, Mavis ran down the stairs and flung open the door but it wasn't Jenny on the doorstep. Instead it was two uniformed policemen.

'Mrs Pugh?' the shorter one asked.

Mavis wanted to reply 'not for much longer' but stopped herself. She hoped nothing had happened to Jenny and Greg on their way over. 'Yes,' she said hesitantly, her voice faltering. 'What is it? Is somebody hurt?'

'Just routine, ma'am,' the taller one answered. 'May we come in?'

Lily came down the corridor to see what was going on. 'Is everything all right?' she asked worriedly.

'Yes, this is just routine, ma'am,' was said again.

'Then you'd better come through,' said Lily, leading the way.

'And you are...?' the short one asked when they reached Lily's kitchen.

'This is my mother,' said Mavis, growing increasingly worried. 'Please, can you tell us what this is about?'

'Mrs Culling, is that right? That saves us some time then as we want to talk to you too.'

'About what?'

The tall one leant against the countertop and

255

took a moment to get out his notebook. 'We're making enquiries about the holiday you just took in Torquay,' he began, turning to look at Mavis. 'We understand that while you were there, your husband died, Mrs Pugh.'

'Yes, but we were separated. We didn't even know he was there, did we, Mum? We only went there because our friends knew a good B and B.'

'The bloody man buggered off and left her and the kids without two pennies to rub together,' Lily said angrily. 'He's no loss.'

The short policeman leant forward with interest. 'Is that right, Mrs Culling?'

Mavis put out her arm to restrain Lily. 'Mum,' she warned in a low voice. 'That's all water under the bridge.' She turned back to the short policeman. 'It's sad that Alec died but we'd had no contact for two years.'

The tall officer checked his notebook. 'We understand that you are now engaged to be married, Mrs Pugh.'

Mavis was startled but managed to answer. 'Well, yes.'

'And that your fiancé, Thomas Wilson, was also on holiday with you in Devon.'

'Yes, that's right.'

'Now hold on. What's this all about?' Lily demanded.

'There's no need to get overexcited, Mrs Culling,' the short officer said firmly. 'We are simply making preliminary enquiries. What we need to establish is exactly when you learnt Mr Pugh was in Torquay.'

Mavis thought back to when Tommy had come

to break the news to her. He had seen Alec in Devon but hadn't told her, and some instinct told her not to pass on that bit of information. Anyway the policeman had only asked when they had learned he was there, not when anyone else had found out. 'Not until we got back,' she said. 'I saw his photo in the paper. The *Daily Mail*, I think it was.'

'We had no bleeding idea he was just down the road,' Lily agreed. 'I'm glad we didn't know. He used to beat Mavis and the children and it would have ruined the kids' holiday if they'd seen him.'

The tall policeman shut his notebook. 'Very well, Mrs Pugh, Mrs Culling. We may have more questions for you at a later date. However, we can also inform you that your fiancé, Thomas Wilson, was arrested this morning.'

Mavis gasped and put her hands to her face. 'Arrested? Why?'

'For the suspected murder of Charles Collier, otherwise known as Alec Pugh.'

Pete stared at the envelope in his hands as he sat in the café, his tea growing cold in front of him. His hands shook. The letter of final notice from the bank had arrived that morning and he could no longer delay the inevitable. He'd been kidding himself that if he kept his fingers crossed a miracle would happen but it wasn't to be. The bank wanted their money back and they wanted it now. He knew he didn't have it.

He'd been first up at home and had checked the post, as he had done every day since they'd got back from holiday. Thank God Lily was too

257

busy getting Bobby ready for the picnic and going on about having her roots done. He'd told her he had something to sort out at work and left early, and had come round to the café near the market to read the details of the letter. He didn't want to risk a repeat of the other day, with Mavis or Lily catching sight of it.

'Do you want a top-up?' asked the waitress. 'A drop of hot?'

'Nah, I'm all right.'

'Do you fancy something to eat; a fry-up?'

Pete shook his head, the thought of food turning his stomach. 'No thanks. I had something earlier,' he replied with a forced smile.

The waitress moved off as a group of shoppers arrived, struggling with heavy bags of fruit and veg. Pete slumped in relief. He didn't want to be disturbed. He had to think hard. He'd kept going by robbing Peter to pay Paul, but now he'd been caught out. He hadn't been able to drum up anything extra over the past weeks. His last hope had been that the council bigwig had returned to London by the time they all got back, but there was still no word. He had to face it: the major project wasn't happening. Or, if it did, it would be too late for him. He'd be bankrupt before it began and if he wasn't careful they'd all be homeless as well.

Pete began to run through his dwindling list of remaining options. No other bank would touch him – they'd see he was a bad risk, and he had no remaining family to ask for help. He prided himself on principle never to ask friends for a loan, and when it came down to it most of his mates didn't have much in the bank at the best of times. Pete thought hard. What about Tommy? He'd said that he was doing well and that there had been a flood of enquiries just before they'd left for their trip, and he'd even done some business while they were in Devon. That must mean he was pretty successful.

With a small groan of anguish, Pete slumped over the table. He hated to do this, to ask Tommy for a loan, but he had no choice. It had to be done and he'd have to swallow what was left of his pride and go cap-in-hand to the younger man. At least Tommy was practically family now, and what were families for if not to help one another out in times of need.

That thought made Pete feel slightly better and, abandoning his cold tea untouched, he set off before he lost his nerve.

Chapter Twenty-Six

It was after ten o'clock that morning by the time Rhona left her house. She'd delayed visiting Penny until her conscience wouldn't let her put it off any longer. She should have gone after speaking to Jeff yesterday, but her mum had her dinner waiting and she was late enough as it was. It was the excuse her mind provided and she had still been looking for excuses that morning. Her mother had asked her to run to the shops to get bread and milk, so that had served to delay her, and besides she reasoned, it would look funny turning up at

Penny's house before at least ten o'clock.

Rhona still didn't know what she could say to soften the blow of Gary's desertion. She'd been kept awake for ages fruitlessly trying to think of a way. Realistically she doubted that Gary would have stood by Penny, though Penny wouldn't want to hear that. She still thought the sun shone out of his arse, but Rhona cursed him for being a self-centred, fame-hungry coward who slept with women and then dropped them whenever it suited him.

She ran through the alternatives for Penny in her head. Have the baby, keep it, and get sent to Coventry by everyone. Have the baby, give it up for adoption, never see it again or know what became of it. Try to find a safe back-street abortionist ... no, not an option. Try to find Gary ... no, he was hardly going to drop everything and make an honest woman of Penny when he'd just been given the prospect of an endless line of fans and backing singers to get off with. Whichever way she looked at it, Rhona was stumped.

She had to ring the doorbell three times to get a response. Good, at least that probably meant Penny's parents weren't around. Eventually Penny came to the door, looking more bedraggled than ever in a grubby pale-grey dressing gown, her hair still flat and greasy. She couldn't have been more different to the energetic young woman who'd loved to go nightclubbing. There were bags under her eyes and she looked twice her age.

Rhona tried to hide her dismay. At this rate everyone would know something was badly wrong. 'Hiya,' she said, deliberately cheerful.

'Aren't you going to let me in?'

Penny mumbled something and turned to go back inside. Rhona couldn't help noticing that she didn't smell too good.

'Why don't we sit in the back yard?' she suggested. The late summer sun was shining and there wasn't a cloud to be seen. 'Put a bit of colour in your cheeks.'

'If you like.' Penny didn't seem to care either way. 'As long as none of those nosy old bags who live either side of us see me or hear us talking. They'd love to know I'm pregnant. It would give them something to gossip about.'

'We'll keep our voices down, though can I have something cold to drink first. I'm parched.'

'We've got some lemon barley water. Will that do?'

'Lovely. You having some?'

Penny pulled a face. 'I can't keep anything down, not even that. Anyway it tastes funny.'

Rhona shrugged and accepted the cold drink, downing most of it in one gulp. 'Come on, let's go outside.'

'So, have you had any ideas?' Penny asked, almost whispering as she sank onto a wooden bench that was close to the back door.

Rhona hesitated. There was no going back now. She'd better just come out and say it straight. 'Not yet, but I've got some news,' she began carefully, keeping a close eye on her friend. 'Jeff came to see me yesterday evening after work.'

'Jeff!' Penny sat up in surprise. 'Didn't know you knew him.'

'Well, I don't, not really. I met him once at the

basement bar and well, he ... he had news about Gary.'

'Gary? I haven't been to the club so has he sent me a message?' Penny asked eagerly.

Rhona took a deep breath and then said in a rush, 'Penny, you've got to prepare yourself. Gary's gone. He's got into a group as a guitarist and they've left to go on tour.'

Penny stared at her as if she was talking a foreign language. 'What? Don't be daft. He wouldn't do that. He wouldn't go off without telling me. He loves me, he said so.'

'Yeah, well, he's fond of telling girls that he loves them,' said Rhona, 'me included.'

'Don't be nasty, Rhona.'

'Penny, I'm sorry, I didn't mean to make it worse, but he's gone, love. He didn't leave a message for you, or for anyone. He just went off the moment he got the chance and as they're touring, he won't be back any time soon.'

Penny stared at her. She had gone even whiter and the purple bags under her haunted eyes stood out like fresh bruises. 'He can't have,' she whispered. 'He loves me. He does. He says so all the time. He wouldn't do this to me. It's a mistake.'

'Penny, it isn't a mistake.' Rhona put an arm around her. 'Listen to me. It's the truth. I'm really sorry, but that's what has happened. Gary's gone off to be a pop star and he's left his old life behind.'

Suddenly Penny gave a loud howl and pushed Rhona away. 'Stop it! You're lying to me! It's all a plot so you can get Gary back. Well it isn't going to work! He loves me, not you! He hasn't gone away, he wouldn't. He loves me and chose me

262

over you. Get away from me, and stop telling me these horrible lies. It's not true, he hasn't gone!'

'He has, Penny,' said Rhona as she tried to rub Penny's back to comfort her.

Tears of anguish began to flow down Penny's cheeks. 'He can't have gone, he can't have left me.'

'He has,' Rhona insisted again, 'and I'm really sorry.'

'No...' wailed Penny, burying her face in her hands. She rocked to and fro while Rhona continued to rub her back, thinking that if the neighbours were in earshot and hadn't known before, they certainly would now.

'Come on, Penny,' she urged after a while. 'If Gary had loved you, he wouldn't have just gone off without a word. He's not worth your tears and I'm not just saying that because he dumped me, it's the truth.'

'Oh, Rhona, what am I going to do?' Penny sobbed.

'We'll think of something,' Rhona said gently, but in truth, she had no idea what advice she could offer.

The sun beat down on them and flies buzzed about the dustbin by the back wall, their drone audible between the sobs, but then suddenly Penny abruptly stood up and leaned forward, clutching her stomach as she cried, 'Rhona, something's wrong. Oh, it hurts!'

Rhona saw it then; the pool of red liquid that was seeping through Penny's dirty dressing gown. When it began to run down the inside of her legs, Penny saw it too and screamed, 'What's wrong me? Why am I bleeding? Help, Rhona!'

Rhona felt panic rising in her chest but knew that somehow she had to do something. She put her arm around Penny and said as calmly as she could, 'Come on, we have to get you inside. Lean on me.'

Penny moaned in pain with every step but she kept going, trembling and unsteady on her feet but held up by Rhona. With her free shoulder, Rhona shoved open the back door and almost dragged Penny inside, where she collapsed onto the floor beside the small kitchen table.

Rhona saw a tea towel and hoping it was clean she grabbed it. 'Here, we need to put this between your legs. It'll stem the bleeding,' she said, frightened for Penny and though trying to stay calm, she couldn't put coherent thoughts into order.

There was a gasp then, and looking up Rhona saw Penny's mother in the doorway, looking in horror at the scene before her. 'What happened?' she cried. 'What's wrong with Penny?'

Rhona could have cried with relief and at last her mind cleared. 'Penny needs to go to hospital. I'm going to ring for an ambulance,' she said hurriedly and ran out of the kitchen, down the short hall and out into the sunny street, trying to remember in which direction to turn for the phone box. For a moment Rhona couldn't see it and panicked, but then noticed its bright red paintwork further down the road.

She sprinted towards it, and once inside with shaking hands she picked up the handset to dial the emergency services. It was only when she was told that an ambulance would be sent, that Rhona slumped. She leaned against the glass in the telephone booth, reliving what had just happened. Anger rose that Gary had buggered off without even knowing that Penny was carrying his baby and it was probably the anguish and distress that caused Penny to miscarry.

But slowly Rhona's anger subsided as she realised that though it was awful, losing the baby was probably for the best.

Chapter Twenty-Seven

Tommy sat on the narrow concrete ledge with his head in his hands. The small cell was stiflingly hot, the only light coming from a tiny barred window high up one wall. There was hardly any furniture and the place smelt of strong disinfectant with an undercurrent of something deeply unpleasant. In the distance he could hear muffled voices but there was nobody within calling distance. Not that it mattered because he had nothing to say.

He couldn't believe the events of the past few hours. He'd been asleep in bed early on Saturday morning when the police had pounded on his door. He'd let them in without much concern, but now wished he'd played it differently; that he hadn't been so offhand, but it most likely wouldn't have altered things. He'd still have ended up in a cell.

He'd laughed in their faces until they told him who they'd talked to. The Devon police had been busy, after a tip-off. They'd spoken to Mrs

Hawkins. She'd informed them that before dinner last evening he had ordered a taxi to take him somewhere – she thought for something to do with work. The police had poured scorn on that because they'd talked to the taxi driver, who told them exactly where he'd gone and how long he'd had to wait. In fact it was the driver who had come to them, after recognising the picture of the dead man in the papers, and reading about the appeal for witnesses. He'd seen the man in an altercation with Tommy on the cliffs so had come forward.

They'd asked to check his shoe cupboard and taken away the pair of sandals that he'd bought while in Torquay. There was still sand clinging to the soles which they'd checked very carefully and he was deeply worried because after what the taxi driver had told the police, he couldn't deny that he'd been on those cliffs and that he'd met Alec there.

Tommy wasn't sure exactly what the taxi driver could have seen, but maybe when interviewed again he'd be able to persuade the police that it was just a heated discussion. How he wished now that he'd asked the driver to go after dropping him off, and then found some other way of getting back to the pub.

He didn't know when he'd be interviewed again. For now they had left him in this gloomy hot cell in the local station, probably to make him sweat. He knew that in all likelihood he'd eventually be put up before the magistrate and hoped then that he'd be allowed bail. On a charge of murder it would be set high, but somehow, rather than be stuck on remand, he'd have to raise it. Bearing in mind what he had been prepared to offer Alec Pugh, he could find a decent amount, but even that might not be enough. Tommy groaned. He dreaded to think what Mavis would make of all this. Would the police think that she was an accomplice? No, surely they wouldn't arrest her as well? Angrily he stood up and paced around the cell, just a few steps long and two steps wide. He hit out at the wall in frustration, wincing when he saw the blood on his knuckles.

He had to face it: this might mean he couldn't marry Mavis. Even though they'd waited for it for so long, would it be better for her if he broke off their engagement?

Pete had been expecting an empty house when he got home. Instead the flat was full of people: Grace and Bobby upset because the picnic hadn't happened, James and Greg sullen for the same reason but taking their disappointment out on a football in the yard. Jenny looking stricken and Mavis was in floods of tears.

Loudest of all was Lily, furious about something and saying before he could get a word in, 'You've got to do something about this, Pete.'

'Hang on, hold your horses,' he said, taking a step back. 'Do something about what?'

Lily told him.

Pete felt the room tilt and he grabbed on to the table to steady himself. On top of the injustice of the arrest, there was his last hope gone. Tommy would be in no state to help him financially if he was locked up.

'Oh, Pete, it's awful, isn't it,' exclaimed Jenny, mistaking his reaction. 'We don't believe a word of it. Tommy wouldn't do such a thing.'

'Course not.' Pete tried to pull himself together. 'It was an accident, stands to reason. They're trying to make something out of nothing. They'll have to let him out 'cos I don't believe there's any evidence against him.'

'That's just what I said!' Lily insisted. 'Tommy wouldn't hurt a fly and we all know that.'

Mavis nodded through her tears. 'Thanks, Mum. It has got to be some sort of crazy mistake,' Mavis said, but in her head she kept thinking back to that moment when she realised Tommy had known Alec was in Torquay. She cast her mind back to all the times he'd promised to keep her safe and now couldn't help fearing about what he'd been doing on that last evening in Devon. Had he really been to a business meeting? Then she berated herself. Tommy was a good man and she refused to doubt him. Somehow she had to stay positive. She had to prepare herself. Some people were going to think the worst of him, but she wouldn't be one of them.

Whatever Tommy was doing that last evening, he'd have had his reasons – but killing Alec would not have been one of them.

Rhona spent the weekend in a state of anxiety; waiting for news of Penny. She'd run back to the house and held her hand waiting for the ambulance, as Penny's mother had almost collapsed with shock when she realised what was going on. Rhona could tell that she was going to be very angry with her daughter when all this was over, but for the time being she rallied and by the time the ambulance arrived she told Rhona very curtly that her presence wasn't necessary and that she should go home. Not being a relative, Rhona didn't have a leg to stand on when it came to riding in the ambulance or visiting her friend if Penny's mother was set against it. She didn't even know which hospital they were headed for.

Not knowing what else to do, Rhona thought about ringing Jeff. She had to talk to somebody and he seemed the least likely to gossip. He'd even asked her to ring him once she'd broken the news of Gary's betrayal, to let him know how it went. She'd never met a man who was so concerned and because part of her thought it was too good to be true, she didn't call him straight away.

On Sunday after tea Rhona went to the nearest phone box to her house and took out the scrap of paper with his number on it. Jeff had told her he had his own flat so at least she wouldn't have to cope with an angry stranger picking up the shared phone in the communal hall, as she'd had to when ringing Gary. They were probably used to the calls coming in at all hours for him and resented every one of them.

This time Jeff answered almost at once. He sounded pleased to hear from her.

'So, how was it? Did you tell her?'

'Yeah, of course I did.' Rhona wound the flex from the receiver around her finger. 'It was awful though.' She told him as simply as she could what had happened. 'And now I don't know how she is, because her mother wouldn't let me come with them in the ambulance and she doesn't want to see me at the hospital. I don't even know if Penny's been kept in or which one it is.'

'Bloody hell,' Jeff sounded shocked. 'The poor girl. I don't know what to say. All I know is, even if she had told Gary about the baby, I don't think it would have changed his mind. He'd still have gone with the group.'

'Yes, I think so too,' said Rhona. 'Nothing else would have mattered to him and if she'd told him he would probably have told her to get rid of it.'

'At least she's got you,' Jeff said.

'That's not saying much, is it?' said Rhona bitterly. 'I don't know. I just feel helpless. I didn't know what to do when I saw the blood and I panicked. I've never seen anything like it.' Then she stopped herself saying anything more. Maybe Jeff was one of those men who didn't like to think about such things.

'You did what you could, and it seems unfair that you're not allowed to see her,' he said, not sounding offended or put off. 'I may be able to help you there though. My brother used to work in a hospital and I know how things work. Why don't I ring the local hospitals in your area to see if she's in any of them? I can pretend to be a relative if they ask.'

'Would you?' Rhona was impressed.

'Yes, of course. I'll do it now while it's still early. Do you want to meet for a drink later to cheer you up a bit? I might have an answer by then.'

'Don't you live a good distance away?' Rhona asked. 'I thought you were near Gary's old place.'

'Sort of but I'm closer to the centre. How about

Soho, for old times' sake? Just a pub, nothing special.'

Rhona thought for a moment. 'OK, but I can't stay out late. I've got work tomorrow.'

'So have I, and I don't want to start the week with a sore head. How about the Dog and Duck? Do you know it?'

'Of course,' said Rhona. 'I'll see you there, in about an hour.'

Leaving the phone box, she cast a glance at herself in a nearby window. He'd have to take her as he found her. A few months ago she wouldn't have dreamed of going out with a man without putting on full make-up and the perfect outfit. Now there was no time and, anyway, this wasn't a date. She was only meeting him to find out if he'd traced what hospital Penny was in. Jeff had previously made it clear that they were just going to be friends, and that was definitely all she wanted as well. She certainly wasn't interested in anything else. Gary had put her off men for life.

Somehow Mavis managed to get through the weekend, constantly reassuring herself that even though Tommy was still being held at the station it was all a misunderstanding. She'd done her best to explain to the children but it wasn't easy. None of them knew what would happen next. She tried hard to keep her spirits up, to believe that it would all be sorted out quickly, but she couldn't get over the sensation of being back in limbo, not knowing what was going to happen, and being powerless to do anything about it. It felt like a punishment for daring to be happy so soon after Alec had died; for dreaming of a bright future.

Tommy had got himself a solicitor, who had managed to send her a message to inform her of what had happened so far. It had arrived by second post on Monday, but as she couldn't read it, she'd had to ask her mother what it said.

'He's been before the magistrate and they've set bail ... oh my God, Mavis, that's a huge amount. What have they gone and done that for? He ain't likely to run off anywhere, not with you and his business here in London. Where would he go? All his family's here as well. That's just picking on him, that is.' She read on. 'He says he doesn't like to ask but can we see if Pete could lend him any money? He's going to ask Stan as well. Finally he sends his love of course.'

Mavis blinked back more tears. 'Doesn't he say when we can go to see him?'

'No, but it may be because he doesn't want you to see him in that place. You'll see him once he gets bail. When Pete comes in we'll ask him about the money.'

The new term had started and Mavis had picked the children up from school by the time that Pete came home later that day. She was pouring a cold drink for Grace in her mother's kitchen, because Lily kept Ribena there for a treat. Mavis thought the little girl deserved it. It wasn't her fault that all the adults around her were so upset and distracted.

'All right, Mavis?' Pete said heavily, dropping on to a chair. 'What you got there, Grace?'

'Ribena.'

'Well ain't you a lucky girl,' he said, but it didn't

sound as if his heart was in it.

Lily rushed in, just a minute behind him, back from the hairdresser's where she'd finally had her roots done. Pete reached up to hug her.

'Good to see you're back early, Pete, we've got something to ask you,' Lily said with no pre-amble. 'We've heard from Tommy's lawyer.'

'Oh?' Pete raised his head. Maybe if Tommy was being released he could still ask him for the money.

'They've charged him and set bail. Look.' Lily showed him the letter.

Pete groaned and pitched forward, his head in his hands.

'I know, I know, it's a lot of dosh,' said Lily, 'but we can help him, can't we? He's almost family. You must have some put by from all the work you've had, and Tommy is sure to pay it back when they let him out. They're bound to do that soon too 'cos there's no way Tommy murdered Alec Pugh and I refuse to believe they've got even a shred of evidence against him.'

'Lily, Lily,' Pete's voice cracked. 'I'd love to help, of course I would. Tommy's a great bloke, but I've got something to tell you though I wish I didn't, especially on top of all this. I hoped to avoid telling you, to find a way out, but I can't and you'd have to know sooner or later so it might as well be now.'

'Pete, you're babbling. What are you on about?'

He ran his hand over his forehead and through what was left of his hair, his eyes closing momentarily before looking at her in despair.

'What is it, Pete?' Lily stared at him in sudden concern. 'Don't look like that, you're frightening me. Are you sick or something?'

'I wish I was. You'd all be all right then. No, it's much worse.' Pete paused, unable to get the words out. 'It's like this. I can't lend Tommy any money because I haven't got any. In fact I was gonna ask him if he could help me out, but then he got arrested.'

'No money! Don't be daft, of course you've got money.'

'No, and I'm so sorry, Lily. I didn't want it to come to this. I been working away like mad, trying to sort it all out, but it's no good. If I don't get something in soon, we're gonna lose the house.'

Lily and Mavis stared at him in disbelief. 'No, that can't be right,' Lily gasped. 'I don't believe you. We own the house, it's all done and dusted. You must have got your figures all wrong or something. The stress of what's happened to Tommy must have addled your brain.'

'No, Lil. I wish that was all it was.' Pete sighed heavily. 'Listen to me, both of you.' And he poured out everything that he'd been keeping to himself since they'd moved in: the mortgage loan, the big construction project that he was sure would fund it, the problems at the council with the elusive official who had the final say-so, and then the final letter from the bank. 'So, you see, they'll want the house back.'

'The house?' Lily repeated, as if in shock.

Mavis grabbed the back of a chair to stop herself falling. They were going to be homeless, and this on top of Tommy being accused of murder.

Pete just nodded.

'But you own the house,' said Lily, baffled.

'You do don't you?' Mavis added, dread settling on her like a heavy chill despite the heat of the day.

'Not quite.' Pete sighed deeply. 'I got it on a mortgage, like I said. A big one. If I can't make the payments then the bank will want it back. That's the whole building, but when I took out the mortgage I didn't think there would be a problem. When I did the deal everything was fine, money was coming in regular from small jobs, but there was a big job coming up which I pinned everything on and I was as good as promised I'd get it. There was nothing to worry about, I thought nothing could possibly go wrong.' He spread his hands. 'How was I to know it would all come to a standstill? I've been going to meetings about it since we moved in, and they always say everything's fine, the contract's just around the corner, and I believed them.' For a minute it looked like he was going to break down but he shook his head and straightened his shoulders. 'I've been hoping against hope to spare you this, but things have gone too far. Tommy getting arrested was the last straw.'

Lily gaped at him. 'Oh my God, Pete. What are we gonna do?'

Pete looked at her with desperate sadness. 'As of this moment, sweetheart, I don't know. I just don't know.'

Lily gazed around her kitchen, every bit of which had been put together with such love and hope. She wouldn't let the bank have it. This was hers and nobody was going to take it from her. 'We'll pawn or sell stuff,' she said. 'I've had to do it in the past and I can do it again. I'll sort out

stuff I can get good prices for and though it's
been a while since I did any selling, I doubt I've
lost my touch. Well raise some money. The bank
isn't going to turf us out of our home.'

Mavis nodded resolutely. 'You can have my
locket,' she said as she drew it out from the neck-
line of her dress. 'I think it is worth quite a bit.
Tommy gave it me as an early birthday present,'
and now she had to hold back a sob at the memory of it.

'And the christening presents,' said Lily, determined now. 'Bobby was given all sorts of stuff for
his christening, some of it real silver. We'll use
that and pay it back to him when he's older.'

Pete shook his head. 'I don't want you losing all
your precious things. I know you mean well but
it's a drop in the ocean compared to what I owe.'

'If it puts us off being evicted for even a week
or two, it's worth doing,' Lily said as she held out
her hand. 'Mavis, I hate to take your locket but I
will.'

Mavis handed it over. 'Tommy would understand, and I'll go all out to sell more sketches.'

Pete looked away as if he couldn't bear to watch.
'I hate to do this to you. I should have been able
to stop it but no matter what I did it wasn't
enough. All this trouble because one man is away
from his office. You wouldn't think it could happen
and nobody seems to know when Andreou will get
back.'

'Andreou? That's a strange name,' said Lily as
she took the locket. 'Don't worry, if I pawn it, we
can make sure you get it back one day.'

'Yes, I know, Mum,' said Mavis, more to comfort

Pete than because she actually believed it.

Grace had been sitting there watching them all this time but now she spoke up. 'It's not a strange name. My friend's called that.'

Everyone looked at her.

'Really?' said Lily.

'Are you sure, Grace?' asked Mavis. 'You've got lots of friends. You might be getting mixed up.'

Grace put down her Ribena with dignity. 'I'm not silly. I'm not a baby and I don't get mixed up.'

'No, of course not,' said Lily. 'So who's your friend?'

'She's Maria Andreou and she's in my class at school. She learnt to swim with her granddad, I told you that ages ago. Everyone knows her because she always goes at the front of the line and her name gets called first on the register. It's because it begins with an A,' Grace explained.

'Maria. Maria.' Mavis tried to picture the girls in Grace's class as they poured out of the school gates each day. 'Is she the one with the very dark hair?'

Grace nodded. 'Yes, it's black. Darker than yours, Mummy. It's because her granddad comes from far away.' She stopped as she remembered something. 'She's been sad since we started school again. Her granddad died. You're not going to die, are you?' She looked up anxiously at Pete. 'I don't want you to die. Is that why you're all sad?'

Mavis reached down and hugged her daughter tightly. 'No, none of us is going to die. Not for a very long time. I expect Maria's granddad was very old and got sick, but we aren't old yet so you don't have to worry.' She thought for a moment. 'Is her mummy the one with the black hair too, all piled up on top of her head?'

'Yes, and she puts her sunglasses on her hair,' said Grace. 'I'm going to grow mine so I can do that when I'm big.'

'Sounds like the same family,' said Pete, scratching his head to recall the personal details. 'Someone did say something about family illness, back in Cyprus or somewhere like that.'

Lily looked at Mavis over the top of Grace's head. 'So you know her mother, do you?'

Mavis shook her head. 'Not really. Only in passing, you know, going in and out of the playground.'

'Still, you know her a bit. Enough to talk to her.' Lily gave her a significant stare.

'Mum, I'm not sure if that would be a good thing...' Mavis trailed off. It seemed like such a long shot. The woman was always so glamorous, she'd thought her unapproachable and somebody she was unlikely to mix with. Then again, what did she have to lose? If she did nothing they'd probably lose the house. 'All right,' she said, touching her neck where the locket usually was. 'I'll speak to her.'

Chapter Twenty-Eight

Penny looked up as the curtain that surrounded her hospital bed moved. 'Penny, is that you in there?' said a voice.

Penny gave a small smile. 'Rhona. How did you manage to get in?'

Rhona slipped around the edge of the curtain. 'With difficulty. Bleedin' matrons asking questions, am I related, do I know what the time is.' She gazed heavenwards. 'As if I wouldn't have come earlier if I could have. Jean let me leave half an hour early as it was.'

'You didn't tell Jean you were coming here, or why,' Penny exclaimed, alarmed. 'I don't want anyone to know.'

Rhona settled herself in the visitor's chair. 'I told her I had a dentist's appointment. She won't know any different.' She reached into her bag and brought out a selection of magazines. 'Here. I got you these.'

'Thanks.' Penny looked relieved. 'I thought it was going to be grapes for a minute. I'm sick of the flipping things. Never liked them in the first place, especially when I had to stack the boxes down the warehouse.' She grinned.

'Me neither.' Rhona took in her friend's appearance as she half-sat, half-lay on the bed. 'You look a bit better, Penny. How do you feel?'

Penny's face grew serious again. 'That's the

funny thing. I ought to feel awful but I don't. I was so miserable before, what with being sick all the time and being petrified about what my mum would say when she found out I was pregnant. Then when you told me that Gary had gone without so much as a word I thought my heart would break, but the pain I felt was losing the baby. Now, lying here, I've had time to think and I know now that it was the best thing that could have happened.'

'I know I said you look better, but you still look a bit pale. Are you all right?'

'Yeah, I am now. You don't want to know the details, but I think it was touch and go for a bit. That's why they're keeping me in. The miscarriage was quite an early one but I did lose a lot of blood. They said I was lucky. If you hadn't called the ambulance so quickly, I might not have made it. Thanks, Rhona.'

'Well your mum would have done it if I hadn't,' Rhona pointed out.

Penny looked rueful. 'If you remember the state she was in when she saw me, I doubt she'd have acted as swiftly. She was really nice when she thought I was dying, but as soon as I began to recover she started calling me a disgrace to the family and a slut and everything. She's furious with me and now I dread her visits. I just hope she calms down soon.'

Rhona reached for Penny's hand. 'I feel so guilty. I handled telling you that Gary had left badly. Was it the shock that caused your miscarriage?'

Penny shook her head. 'No, don't worry. I

asked the doctor if he knows why it happened, and he said it was an ectopic pregnancy so there's no need for you to blame yourself.'

Rhona didn't know what an ectopic pregnancy was, but breathed a sigh of relief that she hadn't caused it. She'd been feeling bad ever since that fateful conversation in Penny's back yard. 'How long are you in here for, do you know?'

'They won't say. A few more days at least. Will you come again?'

'If I can,' said Rhona. 'I think your mum is blaming me so I've got to avoid her.'

Penny shrugged. 'She's got to blame someone. She reckons it was you what led me astray in the first place.'

'I didn't have to do much leading,' said Rhona with a grin that she hoped would cheer Penny up.

'She doesn't believe it. She still thinks I'm her little girl, or at least she did,' said Penny. 'I bet she didn't tell you I was in here. How did you find out?'

'Jeff made a few phone calls,' said Rhona. 'He rang all the nearest hospitals, spoke with authority, claimed he was related to you and wanted to check if you'd been brought in.'

Penny looked at her friend with interest. 'Have you been seeing a lot of him, then?'

Rhona shook her head. 'No, only a couple of times. Stop making that face, there's nothing in it.'

'What face?' Penny exclaimed indignantly. 'I'm only asking. I wouldn't have thought he was your type – he's nothing special to look at, though he's quite sweet. You wouldn't call him dishy though.'

Rhona thought for a moment. 'No, I don't suppose you would. Then again Gary was good-looking and the spitting image of Brian Jones, but what good did that do us?'

Penny looked crestfallen again so Rhona added hastily, 'Sorry, I didn't mean to rub it in. My mouth runs away with me at times and I speak without thinking.'

'It's all right. I've done a lot of thinking these past few days and I can see Gary more clearly now. If he'd loved me he wouldn't have buggered off without a word, though maybe if I had told him about the baby it might have made a difference.'

'I doubt it,' Rhona said. 'The chance of joining a group would have been too much for him to turn down.'

Penny sighed. 'Yeah, you're probably right, but anyway, it's too late now. He's gone, I've lost the baby, and to be honest, if he showed his face again I'd tell him to get lost.'

'Good for you,' said Rhona encouragingly. 'You can do miles better than him. Just you wait, we'll get you down the Talisman as soon as you're back on your feet again.'

'Who's "we"?' asked Penny with a gleam in her eye. 'You and Jeff?'

'He's just a mate,' said Rhona firmly. 'I'm done with men. I like him as a friend and that's that.'

When she arrived at the school gates, Mavis spotted Mrs Andreou immediately. It made her nervous. She'd been prepared every day to start a conversation with the glamorous woman, but then found Mrs Andreou hadn't turned up and little Maria went home with various friends. As the days ticked by Mavis grew more anxious. Pete had to know about the contract, and Tommy still hadn't been released. The only thread of hope she could hold on to was the chance of speaking to Melina to find out what was going on with the construction project.

The chilly breeze hinted that autumn was on its way and Mavis shivered. She drew her thin cardigan around her shoulders, as she scanned the crowd of children for Grace. Her daughter should have been easy to spot as she was in a bright purple jumper that Jenny had knitted for her as a surprise, but Mavis couldn't see her yet.

'We've seen the last of summer, haven't we?'

Startled, Mavis almost jumped at hearing the voice. While she'd been looking for Grace, the very person she wanted to talk to had come to her side. 'Y ... yes,' she replied, frantically thinking how she could steer the conversation towards the right direction, 'it's turned colder today. You're Maria's mother, aren't you?'

The woman patted her smooth dark hair and Mavis noticed she was wearing the famous sunglasses, despite the change in the weather. 'Yes, I'm Melina. You must be Grace's mother?'

'That's right. My name is Mavis.'

'Pleased to meet you, Mavis,' said Melina, in a voice that had a very slight accent.

'Have you been away for the summer?'

'Yes, we have. My poor husband lost his father, back in Cyprus. As the oldest son he had a lot to sort out. We have only just returned.'

'I'm sorry to hear that,' said Mavis.

'Maria missed her usual summer holiday, but we will make it up to her.'

'We went to Devon and it was lovely,' Mavis told her, 'but everyone's returned to work now.' She waited to see what the response would be.

'My poor husband must go back to his office next week.'

'Oh, thank goodness,' Mavis blurted out and then could have kicked herself as Melina looked at her strangely.

'You seem very pleased to hear that. Do you know my husband?'

Despite almost putting her foot in it, Mavis decided it was now or never and began nervously, 'N ... no, but I think my stepfather does. He ... he's a builder, Peter Culling, and I think he's waiting for a decision about a new housing project. I ... I seem to remember him mentioning your husband's name.'

Melina's lips tightened. 'Yes, there were several calls from my husband's office while we were away, but it was remiss of them to expect him to make a decision on this matter while he was in mourning for his father.'

'But he's back next week?' Mavis confirmed, thinking how pleased Pete would be at that news.

'Yes, he is,' Melina said bluntly, then looked to the side. 'Do excuse me, there is somebody I must talk to.' She nodded politely but swiftly, and moved away towards another woman in a very smart, short coat.

Mavis remained where she was, and noticed that some of the other mothers were looking at her and whispering to each other. Dread settled cold and hard in her stomach. Had word got round and her name was tainted by association with Tommy? How dare they judge? Tommy was innocent, and when it was proved she would cock her nose at the lot of them. She pushed her shoulders back, determined not to let them get to her, and then a small figure in a purple jumper emerged from the door on the other side of the tarmac yard.

'Grace,' she called, waving at her daughter.

As Grace ran up to her, Mavis was at least pleased that she could tell Pete that a decision about the project might be made next week. However, as she took Grace's hand to set off home, Melina and the other women that she had gone to talk to, turned to look at her. Mavis smiled and raised her hand to wave goodbye, but neither woman responded. Her stomach turned. Had Melina just heard about Tommy? If she had, she was sure to tell her husband and, by association, it could prevent Pete from getting the contract.

Mavis held back a sob and knew it would take every ounce of strength she possessed to get home with Grace without weeping bitter tears.

Chapter Twenty-Nine

Rhona sat on the number 29 bus as it slowly lumbered its way through Camden. She felt nervous at the thought of going to Jeff's flat; not at the thought of seeing him, but of making a mess of playing a guitar. Her lessons with Gary seemed like ages ago. What if she couldn't remember the most basic stuff, like how to hold it properly? She didn't want Jeff to think she was so useless that trying to teach her to play the guitar would be a complete waste of time.

The bus was full of workers coming back from the centre of town, a lot of them struggling to read their newspapers. The pages were too big to turn easily in the crowded conditions but some had mastered the art of folding them carefully and just turning them to the exact story they wanted.

Rhona watched them curiously, glad of something to take her mind off the next couple of hours. Nobody she knew read the broadsheets, and she only read the occasional magazine. She tried to read the headlines over the shoulder of a short man in front, but he must have sensed what she was doing and turned slightly so that she couldn't see.

She looked out of the window and counted the stops. Jeff had said he'd wait for her and she would start watching out for him just after the station. Lots of people got off at that stop and she could see the road ahead more clearly. There he was, leaning against a lamppost, hands in his jacket pockets. She got up to ring the bell, weaving her way down the aisle of standing passengers. One or two men glanced at her, but there had been a lot more looks when she had worn miniskirts. Today she'd settled for jeans.

Jeff stood up properly as she hopped off the bus. 'You found the right place then.'

'Wasn't hard,' grinned Rhona.

Jeff turned off the main road by a row of shops

and after a couple of minutes he stopped outside a door covered in fading blue paint. 'This is it, and it looks a bit scruffy. The landlord says it's not worth painting the door, but he's happy to let me decorate inside. He runs the launderette downstairs so there's not much noise in the evenings,' Jeff said as he unlocked the door, indicating her to follow him as he bounded up the dark stairwell.

When he opened the door to his flat Rhona was surprised. Light flooded out into the corridor from two big windows in the living room. All the walls were painted white. There were lots of shelves with books on and under the windows were rows and rows of records, LPs and singles, with a record player in the corner. 'Wow,' she said. 'That's the biggest record collection I've ever seen.'

Jeff looked pleased. 'I've been buying them since I was old enough to save up pocket money. Then I got a paper round so I could buy more. Some are really rare, but I won't bore you with those.' He raised his eyebrows and grinned, acknowledging that his obsession might not be everyone else's cup of tea.

Rhona nodded gratefully. She didn't want her lack of knowledge of obscure bands to be exposed. She was all right with music in the charts, or from her favourite singers and groups, but not much beyond that. She noticed a pile of copies of the *New Musical Express* in the corner by the record player.

'How about a cup of coffee before we start?' Jeff went on.

'That would be lovely.' Rhona didn't have high

hopes of a decent cup as the only good coffee she'd had was in the Italian bars of Soho, but it turned out this was one of Jeff's interests too. In his kitchen he had a coffee grinder and a special metal pot which he put on the gas ring. The result was pretty close to what she was used to. She was impressed in spite of herself. 'Not bad, in fact it's great,' she said, sipping at it appreciatively. 'Where did you learn to do this?' She won-dered if a girlfriend had taught him – not that he'd ever mentioned one.

'I got fed up with the stuff they get in at work,' he said. 'They know how to make tea but if you fancy a change it's Camp coffee or nothing. I hated the strong flavour of chicory, so I learnt how to make the real thing. Glad you like it.'

He grinned and Rhona thought he seemed a bit shy, yet pleased when she complimented him. Maybe he wasn't used to it.

'Right, let's get started,' he suggested.

They went back into the living room and Jeff picked up the guitar that was on a stand by the door. 'You can use this one. I'll go and get my other one from the bedroom.'

Rhona craned her neck to look as he went to fetch it but she couldn't see what the bedroom was like from where she was sitting. Not that she was interested, of course, she told herself. It was just nosiness.

'Let's see what you know already,' Jeff suggested as he returned and sat opposite her on the sagging sofa. 'Show me what you can remember.'

Rhona picked up the guitar, and tried to recall what to do. She frowned in concentration. What had Gary taught her? She felt very rusty as she moved her fingers over the frets, then tried a chord. 'No, that's not right…' She readjusted her fingers a little and tried again. 'OK, that was one of them. Or at least I think so.'

'Very good,' said Jeff. 'That's a G major. Useful one to begin with. Any others?'

Rhona racked her brain. 'Yes, I'm sure it'll come back.' After a few attempts she remembered the next one.

'Yes, that's a D,' said Jeff. 'That makes sense, lots of songs use those two chords. Any more?'

'I used to know three.' Rhona tried once more but couldn't quite find it.

'Was it this?' Jeff showed her on his guitar. 'Copy me and see if it sounds familiar.'

Rhona moved her fingers again and strummed the strings. 'Maybe. I can't really remember.'

'That's C,' said Jeff. 'Also useful when you know G. Try to go from one to the other. Slowly at first.'

Rhona had a go but it didn't sound as smooth as when Jeff did it. She kept missing a note or slipping. 'It's no good,' she said, angry at her lack of progress. 'I thought I had mastered this bit at least, but now it sounds like I've never played a guitar before. I can't have any talent at all.'

Jeff looked at her and a smile crept over his face. Rhona realised he had a lovely smile, one she had noticed briefly when he came to the factory. She'd been too busy focusing on what he'd told her about Gary and how it would impact on Penny to realise that when he smiled, Jeff was not bad-looking at all – just not as obvious as the men she used to go for.

'Don't be daft,' he said. 'It been a long time since you've had a chance to practise, that's all. You'll be fine. You just need to keep at it until you get it right.'

Rhona hoped he wasn't patronising her. That would be unbearable. She really wanted to do this, not just for her, but to please Jeff too. He'd given up his evening when he could have been out at a concert or even out with another girl. She owed it to him to concentrate and get this right. She nodded, 'Yeah, all right. I'm impatient, that's the trouble.'

Jeff turned serious. 'You won't get far with this unless you work at it, and there's no way round it. Yes, you could be flash like Gary, learn lots of tricks but have hardly any real musical technique. That's not what you want, is it?'

Rhona shook her head. She knew this was her chance to learn properly, and without all the overtones that had come with playing Gary's guitar. 'I really want to get it right,' she said, her voice full of determination. 'I love listening to other people play but it's not enough. I want to see if I can do it too. I'm fed up with everyone saying girls can't play guitar.'

'No reason why you can't,' Jeff assured her. 'You can keep rhythm – well, you will when you've got the chords sorted out. I've seen you dance, and heard you sing along to songs in the pub. You've got music running through you. You'll be fine.'

'Really?' Rhona didn't feel any confidence but she desperately hoped he was right and wasn't just saying it to make her feel better. He really did have the kindest eyes, so was that all it was. He was trying to be kind.

'Yes, really,' Jeff echoed.

He looked at her directly and Rhona felt the atmosphere shift. He was looking at her in a new way ... or was she imagining it? She told herself not to be silly and to concentrate.

'Look,' he said. 'Try this one. This is an A major.'

Rhona tried to copy the position of his fingers and strummed but it sounded totally different. She couldn't work out which string she wasn't pressing correctly. She plucked each one in turn but every time it sounded worse than before. 'No, I can't get that. I can tell what it ought to sound like, but I just can't get it right.'

'Like this, on this fret.' Jeff tried again. 'No, further up ... no, too far. Hang on.'

He got up, came behind her, and she could feel the warmth radiating from his body. She went completely still, not sure what he was about to do, but found herself willing him to come closer. He slid in and put one arm around her, hardly touching her, so that he could move her hand along the neck of the guitar.

'Like that,' he said. 'Can you see where you went wrong now? You were nearly there.'

He turned his head so that he was looking straight into her eyes. Their faces were very close and Rhona could feel his breath on her cheeks. 'Yes, I see,' she husked, sure that he was about to kiss her and found that she actually wanted him to.

'Good,' he said, and slipped back again, returning to his chair.

Rhona looked down, hiding her disappointment. She was embarrassed. This was nothing like anything she was used to. Men usually kissed her with confidence and she kissed them back Sometimes she kissed them first. But she didn't want to do that to Jeff – she wasn't sure he'd like a girl who was too forward. Hell, she couldn't tell what he wanted.

Stop it, Rhona told herself. Jeff is just teaching you the guitar, there's nothing else to it. 'OK,' she said, looking up. 'Got it.'

Mavis was shaking as she stood waiting in the corridor. It smelt of disinfectant. She wondered if the cells smelt the same. She was finally about to see Tommy for the first time since his arrest and she was nervous. The solid brick walls of the prison were unforgiving and her heart ached at the thought of him shut up in here. At least the authorities had stopped moving him round, but as he'd ended up on the other side of London she had thought she'd never manage to get there for the short time slot allowed. In the end, seeing as he didn't have any work on at the moment, Pete had offered to drive her. He refused to come in with her, saying he didn't want to infringe on the short time she and Tommy had together, and that anyway, prisons gave him the creeps. Mavis knew exactly what he meant – it was as if the building itself was full of fear and violence – but she couldn't let that put her off. At last Tommy had agreed to see her and she was desperate to see him. It had been weeks since his arrest – the autumn term was well underway and the leaves were falling from the trees, but he wouldn't be able to see them.

It seemed like hours before the guard unlocked the door. 'Here you are. Ten minutes. No personal contact of any kind.' He stood back but didn't leave them alone.

Tommy was thinner than when she'd last seen him, and it was strange to find him in prison scrubs rather than his usual clothes, but his smile was the same, that smile she'd dreamed of so often while they'd been apart. She rushed towards him but the guard called to remind her: 'No personal contact.' She wasn't allowed to touch him, to hug him, no matter how much she wanted to.

'Mavis, you came.' Tommy stood as close to her as he could, hungrily taking in every inch of her with his eyes. 'It's such a long way. I didn't know if you'd make it but I'm so glad you did.'

'Of course I came.' Mavis looked at him longingly. It was unbearable, to be this near and yet not be able to reach out for him. 'Pete brought me, but why didn't you want to see me before? I miss you so much and I wanted to see you to make sure you're all right.'

'I didn't want you to see me like this, in a place like this, and I'm fine,' Tommy said and shuffled a little. 'Look, we can sit down, either side of this table.'

'Are they treating you well?' Mavis began, but Tommy raised his eyebrows and she realised he wasn't going to say much on that subject while there was a prison guard listening in. 'You won't be here for much longer, Tommy. They'll have to let you go because it's plain that you're innocent.'

Tommy shook his head. 'Unless something

comes up to prove that, they'll keep me here until my trial. I'm trying to get my head around it, and so must you, but at least it's great to hear that you think I'm innocent.'

'Of course I do!' Mavis burst out. 'I know you'd never hurt anyone.'

'The fact that you believe in me means a lot.'

'Tommy, it isn't just me who believes in you. We all do, my mum, Pete, Stan and Jenny, and so many others. I'm sure the police will realise that you're innocent soon and then you'll be home.'

'I don't think so, Mavis.' Tommy sighed deeply. 'We have to face it, I might not be out of here for a long time. They've got reason to keep me here. I don't have any alibis for that night, you know that. Mavis, look at me. I hate to say this but they could find me guilty even though I've done nothing.'

'No, Tommy!'

'There are plenty of people in here who haven't done what they're accused of. Things don't always work the way they should. You have to be prepared for me to be in here a long time. If they find me guilty...'

'Tommy!' Mavis was close to crying now, trying hard not to because she didn't want to upset him more than he was already, but the thought was so overwhelming that she couldn't help herself and tears began to roll down her cheeks. 'No, that won't happen, you aren't guilty and they can't lock you up for something you didn't do. I need you back home, and the children keep asking where you are. You have to get out of here. I can't live without you.'

'Mavis.' Tommy swallowed hard. 'Mavis, listen to me. You don't want to be an old maid, shackled to a lifer. I love you more than I can say but I don't want to think of you on your own because of me. Maybe we should call it a day and then you can find someone else, make a go of your life rather than sitting around waiting for me when I might not get out. I'm saying it because I love you, not because I want to get rid of you, but I can't forgive myself for ruining your life.'

Mavis gasped then sat up straight and looked him in the eye, her sobs subsiding. 'Never, Tommy. I don't want anyone else and if I can't have you, I'd rather be on my own. There's no one else for me and there never will be. You're the man I love more than life itself; so don't ever say anything like that to me again. I'll love you forever, whatever happens.' She put her hand to her neck out of habit, but there was nothing there.

'Your locket. It's gone.' Tommy realised at once what she was reaching for.

Mavis could have kicked herself. She didn't want to add to his worries but she'd been found out. 'I'm so sorry, Tommy. We had to pawn it. You know we couldn't raise your bail money because of Pete's work problems. Well, it wasn't just because they set it at such a huge amount. It's because his firm is probably going bust and we're struggling to pay for the house. So Mum took everything valuable to the pawn shop and that got us enough to tide us over. But I will get the locket back as soon as I can, honest.'

'Blimey, that's a relief. I thought you might have taken it off because you'd gone off me,' Tommy tried to joke.

'Never, Tommy,' Mavis replied fiercely. 'Don't you ever think that! I didn't want you to find out about our money problems, or that we might lose the house. You've got enough on your plate.'

Tommy shook his head. 'It's not looking good, is it? Pete's going bust and so am I. Jerry wrote to say all the work I was getting has dried up now I'm in here. Word has got round and everyone's turning their back on the firm. Nobody wants to be tainted by scandal. All those leads I had before we went to Devon, all those promising new contacts have faded away. My name is ruined now. All those years of working to get the firm set up and it's disappearing before my eyes like water down a plug hole. Even if I do get out of here, I'll be back to square one and with hardly a penny to my name.'

Mavis tossed back her hair. 'I don't care, Tommy. Rich or poor, as long as we're together, I'll be happy.' Instinctively she reached for him but once again the guard's voice brought her up short. 'No personal contact, madam. Anyway your time is up.'

Mavis reluctantly rose to go, another sob breaking through. 'Oh Tommy. I'll come again. I love you.'

'I love you too, Mavis,' said Tommy, his dark eyes full of pain. 'I'm sorry I'm putting you through this.'

The guard came forward and began to usher Mavis towards the door. She turned, dashed the tears from her cheeks and said, inwardly praying she was right, 'Don't give up, we're going to get you out of here.'

Tommy watched her go, and had Mavis turned back for a second time before the door closed, she would have seen the look of utter despair on Tommy's face.

Chapter Thirty

Despite everything that was going wrong in her life, Mavis found herself laughing the next evening when Rhona came round to see her. 'Did I hear you right? You're asking me advice about a man? Surely that has got to be a first.'

'Mavis, I'm serious,' Rhona said. 'I know it must sound funny, but I don't know what to do. I can usually tell if a bloke likes me or not, but Jeff is different and I can't read him at all. Oh, I know he likes me as a friend, but I'm not used to that. Men usually make it obvious that they fancy me, but not Jeff. Of course it could be that I've lost a lot of weight and I'm too skinny now, but I'm going to put that right.' She paused to take a bite of the cake Mavis had made and with a mouthful she mumbled. 'Mmmm, this this is gorgeous, Mave, you have got to give me the recipe.'

'You never cook,' Mavis pointed out. She felt better for having her friend round. Something about Rhona made her shake off the all-enveloping despair that was always one heartbeat away these days, and to believe that there might be light at the end of the tunnel after all.

'I'll give it to my mum. She keeps going on about feeding me up. Anyway, where was I? Well, I was round Jeff's place, and he's teaching me these guitar chords, and he practically has his arm round me, but then ... nothing. He just stands back and we go on practising music. I'm really confused.'

Mavis leant forward and put down her own plate. 'Maybe he respects you and wants to get to know you a bit first.'

Rhona pursed her lips in thought. 'Maybe. But he was so close! I could have kissed him. I nearly did but something held me back.'

'What was it, do you think?'

'It's hard to say. I mean, Jeff didn't have to get that close to me, so he must have wanted to, but I'm so unsure of myself when I'm with him.' Rhona tutted impatiently. 'Oh, I don't know why he's getting to me like this. He's not really my type. He's a bit quiet and his clothes are nothing special and yet ... I can't quite describe it. He's really cute, but just not the type of bloke I'm used to. When I'm with him I feel different. He's teaching me the guitar, and is so patient with me, but unlike most blokes who just want to get me into bed, Jeff doesn't ask for anything back. It makes me feel ... I don't know. Special. Like I'm worth something.'

Mavis paused for a moment. 'You know, I've never really put it into words but that's how I feel when I'm with Tommy.' Her voice caught on the last word.

'Oh, I'm sorry!' Rhona cried. 'How stupid of me, boring you with my love-life problems when you must be worried sick about Tommy. I didn't mean to upset you.'

'You haven't,' Mavis assured her. 'I'm glad you're here. I haven't seen you for ages, and it takes me out of myself for a bit. I'm flattered you've asked for my advice. God knows I haven't got much experience with men. I married Alec, and what a mistake that was. Then I met Tommy and it's true, I do feel differently about myself when I'm with him. He makes me feel safe, treasured, cared for, and even now, when just about everything has gone wrong and we are being forced apart, I still feel like that when I think of him. I love him, Rhona, and I always will.'

Rhona gazed out of the window in thought. The curtains were still open but it was nearly dark and she could see the lights on in the houses opposite. Normal daily life was going on, and yet she was full of an emotion she'd never encountered before. She got up and stood by the window, staring out. 'I don't know what to do. I always knew exactly how to handle men before. It was easy. Flirt a bit, let them buy you a drink, giggle, laugh at their jokes, hope they'd be able to get you into clubs and concerts. Nice and straightforward, good clean fun. Now I feel so unsure of myself. What if he really only wants me as a friend?'

Mavis's eyes widened. It didn't seem possible that there was a man on earth who'd be immune to Rhona. 'Has he never asked you out? Not even for a drink?'

'Well...' Rhona remembered the phone call that Sunday evening. 'Sort of. But that was because we had to meet up to discuss a mutual friend.'

She hadn't told Mavis what had happened to Penny because it wasn't her secret to reveal.

'But you did go out?'

'Yeah, we had a few drinks in the pub then went home, separately. He didn't try to kiss me or anything.'

'Maybe that was his way of trying to get to know you first,' Mavis suggested. 'Did you enjoy talking to him?'

'Oh yes. He knows heaps about music, and he doesn't laugh at me when I say I want to learn to play the guitar.' Rhona sighed. 'It just isn't what I'm used to. To be honest, there was never much conversation with other men. I only cared about what they looked like, how they dressed, who they knew and what clubs they were taking me to.' She pulled a face. 'I'm shallow, Mavis. I realise that now.'

'Just because you enjoy having a good time and like ... well ... sex, it doesn't make you a bad person. You haven't robbed anyone, or harmed anyone.' Mavis assured her. 'And now, maybe you just want something more.'

'Yeah, maybe.' Rhona had to admit there was some truth in what Mavis said. 'When I was trapped in that cellar, I kept thinking about my life and sort of felt it flash before my eyes. I knew then that something had to change. I just didn't think I'd end up like this, not knowing what to do about a bloke, and one I have to admit I really like.'

Mavis thought back to when she'd found out about Rhona being attacked and then trapped in a cellar. She'd been horrified at the thought that she might never have seen her friend again, and what a gap that would have left in her life. Rhona could have died from her head injury and no one would have known where she was until it was too late. Perhaps being that close to death was enough to alter anybody's outlook on life. Another memory surfaced then; of Larry cornering her in the alley, the fear of being raped, the horror of being unable to get away, but that had been nothing in comparison to Rhona's dreadful experience.

'What do you think I should do, then?' Rhona asked now.

Mavis knew the main reason that she had been able to put Larry's attack behind her was because she'd had Tommy's love and protection. She hoped that this Jeff was as good a man as Tommy and one who would truly care for Rhona. 'Why not ask him out?'

'But what if he says no? I'd be so embarrassed.'

'You could invite him to join you at a concert, one you know he'd enjoy and then it wouldn't feel like you're asking him on a date.'

'Yes, I could try that I suppose,' Rhona said. 'I'll check the papers to see who's on over the next few weeks. There's bound to be someone we both like. Then at least I'll get a good night out even if he's not interested in me. Oh, I didn't mean that, it sounds selfish, but it's all bravado really. It's just that I seem to have lost my confidence and I hate feeling like this.'

'Just do it, Rhona. Ask Jeff out.'

'Yeah, all right,' she said, wrinkling her nose. 'I keep thinking I can smell something funny.'

'Funny like what?' Mavis wrinkled her nose.

'Like oil or something? Rhona looked around.

'I can't see anything, so I'm probably imagining it. Perhaps that head injury has done something to my sense of smell.'

'Don't be daft,' Mavis said, smiling as she got up and went to a corner of the room to bring something out from behind a chair. 'I think you can smell this?'

Rhona came closer and sniffed. 'Yeah, that's it. What is it?'

Mavis turned it around. 'It's a picture of Grace, James and Bobby. Careful, it's not quite dry, that's why you can still smell it I expect. It's been painted in oil and I did it to take my mind off everything that's going on. It kind of worked, or at least for a while.'

Rhona took a step back in amazement. 'Wow, Mave, I know you used to do a bit of drawing but I never knew you could do stuff like this. It's brilliant. It's almost like a photo but better. How long have you been doing this?'

Mavis looked down in embarrassment. She still felt uneasy when anyone praised her work. All those years of everyone putting her down for being stupid had left their mark. 'For a while now. I did one of Grace on her own, then one of the boys together, which was really hard because Bobby can't sit still for two minutes. I can't bear to think about having to give up this place, so instead of just doing sketches I was thinking of showing these to see if I can get a few commissions. We've already pawned everything we had of any value, and now my mum is talking about going back to collecting secondhand goods and selling them on.'

'Oh no, I bet you thought you'd left all that

behind,' Rhona said sympathetically.

'With things so tight, there isn't any choice. We'll both do pretty much anything we can to keep this place and now that Tommy's landlord has taken his flat back, he'll need somewhere to stay when he's released from prison. Stan and Jenny had to go and get all his furniture and things to put into storage so I'm damned if I'll let the bank take this house away from us. Until we can arrange to get married, we'll just have to live together.'

'I never thought I'd hear you say that.'

'I've changed too, Rhona. I was daft to make Tommy wait so long before I slept with him and I realise that now. I was too frightened to put my trust in a man again, but all Tommy ever seems to think about is my happiness. When I went to see him in prison he even said that if he goes down he doesn't want me to waste my life waiting for him, and suggested that we split up. I wouldn't hear of it.'

'Of course not, and anyway he's sure to be found not guilty.'

'That's what I told him and if the worst happens, which I can't bear to think about, Tommy is the man for me and if I have to wait for him until I'm old and grey, I will.'

'Let's hope that doesn't happen,' Rhona said worriedly.

'Tommy said there are innocent men who have been convicted and I'm so scared, Rhona. What if that happens to Tommy?'

'That isn't going to happen,' Rhona said firmly. 'You wait and see, he'll be home soon and then you can start planning your wedding. I hope you're going to ask me to be a bridesmaid.'

'Of course I will,' Mavis said, pushing her fears to one side. 'I haven't got any sisters and Grace is too little.'

'Mavis, I only suggested that to cheer you up. With my reputation, you won't want me as a bridesmaid.'

'I don't give a damn about what's said about you,' Mavis said. 'You've been a good friend to me through thick and thin. When Tommy gets out we're going to have a wedding that nobody will ever forget and I want you there, right behind me. Do we have a deal?'

'Deal,' said Rhona, giving her friend a big hug. Then she sat back and looked at the oil painting again. 'Mave, I don't know, much about this sort of thing but your picture really is terrific, it really is. If you show it, I feel sure you'll get loads of commissions.'

'I don't know, Rhona. I know this flat is a fair size, but there isn't a proper studio so I can't ask anyone here to sit for their portrait. Not only that, I've seen how the other mothers look at me now when I go to collect Grace from school and it gave me second thoughts. There's so much gossip about Tommy being accused of murder, and orders for sketches of children have all but dried up. I think it's doubtful that anyone will want me to paint their portrait now so I think I'd better stick to helping my mum with selling second-hand goods.'

Rhona stood up and placed her hands on her hips, arms akimbo. 'Yeah, right. Do you really want to go out hoicking stuff about now the

304

weather's getting colder? Come off it, Mave. And people will be a damn sight ruder too, looking down their noses at you. You've got a talent, a proper one, and you've got to use it.' She went across to her friend and stared intently into her eyes. 'Don't you want to make Grace proud of you? You once said she's showing signs of talent too and she might just follow in your footsteps, as an artist, not as a bloomin' hawker.'

'That's a bit below the belt, Rhona.'

'I'm just trying to make you see sense. It's not just you, or even the house, it's for Grace and James too. They don't want to be seeing you flogging tat down the market or wherever. You can do a lot better than that.'

Mavis squirmed under her friend's serious gaze. 'It's so hard, Rhona. It's just me and that box of paints ... and now with all the gossip, I don't have the confidence. I wish I was more like you. You wouldn't take any nonsense from anyone, but I'm really down after all this with Tommy. I feel sort of raw inside and don't want to give people an excuse to hurt me even more.'

Rhona backed off a little, sensing she was pushing Mavis too hard. 'OK, OK,' she said. 'But at least think about what I said. If you show your oil paintings, I'll come with you if you like to boost you up. And in the meantime I might ask a few people if they're interested, just in case. You wouldn't mind that, would you?'

'No,' Mavis admitted.

'Well, then.' Rhona stood up. 'We're going to get you out of this mess, Mavis. You just wait and see.'

'Mavis not here?' asked Stan, bending down to fend off Bobby who'd rushed towards him as he came in through the front door. 'Blimey, Lily, this boys going to be a rugby player, he nearly brought me down with a tackle there.' He rubbed his knees. 'You knew we were picking up James for the afternoon, didn't you?'

'Come on through,' Lily invited. Stan, Jenny and Greg followed as Lily led the way into her sitting room with furniture she'd been so proud of only a few months before. Now she could only look at it and calculate what she might get if she put it up for sale. Pete was sitting silently in the chair beside the window, staring morosely into space.

'Isn't Mavis here?' Stan asked again.

'You're a little bit early and she's just popped to the shops. She doesn't go far nowadays because every time she goes out, she thinks people are talking about her behind her back. I don't like to tell her, but she's right. Everyone's gossiping and pointing the finger, like we're all criminals now.'

'Oh, that's awful,' Jenny said.

'James is getting a few things to take with him. He'll be down in a mo, but in the meantime take the weight off your feet. Greg, you can go upstairs to hurry him up 'cos no doubt he'll be lost in his own world as usual.' She sighed as the boy dashed out of the room, followed by Bobby, who couldn't bear to be left behind.

Jenny stretched her legs in front of the electric fire where one lone bar was burning dull orange. 'God, Lily, who'd have thought it. I don't like to say anything in front of Greg but this just gets worse and worse.'

'Fancy a cuppa?' Lily tried to act the polite hostess but her heart evidently wasn't in it.

'No, don't bother. We'll have to be off as soon as James is ready.' Jenny shook her head. 'I can't get over it, you know. This doesn't make sense, keeping Tommy locked up, and yet ... and yet...'

Stan looked at the ceiling as if willing her not to say it.

'What, Jenny?' Lily stared at the younger woman.

'I can't get that night out of my head,' Jenny confessed. 'You know, when Tommy told us he had a bit of business to do and left before six. He didn't turn up again until just after we were all in the pub and was I the only person to notice what he looked like? He was all sweaty and he was in a really strange mood. He kept trying to make jokes that weren't funny and it wasn't like Tommy at all. Come on, Stan, you know exactly what I mean.'

Stan rubbed his hands in discomfort. 'That doesn't mean he pushed that bastard off the cliff,' he muttered. Then he met his wife's stare. 'All right, yes, of course I noticed. He was out of breath when he got to the bar. Said he was too unfit to run, but he'd been out playing football all week and never got out of puff. I knew something wasn't right, but it doesn't mean...'

'It doesn't mean anything,' protested Lily, trying to give Tommy the benefit of the doubt. 'Fit or not, people can get out of breath when they run. Take me, for instance, I can hardly get up the stairs to Mavis's flat if Bobby's been running me ragged some days. But I know what you mean, he wasn't himself. It was peculiar and it's been bugging me, but I didn't like to say.'

Pete grunted. 'Can't blame a man for having a funny mood.'

Lily glared at him. 'I'm just saying. Something wasn't right, you know that as well as I do.' She folded her arms and turned towards the meagre warmth of the fire.

'I haven't told the police about it, and I'm not intending to,' Stan reassured them, 'but something about Tommy's story isn't right. There's something fishy about it, though I hate to say it.'

'Say what?'

Nobody had heard Mavis come in, and they turned to see her standing in the living room doorway, her arms full of bags of painting materials. Her hair was wild, as if blown by the wind.

'Say what?' she repeated. 'No, don't bother. I heard some of it. I can't believe it. Not you as well? Surely, even if the rest of South London is against Tommy, you don't think he's a killer too?'

Jenny's hand flew to her mouth and Stan flushed beetroot red. Lily, however, hastened across to her daughter. 'No, no, you've got it all wrong,' she said. 'We were just wondering what was going on with Tommy that last night.'

'Don't.' Mavis stopped her with one word. 'Don't you badmouth Tommy. He's a good man, and he had nothing to do with Alec's death. If you don't believe that, you're no family of mine.' She whirled around but Lily caught her by the arm.

'We don't think he killed the man, but if we can't say what we saw with our own eyes within these four walls, then where can we?' Lily flashed. 'We all noticed something was up with him, that's all.'

'So what?' Mavis cried. 'So he was a bit agitated, and he admits he saw Alec on those cliffs, but that doesn't mean he killed him! I know in my heart that he's incapable of murder, I just *know*. He ... he's my soul mate, and I'd know if he lied to me.' She dropped her bags to the ground with a dull clatter. 'Tommy is a good man, you all know that and we're all he's got. We have to stick together to get him out of there.' Her chest heaved and she fought to take a breath. 'He's innocent. You know it in your hearts as well as I do so don't talk about him as though he's guilty.'

'Mavis, don't take on so,' Lily appealed.

'But, Mum, there isn't a shred of truth in those accusations, and somehow we've got to prove it. He must be set free, he just must, and then we're going to have our big wedding, you see if we don't.'

It was Jenny who gave way to tears. 'Mavis, despite what you heard, I don't for one minute think that Tommy is guilty. I know my cousin and I too know he's incapable of killing anyone.'

'Then I don't understand why you're all questioning what happened that night,' Mavis cried, and with that she bent to pick up her bags and left the room.

Chapter Thirty-One

Jean walked over to Rhona in the canteen when they were on their lunch break. She was halfway through a packet of crisps, and she offered them to the younger woman. 'Go on, you still need building up. Mind if I sit here?'

'Of course not and thanks,' Rhona said as she took a handful. She'd chosen a big bowl of oxtail soup, keen to warm up after hours standing in the chilly packing room. 'Well? Did you ask him?' She'd suggested to Jean that her fiancé might like a portrait done of her now that their wedding was drawing closer, not sure if he'd dismiss the idea as nonsense.

Jean beamed. 'I did. And guess what? He said yes. He was dead keen, and was really lovely about it. He said he wants to remember how I look now when we're old and grey together. Isn't that romantic? Don't pull that face, Rhona, he's a kind man and I love him, even though I know he's too staid to be your type.'

'Type? I don't have a type. I'm off men,' insisted Rhona, flicking her hair, but secretly she was delighted. She was a little embarrassed that she hadn't managed to hide her opinion of her boss's boyfriend, but by the looks of things Jean didn't hold it against her.

'Of course you are,' Jean gave her a meaningful glance. 'You sort out when your painter friend is free and I'll get my best twinset ready. Might even put on a bit of lippy.'

Rhona paused in the act of dunking a bread roll in her soup. 'Never seen you in lippy, Jean. Didn't even know you had any. What about mascara? Do you want to borrow my false eyelashes too? I don't have no use for them now.'

Jean threw back her head and laughed. 'You've got to be joking. Those old things? Ugh, thanks but no thanks. But yes, of course I've got lippy. There's just no point in wearing it round here, the dust will only stick to it.' She gave Rhona a determined look. 'I'm going to get all dressed up then your friend can go to town and make me look gorgeous for posterity.'

'Oh, hark at you,' Rhona laughed. 'Posterity! Have you swallowed a dictionary and gone all posh now that you've been promoted?'

Jean just smiled and Rhona finished her soup, wiping the bowl with the rest of the roll. So her idea had been a good one after all. She'd keep on asking around to see how much business she could drum up for Mavis. If they ended up losing the house it certainly wouldn't be for lack of trying.

It was late when the doorbell rang and Mavis hesitated as she made her way along the corridor. Pete and Lily were out, and Bobby had jumped at the chance to sleep upstairs, so the ground floor was empty and echoed with her slow footsteps. She didn't like it when she didn't know who it was calling at this hour and tensed with nerves.

The nights were drawing in and at first Mavis

311

could barely make out the shape of the person on the doorstep. By the way he stood he was almost blocking the light from the streetlamp as she opened the door, but then the moon came out from behind a cloud and she could see him more clearly. His hair was greasier and longer than when she'd last seen him and he had put on more weight, but there was no question as to who he was.

She gasped, pulling her threadbare cardigan more tightly around her. 'Larry Barnet. What are you doing here? How did you know where I lived?' Nervously she found the light switch and turned on the bare bulb that swung from the hall ceiling. Lily had already pawned the glass shade.

Larry smiled thinly. 'That's no way to greet an old friend, is it? Aren't you going to invite me in?' He made as if to step inside.

Mavis folded her arms and stood her ground. 'After what you tried to do to me last time, I don't think so, Larry. Now what do you want?' She managed to keep her voice from shaking but she could feel her legs were trembling.

He leaned against the door jamb. 'So that's how you want to play it. No skin off my nose, Dumbo. I can do what I came here to do from here or you could make it easier for all of us by asking me to come up to your lovely flat.'

Mavis shook her head. Every cell in her body screamed out against letting this foul man into her property and any closer to the children. 'You aren't coming in, Larry.'

He shifted his weight slightly. 'Pity. I'd like to see what sort of love nest you and that murdering boyfriend have got up there. It was so easy to follow you back from the school playground. Didn't even think to look behind you, did you?'

'Larry Barnet, you stay away from my children,' hissed Mavis, instantly on her guard where their safety was concerned.

'Or what, Mavis? You can't get your boyfriend to scare me away a second time.' He leered at her in the pale light. 'He's not here to protect you anymore, is he, nor is he here to tell his snitching tales. No, Tommy can't help you now.'

Despite herself she shuddered. 'What do you want, Larry?'

'What do I want? What do I want? Now there's a question. I think you know *one* of the things I want.' He tried to come nearer but she managed to half-close the door on him. He laughed. 'That won't help you, Dumbo. You know I can get in if I want to. Like this.' He shoved the door and it swung open, leaving the corridor horribly exposed. Mavis wanted to shrink back against the wall but something told her he'd take that as an invitation. Instead, she forced herself to keep still.

'Just tell me,' she breathed. 'Let's not pretend you're here for a social visit, Larry. Tell me what you're after then go.'

He reached forward and stroked her face menacingly. 'Maybe you will keep, Dumbo. You'll still be around, won't you? I can make myself wait. I can come back here any time I like if you ain't got your protector hanging around.' He arched his back slowly. 'So, I need you to pass on a message to your precious boyfriend in the nick. The word is he's going to be sent down and when he is, one of

313

my very good friends is going to be waiting for him along with a few of his mates. Really looking forward to that, he is. Has a score to settle. Name of Fenton. Got that, have you, Dumbo? I know you can't write it down, but see if you can get it to stick in that thick head of yours. Fenton.'

'Why should I?' demanded Mavis, suddenly angry at being told to be a messenger for the man and his criminal mates.

'Because if you don't you're going to be very sorry,' said Larry, leaning in so that she could feel his foul breath on her face. 'And it'll be the worse for Tommy too if you don't. As I said, Fenton and his mates are waiting for him and at least this way Tommy will be prepared. They've got a special welcome for him, and they are very much looking forward to it.'

'What ... what do you mean?' Mavis asked, faltering despite herself now. She drew back from his fetid stink.

'They've got a few nice weapons stashed away and they're keen to try them out,' Larry said confidently. 'They'll get Tommy at close range, and as they'll be behind closed doors, there won't be anywhere for him to run. So you be a good girl and pass this on to your lover boy the next time you see him.'

'So ... so ... Larry, what you're saying is ... your mate Fenton and his accomplices have got hold of some weapons, hidden them, and when Tommy's sent down they're going to use them on him?'

'Blimey, Dumbo, maybe you're not so thick after all.' Larry pretended to clap. 'That's exactly it. I managed to let it be known that your darling

Tommy made the phone call that got Fenton banged up. Of course he isn't happy that Tommy got the information about him because of me and my big mouth, but I'm not too worried about that. Fenton and his cronies can't touch me while they're in prison, and I can soon disappear again when they get out.' He stretched and smiled. 'Still, at least they'll be delighted to take some of their revenge out on Tommy. They've still got a few mates on the outside that I've managed to steer well clear of, and some of them in uniform have done what they could to make things difficult for Tommy while he's been on remand, making sure he was moved from place to place. But that's nothing compared to what Fenton and his mates will do to him when he's on the inside proper. It'll give them something to look forward to and who knows, it might take the heat off me. Your man thinks he got them all turned against me but let's see how funny he finds it once he's in their hands.'

Mavis stood up straight. 'Did you get all that?'

Larry looked puzzled. 'Get all what?'

There was a noise from further down the hall and Rhona emerged from the staircase, swinging her handbag. 'Yeah, got the lot. Clear as anything.'

'Who are you? What do you mean?' Larry blustered. He was thrown off his stride by this other young woman. He was happy to bully one at a time but he didn't fancy taking on two. And this new one looked like trouble.

'It doesn't matter who I am,' she said, 'but I know who you are. I've heard a lot about you and there are quite a few people who'd like to know you're back, ain't there? So don't you go making

315

threats to Mavis.'

'I'm not worried about a couple of bloody women,' snarled Larry, unsure which of them to look at.

'Suit yourself.' Rhona shrugged and tossed back her hair. 'We'll just tell the police about your friend Fenton and let them know how we came by the information. It's up to you.'

Larry laughed derisively. 'Yeah, right. As if they'd believe you. They can come looking for me if they like, I'll deny everything.'

Mavis nodded. 'Yes, you can try. But I think you'll find they will definitely believe us.'

Larry glared at her as if she was still the stupidest girl in the class. 'Dream on, Dumbo. You was always good at making up stories. The police have got nothing on me and you can't change that. If it's my word against yours, with your boyfriend accused of murder, who do you think they'll believe?'

'Tell him, Rhona,' Mavis said.

Rhona pulled what looked like a little black plastic tube out of her bag. 'See this? Do you know what this is?'

Larry barked out a laugh. 'Somewhere you keep your make-up, is it, darlin'?'

Rhona shook her head. 'Oh, no. It's way better than that. It's a microphone.'

Larry shook his head in bafflement, none the wiser.

'It's really clever,' Rhona went on. 'It picks up sound and records it on a little tape. When we play the tape to the police, they'll hear every word you said and Bob's your uncle.'

316

Larry swung around, cornered. 'They won't know it was me,' he said wildly.

'But your name's on it. If you remember, Mavis said your name several times so it's got everything recorded that they'll need.' Rhona shrugged. 'So, Larry, you'd better piss off back to where you came from, and we'll make sure that this tape is good and safe. If you make any more threats against Mavis or anything happens to Tommy, you're done for.' She pointed at the street. 'Better go before you say anything else.'

Larry's eyes darted here and there, as if weighing up his options, but then he saw a man walking along the street and knew he couldn't risk it. If they screamed it would attract attention, and he remembered from their previous encounter that Mavis wasn't shy of fighting back. There were also two of them, along with the bloke drawing closer who might come to their rescue.

Larry hesitated for another moment. He wasn't totally sure what the younger one was talking about, but he'd heard of these portable tape things even though he'd never seen one. With a howl of frustration he ran off, but not before shouting, 'You fucking bitch! Tommy's fucking welcome to you. He's going to be inside for life anyway and if he ever gets out I pity him coming back to a dozy mare like you.'

Mavis collapsed on Lily's sofa, trembling but elated at the same time. 'We did it, Rhona,' she said. 'We got rid of him. I can't quite believe it. We did it.'

Rhona was too wound up to sit still. 'I know. It

317

was brilliant. How lucky was that, me bringing the tape recorder round to show you this evening? And you were so brave, just standing there and taking all his bullshit. I was afraid he was going to hit you and I'd be too far away to help.'

'Yes, I thought so as well,' Mavis admitted, 'but he was too full of himself and thought he had me just where he wanted. You were so clever to follow me down like that. What a good job Jeff lent you that little machine. I know you were meant to use it to learn chords but the timing was spot on.'

'Yeah, I've gone and recorded over the tunes he did for me now,' said Rhona, 'but it don't matter. I don't know what it'll sound like as I was so far away so you might not be able to hear what was going on. Still...'

'As long as Larry thinks we recorded him saying all that, it won't matter,' Mavis said decisively. 'The man's a bully, and bullies are cowards. He won't dare do anything now.'

Rhona sank down on the sofa beside her. 'We did it. Blimey, I'm sort of deflated now. It must be all that excitement.'

'I know what you mean. I feel the same.'

'We had better get back upstairs then. We can't have you flaking out down here. It's a big day tomorrow and you need your beauty sleep. You've got to do that painting for that woman, what's her name,' Rhona asked.

'Yes, I know, and her name is Melina.'

'Yes, that's it. I thought she was going to be a bit of a mare to be honest. She looked a bit stuck up what with those glasses and the hairdo, but when you got talking to her she was all right. I don't know what you're so nervous about. You've got a knack for it.'

Mavis laughed. 'I don't think so. It was worse outside Grace's school when I tried to talk to her about her husband. I thought she made an excuse to walk away because she didn't trust me, but now I know I was making a mountain out of a molehill.'

'Yeah, well, we've all done that.'

'In a funny way I'm looking forward to to-morrow. While I'm painting her, I might be able to dig a little to find out if she can tell me if her husband has made a decision about who is going to get the contract for the new housing project. Grace likes Melina's little girl, and you never know, when Melina shows her portrait to her friends, it might bring me more commissions. There's also that commission you got for me to paint Jean and I hope her fiancé will like it.'

'He's sure to.'

Mavis stood up. 'You're right, we should go upstairs now in case any of the kids wake up and wonder where we are.'

As they climbed the stairs, Mavis was still reeling a little from her encounter with Larry Barnet, and there had been other incidents that hadn't been easy to shrug off; people pointing at her in the market, crossing the street to avoid her, women like Mrs Burns. Mavis thought she had grown a hard shell, but now found it cracking.

When they reached the upstairs living room, Rhona took the portable recorder out of her bag. 'I'd better make sure this is still OK.'

Mavis looked at the small machine and said, 'Do you know what, Jeff must think a lot of you to lend you that. They cost a lot, don't they?'

'Yes, I think they do, and maybe Jeff does really like me, but I'm trying not to get my hopes up. I'll find out when I get the nerve to ask him out, won't I?'

Mavis looked at her friend, still surprised by the change in her. The old Rhona had never lacked confidence where men were concerned, but now she seemed vulnerable. Surely Jeff wanted more than friendship? Mavis hoped so.

Chapter Thirty-Two

It was strange being back, thought Stan, the only guest now as he gazed around the quiet dining room at the B and B in Torquay. It was his first visit since the holiday. He hadn't wanted to be reminded of how brilliant the holiday had been, marred by what had happened when they got back, with poor Tommy accused of murder. Stan had made excuses at work, inventing plausible reasons not to travel to Devon, but now it was autumn, out of season, and he'd run out of excuses.

He hadn't liked leaving Jenny, who was beside herself with worry about Tommy. There was also the constant threat hanging over Mavis and her family of losing their house. Stan had felt torn, wondering if he should give what savings he had to either Pete or Tommy. The decision had been made for him when he realised that Pete's debt was for the full price of the house, and Tommy's bail was set absurdly high. Even though he'd managed to put by what he considered a very respectable amount, it would barely scratch the surface in either case. He'd lent Pete a bit to buy him some time but there was no way he could do more.

Stan sighed. He'd always been cautious, and in case of something unforeseen happening, he liked to have savings to fall back on. However, at this rate he fully expected to have Pete, Lily, Bobby, Mavis, James and Grace sleeping on his living-room floor before too long. They already had all Tommy's belongings stored and were paying the fees, and although it wasn't expensive and he didn't mind, he had suggested to Jenny that Tommy's mother, Olive, might like to make a contribution.

Jenny wouldn't hear of it. 'I don't even want to speak to her,' she'd said. 'My mum saw her the other day and she's convinced that Tommy, her own son, is guilty of murder. She's even going round telling anyone who asks. What sort of mother is she? I don't want anything to do with her.'

Stan wanted to believe in Tommy's innocence but he was certain of one thing – Tommy would have done anything to protect Mavis and the children. Would he have gone as far as to murder Alec? He found it hard to imagine that his wife's cousin, his own good friend, could have done something that cold-blooded, but the conversation they'd all had at Lily's had opened the floodgates of doubt. How he wished he'd never said anything to him about Collier's real identity, or at least waited until they'd all got home. Too late now.

Mrs Hawkins came in with a plate of hot food: a steaming beef pie with carrots and peas on the side. It smelt wonderful. She set it down before him and then sat opposite.

'I hope you don't mind me joining you,' she said hesitantly. 'I've eaten already but it can get lonely now that it's out of season, rattling around this big house on my own in the evenings.'

'Of course I don't mind,' said Stan, ever the gentleman. 'It's always a pleasure to talk to you.'

Something seemed to be bothering her. Eventually she spoke again. 'I do hope I did the right thing,' she began.

'What do you mean?' said Stan, wondering whatever could have worried the usually calm landlady.

'When the police came. To ask about ... you know. What happened on your last night here, I didn't know what the police were after or I'd have been more careful.' She was almost crying. 'I can't bear to think of that lovely man in prison and his poor family having to manage without him. They all seemed so happy.'

Stan sighed. Yes, they had been happy that holiday. Mavis and Tommy had had a glow about them. Anyone could have seen it.'

'I only told them that Mr Wilson left just after dinner, and that he had ordered a taxi to go to some sort of business meeting. Surely that wasn't what got him arrested?'

'Don't you worry, Mrs Hawkins,' Stan reassured her. 'They'd have found out sooner or later. It was the taxi driver who came forward, and he told the police that he'd seen Tommy on the path looking as if he was having a row with Alec, and how long they were there. That sealed it, I reckon.'

'He might have had a row with the man, but it doesn't mean he pushed him off the cliff,' the landlady protested. 'There has to be another explanation. I have had many, many guests over the years and I think I've learned to be a good judge of character. Mr Wilson is no murderer, I'd stake my life on it.'

His mouth full of the last bite of pie, Stan nodded, hoping that the woman was correct. The alternative didn't bear thinking about – but he couldn't put it out of his mind.

'Would you like some apple crumble?' she asked sadly. 'I'll make some custard if you want it.'

'Thank you, but no. The pie was delicious and I've had more than enough to eat,' Stan said. He felt sickened just considering the possibility of Tommy pushing Alec over a cliff. Not that the odious man didn't deserve to be punished for what he'd done to Mavis and his own children, but surely Tommy wouldn't have gone that far. 'I might just go for a bit of fresh air, take a little walk down to the seafront.'

'Surely you'd like a nice cup of tea first?'

Stan shook his head, standing up. 'Maybe later.' He didn't want to be rude to this kind woman who'd done so much for him and his family, but suddenly he couldn't stay inside a moment longer.

Being in this house brought it all back and he couldn't control the suspicions that were whirling around his head.

Hurrying out, Stan let his feet take him along without thinking where he was going, and before too long he found himself down near the seafront. It was cold, yet he didn't care. He saw the peculiar stamp shop, its front all shuttered and locked now, with a 'To Let' sign above the door, looking the worse for wear, battered by the onshore wind. Stan wondered who would rent it. Would they worry about the previous occupant having fallen to his death? Would it put off customers, or would people soon forget?

Standing there, listening to the sound of the sea, thinking about the time he'd come to this very spot with Jenny and they'd laughed at the building, he didn't notice at first that there was a light on in the shop next door. Then the shadow of a figure passed across the front window. Stan blinked, wondering if he'd been mistaken. It was getting on; not many places were still open around here at this time of the evening. Then he remembered that this place sold tobacco. He could do with a smoke, and as Jenny wasn't here to tell him off, it was worth a try.

His feet were numb with the cold as he went across to the shop door and tried it. It didn't open. Not wanting to give up now he could see the rows of cigarettes behind the counter, he knocked on the glass panel. The figure reappeared and he could tell it was the same man as last time, the one he'd spoken to in the summer.

'What do you want?' the man asked, cautiously

opening the door. 'We're shut.'

'I'm very sorry,' said Stan, his teeth chattering after standing in the biting wind. 'I saw your light on and wondered if there was any chance of a packet of fags? I'm down here on business and I've run out. I wouldn't ask otherwise.'

The man looked at him and then appeared to take pity on him. 'Oh I suppose you can have some,' he said wearily. 'Come in and shut that door behind you. That wind is perishing.'

Stan gladly obliged and followed the man over to the counter.

'I've seen you before,' the man said.

Stan was impressed. 'You've got a very good memory. Yes, I was here in the summer, yet I only came in once.'

'I do have a good memory as it happens,' the man said. 'Packet of Embassy, wasn't it?'

'Blimey, fancy you still knowing that,' said Stan, amazed.

'Well, I remember that day particularly well because it was the very day I got called away, and just after selling you those cigarettes,' the man said. 'Normally I wouldn't dream of shutting up shop in the height of the summer season, but my dear old mum was taken ill and I had to go to her. I'm glad I did, we had that time together before she passed away, God rest her soul.'

'I'm so sorry.'

'Thanks. I only got back this afternoon. My nephew took over for me and kept things going but will you look at this?' He indicated a large pile of envelopes, leaflets and catalogues which looked about to fall over. 'He didn't open a single letter.

This has all built up since August. It's not that I'm ungrateful, but he might have missed an important bill. I can't afford to annoy my creditors. Reputation is everything in business, you know.'

'I completely agree,' said Stan, beginning to wonder when he could escape. Still, it was warm in here and as the man had done him a favour, he didn't begrudge him a bit of conversation.

'Honestly, he hasn't even divided it into official and personal,' grumbled the man. 'That's from the electricity company, and that's water rates ... that's a postcard from my sister, you'd have thought he'd have put that separately ... that's a circular, he could have binned that, he knows what I think of them ... now what's this?' He had come to a hand-written envelope with no stamp. 'That writing looks familiar. It's from my neighbour if I'm not much mistaken.'

'Your neighbour?' Stan felt as if an icy finger was touching the back of his neck.

'Yes. Alec Pugh. Maybe you'll have read about him in the papers? A sad affair, though it's old news now. He ran the shop next door, which I seem to recall you were interested in, was discovered at the foot of some nearby cliffs. I only heard after I left, as I must have gone that very same day, and I was terribly shocked. Mind you, he had been acting out of character the night before. He was usually so quiet.'

Stan was fully on the alert now. 'What do you mean, the night before? The night before he died, you mean?'

'Well it might have been on the day he died for all I know,' the man said. 'From what I read they weren't exactly sure when he died, which side of midnight it was, I mean. All I know is that when I was shutting up the shop, about nine it must have been because I like to stay open late on summer evenings, he was making a tremendous racket next door. He used some of the upstairs rooms for storage, as I do, and I was up there cashing up. I could hear him through the dividing wall. It was like he was having a row with someone but there was only one voice. Extraordinary behaviour, but I recognised his plummy accent so it was most definitely him.'

'Wait. You mean he was alive at nine that evening?' Stan couldn't believe his ears. Tommy had joined them in the pub well before nine on that fateful night.

'Oh, without a doubt. Raving, he was. Actually using quite disgusting language, I was surprised at him.'

Stan realised he was shaking at this revelation. 'Do you mind if I light up in here?' he asked when he found his voice.

'Be my guest,' said the shopkeeper. 'I suppose I should see what this letter's about. Maybe he's apologising for making such a din. For the first time ever, I had to bang on the wall. Not that it stopped him. If I hadn't been so worried about my mother I'd have gone round to have a word with him, complain about the racket. Somewhere round here I have a letter opener. Let me see ... here it is.'

Stan could hardly contain himself as the man fussed about, before finally slitting open the envelope. It contained just one page. The shopkeeper read it carefully and the colour of his face changed from a healthy pink to grey in a matter of seconds. 'Oh no. Oh dear. This is terrible.'

'May I see?' asked Stan, craning his neck, but the man backed away.

'I don't think so. This is very personal. It certainly explains the shouting. Oh, if only I'd known, I could maybe have stopped him.' He seemed on the verge of collapse.

'Can I get you anything?' asked Stan. 'Water? Something stronger?'

The man had sunk on to a stool behind the counter and was staring blankly into space. 'No, no. I've never had to deal with anything like this. He kept himself to himself, but I think as we sometimes spoke, he counted me as a sort of friend. Oh, but this. This is terrible.'

'What is,' Stan asked. 'What does the letter say?'

The man shook his head. 'I don't know that I should tell you. It's very private...'

Stan noticed some soft drinks on the shelf beside him and took a small bottle of dandelion and burdock to give to the man. 'Have some of this. You're in shock, the sugar will do you good.'

The shopkeeper took it gratefully. 'You're very kind. Really, there's no need, but ... I don't know what to do. I fear there's no mistaking what it means.'

'Look, you're obviously very upset about it, so it might help you to tell me,' Stan urged.

The man shook his head in distress. 'It's dreadful. I think he must have lost his mind. That would explain all the noise that night. But ... I can't quite

'... well. The thing is, this is a suicide note.'

Stan stared at the man. 'What? Are you sure?' He couldn't square the idea of suicide with the Alec Pugh he had known and loathed.

The tobacconist seemed more in control of himself now. 'Yes, I'm afraid there's no doubt.'

'I don't believe it. Not Alec Pugh. He just isn't the type to do such a thing.'

The shopkeeper seemed to overcome his scruples. 'Here you are, then. Read it for yourself.'

Stan stared in disbelief at the letter and squinted to make out the handwriting, which grew more and more illegible as the message went on:

My dear friend,

Forgive me for imposing in this way but you are right to be angry with me for the disturbance I caused earlier this evening. I feel I must offer you this by way of explanation. Once this letter is complete I shall bother you no further.

I fear I have deceived you these past two years. You know me as Charles Collier but I was formerly Alec Pugh. I fled London and left that name behind, but now my earlier life has caught up with me. My wife and her fancy man are here, plaguing me with the sight of them flaunting themselves in front of my two children. It was my intention to expose her for the adulterous slut that she is and take custody of the children myself but, after much soul-searching, I now realise that would be the wrong thing to do. They are tainted with her blood and no discipline will be enough to put them right. I am sickened to the core that her fancy man repeatedly attempted to bribe me, but I turned him down and now I shall return to the spot where he made his foul offer and end it all. Seeing my wife again has dragged up the past, and reminded me of my mother's deception that causes me to suffer bouts of deep anger and depression. When I sold my mother's house in London, I thought I would be rid of her, but no, she continues to taunt me, to haunt me, and I can't stand it anymore. It is unbearable.

I am truly sorry for any inconvenience I have caused you.

Yours sincerely,
Charles Collier

There had been no murder. It hadn't been an accident either. The one explanation that nobody had even entertained was that Alec had taken his own life. If it had been suggested, Stan would have totally ruled it out, thinking that his old neighbour was just the sort of self-righteous bastard to stay around and make everyone's lives a misery for as long as possible. But he would have been wrong. Alec Pugh had thrown himself off the cliff. Tommy hadn't pushed him. Suddenly Stan felt horribly guilty; knowing he had had those suspicions ever since the arrest, believing his friend might be capable of killing. Mavis had believed in Tommy, but surely he wasn't the only one who'd had doubts?

'So Alec Pugh killed himself,' he breathed. 'Thank God he wrote to you to explain or they'd have carried on trying to fit Tommy up for murder.'

'Pardon?' asked the man, only now realising that this customer had a very keen interest in the case. 'I don't know what you're talking about, but from reading the letter it would seem that poor Alec lost his sanity. He said his mother was haunting him, delusional of course, but who is this Tommy?'

Stan sighed and took a final drag of his cigarette. 'I'll tell you about him as we go.'

'Go where?' asked the man.

'To the police,' said Stan. 'We have to go right away. There's an innocent man due to stand trial for the murder of Charles Collier or Alec Pugh, and you're the only one who can stop it happening.'

Chapter Thirty-Three

The next morning, Jenny sliced some bread for toast, although she didn't, really feel like eating. She always lost her appetite when Stan was away. Not only that, she was worried sick about Tommy and concerned for Mavis and her family. All in all she would rather have gone back to bed and pretended the day hadn't started, but she knew she had to keep going for Greg, who was still settling into his new class though apprehensive about his form teacher.

They'd had the phone put in so that Stan's company could reach him whenever they needed him, which on the one hand was a good thing as it showed how much they valued him, but on the other was a nuisance because nobody she really wanted to speak to had a telephone. She'd hoped that Pete would have installed one when he was doing up the house but it hardly mattered now; it looked as if he'd be losing it anyway. Mavis sometimes used the call box down her road, but as she was spending every waking moment on her paintings in an attempt to keep the wolf from the door, Jenny knew it was unlikely to be her ringing to say she was coming to see her. They had fallen out when Mavis had caught them talking about Tommy, when she had thought they were casting doubts about his innocence, but Mavis wasn't one to bear grudges and they'd soon made up.

She had only just returned from taking Greg to school, but perhaps something had happened and her heart fluttered anxiously as she reached for the receiver in the hall. 'Hello?'

'Jenny, thank goodness you're in!'

'Stan? Is everything all right?' Jenny couldn't tell what was wrong from one brief sentence but she recognised that Stan was extremely tired from his tone of voice. 'Haven't you slept well?'

'I haven't slept at all!' said Stan, and yawned. 'You'll never believe what happened last night.'

Jenny put one hand out to the hallway wall and steadied herself in readiness, as she couldn't tell if this was good or bad. 'What is it, Stan? Tell me.'

Stan began the extraordinary story of going to the tobacconist on the seafront and what had followed. The police took a statement in which the tobacconist insisted that Alec Pugh was still alive at nine o'clock. They then said they would have to interview the bar staff and anyone else in the pub to establish where they had been that evening to establish what time Tommy had arrived, and how long he had remained. They would also have to verify Alec Pugh's handwriting. 'Once they've done that, with all this new evidence,' Stan finished, 'it will mean that Tommy will be released.'

'Oh my God, Stan. Are you sure? Are you absolutely sure?'

'Well I rang his lawyer this morning and he said he's going to do everything he can to set the wheels in motion.'

'Oh, Stan, this is wonderful news, but why didn't you ring to tell me all this last night?'

'It was getting on a bit before we left the station, and then ... well ... I went for a drink to sort of celebrate. By the time I got back to the B and B, it was late and I thought you'd probably be in bed and asleep.'

Jenny couldn't berate him. She was too happy and realised she was crying. She scrabbled in her apron pocket for her hanky. 'I've got to tell Mavis.'

'That's partly why I rang,' said Stan. 'They haven't got a telephone, so you'll need to go over to Peckham to pass on the news.'

'I will. I'll go now.' Jenny stuffed her hanky back into her pocket.

'I've got to see a couple of clients now, but I'll ring you again this evening.'

'All right, darling. Love you,' Jenny said, barely taking in Stan's return affirmation before she replaced the receiver.

She dashed to the kitchen, found her purse and keys and ran to the door, leaving any further thoughts of having a couple of slices of toast behind.

Lily opened the front door. 'Blimey, Jenny, what's up with you? You're jumping about like you've got ants in your pants.'

'Lily, let me in, I've got important news,' panted Jenny, who'd run all the way from the bus stop. 'Is Mavis upstairs?'

'She's bound to be. She hasn't put those paint brushes down for weeks,' said Lily. 'Come on, if you don't mind me joining you, we'll go up there now.'

They could smell the turpentine from the stairwell before they even got to the flat. Lily called out that she had a visitor outside and Mavis appeared at the living-room door, paint on her face and in her hair. 'Jenny! This is a surprise. I'd offer you a cup of tea but I'm a bit messy.'

'Never mind that,' breathed Jenny. 'Sit yourself down, Mavis. Stan just rang, he's down in Torquay, and thanks to him going into a tobacconist's, new evidence that proves Alec killed himself has come to light. He wasn't murdered and now Tommy's lawyer is doing all he can to get him released.'

Mavis just stared at her. 'Say that again, Jenny. I want to make sure I heard it right. What new evidence?'

So Jenny explained everything that Stan had said, from the visit to the tobacconist to him giving a statement. Lily had stood open-mouthed, but Mavis was in tears by the time Jenny finished speaking.

'We'll ring the lawyer to see when he's being released,' Lily said. 'Once we know, Pete can drive you to the prison gates to meet him.'

Mavis wiped a tear from her cheek. 'I can't seem to take it in. I've never doubted that Tommy is innocent, but with the taxi driver's evidence against him, I was so frightened that a jury would find him guilty.'

'Well it's all over now and he'll be coming home,' Lily said.

Mavis sprang to her feet. 'Look at the state of me, and this place,' she cried, wiping her hands on the old, baggy shirt that she wore when painting.

'Don't panic,' Jenny said, smiling. 'I doubt he's going to be released just yet.'

'Maybe not, but when he is, I think we should give him a proper welcome,' Lily suggested. 'We should throw him a party, show him how much he's been missed, and all those scandalmongers, the gossiping bitches, won't get a foot in the door. They can all get stuffed.'

'A party would be lovely, Mum, but can I have a bit of time alone with Tommy first?' Mavis asked.

'Of course you can darlin',' Lily agreed, 'and then after the party we've got a wedding to plan.'

Pete had gone to his office, which was deathly silent. He'd had a few small jobs to do, a wall outside a house to build, along with fitting a new front door, but the money earned barely paid the rent on the premises. He'd only come to the office for a bit of peace and quiet, which was hard to come by at home. Lily meant well, always finding him things to do, but it made him sadder than ever, because whatever improvements he made, the likelihood was that they wouldn't be there to enjoy them for much longer. The money Stan had lent him was nearly gone, and while Mavis's paintings were bringing in enough to pay the interest on the loan, there were still bills outstanding.

He plugged in the kettle and set it to boil before remembering there wasn't any milk. He didn't really feel like tea anyway, it was just for something to do. He watched the steam coming out of the spout and misting up the cold window. The wind was blowing outside and a few dry leaves whirled around.

Some post had arrived. Pete shook his head, doubting it could be anything good. Probably another demand for impossible sums of money to stave off the imminent repossession of the house. One of the envelopes on the dusty floor looked official and he bent down to pick it up, his back stiff and his knees sore. That'll be your age, he told himself. Age and sitting around doing nothing, not getting enough exercise. But what was the point when he was about to lose everything he'd worked so hard for?

He struggled with the flap of the envelope and stuck a pen in the corner to rip it open, almost tearing the letter inside. He could barely summon the energy to read it anyway. His eyes were red and dry from the wind he'd walked against on the way here, and from tiredness. He also hadn't been sleeping properly for weeks, certainly not since Torquay. They watered as he squinted to read the paragraphs which blurred as he looked at them.

Then he stood up straight. This was it. Here it was in black and white: approval for the construction project had come through at last. He was to be the major contractor. It was a definite commission. The price he'd so optimistically agreed back at the start of the year was confirmed. He would be paid partly on signature of the contract, which would be ready within the week. It was from Andreou's assistant. The man had come good at last.

Pete was so overwhelmed that he struggled to bring coherent thoughts into order. He tried to think sensibly, to work out if the partial payment on signature would be enough to stave off the bank. It had to be. If he took this letter to the branch manager it would be proof that he would be able to pay off his debts. They wouldn't evict him. The house was safe.

He would go to the bank now and then rush back to tell Lily. Pulling his van keys out of his pocket he ran out of the door, slamming it behind him, the letter clutched tight in his fist.

Rhona had done an early shift for once and immediately set off for Camden. She knew Jeff finished work by four-thirty most days and thought she'd surprise him at his flat. She had something in her bag that she was sure he'd like.

They'd had a couple more lessons since he'd lent her the portable cassette recorder with which they'd outwitted Larry and his threats, but she was still none the wiser about how he felt about her. Sometimes he seemed on the verge of touching her, or kissing her, and she had waited for it to happen, yet all that had taken place was he had adjusted her hands on the guitar, just as he had before. That was the only real physical contact they'd had. She could have sworn the air was full of electricity between them, but as Jeff didn't seem to notice it, maybe it was all one way.

The more Rhona got to know Jeff, the more special she realised he was, and so unlike the other men she'd known. She loved the way he explained what they were doing, how he helped her to see things for herself, how he never directly criticised her. He praised her progress and never complained that she was wasting his time. On the other hand he didn't seem to appreciate her as a woman, no matter what she wore. She couldn't make him out.

Following Mavis's advice, she had studied the music press and local papers to find the perfect concert to ask him to. She couldn't believe her luck. The Rolling Stones were playing at the Granada Theatre in Tooting. It was fate, she decided. It couldn't have been better if she'd planned it herself. Jeff was almost as keen on the band as she was, and would definitely want to go.

Now she was going to present him with the ticket and wait to see how he reacted. If this didn't work Rhona wasn't sure what to do. She hadn't told anyone what she'd planned. Mavis had enough on her plate, Penny was still getting over her near fatal miscarriage and as Jean was now her boss she wasn't as easy to confide in as she used to be.

Rounding the corner towards the launderette, Rhona took a moment to check herself in the tiny mirror she carried in her bag. She'd slicked on some mascara and lipstick after work, nothing too showy but a step up from how she usually arrived for guitar lessons. It still looked fresh, even after the trek across London. She glanced at her watch. Perfect. He'd be back from work, but it was still too early for him to have left again for whatever he did in the evenings when she wasn't there. She straightened her jacket and adjusted her dangling earrings, tucking her hair behind her ears. This was as good as she was going to look after a day at the factory. It was time to gather her courage and knock on the door.

Before she could get any closer, a laugh rang out and two people emerged from the shabby door beside the launderette. One was Jeff. The other was a young woman, wearing a brightly coloured mac with a tight belt. Rhona thought she was about her own age, although they were a little too far away to see clearly. They hadn't noticed her. She drew closer to the nearest wall to watch.

The woman was leaning back and laughing, looking up into Jeff's face. Rhona couldn't see his expression but suddenly he bent forward and hugged the woman. She hugged him back and they stood for what seemed like ages, arms wrapped around each other. Then the woman broke away and ran off, turning to wave, before she headed towards the far end of the road. Jeff stood where he was, waving back, and when the bright mac was no longer visible he went in through his front door.

Rhona felt as if she had been punched in the stomach. So he had a girlfriend after all, a young, pretty and fashion-conscious one. He'd never mentioned her but she'd never asked him directly about the subject so she shouldn't be surprised, or blame him. Yet she was stunned. Had she misread his signals? Was there really no buzz between them? How could she have got this so wrong? There was no way she was going to ring his doorbell now.

Turning, she went back the way she had come, towards the familiar bus stop. The wind was blowing hard and that's what must be making her eyes water, she told herself. They weren't tears. Rhona Foster didn't cry over men.

'Lily? Mavis? Blimey, what's going on?' Pete stuck his head around the kitchen door and couldn't believe the sight that met his eyes. 'Have I walked into a NAAFI kitchen or what? I've never seen so many loaves of bread. Stop what you're doing for a minute. I've got news.'

Lily turned from the sink, wiping her hands on her pinny. 'Pete! We wondered where you were. We got news too! We're getting ready to have a party. Tommy's going to be released.'

Pete blinked in amazement. 'What, now? Just like that? What's happened?'

Lily and Mavis competed to tell him, speaking over each other so much that he had to ask them to repeat everything over and over. Jenny emerged from the flat upstairs, bearing a stack of plates and joined in until they were sure he'd understood. When they had finally finished he laughed, in what felt like the first time in weeks. 'You'll never believe it,' he said. 'It's too much, I can't take it in, but wait till you hear what I've got to say.'

'Is it really important?' Lily was on to him in a

flash. 'We've got a lot of arrangements to make and we're pooling our plates and things. I need you to run over to Jenny's with her. She's going to lend us some glasses.'

In reply he drew two letters from his well-worn jacket pocket and flourished them. 'Is it important, she says?' Even though Lily expected him to take Jenny to Battersea, he wanted to get every ounce of joy from his announcement.

'Pete, get *on* with it.' Lily folded her arms and gave him a straight look.

'Now listen, what's the rush? I doubt that even with all this new evidence, Tommy will be released today. I should think there are procedures that have to be gone through, and see this?' He flourished the letters again. 'This one is from the council. You are now looking at the principal building contractor for the whole new Peckham improvement scheme. What do you say to that?'

For once Lily was left speechless. Mavis gasped, but then smiled broadly, thinking of what might have gone on behind the scenes. 'I think it worked. I think Melina spoke to her husband and the wheels started turning. Well, I know they would have done eventually but she hurried them up. You don't say no to that woman when she wants something.'

Lily too smiled broadly. 'All this happening in one morning? It's too good to be true. You did it, Mavis, you said the right thing to that woman at the right time and it worked. Come here, I want to give you a hug.'

'And see this other letter?' Pete interrupted, as he waved the second envelope. 'I've just been to

341

the bank. This is the confirmation that the mortgage still stands and they aren't repossessing the house after all. We're safe and I can't tell you how long I've waited to say that. We're safe, we can stay here.'

For a moment nobody spoke. The impact of what he'd said hit them and Lily and Mavis looked at each other, their eyes bright with tears of relief. Then Mavis came to her senses.

'Pete, get in that van and take Jenny to Battersea to fetch some glasses. We're going to throw a party and it's a double celebration now. I don't care what you say, I'm sure Tommy will be released almost immediately. They can't keep him locked up now that they know he's innocent. And, thanks to you getting that contract, this is going to be his home now too.'

'Yes, your ladyship,' Pete said, tugging his forelock.

'Oh, you daft sod,' Lily said, but her eyes were still glistening.

Chapter Thirty-Four

'What's all the bleedin' fuss about?' demanded Muriel Burns the next afternoon, her face grim. 'What do you call this? You're making a right spectacle of the place.'

Lily stopped what she was doing and stood with her hands on her hips, confronting her neighbour on the pavement. 'I'll tell you what we're doing.

We're going to be welcoming Tommy home. He's an innocent man whose been banged up for something he didn't do and it's no thanks to you he's been set free.' Her eyes narrowed with contempt. 'We heard what you did. You gave evidence against him.'

'That young man with the dark hair what's been hanging round your daughter? He was downright rude to me. Of course I told the police that, it's my duty as a citizen.' The woman sniffed self-righteously.

'My God, Muriel, if you reported everyone who was rude to you then you'd be spending all your flaming time down the station,' said Lily. 'You are a miserable old bag, but you know what? I ain't got time to waste on you. We got a party to organise and less than an hour to do it so like it or not there's going to be a bit of noise round here and, you won't want to hear this, but people will be enjoying themselves. Jenny!' she shouted up at the first-floor window, the one to Mavis's lounge. 'Chuck one end of that bunting down here and I'll tie it to the gate post.' Or around Muriel's neck, she thought but didn't say.

'If you're going to have a party in the street then you need a licence from the council...' Muriel began.

'Oh piss off,' said Lily. 'I'm having it in my house so go and shut yourself behind your front door and do whatever it is you do alone in there all day. I got a celebration to sort out.' She turned her back on her neighbour and started to tie the tape of the bunting to the front fence. Muriel gave her a look like thunder and went into her house, slamming the door so hard the windows rattled.

'Hurry up, Lily!' shouted Jenny from above. 'We need you back in here!'

Lily raced back up the stairs. 'That woman gets my goat,' she muttered. 'She never has a good word to say about anybody. It's as if she enjoys being miserable.'

'Oh no,' said Mavis, overhearing this. 'That's made me think. I suppose Olive will have to know Tommy's free. Should we ask her along today?'

Jenny looked up from the table, where she was stacking a huge tray of ham sandwiches. 'Are you joking? Seriously, Aunt Olive? Seeing as she thought Tommy was a killer, I don't think she'd want to come and I really don't think Tommy would want her here. Isn't the idea that we fill the house with people who love him? And that,' she added firmly, 'rules her out.'

Mavis nodded. 'You're right of course. I'm glad you let Greg come over after school, even if he did have to get the bus on his own for the first time.'

'You mollycoddle that boy,' said Lily bluntly. 'About time he did that journey. He's done it often enough with one of us, he's a sensible lad.'

Jenny shrugged. 'I knew you needed help, which meant I wouldn't be there when he finished school. I wasn't really happy about it, but he's here now and no harm done. I'm proud of him and he can't wait to see his uncle Tommy.'

Mavis thought for a moment. 'There's someone else I'd like to invite. Maybe Greg and James could go to fetch her – she only lives on our old street.'

Lily looked up at her daughter. 'You mean Rhona? I'm still not sure about that girl. She's man-mad, and fast.'

'I don't care what people say about her and neither should you. Rhona has got a heart of gold and she didn't believe that Tommy was guilty. She helped me so much, Mum. She persuaded me to ask for permission to display the oil painting of the children in Grace's school. Melina saw it and when the other mothers heard that she'd commissioned a portrait, a lot of them wanted one too. Rhona also persuaded a woman at the factory to have a portrait painted. It was also thanks to Rhona that I found the nerve to talk to Melina about Pete, but you know all this.'

'Yeah, you're right. Sorry love.'

'Rhona loves a party and she'll be finished work by now.'

Lily stuck her head round the door to call out, 'James! Greg! We've got a job for you.'

As time went on and the evening closed in, Mavis watched anxiously from the window. 'I had wanted to spend a bit of time alone with Tommy, but then the plans for the party sort of took over and I felt bulldozed into it.'

Jenny put an arm around her Mavis's shoulder as she too peered out of the window. 'You'll have all the time in the world to be alone with him soon.'

'Yes, there is that, but how long do you think it'll take them to get back from the prison? It's such a long way and the traffic might be bad.'

'Don't worry. He'll here soon, and now we

345

know you won't have to move out of this house it's a double celebration.'

'I know. It's wonderful,' Mavis smiled through her nerves. 'It's lovely too that Melina and I have become friends. It was nice of her to suggest taking Grace to her house to play with her daughter after school. She said it would keep Grace from getting under my feet, but she'll be bringing her home soon. When she drops her off, Pete is going to thank her in person for putting the pressure on her husband behind the scenes.'

There was the sound of a car and Mavis craned her neck to see. It wasn't Pete's van, but a big black limousine. 'That must be her now,' she said. 'I can't think of anyone else round here who'd have a car like that.'

Sure enough the impressive vehicle pulled up in front of their house and Grace tumbled out, followed by Maria, and finally from the driver's side stepped Melina, complete with the latest fashionable coat. Mavis ran to let them in and the girls rushed past her, eager to see the party preparations.

Melina looked up approvingly at the bunting. 'This is very good. I expect you made it?'

Mavis nodded. 'Yes, well, myself and my mum. We did it for one of the children's birthdays back in the summer so it seemed the right idea to use it again.' She paused. 'I wanted to thank you, Melina. You'll know that Pete got the news we've been waiting for today. I can't even begin to say what that means to us all. Please come inside as he wants to thank you personally.'

'It isn't necessary, it was nothing. When you told

me of the problems the delay had caused, I'm only sorry it took this long. Oh, I have brought you this.' She turned to the car and lifted a large box from the back.

'Champagne? You've brought champagne?' Mavis gasped. She'd never tried it and neither had any of her family, as far as she knew.

'Of course. It is a celebration, isn't it?' Melina widened her beautifully made-up eyes. 'We must do it properly.'

At that moment there was the sound of another car engine. Mavis looked up. It sounded familiar and there coming down the street was Pete's van. As Melina's car was on his usual spot, he pulled up outside Mrs Burns' house and her door immediately swung open.

'Don't you be thinking you can leave that rust heap there!' she began, but a look from Pete as he climbed out silenced her.

'Don't you reckon you've caused enough trouble?' he asked mildly. 'If you've nothing pleasant to say, then keep quiet.'

Stunned, Mrs Burns glared at him in silence and then retreated.

Mavis took hardly any notice of this exchange. Her eyes were fixed on the passenger door. It seemed like ages before it opened and finally Tommy got out. He gazed at her, and then the house with its decorations, and his face broke into a huge smile.

Mavis almost flew into his arms. 'At last!' she gasped, Tommy hugging her tightly before his mouth dropped to hers, their kiss deep.

Time stood still and all the fear and dread of

the past few months faded away as Mavis melted into his warm, familiar arms. Gradually she became aware that there was cheering from the window as Lily and Jenny had thrown it open to poke their heads out.

'Welcome home!' they shouted, and eventually Tommy stopped kissing Mavis and waved up them.

'Oh my God,' said Mavis. 'I can hardly believe you're here, Tommy. Let me look at you properly. That time I saw you in prison, I was sick with worry, even though I knew you were innocent.' She struggled against the weight of emotion that threatened to overcome her and wrapped her arms around him again. 'Oh, Tommy, I never, ever, want to lose you again.'

'You won't, love,' he said, drawing back to look into her eyes. 'It doesn't matter what I went through in prison now. I'm here with you and I'm staying. God, I love you, Mavis.'

Mavis gazed at him, taking in every inch of his beloved face. 'You're home, my love, you're home. It's ... it's ... I don't have the words to describe it. You know, when I remembered how you looked when you came back to the pub that night ... I knew you couldn't have killed Alec, but I could tell something was wrong.'

Tommy sighed and held her tightly. 'I'd just messed up the most important conversation of my life. I'd totally failed to get Alec to agree to divorce you and he even said he wanted custody of the children. I knew that would break your heart, so I did row with him, I don't deny it. We almost had a scuffle too, but he was slippery and pushed past me. I felt so useless, and furious with him for messing up your life. And I was angry with myself for losing my temper; for not keeping a level head.'

'Oh, Tommy, you should have told me.'

'I was too ashamed of making such a mess of it.'

Mavis hugged him again. 'It doesn't matter. It's all over with now and you're here.'

He stroked her hair tenderly. 'Yes, you're right. It's all behind us now.'

Pete came up to them, carrying Tommy's bag. 'Come on you two, that's enough canoodling for now. Let's get to that party or your mum will have kittens, Mavis.'

She gazed up into Tommy's eyes. 'Are you ready for this?'

He nodded. 'Yes. Let's get this party over and then hopefully I can have you all to myself.'

'Forever,' she whispered, taking Tommy's hand and leading him past the banner that read, 'WELCOME HOME TOMMY'.

He looked at the huge spread of food and the booze, and grinned. 'I haven't seen grub like this since before I was inside, and I can't wait to drink a bottle of that beer.'

'Coming up,' said Pete.

Tommy hugged Jenny and then Lily, but then frowned quizzically, puzzled when he caught sight of Melina. Mavis hastily introduced them and Melina offered them both glasses of champagne. Mavis took one and sipped it dubiously, but Tommy shook his head. 'That's very kind of you but to be honest I'd rather have the drink that Pete has poured me.'

'I'm with you on that,' said Pete.

Melina shrugged prettily. 'You English men. You are all the same. But it is your party and you must drink what you like.'

There was more noise from the front path and James and Greg raced in, both wanting to get to Tommy first. Behind them came Rhona, followed by a tall young man with brown hair and kind eyes.

'Rhona!' Mavis exclaimed in delight, and came across the room to hug her friend. 'You made it. I'm glad the boys found you. And who's this?' She hoped it was who she thought it was.

Rhona looked unusually shy. 'This is Jeff. Jeff, here's Mavis, the one I told you about.'

Jeff shook her hand. 'I'm pleased to meet you. I understand it's you I have to thank for this Rolling Stones ticket?'

Mavis's eyes widened. 'Oh, you didn't say you'd managed to get tickets for the Stones, Rhona. Lucky you.'

'Yeah, well, earlier today I thought I'd be going with Penny,' Rhona said sheepishly. 'I'd gone round to Jeff's with them and saw him outside his flat, hugging and saying goodbye to a gorgeous girl. I nearly gave up on him then and I was about to go home. Then I thought that seeing as I'd travelled all the way to Camden, I might as well drop in anyway even if Jeff had a girlfriend. I was a bit shook up, but I had to find out for sure.'

Jeff looked down at her, his face radiant. 'You daft woman. Didn't you notice how alike we are?' he said, then turning to look at Mavis, 'As I told

350

Rhona, it was my sister. She doesn't live in London, but as she had a meeting to attend she decided to visit me and to stay overnight.'

'Yeah, well, I didn't know you had a sister.'

'It didn't occur to me to mention her,' he said, but then his face grew serious. 'Why would I look at another girl when you're in my life? I just didn't think you were interested in me, that's all. You always acted so cool, and anyway, I knew you went for flash men, like Gary.'

'Oh, him!' Rhona made a disgusted face. 'All talk, no trousers. No, I've grown up a bit since he dumped me. Mave, you're a star. Your advice was spot on.'

'Champagne?' asked Melina, coming over with two brimming glasses.

'Don't mind if I do,' said Rhona. 'Makes a change from Babycham. I bet you haven't had this before, Jeff. See, I only bring you to the best places.'

'I've had it once or twice,' he said, taking a sip. 'Oh, this is good stuff.'

'It seems that Melina has brought us nothing but the best,' said Tommy, joining them, holding on to his pint. 'But as I said before, give me this any day. Mavis, you'll have to introduce me. Well, I know Rhona, of course.'

Rhona sparkled. 'Yeah, I used to flirt with you when I was young and didn't know any better. Not that you aren't gorgeous of course, but there has only ever been one woman for you.' She raised her glass. 'Cheers. Welcome back to where you belong, Tommy, and that's with Mavis.'

Tommy hugged Mavis again. 'You're right and

351

as I think we've waited long enough. Mavis, how soon can we get married?'

'As soon as you like,' Mavis said at once. 'Rhona has already agreed to be a bridesmaid, and now we can add Jeff to the guest list.'

Jeff raised his own glass in acknowledgement. 'I'd be flattered to come.'

'Tommy, what about your mother?'

He sighed. 'Yeah, well, that's up to you, Mavis. She hasn't exactly been a fan of yours, and she's a bitter lonely woman.'

Mavis gazed up at him and even though the room was filled with the people she loved most in the world, they seemed to fade into the distance. 'I don't mind either way, Tommy. If you want her there, that's fine with me.'

'I don't want anyone to spoil our wedding day and if I do decide to invite her, I'll make that clear. No one else matters except you now.'

'Oh, Tommy. I love you so much,' Mavis said as all the horrors of the past, and all the fears she'd had, melted in the safety of Tommy's arms.

The publishers hope that this book has given you enjoyable reading. Large Print Books are especially designed to be as easy to see and hold as possible. If you wish a complete list of our books please ask at your local library or write directly to:

Magna Large Print Books
Magna House, Long Preston,
Skipton, North Yorkshire.
BD23 4ND

This Large Print Book for the partially sighted, who cannot read normal print, is published under the auspices of

THE ULVERSCROFT FOUNDATION